RANDOM
HOUSE
LARGE
PRINT

DEATH AT NUREMBERG

A CLANDESTINE OPERATIONS NOVEL

★

DEATH
AT
NUREMBERG

★

W.E.B.GRIFFIN
AND WILLIAM E. BUTTERWORTH IV

R A N D O M   H O U S E
L A R G E   P R I N T

Copyright © 2017 by W. E. B. Griffin

Published in the United States of America by Random House Large Print in association with G. P. Putnam's Sons, an imprint of Penguin Random House LLC, New York.

Cover design by Eric Fuentecilla;
Cover images: (Officer) © Collaboration JS / Trevillion Images; (Buildings) Slow Images / Getty Images

The Library of Congress has established a Cataloging-in-Publication record for this title.

ISBN: 978-0-5255-2427-4

www.randomhouse.com/largeprint

FIRST LARGE PRINT EDITION

Printed in the United States of America

10 9 8 7 6 5 4 3 2 1

This Large Print edition published in accord with the standards of the N.A.V.H.

26 July 1777

"The necessity of procuring good intelligence is apparent and need not be further urged."

George Washington
General and Commander in Chief
The Continental Army

FOR THE LATE

WILLIAM E. COLBY
An OSS Jedburgh First Lieutenant
who became director of the Central Intelligence Agency.

AARON BANK
An OSS Jedburgh First Lieutenant
who became a colonel and the father of Special Forces.

WILLIAM R. CORSON
A legendary Marine intelligence officer
whom the KGB hated more than any other U.S.
intelligence officer—and not only because he wrote the
definitive work on them.

RENÉ J. DÉFOURNEAUX
A U.S. Army OSS Second Lieutenant
attached to the British SOE
who jumped into Occupied France alone and later
became a legendary U.S. Army intelligence officer.

FOR THE LIVING

BILLY WAUGH
A legendary Special Forces Command Sergeant Major
who retired and then went on to hunt down the
infamous Carlos the Jackal.
Billy could have terminated Osama bin Laden in the
early 1990s but could not get permission to do so.
After fifty years in the business, Billy is still
going after the bad guys.

JOHNNY REITZEL
An Army Special Operations officer
who could have terminated the head terrorist of the
seized cruise ship **Achille Lauro** but could not get
permission to do so.

RALPH PETERS
An Army intelligence officer
who has written the best analysis of our war against
terrorists and of our enemy that I have ever seen.

AND FOR THE NEW BREED

MARC L
A senior intelligence officer who, despite his youth,
reminds me of Bill Colby more and more each day.

FRANK L
A legendary Defense Intelligence Agency officer
who retired and now follows in Billy Waugh's footsteps.

AND
In Loving Memory Of
Colonel José Manuel Menéndez
Cavalry, Argentine Army, Retired

OUR NATION OWES THESE PATRIOTS
A DEBT BEYOND REPAYMENT.

I

[ONE]
Schlosshotel Kronberg
Hainstrasse 25, Kronberg im Taunus
Hesse, American Zone of
   Occupation, Germany
1955 17 February 1946

Captain James D. Cronley Jr. sat in the back of an olive-drab 1942 Chevrolet staff car in his "pinks and greens," which is how officers referred to the "Class A" semi-dress uniform, puffing on a long black cigar, despite a sign on the back of the front seat that read both NO SMOKING! and RAUCHEN VERBOTEN!

Jim Cronley was a six-foot-tall, blond-haired and blue-eyed Texan. The crossed sabers on his lapels identified him as a cavalryman, and his shoulder insignia—a three-inch yellow circle outlined in black, with a C in the center pierced by a red lightning bolt—identified him as a member of the U.S. Constabulary, which policed the American Zone of Occupied Germany.

Three and a half hours before, the telephone

on his desk in the Compound, which housed the Süd-Deutsche Industrielle Entwicklungs-organisation (South German Industrial Development Organization) in Pullach, a small village about twenty miles from Munich, had flashed a red button, which had caused him to say "Shit!" as he reached for it.

His office was in a small, neat building identified by a sign on its small, now snow-covered lawn as the Office of the OMGUS Liaison Officer. OMGUS was the acronym for Office of Military Government, U.S.

It was, de facto, the headquarters of DCI-Europe, the Directorate of Central Intelligence, which had been formed several months before to replace the Office of Strategic Services by President Harry S Truman and answered only to him.

The OMGUS sign was an obfuscation, a smoke screen, so to speak, to conceal the truth. So was the Constabulary shoulder insignia on Jim Cronley's tunic. He was not assigned to the Constabulary. He was listed on the War Department's "Detached Officer Roster," which is classified Secret, as being assigned to the Directorate of Central Intelligence.

He was, in fact, chief, DCI-Europe.

So was the South German Industrial Development Organization an obfuscation to conceal what had once been Abwehr Ost—Intelligence

East—of the Wehrmacht. Generalmajor Reinhard Gehlen had made a deal with Allen Dulles, then the OSS station chief in Switzerland, not only to surrender to the Americans but to bring with him all his assets, which included agents inside the Kremlin, and to place him and them at the service of the Americans. In exchange, Dulles agreed to protect Gehlen's officers and enlisted men, and their families, from the Russians.

"Cronley," Cronley had said into the handset of the secure telephone.

"ASA Fulda, sir. Hold for Major Wallace."

The Army Security Agency was charged with making sure the Army's communications network was not compromised, and, in addition to other services, providing secure encrypted telephone, Teletype, and radio communications.

"Major Wallace, we have Captain Cronley on a secure line."

"You're invited to Colonel Bob Mattingly's 'Farewell to USFET' party."

"I must regretfully decline the kind invitation."

"It will be held at Schlosshotel Kronberg."

"As I have a previous social engagement."

"So put on your pinks and greens and get in your airplane within the next thirty minutes. A car will be waiting for you at Eschborn."

"No."

"And wear your DSM."

"I was told I wasn't supposed to wear it."

"This is a special occasion."

"I ain't gonna wear the damned thing, which is sort of moot, since I ain't going to fly up there to play nice with Mattingly."

"When you get an order, Captain Cronley, the correct response is 'Yes, sir.'"

After a ten-second pause, Cronley said, "Yes, sir."

More obfuscation was in play here.

In order to make DCI-Europe seem less important than it was, to have it sort of fade into the background, it was decided that it be commanded, as far as anyone outside of DCI was concerned, by a junior officer. Such an officer was available in the person of Jim Cronley, who had just been awarded the Distinguished Service Medal and promoted from second lieutenant to captain at the verbal order of the President of the United States. The Citation stated that he had demonstrated **at the risk of his own life not only valor above and beyond the call of duty but a wisdom far beyond that to be expected of an officer of his age and rank while engaged in a classified operation of great importance**.

DCI-Europe was important, and not only because it was involved in surreptitiously keeping former members of Abwehr Ost, and their families, many of them Nazis, out of the hands of the Russians by surreptitiously flying them to Argentina. This activity, should it become public knowledge, would have seen Truman—who had authorized Allen Dulles to make the deal with Gehlen—very possibly impeached, even if Eisenhower, who had brought the deal to Truman, agreed to fall on his sword to save the commander in chief.

Under these conditions, it was obviously necessary to have some experienced intelligence officer looking over Cronley's shoulder to "advise" him and, should it become necessary, to take DCI-Europe over. Such an officer was available in the person of Major Harold Wallace, who had been commander of OSS-Forward until its dissolution, and was now assigned to USFET Counterintelligence.

And there was more obfuscation here, too. In order to keep "Army G-2 off my back," as Wallace, a full colonel, had phrased it, he had taken the eagle off his epaulets and replaced it with the golden leaf of a major and allowed the Army to think Colonel Robert Mattingly was actually commanding OSS-Forward.

Major Wallace was given command of the XXVIIth CIC Detachment in Munich, from which position he was able to look over the activities of the XXIIIrd CIC Detachment, commanded by Captain James D. Cronley, which had been established to provide Cronley with a credible reason for being in Munich, in the hope that people would not connect him with DCI-Europe at the Compound.

Originally, Cronley was not told of Wallace's role, but he soon figured it out. They worked out an amicable relationship, largely because Cronley accepted that Wallace could give him orders.

[TWO]

As Cronley entered the lobby of the Schloss-hotel, a bellman snatched his canvas Valv-Pak from his hand and led him to the desk.

"I'm going to need a room," he said to the clerk.

"I'm very sorry, Captain, the Schlosshotel Kronberg is a senior officers' hotel."

"I thought this was a low-class dump the moment I walked in," Cronley said, his automatic mouth having gone into action.

Another clerk rushed over.

"Sind Sie Hauptmann Cronley, Herr Hauptmann?"

"Ja."

The clerk switched to English.

"We've put you in 110, Captain. Your bag will be there whenever it's convenient for you to go there." He handed Cronley a key, which came attached to a brass plate with the number on it.

"Captain Cronley," a voice said in his ear, "if you'll come with me, sir?"

He turned to see a naval officer, a full lieutenant, who had the silver aiguillettes of an aide-de-camp dangling from his shoulder.

"Who the hell are you?"

"I'm the admiral's aide, sir," he replied, his tone suggesting "dumb question."

"What admiral?"

The lieutenant didn't reply, instead gesturing for Cronley to follow him. Cronley did so, out of the lobby and down a corridor, where the lieutenant opened half of a double door, gestured for Cronley to precede him, and then bellowed, "Admiral, Captain Cronley."

Cronley looked into the room. There were six people sitting around a table on which were three bottles of whisky, an ice bucket, and a soda siphon. He recognized two of them. Harold Wallace and Oscar Schultz. He saw that Wallace had the silver eagles of his actual rank on the epaulets. Oscar was in a business suit.

And that has to be Admiral Souers. All that gold on his sleeves.

What the hell is going on here?

"Well, come on in," Schultz called. "Don't just stand there."

Cronley walked up to the table.

"Sir," he said. "I don't know the protocol. Am I supposed to salute?"

"Try saying, 'Good evening, gentlemen,'" the admiral said, as he stood up.

"Good evening, gentlemen."

The admiral put out his hand.

"I'm Sid Souers, son, and I'm glad to finally meet you. You know Colonel Wallace, of course, and Mr. Schultz, and you've just met my aide, Tommy Peterson. These fellows are, left to right, Bill Conroy, Jack Kingsbury, and Tony Henderson. All are DCI."

Cronley went to each and shook his hand.

"Where's your DSM, Jim?" Wallace asked.

"In my pocket. In the box it came in."

Wallace put his hand out, palm up.

Cronley took an oblong blue-leather-covered box from his tunic pocket and laid it in Wallace's hand. Wallace opened it and withdrew the Distinguished Service Medal.

"I see you also brought your 'I Was There' ribbons," Wallace said. "Good."

He referred to the small colored ribbons Cronley and millions of others had been awarded, the World War II Victory Medal testifying that they had been in the service when the war had been won; the European Theater of Operations Medal, awarded to everyone serving in Europe; and the Army of Occupation Medal–Germany, awarded to everyone serving in Occupied Germany.

Cronley's mouth went on automatic. "Modesty prevents me from wearing them," he said.

That earned him a dirty look from Wallace, but he saw Admiral Souers and the others smiling.

"Tell me about the Legion of Merit, Cronley," the admiral said.

Cronley knew the Legion of Merit ranked immediately below the Distinguished Service Medal but his mouth was still on automatic: "Isn't that what they award majors and up for ninety days' service in the Army of Occupation for not coming down with either the clap or syphilis?"

"Watch your goddamn mouth!" Wallace snapped.

"I don't think I'll tell President Truman you said that," Admiral Souers said.

"Sir, I'm sorry," Cronley said. "My automatic mouth ran away with me."

"As it often does. Jesus, Jimmy!" Wallace said.

"What I think I'll tell the President is that you said, with becoming modesty, that you didn't deserve the Legion," Souers said.

"Sir?"

Souers gestured for the others at the table to stand up.

"Where do you want us, Jack?" the admiral asked.

"There were supposed to be flags, Admiral."

"Bill, go find the goddamn flags!" the admiral snapped.

Bill Conroy hurried to do the admiral's bidding and returned a minute later with two bellmen carrying two shrouded flags on poles and bases for them.

The flags were unshrouded and set in their bases against the wall. One flag was the national colors, and the other the blue flag with two silver stars of a rear admiral.

"Where do you want us, Jack?" the admiral said again.

"You by the colors, sir, with Tommy standing beside you. Colonel Wallace on the other side, and Cronley in the middle."

Cronley now saw that Jack had a Leica camera.

What the hell is going on?

The admiral motioned for everyone to follow Jack's instructions.

Colonel Wallace pinned the "I Was There" ribbons to Cronley's chest, and then hung the Distinguished Service Medal above them.

"Okay," the admiral ordered, "go ahead, Tommy."

"Attention to orders," the admiral's aide barked. "'The White House, Washington,

D.C., seventeen February, 1946. By direction of the President, the Legion of Merit is awarded to Captain James D. Cronley Junior, Cavalry, Army of the United States. Citation: Captain Cronley was called upon to assume command of the Directorate of Central Intelligence–Europe when circumstances did not permit the assignment of an appropriately senior officer to that position. During his tenure as chief, DCI-Europe, Captain Cronley demonstrated characteristics of leadership and professionalism far above those to be expected of someone of his rank and length of service. He also proved his willingness to risk his life above and beyond the call of duty on many occasions when carrying out his duties. His outstanding performance and his valor reflected great credit upon the Directorate of Central Intelligence and the Office of the President of the United States. By Order of Harry S Truman, President of the United States and commander in chief of its Armed Forces.'"

What that sounds like is that I am no longer chief, DCI-Europe.

"Wipe that confused look off your face and try to look serious while I pin this thing on, Cronley," the admiral said. "The pictures are for President Truman."

Cronley did his best to comply with the order.

"You got enough, Jack?" the admiral asked of the man with the Leica.

"Yes, sir."

"Okay. Now I suggest someone pour Cronley a drink before he starts asking questions."

He walked back to the table, sat down, and motioned for Cronley to take the seat beside him.

"Scotch or bourbon, Captain?" the admiral's aide asked.

"Scotch, please."

The drinks were poured.

The admiral raised his glass.

"To Captain James D. Cronley, DSM, LM," he said.

Everyone raised their glasses. There was a chorus of "Hear! Hear!"

"The chair will now entertain any questions the captain may have," the admiral said.

"Why wasn't I just relieved? And you know I don't deserve the Legion of Merit."

"You mean, son, that you did come down with the clap?"

There was laughter.

"Okay, serious answers. You ever hear, son, what Eisenhower replied when someone asked him the secret of his success at Supreme Headquarters Allied Expeditionary Forces?"

"No, sir."

"Ike said, 'I think it's my knack of getting people who, with reason, hate each other to work together.'

"Ike came to see me. Somehow, he had learned of us going to G-2 at the War Department with those movies you had made with those two Peenemünde Nazis. The Blackmail Movie, as Jack put it. **Lay off DCI or we'll show these movies to the President.**

"Ike said, 'Sid, you—we—won this one, but the war between your man Cronley and General Seidel has to be called off. General Seidel is not going to quit until he buries Cronley. His ego is involved. And in trying to bury your young captain, he's likely to do something that will cause Operation Ost to blow up in our face, which means the President's face, and our primary obligation is to protect him.'

"I asked Ike what he had in mind, and surprising me not at all, it made a hell of a lot of sense, so I took it to the President, and he agreed, a little reluctantly, to it. Harry said it looked like you were getting the shitty end of the stick, and he didn't like that. Hence, the Legion of Merit, and his own contribution to Operation Peace.

"What Ike is going to do is transfer General Seidel to the Pentagon, where Ike will tell him to lay off DCI. He will also tell him that you've been relieved as chief, DCI-Europe, and that an officer of suitable rank and experience has been appointed to that position, Harold Wallace. When a new man is sent to be USFET G-2, that's who he'll deal with.

"There were a number of reasons Harold got the job. DCI-Europe is about to be greatly expanded. The President is really worried about the Russians. So I started recruiting people who had been in the OSS. Bill, Jack, and Tony, for example, all ex-OSS. Bill and Tony had the bad luck to work for Harold in London. But they're willing to give him a second chance."

"But they would be unhappy working for me?"

The admiral did not reply directly, instead saying, "What you're going to be doing, Jim, is making yourself useful to Justice Jackson."

"Who?"

"You don't know? I'm really surprised. He's our chief prosecutor at the Nuremberg trials."

"So I'm really out of DCI?"

"Oh, no. What you are now is commanding officer of Detachment 'A' of DCI-Europe, which is charged with protecting Justice Jackson, under the cover of the Thirty-fourth CIC Detachment, which of course will be commanded by CIC Supervisory Special Agent Cronley."

"What's that all about?"

"The decision to provide Bob Jackson with additional security had already been made, and General Greene had set up the Thirty-fourth to do that before Ike came to see me. The kidnapping of Bob Mattingly showed—in case anybody didn't already know—that the Soviets are now playing hardball. After Ike, so to speak, I called Greene, explained the situation, and suggested you were just the guy to protect Justice Jackson. He agreed."

"And what is Mr. Justice Jackson going to think when all he gets to protect him is a young CIC agent?"

"That potential problem came up and the President dealt with it. He and Jackson are old friends. He shared—the three of us shared—many a dram or two when Bob was attorney general. So Harry called him and told him he was concerned with his safety and the way he was dealing with that was to send the DCI man who'd gotten Mattingly back from the Russians to protect him."

"I don't suppose the President said 'the twenty-two-year-old DCI man'?"

"No, he didn't. I was there. You're going to have to deal with that problem yourself. It never seemed to bother you before."

"It doesn't bother me, but it seems to bother the hell out of senior officers."

"I've noticed," Admiral Souers said drily. "Well, finish your drink, and then we'll go and make nice with those senior officers who are now gathered in the main ballroom to say **auf Wiedersehen** to Colonel Mattingly."

"No way I can get out of that, Admiral?"

"By now you should have learned that serving with the DCI often requires that one must endure distasteful, even painful, situations while smiling broadly."

"And if you behave, Jimmy," Oscar Schultz said, "you get a prize."

"I'm afraid to ask what."

"Mattingly's Horch. He asked me what to do about it. I think he wanted me to help him get it to the States. I told him it belongs to the government. So it's in the provost marshal's impound lot, where they put it after he was grabbed. If you behave in the ballroom, you can have it. Otherwise, I'll ship it to Clete in Argentina. He can use it for spare parts."

"I will behave."

"I expect nothing less of you, Captain Cronley," Admiral Souers said.

[THREE]
The Main Ballroom
Schlosshotel Kronberg
Hainstrasse 25, Kronberg im Taunus
Hesse, American Zone of
**   Occupation, Germany**
2020 17 February 1946

There was a small stage, on which a string orchestra was playing Viennese music. The ballroom itself was filled with officers and their ladies either lined up at a bar or at an hors d'oeuvre–laden table or sitting at tables set for eight.

There was a reception line, with Colonel Robert Mattingly, a tall, handsome, splendidly turned-out thirty-six-year-old standing at its end next to Major General Bruce T. Seidel, U.S. Forces, European Theater EUCOM G-2, and Brigadier General Homer Greene, chief of CIC-USFET.

For the first time, Cronley wondered how the Army was going to deal with the facts concerning Colonel Robert Mattingly's **auf Wiedersehen** party, and immediately upon starting to think about that, wondered why they were having a party at all.

The facts were that Colonel Mattingly, deputy chief of CIC-USFET, had been kidnapped by the Russian NKGB not far from the Schlosshotel Kronberg.

At the time, officials didn't **know** that he had been kidnapped, just that he had disappeared. Cronley suspected from the start that the NKGB was involved. The NKGB had tried to kidnap two WACs assigned to DCI-Europe in Munich. The attempt had failed when one of the women took a snub-nosed .38 from her brassiere and killed three of the attackers and wounded a fourth, later reported dead.

The incident had been reported in the **Stars and Stripes**—and for that matter around the world—by Miss Janice Johansen of the Associated Press. But that story, after Miss Johansen had struck a deal with Cronley, had said the "would-be rapists" were escapees from a displaced persons camp, rather than suspected NKGB agents. Cronley had admitted to her that he suspected the attackers were NKGB officers not at all interested in rape, and also he knew no displaced persons who had taken off from DP camps and resembled at all the three bodies he had cooling in the morgue of the 98th General Hospital.

Janice's story had been about the bravery of the WAC sergeant who had taken down the would-be rapists with a pistol drawn from her brassiere.

The deal Janice had struck with Cronley was that he would tell her, and no other member of the press, everything that was going on vis-à-vis Mattingly, and tell her what would hurt his efforts to get him back if it appeared in print.

They both lived up to the bargain struck. Janice was on the Glienicke Bridge in Berlin with her camera when Cronley exchanged the fourth "rapist," actually a former senior SS intelligence officer whom the Russians had turned, for Mattingly.

He had told her all the details about that: The NKGB had contacted General Gehlen and in effect said, "You have something we want, and we have something you want, so why don't we talk about it as civilized gentlemen?"

The Russians wanted Gehlen to meet with Major of State Security Ivan Serov in the Drei Husaren restaurant in the Four Power Zone of Vienna. Suspecting the Russians would try to either assassinate Gehlen or kidnap him, Cronley had refused to let him go. He went himself, taking with him Gehlen's deputy, former Oberst Ludwig Mannberg.

In the restaurant, over a meal that could only be described as sumptuous, Serov showed them a picture of Colonel Mattingly wearing a bloody bandage and chained to a chair. He said that Mattingly would be on the Glienicke Bridge, which connected the Russian Zone of Occupied Berlin with the American Zone, two weeks later at nine in the morning. If the Americans showed up there with NKGB colonel Sergei Likharev, his wife, Natalia, and their young sons Sergei and Pavel, an exchange could be made.

Serov explained that it was important, **pour encourager les autres**, that Likharev, who had been captured attempting to make contact with a mole in the Gehlen Organization, and turned by Cronley, be returned to Russia. Likharev and his family—Gehlen's agent in Russia had gotten Likharev's family out of their Leningrad apartment to Thuringia in East Germany, where Cronley and Kurt Schröder, who had been Gehlen's pilot in Russia, picked them up in Storch aircraft—were now in Argentina.

Cronley had left the Drei Husaren restaurant rather desperate. He had no intention of swapping the Likharevs for Mattingly. He knew what Serov had in mind for him and his family. They would be examples to other NKGB officers of what happened to NKGB officers and their families who tried to switch sides. And Colonel Likharev, according to Oscar Schultz, who had flown to Argentina to meet him, had lived up to his side of the bargain. He was "singing like a canary," and the information he provided was "right on the money," according to Schultz.

And then, virtually at the last minute, Cronley had gotten lucky. He had moved the fourth rapist/kidnapper, whom he had dubbed "Lazarus" because he had, so to speak, risen from the dead, from the 98th General Hospital to Kloster Grünau, a DCI installation in a former monastery, where he had learned he was major of State Security Venedikt Ulyanov.

Cronley told General Gehlen that he didn't think Serov would swap Lazarus for Mattingly, as he was of far less importance than Likharev and his family, but he was all that he had, and he was going to try. Gehlen agreed, and then said, almost in idle curiosity, "Let's have a look at him, maybe something will pop up."

Cronley had taken Gehlen and Mannberg to Lazarus's cell below what had been the Kloster Grünau chapel.

Ludwig Mannberg took one look at Lazarus and breathed, **"Ach, du lieber Gott!"**

Lazarus had said, "The Herr General will understand why I am not overjoyed to see him again."

Gehlen had said, "Cronley, permit me to introduce former SS-Brigadeführer Baron Georg von Deitelberg."

Gehlen had later explained that von Deitelberg had been his deputy in Abwehr Ost until Gehlen had decided that the SS-**Brigadeführer**'s loyalty was not to the Wehrmacht, but rather to Heinrich Himmler and the SS. He had then assigned von Deitelberg to General von Paulus's Sixth Army, then attacking Stalingrad.

Realizing that Stalingrad was going to be a disaster, and that Germany was going to lose the war, von Deitelberg had changed sides before von Paulus had to surrender. He had been taken into the NKGB with the equivalent rank to SS-**Sturmführer** and subsequently promoted.

It was clear to both Gehlen and Cronley that

he was the man behind the kidnapping operations, and equally clear he was not about to tell them anything that could be believed about its purpose. And it was also equally clear that the NKGB probably would want him back, both because of his rank and to learn what he had told Gehlen and the DCI while they had him.

He was taken to the Glienicke Bridge at the hour Serov had specified for the Mattingly–Likharev exchange.

As Janice Johansen snapped pictures of everything, Lazarus got out of a Ford staff car. Cronley led him to the white line in the center of the bridge, where Ivan Serov waited for them, standing before the open door of a truck in which Colonel Mattingly sat chained to a chair.

"Turn Colonel Mattingly loose, Ivan," von Deitelberg ordered. "The operation didn't go quite as we planned it."

After a moment's hesitation, Serov obeyed.

"You realize, Janice, that you can't use this," Cronley said. "We have to find out what this kidnapping operation is all about . . ."

"I know," she replied, "but you are going to have to be very nice to me, sweetie, while I'm weeping for all the money I'm not going to get from Hollywood for this natural-for-a-movie yarn."

WAYWARD OFFICERS GO HOME TO FACE REPRIMAND

By Janice Johansen
Associated Press Foreign Correspondent

Berlin February 13—

What at first appeared to be an international incident in the making turned out to be nothing more than two officers, one Russian and the other American, drinking too much in the wrong places.

The issue was resolved at nine o'clock this morning in Berlin, when Russian officers marched Colonel Robert Mattingly, of USFET headquarters, to the center of the Glienicke Bridge while simultaneously American officers marched Major of State Security Venedikt Ulyanov, of the Allied Kommandatura, to the same place.

A white line in the center of the bridge over the River Havel marks the dividing line between the Russian and American zones of Berlin. Once the two officers reached that line, Russian officers released Colonel Mattingly into the custody of an American captain, probably a military policeman, who in turn released

Major Ulyanov into the custody of a Russian major, also probably a military policeman.

This reporter has learned exclusively that despite early reports that Colonel Mattingly was missing and kidnapping was suspected, and that Major Ulyanov had been kidnapped in retaliation, the truth seems to be that prior to their exchange on the Glienicke Bridge, Colonel Mattingly was sitting in a jail cell in Thuringia, in East Germany, after his arrest for driving under the influence, and Major Ulyanov was sitting in a West Berlin jail after his arrest for public intoxication on the Kurfürstendamm.

Both headquarters, Berlin Command and the Allied Kommandatura, refused to confirm or deny what this reporter had learned, but a U.S. Army spokesman said "the incident is under investigation."

Janice Johansen walked up to where Cronley and the others were standing just inside the door of the hotel's main ballroom.

"Hi, Harry," she said. "Is the sailor who I think he is?"

"Admiral, may I introduce Miss Janice Johansen of the Associated Press?" Colonel Wallace said.

"I'm very pleased to meet you, Miss Johansen," Souers said. "I want you to know how much I appreciate your cooperation."

"When Jimmy asks me to do something in our noble war against the Soviets, as a patriotic American girl, I'm putty in his arms."

"How fortunate for all of us," the admiral said.

"Speaking of Jimmy—what's with the medals, sweetie?"

"Don't ask," Cronley said.

"What is it you don't want me to know?"

"On his relief as chief, DCI-Europe, President Truman decided the award of the Legion of Merit was appropriate recognition for his superb performance of that duty," the admiral said.

"That raises several questions in my mind," she said.

"Shoot," Souers said.

"Why is he getting relieved? That looks to me like you're handing him the shitty end of the stick. If it wasn't for Jimmy, Mattingly would still be chained to a chair in Potsdam, or on his way to Siberia."

"That's one of the reasons President Truman gave him the Legion of Merit," Souers said.

"I don't know how it is in the Navy, Admiral, but around here, majors and up get the Legion of Merit for dodging the clap, or other social diseases, for six months."

"So I've heard," the admiral replied. "I guess Jim qualifies that way, too."

"Actually, I was asking about the other medal dangling from Jimmy's manly chest. I recognize the Distinguished Service Medal when I see it. You going to tell me where you got that, sweetie?"

"Sweetie can't tell you that, Janice. It's classified."

"You think I work for the NKGB, right?"

"It never entered my mind. Female NKGB agents usually weigh two hundred and fifty pounds and have at least two stainless steel teeth."

"I'm starting to like you," Janice said. "That'll stop if you don't tell me why Jimmy's being relieved."

"Fair enough. Out of school, DCI-Europe is about to be tripled in size. It needs a senior officer to run it. It's as simple as that."

"So Harry gets to pin his eagle on, and Jimmy gets to do what? Run the motor pool for the tripled-in-size DCI-Europe? Something like that?"

"He gets to do something he's uniquely qualified to do."

"Like what?"

"For example, acting as liaison between General Gehlen and Mr. Schultz and me, and between DCI-Europe and DCI–Southern Cone, and keeping Justice Jackson from being kidnapped by the NKGB."

Janice considered that a moment.

"I think you're too smart, Admiral, to try to con me . . ."

"Thank you."

"So I'll take that as the truth. I think our Red friends are going to cause trouble at Nuremberg, and Jimmy's good at screwing up their evil intentions. But what's with him wearing his medals? For that matter, what's he doing here at Mattingly's farewell party?"

"Since your interest in Captain Cronley's welfare touches the cockles of this old sailor's heart, Janice, I'll tell you. You see General Seidel standing in the line with General Greene and Colonel Mattingly?"

"Uh-huh."

"Well, he's being transferred to the Pentagon. He and his staff—who are not going to Washington with him—think it's a promotion, and that means they think G-2's war on the DCI is going well. When they see me—and Jim wearing his new Legion of Merit—they will know that's not so. And when Homer Greene drops into the conversation that DCI, in the person of Jim, is taking over protection of Mr. Justice Jackson, they'll really get the message."

"How does General Greene feel about me doing that?" Cronley asked.

"He said he thinks you're just the guy for the job," Souers said. "His CIC people there now—the Twenty-first CIC Detachment—are of course Army. The Army—the 1st Infantry Division—who has been charged with providing security for the trials thinks that includes protecting Bob Jackson and his people. There have been conflicts between the 1st Division and Greene's people."

"I suppose it's occurred to you that you guys spend as much time in turf warfare as you do fighting the Red Menace?" Janice asked.

"Oh, yeah," the admiral said. "That thought has passed once or twice through this old sailor's mind. If you have a solution to our problem, Janice, I'm all ears."

When she didn't immediately reply, the admiral said, "That being the case, why don't we all go over and make our manners to Generals Seidel and Greene and, of course, Colonel Mattingly?"

"That should be fun," Janice said. "Homer Greene told me that Mattingly was practically in tears about my yarn about his drunken driving in East Germany. He said it would follow him for the rest of his life and ruin his career. Homer said what he said was 'I'd like to strangle that bitch.'"

She put her hand on Cronley's arm.

"Let's go, sweetie," she said.

"Into the valley of death," Colonel Wallace said, "marches the noble DCI."

II

[ONE]
Farber Palast
Stein, near Nuremberg
American Zone of Occupation,
  Germany
1905 20 February 1946

A three-vehicle convoy rolled up to the palace, which was red-roofed and three stories tall. In the lead was a gleaming Horch touring car. Following it was an olive-drab 1941 Ford staff car whose bumper markings identified it as the eleventh vehicle assigned to the 711th MKRC. Bringing up the rear was a U.S. Army three-quarter-ton ambulance. The red crosses that had once adorned the vehicle's sides and roof had been painted over, and its bumper markings identified it as the twenty-third vehicle assigned to the 711th MKRC.

Captain James D. Cronley Jr. was at the wheel of the Horch. It was an enormous vehicle. Its fenders and hood were painted black, and the sides canary yellow. Spare tires encased in gleaming black covers were mounted in the front fenders, and there was a gleaming black trunk mounted above the rear chrome bumper.

There were two bullet holes in the left rear door of the car, and another in the left front door. The damage had occurred while the NKGB was kidnapping Colonel Robert Mattingly as he was en route from Schlosshotel Kronberg to the I.G. Farben Building.

The vehicle had come into Captain Cronley's possession via Mr. Oscar Schultz, executive assistant to the chief of the Directorate of Central Intelligence, who had decided that Cronley had behaved himself at Colonel Mattingly's farewell party.

Sitting beside Cronley was Miss Janice Johansen of the Associated Press. Seated in the back were DCI special agents August Ziegler and Karl-Christoph Wagner. Ziegler was thirty-one but looked younger. "Casey" Wagner had the innocent face of a seventeen-year-old, but was six-feet-two, weighed 232 pounds, and could pass for, say, eighteen or nineteen.

At the wheel of the Ford staff car was DCI special agent Maksymilian "Max" Ostrowski.

Beside him sat another former member of the Free Polish Air Force, and there were two more men with a similar background in the backseat, and four more in the trailing ambulance.

All the males, who were all wearing OD uniforms with civilian triangles identifying them as civilian employees of the U.S. Army, comprised the entire complement of the newly formed Detachment "A" of DCI-Europe, and also of the newly formed XXXIVth CIC Detachment, which had been established in the hope it would obfuscate the existence of Detachment "A."

They were going to Farber Palast at the recommendation of Miss Johansen, who said the accommodations of Farber Palast, which housed the press corps covering the Nuremberg trials, were far superior to the Bachelor Officer quarters in Nuremberg. She said she was sure Cronley's DCI credentials would dazzle the officer in charge of assigning rooms to the press.

Cronley agreed. DCI credentials did dazzle people.

**Office of the President of the United States
Central Intelligence Directorate
Washington, D.C.**

```
        The Bearer of
      This Identity Document


      James D. Cronley Jr.


   Is an officer of the Central
     Intelligence Directorate
     acting with the authority
      of the President of the
   United States. Any questions
      regarding him or his
   activities should be addressed
      to the undersigned only.


              Sidney W. Souers
            Sidney W. Souers,
                Rear Admiral
         Director, U.S. Central
        Intelligence Directorate
```

The convoy rolled into a parking lot half full of vehicles, most of them Army staff cars and jeeps but with a few American and German passenger cars among them. All the jeeps had PRESS painted on the panel below their windshields.

"Casey," Cronley ordered, "you come in with Janice and me while I see if we get to rest our heads in this palace."

The three got out of the Horch and walked into the palace's lobby.

There was a wide-curving staircase leading up from the lobby. At the foot of the staircase was a life-size statue of Diana, the goddess of the hunt. She was almost naked, bow and arrow in hand, standing on one foot as she presumably looked for game.

She was also wearing a pink brassiere and matching panties, and a six-inch cigar was planted between her lips.

"I think I'm going to like this place," Cronley said.

"Ernest Hemingway found it satisfactory," Janice said. "The bar offers Hemingways, which are gin martinis made to his personal recipe."

"Now I know I'm going to like it," Cronley said.

To one side of the stairway was what had once been, before the castle had been requisitioned by the Army of Occupation, a cloakroom. Now it bore a sign: REGISTRY.

It was not attended, but there was a bell on its counter. Cronley thumped it, and a moment later a sergeant appeared. He looked to be about as old as Casey, which caused a statistic to pop into Cronley's mind. The average age of enlisted men in USFET was eighteen-point-something years.

"Hello, Miss Johansen," the sergeant said. "Welcome back. Would you like your usual room?"

"Please. Thank you," she said, and then added, "It has a large bed, sweetie, with a marvelous feather-filled mattress."

"And what can I do for you, sir?"

"I'm going to need rooms for myself and ten of my officers."

"No problem, sir. The palace is half empty. May I have a copy of your orders, please?"

"I think I better speak to the officer in charge, Sergeant. Would you fetch him, please?"

"He's not available at the moment, sir."

"Be a good boy and go in the bar and get him," Janice ordered.

"Yes, ma'am."

A plump Quartermaster Corps major appeared three minutes later.

"Hello, Charley," Janice said. "Sweetie, this is Major Levin, the innkeeper. Charley, this is my pal Jim Cronley."

"Welcome back, Janice. What can I do for you?"

"My pal here needs rooms for himself and ten of his officers."

"Is there a problem?"

"He doesn't have any orders."

"We're CIC," Cronley said.

"That is a problem. The palace is for press only. The CIC has a **Kaserne** downtown. I'm afraid you're going to have to go there."

"Actually, we're not CIC," Cronley said, and produced his DCI credentials.

The major was dazzled.

"I've never seen one of these before," he said.

"Few people have," Cronley said. "And please don't tell anyone you've seen that one."

"Or else Sweetie will have to kill you, Charley," Janice said.

"Is that going to get us in here, Major, or am I going to have to work my way up your chain of command?" Cronley asked.

The major considered the situation for a full thirty seconds. Finally, he asked, "How long will you be staying with us, Mr. Cronley?"

"Three or four days, anyway."

"Sergeant, take care of these gentlemen," the major ordered. "Put Mr. Cronley in the Duchess Suite."

"That has a bed big enough for six people," Janice said. "I know, because it's right down the corridor from my room."

"Casey, go get everybody," Cronley ordered. "Tell them when they get settled to come to the bar."

"Yes, sir."

[TWO]
The Palace of Justice
Nuremberg, American Zone of
Occupation, Germany
0855 21 February 1946

As they had left Farber Castle, Cronley had seen a table in the lobby with a sign on it reading "Help Yourself." It was cluttered with all sorts of information about the Nuremberg trials and the city of Nuremberg that might be of use to the press corps.

"Casey," Cronley ordered, "take one of each. Two of the road map, which will, God willing and if the creek don't rise, guide us to the Palace of Justice."

"Yes, sir."

Casey scooped up an armful of the material and followed Cronley, Ziegler, and Ostrowski out of the building and to the staff car. Everyone was now wearing pinks and greens with civilian triangles on the lapels.

Cronley was slightly hungover. There had

been at least two too many Hemingways in the bar, as Janice had successfully convinced a half dozen of her very skeptical peers that her story about Mattingly and Ulyanov was all there was to the first story that Mattingly had been kidnapped. She had introduced CIC Special Agent Cronley and then named him as her source.

Afterward, surprising him not at all, he and Janice had carnal knowledge of one another in the bed—which really was large enough for six people—in the Duchess Suite. He didn't really understand his relationship with her. The simple answer, that she liked to screw without any strings attached, which solved his problem in that regard, seemed too good to be true. He genuinely liked her, but as a buddy, with no more romantic involvement than he had with, say, Max Ostrowski or Augie Ziegler.

All he could do was hope the relationship would continue on its present terms, which seemed unlikely. Cronley was a devout believer in the theory that good situations never last long.

Finding the Palace of Justice wasn't as difficult as he thought it would be. Directional signs had been put up at the major crossroads of the city, which, like most German cities, had been reduced to a sea of rubble by a thousand plane bombing raids, one after the other.

Somehow, the Palace of Justice, like the I.G. Farben Building in Frankfurt—now housing USFET headquarters—had apparently escaped destruction. Cronley had heard that the Farben Building had been spared on purpose. He had also heard that Marburg an der Lahn, where he had been briefly stationed as a CIC second lieutenant, had been spared because an Air Corps general had threatened the colonel leading a raid on Marburg's railroad yards with castration if one of his bombs came anywhere near Philipp University, from which he had graduated.

When they reached the Palace of Justice, it turned out to be a four-story building with a two-floor red-roofed attic that didn't look at all like the castles on picture postcards.

It was surrounded by fences topped with concertina barbed wire, and guarded by soldiers wearing the shoulder insignia of the 1st Infantry Division. Their web belts and the leather pistol holsters attached to them were white, and they wore highly polished combat boots, into which their trousers had been "bloused," and plastic helmet liners also painted white.

They were passed into what was now obviously a compound without trouble after Casey Wagner, who was driving, flashed his CIC credentials at the sergeant in charge of the striped pole across the road.

And they found the building that housed the

Office of the Chief United States Prosecutor without trouble. Getting into the building required that they each show identification. Once inside the building, the trouble began.

A 1st Division captain and a sergeant sat behind a counter.

Cronley extended his CIC credentials and announced that he was there to see Justice Jackson.

"That's **Mr.** Justice Jackson," the captain said.

He consulted a loose-leaf notebook and then announced, "You don't seem to be on the appointments schedule, Mr. Cronley."

"I don't have an appointment," Cronley replied. "But I'm expected."

"If you were expected, you would be on the appointments schedule," the captain said.

"Tell you what," Cronley said, "why don't you call Mr. Justice Jackson's office and tell them I'm here?"

"I'm afraid I can't do that."

Cronley took out his DCI credentials and showed them to the captain.

"Get on the goddamn phone, and now!"

They were marched, escorted by two 1st Division sergeants, down a long corridor and passed through a door under a sign reading CHIEF UNITED STATES PROSECUTOR.

There a man in his late twenties wearing

pinks and greens with triangles on the lapels sat behind a desk.

"What's this all about?" he asked. "Who are you?"

"My name is Cronley, and I was led to believe Mr. Justice Jackson expects me."

"If that were so, I'd have been so informed."

An interior door opened. A fiftyish, trim man in a dark business suit stood there.

"Am I interrupting anything?" he asked.

"Sir, my name is Cronley."

"They just bullied their way in here, Mr. Justice."

"Well, Ken," Jackson said, "consider yourself lucky to be alive. Mr. Cronley's reputation precedes him. Please come in, Mr. Cronley."

"Sir, may I bring my deputies with me?"

"Why don't you leave them here with Ken while we have a private word? Would that be all right?"

"Yes, sir."

Jackson waved him into his office, closed the door, and then signaled that Cronley should take a seat on a leather sofa against the wall, behind a small table.

"Coffee?" he asked, and then without waiting for a response, bent over the table and poured coffee into two cups and then sat down beside Cronley.

"I knew you were coming, Mr. Cronley, because I had a telephone call from General Seidel. You know who I mean?"

"Yes, sir."

"He said that he had just heard that you were being assigned to the trials and thought I should know something about you, and then went on to tell me that you, quote, were a poster child for Too Big for His Britches, end quote, and that, quote, that would be amusing were you not a dangerous loose cannon with two much authority for a twenty-two-year-old. End quote. Is that true?"

Oh, shit!

"General Seidel is not one of my admirers, sir."

"I mean about you being twenty-two years old."

"I'm twenty-two, sir."

"Neither the President nor Admiral Souers mentioned that when they called me about you. The President said I needed protection, and that I was going to have it whether or not I wanted it, and he was sending me the best man he knew to protect me, and I should do whatever he—you—told me to do. Sid Souers said that you managed to get Colonel Mattingly back from the Russians when everybody else had written him off as lost, and that I should pay attention to what you had to say about my personal security. Inasmuch as I have had the privilege of the friendship—the close friendship—of the President and the admiral for many years, it wasn't hard for me to accept their opinion of you, rather than General Seidel's."

Cronley didn't reply.

"What's the problem between you and General Seidel, Mr. Cronley?"

"Sir, how much do you know about the formation of DCI?"

"The President told me he had realized, just about as soon as he'd ordered it, that shutting down the OSS was a mistake. He said there were several reasons, including that everyone pressing for its dissolution wanted to take over its missions. And so he was establishing DCI and putting Sid Souers in charge."

"Sir, does 'Operation Ost' mean anything to you?"

"Oh, you know about that, do you?"

"Yes, sir, I do. The President gave responsibility for that to DCI-Europe. And until three days ago, I was chief of DCI-Europe."

"And what has that to do with your problems with General Seidel?"

"General Seidel and Army G-2 generally think DCI is a threat to their turf and want to either take it over or abolish it. I was—am—in their way."

"So you know all about Operation Ost? Including what a threat it poses to the President?"

"Yes, sir."

"I am having difficulty understanding—no offense, Mr. Cronley—why such a responsibility would be handed to a twenty-two-year-old captain. And also how you got to be a captain at twenty-two."

I have to tell him, Cronley thought.

And did.

"So you know Generalmajor Gehlen?"

"Yes, sir."

"There are those who believe Generalmajor Gehlen and his entire staff should be here, in cells next to Hermann Göring, Rudolf Hess, Field Marshal Alfred Jodl, and the other senior Nazis awaiting trial, like Martin Bormann, but he seems to have dropped off the face of the earth."

"Yes, sir, I know."

"But what he's given us, in an intelligence sense, is worth the President allowing him . . . hell, ordering that he be allowed to vanish?"

Before Cronley could frame a reply, Jackson added, aloud but as if he was speaking to himself, "I can't believe I'm asking that of a twenty-two-year-old captain."

And then, as if he had heard what he had said, he added: "Again, no offense intended, son."

"None taken, sir. Sir, when General Gehlen surrendered to Colonel Wallace—"

"Who?"

"Colonel Harold Wallace, sir. Then of the OSS and now chief, DCI-Europe. The man I told you was looking over my shoulder when I was chief in case I fuc—didn't perform as expected."

"Oh, yes."

"When he surrendered to us, General Gehlen was two jumps ahead of the Sicherheitsdienst."

"Who had heard that he wanted to switch sides?"

"The Sicherheitsdienst didn't know about that. What they wanted to do was take him, and his staff, to the Flossenbürg concentration camp and hang him and his deputy, Oberst Ludwig Mannberg, beside Admiral Canaris for their role in the attempted assassination of Hitler."

"I didn't know that," Jackson said. "But I heard that when we liberated the Flossenbürg camp, they found Admiral Canaris's naked body still hanging from the gallows on which he had been hung two weeks before."

"I heard that, too, sir. My point is that General Gehlen and most of the members of Abwehr Ost were not Nazis. Quite the opposite."

"Most, but not all?"

"Not all. The 'Russian' we swapped for Colonel Mattingly, Major of State Security Venedikt Ulyanov, had once been SS-Brigadeführer von Deitelberg, a Nazi on Gehlen's Abwehr Ost staff. Gehlen had gotten rid of him by assigning him to the Sixth Army at Stalingrad, where he changed sides."

"Incredible," Jackson said. "And while I really would like to continue this conversation—and we will, later—let's turn to a subject really dear to my heart, my personal safety."

"Yes, sir."

"Am I really at some risk? Or are Sid Souers and the President being overly cautious?"

"I don't know how much of a risk, sir, because we don't really know why the Russians started the kidnapping, or what they hope to accomplish. But they are kidnapping or trying to kidnap people, and I think that means you are at risk, sir."

"And how do you propose to protect me?"

"I think the best way to do that is to get the Army—the 1st Division—out of the picture. They don't know what they're up against. The CIC—General Greene's CIC—is already charged with the basic security of the trials, sort of supervising the soldiers from the 1st Division . . ."

"And making sure Göring and his friends stay in their cells."

"Yes, sir. Sir, that really breaks down into two functions. One, which I think the Army can handle, is physically keeping them in their cells or from breaking out of them. The second part of controlling the bastards—"

"I like to think of them as 'the accused,'" Jackson said. "You know, 'innocent until proven guilty.' I find that difficult, but I think it is incumbent upon me to think of them that way, and treat them accordingly."

"Yes, sir. I was about to say that the second part of keeping **the accused** in their cells and from causing trouble, or have them harmed—"

"Have them harmed? By whom?"

"For example, sir, by Mossad, or other Jews. Or by some Odessa Nazis still on the loose who are afraid of what **the accused** might say to save their skins."

"Mossad? The Zionist intelligence service?"

"They are determined that the Nazis not escape punishment."

"You sound as if you're familiar with Mossad?"

"Yes, sir, I am. More accurately, General Gehlen is. I've only met one of their agents."

"The current wisdom around here is that Odessa is a myth, like the 'National Redoubt' the SS was supposed to have had at Berchtesgaden."

"Sir, Odessa exists. We just caught two really bad SS officers Odessa was trying to sneak out of Germany and through France into Spain."

"Two questions, Mr. Cronley . . . or do I call you 'Captain Cronley'?"

"That's your call, sir. Most of the time I don't wear my railroad tracks."

"Why not?"

"People are not surprised to see somebody my age wearing civilian triangles. They often look curiously—"

"At someone your age wearing 'railroad tracks'?"

"Yes, sir."

"People are going to look curiously at you for just being here. How are you going to handle that?"

"Sir, one of the ways we're going to try to keep you safe is for you to add a translator to your personal staff. One of the men I have with me, Maksymilian 'Max' Ostrowski, is a former Free Polish Air Force fighter pilot. He speaks German, Russian, French, and a couple of other languages."

"How is he at protecting people?"

"He was the same thing as a lieutenant in the PSO—the Provisional Security Organization—when he saved the life of one of my sergeants by killing the NKGB people who were trying to . . . I don't know, make contact with a mole, or kidnap or murder one of us in Kloster Grünau."

"Kloster Grünau?"

"It used to be a monastery. It's near Scholl-brunn in the foothills of the Alps. The Vatican turned it over to us. It's where we had General Gehlen until we got the Süd-Deutsche Indus-trielle Entwicklungsorganisation Compound up and running."

"Why did the Vatican do that?"

"They had people they wanted to get out of Europe and to South America. We had the means to do that. I'm told Mr. Dulles made the deal."

"I want to hear more about that, but I'm hearing so much it's overloading me. Let's start again. With what do I call you? How about by your first name?"

"That would be fine with me, sir. It's James. Jim. But what do I call you?"

"It wouldn't bother me, Jim, if you called me by my first name. But it would bother Ken . . . Ken Brewster . . . the man in the outer office. He was—still is—clerk to Supreme Court Jus-tice Jackson, and takes that role, and Mr. Justice Jackson's dignity, very seriously. He would have a heart attack if he heard you calling me 'Bob,' so that won't work. Can you live with calling me 'Mr. Jackson'?"

"Yes, sir, Mr. Jackson."

"'Sir' would also work. But in Ken's hearing, 'Mr. Justice' would be better."

"Yes, sir, Mr. Justice."

The two were smiling at each other.

"Ken's a very bright—brilliant—lawyer. He was top of his class at Yale. And I really need him around here."

Cronley's mouth went on automatic: "He's a lawyer and a clerk?"

"That's the way the system works, Jim," Mr. Justice Jackson said, smiling. "Now tell me about my interpreter."

"After he whacked the three NKGB guys at Kloster Grünau, I took him into DCI, which proved to be one of my rare good ideas."

"You had that authority?"

"Yes, sir. Or I took it because it was the right thing to do."

"And you want him to be my bodyguard?"

"I want him to be in charge of your security detail. We're going to cover you twenty-four hours a day. I brought the men to do that with me."

"All multilingual former members of the Free Polish Forces?"

"Most of them. But two of them are German-speaking Pennsylvania Dutchmen. One is a former Criminal Investigation Division agent, and the other one graduated from high school last year. Really bright kid. He came up with how Odessa was moving Nazis out of Germany."

"You touched on that."

"They were concealing them on the trucks

that deliver **Stars and Stripes** all over Europe. That's how we caught SS-Brigadeführer Ulrich Heimstadter and SS-Standartenführer Oskar Müller."

"Who are?"

"The guys responsible for massacring the slave laborers at Peenemünde."

"I saw the story in **Stars and Stripes**. It didn't say what they had done, and I got the impression that alert Constabulary troopers had caught them trying to cross the Franco–German border."

That's his very polite way of saying he thinks I'm lying.

"Casey—the young Pennsylvania Dutchman— wondered why the **Stripes** trucks were crossing into France at that remote location. When we learned from the French, from Commandant Jean-Paul Fortin of the DST—the Direction de la Surveillance du Territoire—that a man named Luther Stauffer with known connections . . ."

I don't think I should tell Mr. Justice Jackson that Luther is my cousin.

". . . to Odessa had been spending a lot of time in that little **Dorf** Wissembourg, we put two and two together and borrowed some Constabulary troopers from General White and staked them out along the Wissembourg road. The sergeant, First Sergeant Abraham Lincoln Tedworth, in the picture is top kick of the Constab unit that guards Kloster Grünau and the Compound. Tedworth grabbed the bastards because we knew that Odessa was going to try to get somebody through that checkpoint."

Major General I. D. White—a stocky forty-six-year-old who had led the 2nd Armored Division to the Elbe River, and then into the German capital after the Russians had been allowed to take Berlin—had assumed command of the Constabulary on 1 February.

"General White and the Constabulary have a connection with DCI?"

Do I tell him?

My gut tells me he's a decent guy, a really decent human being.

Fuck it! In for a penny, in for a pound.

"As I understand it, sir, General White has been tasked to support us. Not publicly, of course."

"You just said the Constabulary is providing security for your two bases. Isn't that public?"

"Tedworth's people wear Constabulary insignia, but they're really assigned to what we call the 'Military Detachment, DCI-Europe.'"

"How did you get the **Stars and Stripes** to run the story that an alert Constabulary PFC was responsible for catching those two?"

"I struck a deal with Janice Johansen of the Associated Press."

"And she also . . . cooperated . . . in the story

that Colonel Mattingly was in an East German jail for DUI?"

"Yes, sir."

"Perhaps that's why General Seidel thinks you're a loose cannon. My experience has been that any association with the press is dangerous."

"I'm aware of that, sir."

"We were talking a while back about Mossad, Jim. How does Mossad feel about Operation Ost—or should I say, DCI?—shipping Nazis to Argentina?"

"I'm sure they don't like it, but they're patient. Their primary objective now is to get Zionists out of Russia and to Palestine. That requires money. We're giving it to them, so for the moment, money talks."

"The DCI is giving money to a Zionist intelligence organization? Does the President know about this?"

"I don't know about the President, sir, but Admiral Souers does."

"Fascinating."

"Sir, getting back to Miss Johansen. She got us in the press billet in Farber Castle—"

"You mean you and your men, or just you and Miss Johansen?"

"All of us, sir."

"That was very nice of her."

"We're friends."

"Of course you are."

"Obviously, sir, we can't stay there indefinitely."

"Or people would talk, right?"

"Yes, sir."

"Aren't people going to talk, be curious and then talk, about you and your men just because you're here?"

Before Cronley could reply, his office door opened.

"Mr. Justice, I simply have to advise you that you have an appointment with Sir Geoffrey in fifteen minutes," Ken Brewster announced.

"Ken, how many times have I told you the Brits call him 'Sir Geoffrey' and we Americans should call him Justice Lawrence? That's his surname," Jackson said.

"Sorry, sir."

He turned to Cronley. "Sir Geoffrey Lawrence is the chief judge of the Tribunal, Jim. I call him 'Justice Lawrence' to remind him we Americans won the Revolutionary War."

"Yes, sir," Cronley said, chuckling.

"Mr. Cronley is about to leave, Ken. He will return at nine tomorrow morning. Please see that he and his people have no trouble getting in." He turned to Cronley and added, "See you then, Jim."

"Sir, I'd like to leave Ostrowski with you."

"You must think that's important."

"Yes, sir. And so do those two close friends of yours."

"Point taken," Jackson replied. "Okay." He smiled. "If your man speaks, Justice Lawrence will be most curious about the Pole I brought with me. And much too polite to ask."

"If Max says anything at all, sir, I suggest Justice Lawrence will wonder who the Englishman you have with you is. Max sounds like the King of England."

"Even better," Jackson said. "That will really trigger Sir Geoffrey's curiosity."

[THREE]
Farber Palast
Stein, near Nuremberg
American Zone of Occupation,
   Germany
1150 21 February 1946

"Over here, sweetheart," Janice Johansen called, as Cronley came down the wide staircase into the lobby.

He went to where she was sitting at a small table next to the closed door to the bar. With her was a rumpled, chubby man in his forties.

He had an unkempt mustache and was wearing ODs with a War Correspondent patch.

"Say hello to my boss, sweetie," Janice said.

The man extended his hand.

"Seymour Krantz," he said. "My friends call me Sy."

"Jim Cronley."

"Janice has been telling me all about you."

"I was afraid of that."

"Sy's one of the good guys, sweetie."

"Have a seat," Sy said. "In ten minutes, the bar will open and we can have a breakfast beer."

Cronley sat down.

"How did things go at the Palace of Justice?" Janice asked.

"Fine."

"How did Jackson react to being told he now has a bodyguard?" Sy asked.

Cronley gave Janice a dirty look.

Sy saw it.

"They call that the boss–underling relationship," Sy said. "Janice tells me everything, otherwise I send her home to cover vice presidential social events."

"Jesus Christ!"

"Let's clear the air," Sy said. "Sometime ago, a decision was made at the highest executive level of the Associated Press–Europe—in other words, by me—that the world really doesn't have to know what DCI-Europe is up to. I happen to be one of the few people, like Harry S Truman, who thinks Uncle Joe Stalin is dangerous as hell, and I'm certainly—the AP certainly—isn't going to fuck up anything he's doing to fuck up Uncle Joe by letting the Russians know what he's doing.

"As proof of that, I have known from the git-go that the OSS and now the DCI has shipped Nazis to South America as part of the deal Allen Dulles made with Generalmajor Reinhard Gehlen. And we haven't written about it. What I did do was tell Janice to keep an eye on it, which brought her into your life. Getting the picture?"

Oh, boy! Here we go again.
How the hell do I handle this?
I certainly can't piss this guy off.
And I will if I get on my high horse.
Or play dumb.

"Justice Jackson told me that General Seidel had called him and told him all about me. Not nice things. And then he told me that both the President and Admiral Souers had called him—"

"And said nice things about you?" Janice asked.

"And said he was going to have protection, bodyguards, whether or not he liked it."

"And how did he react, to get back to my original question?" Sy asked.

"One of my guys, Max Ostrowski, is with him now, as his interpreter, and I just sent two more guys to his office."

"You're here on the sly, right? You don't want it to get out that the DCI is now protecting Jackson and company?"

"No, I don't."

"You open to suggestion?"

Cronley nodded. "Shoot."

"If Jackson now has a new interpreter, why can't he have a new public relations assistant? That would mean you could live here."

"What do I do with the rest of my guys? I've got more coming."

"Move them in with the CIC. They've already got their own **Kaserne**."

"My guys have CIC credentials, but they're not CIC."

The conversation was interrupted when the door to the bar was opened.

"Breakfast time!" Sy cried, as he got to his feet.

Cy was not kidding about his breakfast beer. As soon as they had taken seats at a table, the bartender set a bottle of beer before him.

Cronley read the label and his mouth went on automatic:

"Berliner Kindl? They don't make beer in Nuremberg?"

"Not as good as Berliner Kindl. The PIO is

kind enough to import it for me. It's nice to be head of the AP."

Cronley and Janice ordered coffee and were told that some was being brewed.

Sy carefully poured the Berliner Kindl so that there was just the right amount of foam and then took a healthy swallow that left beer foam on his mustache. He wiped it off with the back of his hand.

"Janice thinks you don't know enough about the trials," Sy said, "and since I know all about them, suggests I should bring you up to speed. So what don't you know about the International Military Tribunal?"

Cronley's mouth went on automatic: "After a fair trial, we're going to hang the bastards."

"In other words, you know little about it?"

"Yeah."

"Winston Churchill thought we should shoot the bastards on the spot whenever we found them. I think that was the thing to do. Franklin Roosevelt thought there should be a trial. I think that was another of his monumental mistakes. Bottom line, there are trials. Four-Power.

"One of the first things ol' Harry did after FDR died in Georgia—in the arms of his girlfriend—was fire Edward Stettinius Junior, the secretary of State, and Francis Biddle, the attorney general. The story I get is that ol' Harry was pissed, and I think justifiably so, because nobody had told him about the atom bomb.

"Or he might have been pissed with Biddle on general principles. Biddle is a Groton-Harvard-Philadelphia lawyer WASP. They tend to look down the noses at ex–Missouri National Guard colonels and their wives. Harry may have caught him looking down his nose at Bess.

"Anyway, he canned him. And almost immediately realized that was a mistake. Biddle has a lot of friends. So Harry threw him a bone and appointed him chief judge of the Tribunal. And then appointed his crony Bob Jackson as chief U.S. prosecutor to keep an eye on him. Getting the picture?"

"I think so. He wanted to make sure they got a fair trial before we hang them?"

"Not quite. As everybody in Washington is learning, Harry isn't nearly as stupid as thought. Harry always thought that just shooting the bastards, as Churchill proposed, was a bad idea. He also thought that just hanging them after a quick trial was a bad idea."

"Why?"

"The Germans were just about one hundred percent behind Hitler. Hanging the bastards would make them martyrs. Unless the German people could be shown what bastards they really were. Hitler and Goebbels had them pretty well convinced that people of my religious persuasion were not only responsible for Germany's problems, but controlled the world, including the United States.

"So, the Jewish-controlled United States won the war, assisted by the German generals and admirals who had betrayed the Führer, and as the dirty Jews could be expected to, promptly hung the nice people who had nobly defended Western civilization and **Gemütlichkeit** to the bitter end.

"Thus making Göring, Goebbels, Himmler, and company martyrs to the noble cause of National Socialism. Germany had been on its back before, after World War One, when the French took twenty percent of its territory and otherwise really screwed them. But, under the leadership of Der Führer, had risen from the ashes. Why couldn't that happen again? You ever hear of Operation Phoenix?"

"Actually, I know a lot about it."

"How come?"

"Well, I've been to Argentina, where the next thing I have to a big brother ran OSS there, and is now running DCI–Southern Cone."

Krantz gestured for him to go on.

"I don't know whether Göring was involved—he might have been—but I do know that Goebbels and Himmler sent huge amounts of money and gold—"

"Much of which had been gold teeth taken

from the mouths of people murdered at Treblinka and other such places after they had been gassed and before they were fed to the crematoria."

Cronley, nodding, continued: "Over there to buy property and influence so the big-shot Nazis could go there, to bide time and eventually rise from the ashes."

"Which is what Phoenix means, resurrected from the ashes. So you're not completely ignorant."

"Only ninety-five percent."

"I suspect that's false modesty," Krantz said. "Okay, so Harry Truman decided the Germans had to be taught what bastards their leaders were. How to do that? A show trial. The courtroom was rebuilt, including extensive provisions for newsreel cameras, and broadcasters. To make the press feel welcome, they took over this place. The trials would be broadcast over the German radio stations, and the newsreels shown over and over in German movie theaters. If it works, and it may, the Germans will learn what bastards their leaders were."

"**May** work?"

"Bob Jackson is not doing a great job. Göring has made a jackass of him several times."

"How?"

"Let me tell you about Hermann. Did you ever hear about his surrender?"

Cronley shook his head.

"He was on his private train. With his wife, Emily, and other members of his family, four aides, a nurse, two chauffeurs, two Mercedeses, a five-member kitchen crew, and several boxcars loaded with art—stolen art—that he had decided not to blow up when he blew up Carinhall—"

"Blew up what?"

"Unser Hermann was not only Reichsmarschall Göring but **Reichsjägermeister**— hunting master of the Thousand-Year Reich. He had his own private hunting grounds, two hundred hectares in the Schorfheide Forest northeast of Berlin. On it he built a mansion— Carinhall—which he then stuffed with stuffed deer and boar heads, and the best of the art he'd stolen from Europe's better museums. When the Russians got close, he blew everything up except his favorite art pieces, and sixty-two cases of the best French champagne, which he took with him on his train. It went to Austria, where he surrendered to we Americans."

"Jesus Christ!"

"It gets better. They loaded him in one of his Mercedeses and brought him here. One of the 1st Division generals—a one-star, I forget his name—walked up to the car. Göring got out, in full uniform, including the Blue Max. He had his **Reichsmarschall** baton in one hand, and a framed photograph of himself in the other.

"He hands the photo to the one-star. It's signed **War is like a football game, whoever loses gives his opponent his hand, and everything is forgotten. Hermann Göring.**"

"Unbelievable! What did the general do?"

"Took the baton away from him right there, and then had Hermann marched to his cell, where they took away his decorations. Hermann was displeased at the quality of his new accommodations—you ever been in the prison?"

Cronley shook his head.

"One-man cells, with a window through which a GI takes a look every couple of minutes. A GI bed, a wooden chair, a little wooden desk, like a table, a washbasin, and a crapper. You should have a look."

"I will. You said Göring made a jackass of Jackson?"

"Yeah. I got the impression that whatever his legal talents are—and he was—is—one of the better Supreme Court justices—he's not very good at being a trial lawyer. I was there, I saw this. Jackson, bubbling over with righteous indignation, asks, 'Is it true, Witness, that together with Adolf Hitler, you were primarily responsible for preparing the plans for the war in total secrecy?'

"Göring, smiling, says, 'I don't seem to recall reading the American plans for the war in the **New York Times**.'

"Everybody in the courtroom, including me and all the bastards in the defendant's dock, laughed out loud. Göring sat down and accepted the congratulations of his fellow prisoners. And Jackson said something like 'No further questions at this time.' And Biddle quickly adjourned the proceedings for the day."

"I hate to say this, but that's pretty classy behavior for a guy who has to know we're going to hang him." He paused for a moment, and then asked, "Or does he think he's going to escape the noose?"

"No. He knows he's going to be hanged. But he wants to be hung as a martyr to the noble cause of National Socialism, not as a murderer. And it looks as if he's going to succeed. If that happens, we become, in the eyes of the German people, the vindictive victors. The only hope, as I see it, is for Jackson to get somebody to say, 'I did it, and Göring told me to do it.'

"And that's unlikely, as just about all the bastards still treat him as if he's still sitting behind his desk in the Chancellery waving his **Reichs-marschall**'s baton around."

" 'Just about all'?" Cronley parroted.

"You know who Rudolf Hess is?"

"The guy who stole an airplane and flew it to talk to Churchill?"

"Who immediately locked him up and kept him there until he sent him here. He's playing nuts. Or he may really be bonkers. He flew to England in 1941, before all the mass murders began, so that may help him to escape the noose. If he tries something like 'I flew to England to tell Churchill what these terrible Nazis were up to,' that would help. But right now he's playing his 'I'm bonkers' card.

"The other guy who might be useful to Jackson is Speer. You know who he is?"

Cronley shook his head and said, "No. Not really."

"Albert Speer. Architect. If Hitler had any personal friends, Speer was in that select, tiny group. Hitler fancied himself to be an architect. Speer was a very good architect, so Hitler enlisted him to help with his plans to turn Berlin into the twentieth-century version of Athens or Rome. They became friends. Speer was a Nazi. He believed, at the beginning, that Hitler was the man God had sent to save the world from Communism and my coreligionists.

"Hitler fitted him out with a uniform and named him minister of armaments. Which included building the wall to keep the Allies off the continent. Speer was very good at what he did. Until just about the end, despite all the bombing, Speer kept the munitions and weapons factories running at full speed. To do this, he had to use slave labor, much of it imported from what the Krauts called 'the occupied territories.'

"That's what he's being tried for by the Tribunal.

"At the end, when Hitler knew the war was about to be lost, he ordered Speer to blow up everything, and I mean everything—factories, the railroads, the sewers, waterworks, universities, everything. At that point, Speer finally opened his eyes and saw that Der Führer was a dangerous maniac.

"So Speer decided it was his duty as a good German to disobey Der Führer. This took a lot of balls. And then he flew to Berlin and went to the Führerbunker and told Adolf that he had countermanded his orders. That took a huge set of balls.

"I have no idea how he escaped with his life, but I have personally checked out Speer's story and I know it's true. And so does Jackson. So Jackson—this is an opinion, Jackson doesn't confide in me—is trying to get Speer to say, 'I did it. I was involved, I knew all about the slave labor, the concentration camps, the extermination squads, and so did everybody sitting here with me in the prisoner's dock.' If he can get him to do that, the good guys win. Göring and company go to the gallows as people who really fucked Germany up, not as National Socialist martyrs."

The coffee was finally served. Krantz ordered another Berliner Kindl.

"You think Jackson will succeed?" Cronley asked.

"Who knows?"

"Who do I have to see to get someplace for my guys to stay?"

"How many guys?"

"At least a dozen more. All Poles."

"That'll be awkward."

"And probably two, three, four Americans. Admiral Souers told me DCI is going to really grow."

"There're three bird colonels who think they run things. One is from Nuremberg Military Post. The second is from the 1st Division. The third runs the CIC detachment. His name is Morty Cohen. German Jew, one who got out just before all his relatives wound up in Flossenbürg or some other resort on their way to the crematoria. Real prick. I suggest you deal with him first, as he has the final say on just about everything."

Cronley stood up.

"I might as well get it over with," he said. "Thanks for the history lesson, Sy."

"Any pal of Janice's is a pal of mine. Good luck, kid."

"Give me a ring when you get back, sweetie. I'll keep the home fires burning."

III

[ONE]
The International Tribunal Compound
Nuremberg, American Zone of
Occupation, Germany
1305 21 February 1946

There were six **Kasernen**—three-story-plus-attic tiled-roof buildings—three on each side of a cobblestone street. What had been the parade ground between them under German control was now essentially a motor pool, filled with Army trucks, most of which bore 1st Infantry Division insignia and bumper markings.

Concertina barbed wire laid on the ground separated one of the **Kasernen** from the others. Two signs read XXIST CIC RESTRICTED AREA AUTHORIZED PERSONNEL ONLY.

There was space for four vehicles in front of the CIC **Kaserne**. A Ford staff car and a jeep were in two of them. Cronley pulled the Horch into one of the empty spaces and only then saw another sign: FIELD-GRADE OFFICERS ONLY.

He debated for about two seconds and then

decided, **Fuck it. As a DCI agent, I'm an assimilated lieutenant colonel, whatever the hell "assimilated" means.**

He got out of the Horch and walked to the door of the **Kaserne**. It wouldn't open.

Then he saw a "Double Eight" field telephone mounted beside the door and one more sign: USE TELEPHONE FOR ADMITTANCE.

He picked up the handset and cranked the telephone.

"State your business," a voice commanded.

"CIC Special Agent Cronley to see Colonel Cohen."

"Wait one."

The door opened.

A man in his early twenties in triangled ODs and wearing a .45 pistol suspended from a web belt appeared.

"Credentials?"

Cronley produced his CIC credentials.

The man examined them carefully and then said, "First door on the left."

Cronley walked to the door, opened it, and stepped inside.

A master sergeant in his late twenties sat behind a desk.

"I'd like to see Colonel Cohen, please. My name is Cronley."

"Send him in," a high-pitched voice ordered from an outer office.

Cronley walked through the open door.

A very slight man in his forties sat behind a desk on which sat a small sign:

COLONEL MORTIMER S. COHEN, MI. COMMANDING OFFICER.

"Good morning, Colonel. I'm Jim Cronley. I command the Thirty-fourth CIC Detachment, which has just been assigned here, and I'm here to make my manners with you."

"You're off to a bad start. For one thing, since we both know you're in the Army, you should have saluted. And for another, you're obviously too young to be a field-grade officer, so you shouldn't have parked where you just did."

Oh, shit!

What do I do now?

Salute this arrogant little sonofabitch and apologize?

Fuck that!

That would put me in his pocket, and I can't let that happen.

The best defense is a good offense!

"For one thing, Colonel, I'm wearing triangles, and civilians don't salute. And so far as being a field-grade officer, that comes with this."

He took out his DCI credentials and laid them on Cohen's desk.

"I'm actually commanding officer of Detachment 'A' of DCI-Europe, which has been charged with protecting Justice Jackson. The Thirty-fourth CIC Detachment is my cover."

"I've been charged with protecting everyone connected with the Tribunal."

"You have just been relieved of that responsibility for Justice Jackson."

"Presumably you have orders giving you the authority to do that? I find that hard to believe."

"I don't need orders. I have that authority. May I suggest you ask General Greene?"

Colonel Cohen stared coldly at him for a full twenty seconds.

"General Greene telephoned me to tell me you were coming. He said I was to cooperate with you. He didn't say anything about you assuming responsibility for Justice Jackson."

"Well, he knows that's one of the things I was sent here to do. Why don't you call him?"

"You wouldn't want me to call him if you didn't know what he was going to say, so I'll give you a pass on that, Captain Cronley."

Cronley didn't reply. They looked at one another for thirty seconds.

"Are you going to tell me what's going on?" Cohen asked finally. "How I'm supposed to cooperate with you? You implied just now—'one of the things I was sent here to do'—that you have more than protecting Justice Jackson on your plate."

"Let's start with Justice Jackson. When the President heard that Colonel Mattingly had been kidnapped, he became concerned with Justice Jackson's security."

"'Kidnapped'? There was a story in **Stars and Stripes** that he'd been arrested for drunk driving in East Germany."

"You can't always believe what you read in the newspapers, Colonel."

"Very true. There was another story in **Stars and Stripes** reporting that my friend, the CIC inspector general, Lieutenant Colonel Tony Schumann, and his wife were killed when his hot water heater blew up. I didn't believe that, either."

"Why not?"

"Because I had an interesting chat with him shortly before that happened. He told me that he was looking into Operation Ost and that when he tried to see what was going on at the former monastery, Kloster Grünau, ostensibly a CIC installation, he was denied entrance by a young captain named Cronley."

"I remember the incident."

"And that you shot the engine out of his car when he tried to drive in."

"One of my men put one round from a .50 caliber machine gun into his engine."

"And that when he reported this incident to General Greene, he was told not to investigate what was going on at Kloster Grünau or with Operation Ost."

"I understand that's what happened. Except that General Greene had told Colonel Schumann that Operation Ost and Kloster Grünau were off-limits to him before he showed up at the monastery."

"Are you going to share with me, in the spirit of cooperation General Greene wants us to have, what was going on at the monastery?"

"You don't have the Need to Know, Colonel. And neither did Colonel Schumann."

"Tony said he suspected that Generalmajor Reinhard Gehlen and many, perhaps most, of Gehlen's Abwehr Ost staff were being hidden there to keep them from being brought here to stand trial with the other senior Nazis."

"I can't speak to that, Colonel, but I can tell you that General Gehlen and all of his former staff have appeared before a denazification court and been cleared. At the time of his surrender, the Sicherheitsdienst was looking for him—for them—because of their role in the failed assassination of Hitler at Wolfsschanze."

"And shortly after you put a round in his engine, and General Greene told him Operation Ost and your monastery were off-limits, Colonel Schumann's water heater blew up."

"What are you suggesting, Colonel?"

"I'm suggesting nothing more than it's an

interesting coincidence. But like you, Captain Cronley, I'm an intelligence officer and we're supposed to be suspicious of everything. I confess I've wondered if General Gehlen might have had anything to do with the explosion of Tony Schumann's water heater."

"Generals Greene and Schwarzkopf personally investigated that tragedy and found nothing suspicious about it."

"So I've heard. I wonder about a lot of things where there are interesting coincidences. For example, I thought it was interesting that Major Tom Derwin, Tony Schumann's replacement as CIC IG, fell under a train in the Munich Ostbahnhof shortly after visiting the Süd-Deutsche Industrielle Entwicklungsorganisation's compound in Pullach. Doesn't former Generalmajor Gehlen run that? Or have I been misinformed?"

Okay.

Battle lines drawn.

Cohen is among those who feel the Schumanns and Derwin were whacked by Gehlen.

Which I strongly suspect to be the case.

The Schumanns deserved it. Both of them were NKGB moles.

I don't know about Derwin, but it's entirely possible Gehlen took him out just to cover all the bases.

So how far is Cohen going to go running down his suspicions?

I dunno. But it's pretty clear he's not going to stop.

Which predicts lots of trouble for me.

"It's no secret that Gehlen runs the South German Industrial Development Organization, Colonel."

"In a compound surrounded by three barbed wire fences and a reinforced company of American soldiers. I don't suppose you're going to tell what's really going on in that compound, are you, Captain Cronley?"

"As far as I know, they're developing industry in South Germany."

"Bullshit!"

"As I was saying before, as I understand the situation, when the President heard that Colonel Mattingly had been kidnapped, he became concerned for Justice Jackson's security—"

"Why Jackson and not Biddle? Biddle is the chief U.S. judge."

"Jackson, like Admiral Souers, is an old and close friend of the President. As I understand it, the President told Souers to send me to do that and then called Justice Jackson and told him he was going to be protected whether or not he liked it."

"You're telling me—and expecting me to

believe—that President Truman personally picked you, a captain, to protect Jackson?"

"Yes, I am. Are we back to why don't you ask General Greene? Or Admiral Souers?"

"I think we're back to what else you're going to do here at the personal order of the commander in chief."

"On my own authority, Colonel, I'm going to see what the prisoners will tell me about Odessa."

"Odessa is bullshit."

"Many believe that Odessa is bullshit."

"Not so. We just caught two bad guys— SS-Brigadeführer Ulrich Heimstadter and his deputy, Standartenführer Oskar Müller— Odessa was trying to slip into France. I'm surprised you don't know that. When I was through with them, I sent them here. They were already indicted for what they did at Peenemünde."

"When you were through with them? What the hell does that mean?"

"You don't have the Need to Know."

"You arrogant sonofabitch!"

"So what I'm going to need from you, Colonel, is to clear me and my people into the jail whenever we want to visit one of the prisoners. You have a problem with that?"

"You're goddamn right I do!" Cohen said. He snatched a telephone from its base and ordered, "Get General Greene at USFET for me."

After about a minute, Cohen said: "General, Captain Cronley is in my office. He just told me he wants unrestricted access to my prisoners—

"Yes, sir, that was an unfortunate choice of words. I fully understand the prisoners are not mine personally. But I am charged with prison security and giving Cronley—

"Yes, sir. One moment, sir."

Cohen extended the telephone to Cronley. "General Greene wants to talk to you."

"Yes, sir?" Cronley said into the phone.

"Jesus Christ, Jim! I thought you were going to bump heads with Colonel Cohen eventually, but you just got there!"

"I'm sorry, sir. But—"

"'But' my rosy Irish ass. Learn to get along with Cohen."

"I'll try, sir."

"And I don't want a telephone call from Justice Jackson three minutes after you walk into his office."

"I've already met with Justice Jackson, sir. And Max Ostrowski, his new interpreter, is already on the job."

"Really?"

"Yes, sir. And Mr. Justice Jackson has a new press adviser named Cronley."

"Well, maybe you're not really as incompetent as most people around here think. But keep in mind, Jim, that Morty Cohen—like most intelligence officers—can be really dangerous when crossed, and obviously that's already happened."

"That already occurred to me, General."

"Keep in touch, Jim," Greene said, and hung up.

Cronley replaced the handset on its base and retrieved his DCI credentials from Cohen's desk.

"Thank you for receiving me, Colonel."

"My pleasure. And please let me know if there is anything else, anything at all, that I can do for you," Cohen said.

That's the kind of sarcasm that can knock down a brick wall.

Cronley walked out of Colonel Cohen's office.

[TWO]
Headquarters, 26th Infantry
  Regiment
The International Tribunal
  Compound
Nuremberg, American Zone of
  Occupation, Germany
1355 21 February 1946

The office of Colonel James T. Rasberry, commander of the 26th Infantry Regiment of the

1st Division, was, like that of Colonel Mortimer Cohen, close to the door of the **Kaserne**. The reception Cronley received was far more cordial than the one he had just received from Colonel Cohen.

"Come on in, Mr. Cronley," Colonel Rasberry welcomed him. "I'm just sitting here watching my soldiers demolish the vehicles in my motor pool." He put out his hand. "Tell me what I can do for the CIC while we have a cup of coffee."

Cronley saw the only thing pinned to the chest of Rasberry's tunic was the Combat Infantry Badge.

I think I'm going to like this guy.

"Colonel, I'm sort of here under false pretenses," Cronley said, and handed him his DCI credentials. The colonel examined them carefully.

"Jesus H. Christ! If I read this correctly, your chain of command is straight up to this admiral, and he answers only to President Truman. Right?"

"Yes, sir. That's it."

"Should I stand to attention and salute?" Colonel Rasberry asked.

"Please don't, Colonel."

Almost immediately, Rasberry, looking out his office window, said, "Oh, shit! One of my six-by-sixes just ran head-on into one of my ambulances. One of the drivers, if not both, has just flunked, probably for the third or fourth time, How to Drive 101."

Cronley laughed and asked, "That bad?"

"You ever hear what the average age of enlisted men in the Army of Occupation is?"

"Eighteen point something."

"And thirty-point-something percent of them are from New York City and other major metropolitan areas, where they don't teach their young to drive. And of that thirty point something, the repple depple sends ninety percent to units like the 26th, where they really need to know how. Despite what Napoleon said about armies moving on their stomach, this army moves on trucks. Six-by-sixes, like the one that just moved to the 'Out of Service for Collision Damage Repair' column."

"That bad?" Cronley asked again.

"Worse. We are now back to what can the 26th do for you, Mr. Cronley?"

He walked to a coffee thermos, poured two mugs, and handed one to Cronley.

"I just got here with a small detachment to provide security for Justice Jackson, and I'm here to make my manners."

"I was afraid, when Sergeant Fuller said, 'The CIC is here,' that you were bearing more complaints from Colonel Cohen. You know who I mean?"

"I just came from making my manners to Colonel Cohen."

"And?"

"I got the impression he doesn't like me."

"I don't think he likes anybody. Or was it something specific?"

"I told him I was relieving him of the responsibility to protect Justice Jackson. He told me I didn't have the authority to do that. I suggested he check with his boss, General Greene. General Greene told him of the authority that goes with the DCI credentials. Things went downhill from there."

"I try to give Cohen a pass, both because he's an intelligence officer and because he lost a lot of relatives in Treblinka or some other hellhole. But sometimes that's hard. So what can the 26th do for you?"

"Two things. I'd like you to pass the word, quietly, to your people that the DCI is here, and are authorized to be anywhere. Most of my people are Poles, former officers of the Free Polish Army and Air Force—"

"—who didn't want to go home to get shot on arrival by the Russians?"

"Right."

"Done. I've been wondering why Cohen worries more about the Nazis, who we have locked up until we can give them a fair trial and hang them, than he does about the goddamn Russians. Half of the Russian delegation here spends ninety percent of their time running around our zone taking pictures of our installations. Yesterday I ran two of them off Soldier's Field."

"What's that?"

"The Army airfield."

"You're responsible for the airfield?"

Rasberry nodded.

"Is there a hangar on the field where I could park a Storch—that's a German airplane a little bigger than a puddle jumper—"

"I know what a Storch is. You've got one?"

"Two. And the Air Corps doesn't like it."

"But you've got two of them. Which means . . . Would your feelings be hurt if I told you you don't look old enough to be a heavy-duty spook who can get away with giving the Air Corps the finger?"

"You're putting me on a spot, Colonel."

"I'll make a deal with you, Super Spook—you give me a ride in your Storch, and I will let you hide it in my hangar."

"Deal. Thank you."

"Can I ask why you need an airplane like a Storch?"

"To move around. In addition to my duties here, I'm trying to shut down Odessa."

"So Odessa must be real. Contrary to popular belief."

"It's real, Colonel."

"What else can I do for you, Super Spook?"

"I've got to find a place for my people to live. Ultimately, there will be about thirty of them, mostly Poles."

"Go see the Nuremberg Military Post liaison officer. Colonel Steve Anderson. Pretty good guy for a quartermaster officer. Make sure he knows you're on Cohen's shit list. That'll give you something in common."

"Thank you."

The door to the office opened and Master Sergeant Fuller put his head in.

"Colonel, there's another CIC guy out here, says he has to see this one right away."

Rasberry waved a hand as a signal to bring him in.

Augie Ziegler came through the door.

"Colonel Rasberry, this is my executive officer, Mr. Ziegler."

"How about a cup of coffee, Mr. Ziegler?"

"Thank you, but no, sir."

"What's up, Augie?" Cronley asked.

Ziegler's face showed that he was reluctant to talk in front of Colonel Rasberry.

"He's one of the good guys, Augie."

"Ziegler sounds more German than Polish," Rasberry observed.

"He's a Pennsylvania Dutchman. Out with it, Augie."

"Right after you left, an ASA team showed up. They'd been driving all night."

"And?"

"They installed a SIGABA. I had to flash the DCI credentials to the manager, Major Levin, to get him to allow putting the antenna on the roof. I had no choice, Jim."

"What's a SIGABA?" Rasberry asked.

"Your dirty little secret was going to come out anyway, Augie. So what's the rush with the SIGABA?"

"Which is a what?" Rasberry pursued.

"A fancy radio they give to us Super Spooks," Cronley answered.

"As soon as it was up, Colonel Wallace was on it. He wants to talk to you immediately."

"About what?"

"He didn't say. What he said was find you and get you on the horn right goddamn now."

"Colonel, duty calls," Cronley said.

"That happens," Rasberry said. "Two things, Super Spook. I'll call Steve Anderson and tell him you're coming and why. And I have just appointed you and your Pennsylvania Dutchman honorary members of the Blue Spade O Club. It's next door. If you would like to buy me a drink, I am usually there every day from 1700 to 1800 and sometimes a little longer."

"We'll be there, Colonel. Thank you, sir."

[THREE]
The Duchess Suite
Farber Palast
Stein, near Nuremberg
American Zone of Occupation,
  Germany
1525 21 February 1946

"There's sort of a closet, Jim. They put it in there," Ziegler said, as he walked across the room and opened a door.

The SIGABA control board and telephone had been installed on a mirror vanity table that looked like it belonged in a museum.

Cronley sat down on a fragile-looking matching chair, picked up the handset, and switched the device on.

"ASA Fulda. The line is secure."

"J. D. Cronley Six Three One for Colonel Wallace."

"Hold One."

"Wallace."

"J. D. Cronley is on, sir. The line is secure."

"Where the hell have you been?"

"Touring scenic Nuremberg. What's going

on, Colonel? I'm now allowed to call you 'Colonel,' right?"

"Spare me your fucking wiseass wit. What's going on is that sometime around 0300, person or persons unknown murdered Lieutenant Moriarty."

"Bonehead was murdered?"

"In your bed, or what used to be your bed, in the Compound. Seven—they're still counting—shots from a silenced Colt Woodmaster .22."

"Jesus Christ!"

"Yeah. I'm sorry, Jim. But I thought you'd want to know."

"Winters is on his way to pick me up, right? When does he get here? Why isn't he already here, for Christ's sake?"

"Because you have been ordered, by the President of the United States, to set up protection for Justice Jackson, and that's the priority."

"I did that yesterday. At least two of Ostrowski's people are sitting on him."

"There's no reason for you to come here, Jim."

"Bullshit! Bonehead and I go back to A&M. I recruited him for DCI. Put Winters in a Storch and tell him to come get me."

"Winters is consoling the widow. And to repeat, there's no reason for you to come here."

"Then put Kurt Schröder in a Storch."

"For the third or maybe fourth time, there's no reason for you to come here."

"I'm coming. If you won't, for some bullshit reason, send Schröder to get me, I'll drive up there in Mattingly's fucking Horch!"

There was a long period of silence. Finally Wallace said, "I'll call when Schröder gets off the ground."

[FOUR]
Office of the Military Government
    Liaison Officer
The South German Industrial
    Development Organization
    Compound
Pullach, Bavaria
American Zone of Occupation,
    Germany
1805 21 February 1946

Colonel Harold Wallace was sitting behind the desk that had been Cronley's, when Cronley and Ziegler walked in. Captain "Tiny" Dunwiddie and Claudette Colbert sat on chairs facing it. Dunwiddie was wearing his captain's insignia, and Colbert was wearing the triangles of a civilian employee of the Army.

"Please don't tell me you left Ostrowski in charge of guarding Jackson," Wallace greeted them.

"Ostrowski was playing chess with Justice Jackson when I called Jackson to tell him I was coming here."

"You're supposed to be guarding Jackson," Wallace said.

Cronley was about to reply when the door opened and former Generalmajor Reinhard Gehlen, former Oberst Ludwig Mannberg, and former Major Konrad Bischoff came into the building.

"We heard the Storch come in," Gehlen said. "Jim, I'm very sorry about your friend."

"Thank you. Colonel Wallace was just about to tell me about it."

"And I will, just as soon as you tell me why you brought Ziegler with you. Which means Justice Jackson is now being guarded by a Polish displaced person. I don't think that's what the President had in mind when he ordered you to Nuremberg."

"Max Ostrowski is a DCI special agent, and I think he makes a better bodyguard than either me or Augie Ziegler. The President ordered me there because he trusts my judgment. I decided that I could leave Jackson in Ostrowski's capable hands. Okay?"

"Not okay. But there doesn't seem to be much I can do about it, does there? You did it, it's done."

Cronley didn't reply.

"What did you tell Jackson about your coming here?"

"I told him that Moriarty, a good friend, had been murdered in the Compound, and that I was coming here to help find the bastards that did it."

"Jesus Christ, weren't you thinking? That's going to scare the shit out of him, and I don't even want to think about what's going to happen when he tells the President, which he damned sure will."

"What I think will happen is Jackson will now do what Max tells him to do. That, and as far as the President is concerned, I think he'll see it as proof he did the right thing by sending me to Nuremberg."

"At the risk of further inflaming your temper," Mannberg said to Wallace, "I think Jim has made his point."

"Let me get this off my chest before I forget it," Cronley said. "I made my manners to Colonel Mortimer Cohen, who has the Tribunal CIC detachment—"

"And?" Wallace demanded impatiently.

"Two things. First, he was upset when I told him I was taking over Justice Jackson's security—"

"Which I'm sure you did with your legendary tact," Wallace said.

"So he called General Greene—"

"Who is on his way here and should be walking through the door at any moment," Wallace said. "And?"

"General Greene told him I had the authority to do so. Which pissed him off. And during the course of our chat, he let me know that he was a friend of Colonel and Mrs. Schumann and had been wondering if perhaps General Gehlen had something to do with that exploding water heater. And with Major Derwin's falling under the train."

"Oh, Jesus!" Wallace said. "So what—I'm afraid to ask this—what did you say, Loose Cannon, when he told you this?"

"I told him that both General Greene and General Schwarzkopf had personally investigated the water heater explosion and found nothing to suggest it wasn't an accident. I don't think he believes that."

Cronley glanced at Gehlen and Mannberg. Neither's face showed anything.

"And Derwin's accident?"

"We didn't get into that, but I told you, he doesn't think that was an accident, either."

"Why didn't you get into it?"

"Because I had pissed him off even further when I told him he didn't have the Need to Know what really goes on here in the Compound. At that point, he made it clear our little chat was over."

Cronley had, without warning, an epiphany.

Jesus, my mouth just ran away again!

By telling Wallace, in front of Gehlen and Mannberg, that Cohen doesn't believe that "an accident, nothing suspicious" bullshit, have I just as much as signed Cohen's death warrant?

If they took out the Schumanns and Derwin because they posed a threat to Operation Ost, why not one more guy they think poses a threat?

"And at that point, Loose Cannon, did it enter your mind that getting into it with Colonel Cohen might cause a little problem or two for you while you're doing what you were sent to Nuremberg to do?"

"Actually, that did pass fleetingly through my mind."

"What I should do is relieve you!"

"I think you'd have to explain why you did to Admiral Souers and maybe even the President. You sure you want to do that, Colonel?"

"Gentlemen," General Gehlen said softly, "may I suggest that before this gets out of hand, we discuss what's happened to Lieutenant Moriarty?"

Wallace, his face flushed, looked between Gehlen and Cronley.

"I told Justice Jackson that I would tell him what happened," Cronley said.

Wallace took a deep breath and then exhaled between pursed lips.

The door opened again and General Greene came into the room, followed by Major General Norman Schwarzkopf, the USFET provost marshal.

"We're late," Greene said. "Sorry. The autobahn was icy. How much have we missed?"

"We haven't even started," Wallace said. "Captain—excuse me, **DCI Special Agent**—Cronley was just telling us about his meeting with Colonel Cohen."

"I heard about that," Greene said. "Morty Cohen is a good man, but sometimes he gets carried away. I made it clear to him, I think, that Cronley has the authority to do whatever he thinks he has to do. I don't think there will be any more problems between them."

"Harold, I'm having some problems with you taking this thing out of my hands," Schwarzkopf said.

"General, I very much appreciate your cooperation. When you hear what went down, I think you'll understand that what happened has to be kept under wraps."

Schwarzkopf nodded.

"So, taking it from the top," Wallace began, "Lieutenant Moriarty, who commanded the American troops who guard the Compound and Kloster Grünau and supervised the Poles—the

Provisional Security Organization—elected last night to fill in for the PSO officer who was duty officer and had fallen ill. He did this routinely.

"The PSO duty officer and the NCOIC of the Americans do their thing in here, which also serves to keep an eye on the SIGABA machine. Last night the American was Staff Sergeant Henry J. Phillips, a very good soldier who had been one of Tiny's Troopers since the Battle of the Bulge.

"Sergeant Phillips told me that after they inspected the guard at 0200, he suggested to Lieutenant Moriarty that since Cronley was no longer living in there"—Wallace pointed to what had been Cronley's bedroom—"he could 'crap out there while he minded the store.' Moriarty at first rejected the suggestion, but then he changed his mind.

"He told Sergeant Phillips that he had been up most of the previous night with his newborn son, who suffers from colic. Moriarty went into the bedroom to lie down on what had been Cronley's bed. He ordered Phillips to wake him for the 0300 tour of the Compound.

"Phillips did not do so. He said he felt sorry for Lieutenant Moriarty, who looked 'really asleep on his feet.' It has been protocol to have two people in the tour jeep since then Technical Sergeant Tedworth—now First Sergeant Tedworth—making a tour alone at Kloster

Grünau nearly lost his life when persons we now believe to have been NKGB agents ambushed him. They had him on the ground with a garrote around his neck when a PSO officer—now DCI Special Agent Ostrowski—happened on the scene and disposed of all three.

"So, to make the tour, Sergeant Phillips called the Pole barracks and had them send him a PSO sergeant—the equivalent thereof—and they made the tour. Phillips kept the PSO man after the tour, and together they made the 0400 and 0500 jeep tours of the Compound.

"At approximately 0550, Phillips went to the bedroom to wake Lieutenant Moriarty. He found him lying on the bed, his bloody head on the pillow. Phillips went to the body and made the immediate judgment that Lieutenant Moriarty had been shot, twice, in the head, with a small-caliber weapon.

"Phillips immediately called Captain Dunwiddie at the Vier Jahreszeiten. Dunwiddie called me. I then called Sergeant Phillips and told him to secure the area, and not, not, to call the military police until I came to the Compound.

"On our arrival at the Compound, Sergeant Phillips told me that a search of the Compound perimeter had detected no signs of surreptitious entry. He said there were no footprints, or any other sign of disturbance of the snow. He then gave me a silenced Colt Woodsman .22 long rifle cartridge semi-automatic pistol that he had found in the snow outside the bedroom window."

"What kind of a gun?" General Schwarzkopf asked.

Wallace opened the desk drawer and, using a pencil, raised the weapon by its trigger guard and laid it on the desk.

"What the hell is that?" General Greene asked.

"We had them in the OSS," Wallace replied. "They were issued to our agents, primarily the Jedburgh people, but to others as well. They were dubbed 'assassination specials.' They are barely audible when fired. The last time I saw one was when OSS Forward was in Paris."

" 'Jedburgh people'?" Schwarzkopf parroted.

"Three-man teams we dropped into France and other places. They were trained in Jedburgh, Scotland. The question now becomes where did Lieutenant Moriarty's assassin get such a weapon? Not, I think, from the OSS. They were kept in safes in London and Paris, and I know for a fact that before OSS Forward moved to Schlosshotel Kronberg, all the pistols had been issued. That suggests this pistol came into the hands of the Germans, or the Italians, the Serbians, et cetera, via a lost Jedburgh. General Gehlen?"

"We had two of them," Gehlen replied. "We

turned them—all our weapons—over to Colonel Mattingly when we arrived at Kloster Grünau. I'm sure there's an inventory somewhere."

"I think I know where it is," Claudette Colbert said. "And last week I was going over our current inventory of weapons and I'm sure—but I'll check—that nothing like that pistol is on it."

"Do that as soon as you can, please, after we break up here," Wallace said.

"Yes, sir."

"We've got a **gottverdammt** mole," Major Konrad Bischoff said. "Most likely one of those **gottverdammt** Poles."

"What makes you think it's one of the Poles?" Wallace asked.

"I think we can presume the NKGB has rosters of Free Polish Army, or Air Force, officers and enlisted men. The NKGB was all over London during the war. The NKGB connects a family in Poland with a name on a roster. Then they connect that name with a name on a roster of Polish Security Organization personnel. They find out what the PSO man is guarding and where from that same roster. And they establish contact with him. 'Do what we tell you, or we kill your family.'"

"Possibly, Bischoff," General Gehlen said. "But equally likely one of our own. Personally, with nothing to go on, I suspect the mole—or moles—is one of us. Same scenario, but run by Odessa."

"But why would either want to assassinate this lieutenant?" Schwarzkopf asked.

"They wanted to take out Cronley, Norman," Greene said. "To show us what happens to someone who has gotten in their way. That fits the NKGB—Cronley got Bob Mattingly back and they didn't get their defected **polkovnik**—"

"Colonel Sergei Likharev," Wallace furnished.

"—whom Cronley turned back, or his family. Or, so far as Odessa is concerned, DCI—Cronley—was responsible for the capture of SS-Brigadeführer Heimstadter and Standartenführer Oskar Müller, whom Odessa had spent a lot of effort to get out of Germany and to Spain. Both wanted to kill Cronley. Lieutenant Moriarty happened to be in Cronley's bed."

"But as much as they might want to assassinate Cronley," Schwarzkopf asked, "why would they want to cause the stink this is going to cause? As soon as Cronley's friend Miss Johansen hears about this, it'll be on the front page of **Stars and Stripes**."

"Miss Johansen is not going to hear about this," Wallace said. "Or what she's going to hear is that a tragic accident took Lieutenant Moriarty's life. You understand that, Cronley?"

"I heard what you said," Cronley replied.

"If we accuse, or even suggest, the NKGB is involved, and it gets in the newspapers or on the radio, (a) the Russians will deny everything, and (b) the world will learn that the NKGB, despite to-be-expected denials, killed one of us and got away with it. They'd like that. Same thing with Odessa. They'd like the word to get out that they got away with murdering a DCI officer."

"How do you plan to keep what happened a secret?" Greene asked.

"We can't keep it a secret, but what we can do is put out the story that it was an accident, and get his body, and his widow and their baby, out of Germany as soon as possible. At seven in the morning, Moriarty's body will be taken by one of our ambulances to Rhine-Main. It will be placed aboard the ten-o'clock MATS flight to Washington. Accompanied by Lieutenant Winters, Mrs. Moriarty and the baby will be on the plane. Admiral Souers and Mr. Schultz will meet the plane, and the party will then proceed to Texas on Admiral Souers's aircraft.

"The family will be told, in confidence, that Lieutenant Moriarty died in the line of duty while engaged in a classified operation. He will be posthumously decorated with the Legion of Merit."

"So that's why you haven't called in the military police," Schwarzkopf said.

"Yes, sir," Wallace said.

"General Gehlen," Schwarzkopf asked, "whom do you suspect did this?"

"I suspect it's one of my people."

"Why?"

"Because it was done with such finesse. In this room we have all of the best intelligence officers—except Colonel Cohen—in Europe. And none of us have any idea based on the evidence we have who did this. And since the only evidence we have is that pistol, that points to one of my people—the Russians and Odessa would have left us something else to work with."

Cronley stood up.

"Where is Mrs. Moriarty now?"

"In her quarters. The chaplain, Lieutenant and Mrs. Winters, and Colonel and Mrs. Bristol are with her."

"I'm going to offer my condolences."

"You heard what I said about keeping this from your lady friend?" Wallace said.

"I heard you, Colonel. But I'll make up my mind about that later, when I've had time to think things over."

He walked to the door.

"Just a minute, Captain Cronley," Wallace snapped.

Cronley went through the door, pulling it closed after him.

Dunwiddie stood up.

"Colonel, I think I better go with him."

"You tell that arrogant sonofabitch what I said about that goddamn reporter is an order!" Wallace fumed.

Dunwiddie hurried through the door in pursuit of Cronley.

**[FIVE]
Officers' Quarters #5
The South German Industrial
    Development Organization
    Compound
Pullach, Bavaria
American Zone of Occupation,
    Germany
1805 21 February 1946**

Lieutenant Colonel Jack Bristol opened the door to Cronley and Dunwiddie.

"She's in the kitchen," he said.

"How's she doing?" Cronley asked.

Bristol shrugged, and waved them toward the kitchen of the cottage.

Ginger Moriarty was sitting at the kitchen table nursing Bruce T. Moriarty Jr. Mrs. Jack Bristol and Mrs. Thomas Winters sat with her, watching. Lieutenant Thomas Winters stood by the refrigerator, carefully averting his eyes.

"Ginger," Cronley said, "I'm really sorry."

She looked away from her baby and at him.

"You goddamn well should be, you sonofa-bitch! This is all your fault. Get the hell out of my house!"

"Ginger," Mrs. Bristol said, shocked and concerned.

"And you know it's your fault, you bastard!" Ginger went on, coldly furious. "You've had my Bruce following you around since College Station. He even went into the Cavalry because of you. He really wanted to go into the Signal Corps, but he followed you into the Cavalry because he wanted to be just like you. And even that wasn't enough. You got him to follow you to this god-damn concentration camp. If he hadn't wanted to be a hotshot intelligence officer like you, we'd still be in Fritzlar. Bruce wouldn't have been in the Signal Corps, but he wouldn't be dead."

"Ginger—" Cronley said.

"Get the hell out of my house, you sonofa-bitch!"

Cronley felt a tug at his sleeve, turned his head to see that it was Tiny Dunwiddie, and then turned and followed him out of the kitchen and ultimately out of the cottage.

"She's upset, Jim," Dunwiddie said, when they were outside.

"Yeah, I picked up on that. Unfortunately, she's right. I got Bonehead to come here, and now he's dead."

"You're not responsible for that, Jim."

"I'd do it again, but I'm responsible. If I had left Bonehead in Fritzlar, he'd still be alive. I thought I was doing him a favor, but that didn't turn out well, did it?"

Dunwiddie didn't reply.

"Have you got a car?"

"No. I came out here in Colonel Wallace's Kapitän. You're going to the Jahreszeiten?"

"I'm going back to the airfield, back to Nuremberg . . ."

"If what I think you're going to do—take one of the Storchs—"

"That's exactly what I'm going to do. I was going to leave Ziegler here to see what he could find out and tell me. But with Greene and Schwarzkopf here—with their resources—he'd be redundant. And you can tell me what Greene and Schwarzkopf find out."

"I don't think Wallace would like you taking a Storch any more than he will like me being your mole here."

"Fuck him!"

"And he will really be cumulatively pissed— maybe to the point of relieving you—if he also finds out you told anything about this to Janice Johansen."

"I will tell her, and Wallace will probably find out. But he won't relieve me without checking with Chief Schultz, and I know El Jefe well enough to know that he'll want to hear my version of the story. I'll take my chances with that."

"I sometimes wonder if you have a death wish, that you really want to get relieved."

"What I want to do is find out who whacked Bonehead. And I don't want Wallace to tell me he'll handle it, butt out."

"I admit I think that's on his mind. And I think you know what kind of a spot you're putting me in."

"Indeed I do. Is that a problem for you, Tiny?"

Dunwiddie looked at him for a long moment.

"Why don't you go get Augie Ziegler and meet me at the motor pool?" he said finally.

IV

[ONE]
XXIst CIC *Kaserne*
The Palace of Justice Compound
Nuremberg, American Zone of
   Occupation, Germany
0805 21 February 1946

"Thank you for seeing us, Colonel," Cronley said, as he and Augie Ziegler were waved into

Colonel Mortimer Cohen's office by his sergeant major.

"I've been expecting you," Cohen said. "General Greene called to tell me he thought seeing me was high on your list of priorities."

What the hell?

"He told me about the murder of Lieutenant Moriarty, and suspected you were about to open your own investigation of the incident against orders, and that you would probably come to me for assistance."

Oh, shit!

Greene almost certainly told him to keep me at arm's length.

"He also told me you'd stolen a Storch airplane, and asked me to help you conceal it from your outraged commanding officer and the Air Corps."

Greene asked Cohen to help me hide the Storch?

"I didn't steal it, Colonel."

"Actually, General Greene said you'd taken the airplane without asking permission."

"That's true."

"He said that you probably did this following the philosophy of Lieutenant Colonel William W. Wilson."

"Sir?"

What?

"Hotshot Billy has been quoted as saying if

you want to do something you know is right, and you know your superiors don't want you to do it, then do it and ask permission afterward."

"I've heard that, Colonel."

"Why do you need that airplane?"

"I'm going to find the bastards who murdered Moriarty, which means I'll have to go all over Germany. The Storch will be very useful."

"Where is it now?"

"Out of sight, in a hangar at Soldier's Field."

"How long do you think it will be before people start asking questions about it?"

Do I tell him?

Does he already know?

Probably.

"Before Moriarty was killed, I asked Colonel Rasberry if he knew where I could hide it. It's now being guarded—no one gets in the hangar—by his people."

"I was about to suggest you bring the subject up to Rasberry. He's a good man. So tell me how you propose to find the people responsible for your friend's murder."

"He was killed either by the NKGB or Odessa. I have no idea right now how to go after the Russians, so I'm going to start with Odessa. The reason I came to see you, Colonel, is that I want to have a chat with Ernst Kaltenbrunner. I'd like you to go with me."

"You don't really think Kaltenbrunner is going

to tell you anything, do you? Anything you can believe?"

"What I'm thinking is that I can dazzle him with my DCI credentials. What I'm hoping is that the word will pass down to his men imprisoned here that an officer from the White House has been to see him. And then I'm going to talk to every last one of them, until I find who I can turn."

"Turning people is very difficult."

"I seem to have a flair for doing it. I turned NKGB Polkovnik Sergei Likharev."

"So General Greene told me," Cohen said, and stood up. "Why don't we go have a chat with former SS-Obergruppenführer und General der Polizei und Waffen-SS Kaltenbrunner? He always hates to see this lowly **gottverdammten Juden Oberst** who has him in a cell and that pleases me. And on the way—this is General Greene's suggestion—I will start your cram course on how really dangerous these people are. He thinks I might be able to enlist you two in my secret army of the righteously indignant."

What the hell is he talking about? Secret army of the righteously indignant?

Colonel Cohen began the cram course just as soon as they left the XXIst CIC **Kaserne** and started to walk to the prison.

"Kaltenbrunner was born in a little **Dorf** in Austria. His father was a lawyer, and Ernst earned a doctorate degree in law at Graz University in 1926. The story he put out was that the scars on his face came from a duel at Graz, part of the initiation ritual to gain entrance into a fraternity, a **Brüderschaft**. Actually, the scars, of which he was—still is—quite proud, were caused when he got drunk and got into an automobile accident.

"Kaltenbrunner joined the Nazi Party on October 18th, 1930. He was not, in other words, one of the originals. He became a Nazi because he thought it was no longer dangerous to become a Nazi—by then three hundred thousand people had signed up—and he thought membership might be good for him, personally. He went on to join the SS in August 1931.

"From mid-1935, Kaltenbrunner was considered a leader of the Austrian SS. His role in the **Anschluss** in 1933 got him promoted to SS-**Brigadeführer**, and he parlayed that into getting himself elected to the Reichstag."

Jesus, this is a classroom lecture.
Colonel Cohen's another Freddy Hessinger!
Take notes! There will be a quiz!

"In January 1934, Kaltenbrunner got married to thirty-year-old Elisabeth Eder of Linz, who was a Nazi Party member. They had three children. But he had a wandering eye and had a long affair with **Gräfin**—Countess—Gisela von Westarp. They had two children, a boy and a girl, twins.

"In September 1938, Kaltenbrunner, while still Führer of SS-Oberabschnitt Österreich, was promoted to the rank of SS-**Gruppenführer**— lieutenant general—in the army. He was also appointed **Höherer SS- und Polizeiführer** for Donau, which was the primary SS command in Austria.

"In June 1940, he was named Police President of Vienna, and in July 1940, he got a commission as SS-**Untersturmführer** in the Waffen-SS Reserve, and later to **Generalleutnant** of the police. On January 30, 1943, Kaltenbrunner was appointed chief of the RSHA, which was the Sicherheitspolizei—the combined forces of the Gestapo and the Criminal Police—the Kripo— plus the Sicherheitsdienst: Security Service.

"When Reinhard Heydrich was assassinated in Prague in June 1942, Kaltenbrunner got his job and was promoted to SS-**Obergruppenführer und General der Polizei**."

"Colonel," Augie Ziegler said, "are you going to take a break anytime soon? You're throwing a lot at us."

"With that in mind, Mr. Ziegler, as we speak, Sergeant Major Feldman is hammering away at his typewriter preparing, with one carbon copy, what I suppose could be called lecture notes for you and Mr. Cronley to study at your leisure. There will be a quiz."

A quiz? Christ, is he reading my mind?

"May I continue?"

"Yes, sir," Ziegler said, chuckling.

"As an illustration of what kind of people we're dealing with, let me tell you what happened in the summer of 1943 at the Mauthausen-Gusen concentration camp. When the camp commander heard that our Ernst was about to make an inspection of the camp, they set up what the U.S. Army would call a 'dog and pony show.'

"Prisoners at Mauthausen were exterminated in one of three ways—by gunshot to the neck, by hanging from a gallows, and by gassing them. For Kaltenbrunner's edification, and to solicit his professional advice, a demonstration was arranged."

"What kind of a demonstration? Dog and pony show?" Ziegler asked.

"Fifteen prisoners were selected to demonstrate for Kaltenbrunner the three methods of killing then in use. Five categories of prisoners—Healthy, Not Healthy, Young, Aged, and Average. A special gallows was erected for the hanging, and a truck with a sealable body brought in to demonstrate the efficiency of Zyklon-B, a pesticide, in ending human life.

"They were exterminated one by one so that Kaltenbrunner could witness the efficacy of the different procedures. After the dog and pony show, Kaltenbrunner inspected the crematorium and later the quarry, where prisoners were worked to death moving hundred-pound rocks from one pile to another and then back."

"Colonel, I heard about really nasty shit like this, but until now, coming from you, I guess I just didn't want to believe it."

"Mr. Ziegler, you ain't heard nothing yet," Colonel Cohen said.

[TWO]

Outside the prison building, a captain, a lieutenant, two sergeants, a corporal, and a PFC of the 26th Infantry regiment guarded the entrance. All of them were armed with pistols. The sergeants had Thompson submachine guns slung from their shoulders. They were backed up by two jeeps, each with a pedestal-mounted .30 caliber machine gun.

Although the captain obviously in charge greeted Cohen by name when he saluted, that recognition didn't get them into the prison building. There was a protocol to follow.

First, they had to produce identification. After their CIC credentials were carefully examined, their names were checked against a roster of **Accredited Personnel** mounted on a clipboard.

Cronley saw another clipboard marked **Authorized Visitors**, but it wasn't consulted.

Cohen, who runs the whole show, must have gotten Augie and me on the Accredited list right after I asked him to.

"And your weapons, if any, gentlemen, please," the lieutenant said.

He was visibly impressed when, after Colonel Cohen had surrendered his .45, Cronley and Ziegler hoisted their Ike jackets, revealing their pistols, holstered in their "Secret Service High Rise Cross Draw" holsters.

"Nice," he said. "I didn't think either of you were armed."

"That's the whole idea, Lieutenant," Cronley said. "We like to surprise people before we shoot them."

When Cronley and then Ziegler took their pistols from their holsters, it was immediately apparent from the drawn-back hammers and the position of the safety levers that they were "cocked and locked." All it would take to fire them was for the shooter to move the safety lever and squeeze the trigger.

The captain and the lieutenant were visibly

surprised. The captain's face showed surprise and disapproval. Carrying holstered pistols in that ready-to-fire condition was forbidden in the Army.

Ziegler picked up on this: "When I was a Boy Scout," he said, "they had a motto. 'Be Prepared.'"

One at a time, the lieutenant removed the magazines from the pistols, and then racked the actions back to eject the rounds in their chambers. Each time, a cartridge flew out of the pistols. When the lieutenant was finished, the captain looked relieved that a dangerous situation had been dealt with.

Cronley saw that both Ziegler and Cohen were amused.

"And which of our guests are you going to visit, Colonel?" the captain asked.

"We're going to have a chat, a brief one, with Herr Kaltenbrunner," Cohen replied, "and we may visit, or at least have a look at, Herr Göring."

A third clipboard was produced. The lieutenant wrote on it, and then extended it first to Cohen, then to Cronley, and finally to Ziegler. This one had to be signed, attesting to the fact that they were entering the prison at 0825 21 February 1946 to visit prisoners Kaltenbrunner, Ernst, and Göring, Hermann.

* * *

One of the sergeants unlocked a door with a massive key Cronley thought probably weighed a half pound and passed them into the prison.

They found themselves in a three-story building. The ground floor was lined with cells on both sides. A 26th Infantry private or PFC armed with only a billy club stood before each door, or leaned on it, peering momentarily through a small window in the recessed cell door. These guards all appeared to be in their teens.

Above the ground floor were two more tiers of cells. Outside them was a fragile-looking metal walkway with a railing. Two even more fragile-looking bridges, one on the second tier, the other on the third, connected the walkways.

There were no soldiers peering into the upper-level-tier cells, and as he followed Cohen down the twenty-foot-wide corridor between the cells, Cronley thought, **Now is not the time, but when we get out of here, I'm going to ask Cohen to explain this to me. Who's in the upper-level cells, and why are GIs standing outside the ground-floor cells and not the ones above?**

Colonel Cohen stopped before one of the cells and told the PFC standing next to it now—suddenly standing at rigid attention in the presence of a colonel—"Open it up, son."

The PFC first put a large key in a lock and

turned it, then moved a heavy wooden slide away from a slot in the door frame. Then he pushed the door inward.

Cronley saw the cell was about twelve feet wide and maybe twenty feet long.

Cohen waved him in.

A very tall, trim man—Cronley judged six-feet-four, maybe a little taller, and about 210 pounds—rose to his feet from a narrow bed, the thin mattress of which was covered with a U.S. Army blanket. He was wearing a sleeveless gray underwear shirt, black breeches, and thigh-high black boots. A double red stripe with a black middle ran down the center seam of the breeches, identifying the wearer as a general officer. There was a scar, looking to Cronley like evidence of a bungled operation, on his left cheek.

So that's what a sword fight/car accident does to you.

Kaltenbrunner looked at Cronley with mingled curiosity and disdain.

"Mr. Cronley, this is the former chief of the RSHA, former Obergruppenführer und General der Polizei und Waffen-SS Dr. Ernst Kaltenbrunner," Cohen said.

"And may I ask who this gentleman is?" Kaltenbrunner asked in good English.

Cronley held out his DCI credentials. Kaltenbrunner examined them as if he was reluctantly doing Cronley a favor.

"And what might I do for the Central Intelligence Directorate?" Kaltenbrunner asked, then added, "Whatever that is."

"I'm surprised you don't know what the DCI is," Cronley said, in German. "But to answer your question, my superior told me I should take a look at you."

"Which superior would that be?" Kaltenbrunner asked, in German. "The admiral or President Truman?"

"Colonel Cohen has led me to believe that the way things work around here is that we ask the questions and people like you answer them, if not often truthfully."

"So you have a question, or questions, for me?"

"Not at the moment. Possibly, even probably, later. But not at the moment. Right now all I'm doing is having a look at you. My superior, my Führer, if you like, asked me to do that. He wants me to tell him what being face-to-face with you and Göring is like."

"You mean President Truman?"

"I didn't say that."

"And what is it like?"

"We're back to who gets to ask questions and who doesn't," Cronley replied.

He turned to Ziegler and asked, still speaking German, "Seen enough, Augie?"

"There's not much to see, is there?" Ziegler replied, in German.

Cronley turned and walked out of the cell. He saw for the first time the sanitary facilities. A tiny, doorless cubicle held a toilet—no seat— and above it a small washbasin and a stainless steel mirror. Ziegler and then Cohen followed him out.

"Close it up," Cohen ordered, and then when the door had been closed and locked, asked, "Göring?"

"No," Cronley said. "Not now. I told him I was going to have a look at Göring. When he finds out I didn't—and I'm sure he will—he'll wonder why."

"You are devious, Cronley. I say that with ad- miration," Cohen said.

When they left the cell block, the lieutenant who had signed them in was waiting for them with the clipboard to sign them out. A sergeant and a PFC were standing behind him holding the pistols they had surrendered. The actions were racked back, and the magazines had been removed.

"This is yours, Colonel," the sergeant said, as the PFC handed him the pistol and the maga- zine he held. "Who gets the .45 with the fancy rubber grips?"

"That's mine," Ziegler said, taking the pistol and its magazine from him. The sergeant then handed Cronley his pistol and its magazine.

Colonel Cohen closed the action of his pistol, inserted the magazine, and then holstered the weapon. Both Ziegler and Cronley inserted the magazines into their pistols before closing the action, which caused a round to be loaded in the chamber before holstering them.

"You always go around with a round in the chamber?" Colonel Cohen asked.

"You know what they say—'You never need a gun until you really need one,'" Ziegler said. "I interpret that to mean 'You never need a gun until you really need a ready-to-fire-right-now gun.'"

"You think that's worth the risk of an accident with a round in the chamber of the ready-to-fire-right-now gun?" Cohen challenged.

"If you're prone to having accidents with a gun, you shouldn't be carrying one," Ziegler replied.

Cohen chuckled. "Point taken. I gather you've had experiences with a ready-to-fire-right-now pistol?"

"Unfortunately," Ziegler replied. "The only thing good about having to take somebody out is that you're alive, and they're not. I was thinking about that just now when we were having our chat with that bastard Kaltenbrunner. What I wanted to do was shoot him in the ear."

"'Vengeance is mine, saith the Lord,'" Cohen quoted.

"I didn't mean it that way," Ziegler replied.

"When I was a beat cop, I had to shoot a lot of rabid dogs. In the ear, if I could get close enough, so that they couldn't bite somebody, or some other dog, and spread the rabies."

"Why in the ear?" Cronley asked.

"You know they're dead right then, and aren't going to take anybody with them on their trip to piss on the pearly gates."

"You're a very interesting man, Mr. Ziegler," Cohen said.

Yes, you are. And I damned sure did the right thing when I recruited you for DCI.

"Are you planning on seeing Justice Jackson this morning?" Cohen asked. "And if so, when?"

"When I get there, if that's before noon. He told me 'anytime this morning' when I telephoned."

"So you have time for me to conclude my lecture on Kaltenbrunner, Ernst?"

"I'd like that, Colonel."

"Then I suggest we walk over to the 26th Officers' Mess. They charge ten cents for coffee and doughnuts. I'll buy."

[THREE]

"One of the nice things about being a senior officer," Cohen began, just as soon as they found seats in a corner of the officers' mess and ordered coffee and doughnuts, "is that junior officers really try to distance themselves from you. That means there will be no ears cocked this way while I finish my lecture."

Cronley and Ziegler chuckled.

Cohen waited until a waiter had delivered their coffee and doughnuts before resuming his lecture.

"After Colonel Count von Stauffenberg's bomb failed to take out Hitler in July of 1944, Hitler put Kaltenbrunner in charge of dealing with the miscreants, including the kangaroo trials, which after an unfair trial saw about five thousand officers executed, most often by strangulation as they were hung by piano wire from butchers' hooks. This procedure was filmed so that Hitler could watch, again and again."

"Nice guy," Ziegler said.

"This of course placed him even closer to the Führer than he had been," Cohen went on. "In December of 1944, many, perhaps most, senior SS officers were given commissions in the Waffen-SS."

"Why?" Cronley asked.

"I presume so they would have prisoner-of-war status when they were captured," Cohen explained. "Kaltenbrunner became the equivalent of a four-star general in the Waffen-SS. And thereafter usually wore that uniform. You noticed the red-striped breeches?"

Both Ziegler and Cronley nodded.

"In April of 1945, Himmler named Kaltenbrunner commander in chief of what Waffen-SS forces were left in southern Europe. He divided that command in two. He put Otto Skorzeny in charge of blowing things up—"

"Skorzeny? The guy that rescued Mussolini from that mountaintop?" Cronley interrupted.

"One and the same," Cohen said.

"I'm missing something here," Ziegler confessed.

"Then let me fill you in," Cohen said. "When the Italians surrendered, Mussolini was arrested—by the Italians—and taken to an Italian ski resort . . ."

Cohen paused, obviously searching his memory, and then went on: "The Campo Imperatore Hotel, which was on top of Gran Sasso Mountain in the Apennines . . ."

Jesus, Cohen's just like Freddy Hessinger—a walking encyclopedia!

". . . Hitler didn't know this, where Mussolini was, only that he was being held prisoner, but he decided to try to free him. He personally chose Skorzeny, then a captain in the Leibstandarte Adolf Hitler and a protégé of Kaltenbrunner, to find him.

"He did. Then Hitler ordered Luftwaffe General Kurt Student, the commander of **Fallschirmjäger**—paratroops—to stage an operation to rescue him. They landed twelve D230 gliders on a small patch of clear land and seized the hotel without firing a shot.

"Then Skorzeny flew in in a Fieseler Storch—"

"A great little airplane," Cronley interjected.

"So you have led me to believe," Cohen said. "May I continue?"

"Yes, sir."

"And flew Mussolini out in the Storch. To Rome. Then he took him by train to Vienna. He was promoted to major and given the Knight's Cross of the Iron Cross. Goebbels put his propaganda machinery in high gear and soon Skorzeny was famous."

"You said he was a protégé of Kaltenbrunner?" Cronley asked.

"At first. Later they became quite chummy. Both enormous men. Skorzeny was—is—also over six feet tall and bears Brüderschaft dueling scars. I think Kaltenbrunner both liked him and was aware that some of Skorzeny's hero publicity sort of shined on him."

"I'd like to see this guy," Ziegler said. "Is he in the slam here?"

"No, he's in Darmstadt in a POW enclosure. But let's take things in sequence."

"Sorry."

"And remember, there will be a quiz, so pay attention," Cronley quipped.

Cohen's face showed he was not amused.

"In October 1944, if I may continue—"

"Aren't we going off at a tangent?" Cronley interrupted.

"No," Cohen said simply, and then went on: "In October 1944, as the Russians got close to Hungary, it looked to Hitler as if Admiral Miklós Horthy, Hungary's regent, was about to strike a deal with them. So he formed Operation Panzerfaust under Skorzeny to keep that from happening.

"Skorzeny took a team of SS men to Budapest, kidnapped Horthy's son, and sent him to Germany as a hostage. Horthy then resigned, which meant no deal with the Russians.

"Hitler promoted Skorzeny to lieutenant colonel. And then he and Kaltenbrunner came up with another idea, Operation Griffin."

"Which was?"

"Part of what the Germans called **Unternehmen Wacht am Rhein** and we called the Battle of the Bulge—"

"During which, for your edification, Augie," Cronley interrupted, "Captain Dunwiddie rose from corporal to first sergeant and acting CO of Company C, 203rd Tank Destroyer Battalion because all the officers and non-coms were hors de combat, which means dead or wounded."

"No shit?" Ziegler asked.

"Who is Captain Dunwiddie?" Cohen asked.

"And Sergeant Finney—you'll love this, Colonel—a CIC agent who had been sent undercover to Company 'C' to look for Communist agitators, finally confessed to Tiny he was a CIC agent after getting a Purple Heart and a Bronze Star and promotion to corporal."

"At the risk of repeating myself, who is Captain Dunwiddie?" Cohen said.

"He was my deputy when I was chief of DCI-Europe. Interesting guy. He's old Army. His father is a classmate of General White at Norwich. White is Tiny's—"

"'Tiny's'?" Cohen interrupted.

"Great big black guy, six-four-plus, two hundred and fifty pounds plus. He's General White's godson. He resigned from Norwich in his senior year and enlisted because he was afraid the war would be over before he got into it."

"Did I hear you say a moment ago something about going off at a tangent?" Cohen asked.

"Sorry."

"Back to the Battle of the Bulge," Cohen resumed. "Skorzeny set up and then executed Operation Griffin. A false-flag mission. He recruited about twenty-five American-English-speaking soldiers from all over the Wehrmacht. Then he put them in uniforms he took away from American POWs and sent them behind American lines in the Ardennes forest.

"They misdirected road traffic, tried to blow bridges, that sort of thing. They had some minor successes, but they were quickly rounded up and most of them, after quickly convened field court-martials, were shot. They did succeed in convincing their captors that not only were there more of them than was the case, that some of them were headed, under Skorzeny, for Paris to assassinate Eisenhower. For the next couple of weeks, Ike was reluctant to leave his headquarters at all, and when he did, he was surrounded by a small army of military police."

"You have to admire the guts of the Germans who did that. I mean, everybody knows if you get caught wearing the enemy's uniform, you get shot," Ziegler said.

"I've thought about that," Cohen said. "It's possible they were dedicated Nazis, or even simply dedicated soldiers. I think it was equally possible that they were offered the choice between refusing to obey the order, in which case they would be shot on the spot for disobedience, or taking their chances in the Hürtgen forest.

"In any event, Hitler was pleased with Skorzeny. He named him an acting **Generalmajor** and sent him to the East, to command

Waffen-SS troops defending Frankfurt-on-the-Oder against the Russians. He did that well enough to get Oak Leaves for his Knight's Cross. But the Russians took Frankfurt anyway.

"By then, just about everyone but Hitler recognized the war was lost, but Hitler, and some others, decided to fight to the last man. In mid-April 1945, Hitler ordered Kaltenbrunner—which brings us back to him in my lecture—to reorganize his intelligence agencies as a stay-behind underground net. Kaltenbrunner picked Skorzeny to be in charge of the scorched earth—leave nothing standing the enemy can use—policy, and a fellow named Wilhelm Waneck to both keep an eye on Skorzeny and to set up a program of stay-behind agents."

"Two questions, if I may," Cronley said.

"Ask away."

" 'Keep an eye on Skorzeny'?"

"Somebody, probably Himmler, but maybe Hitler himself, worried that Skorzeny would have problems with blowing up everything in what was left of Germany. As it turned out, the suspicions were justified. Next question?"

"Who is Wilhelm Waneck?"

"I'd really like to know. All I really know about him is that he was very close to Himmler. I've seen him identified as both a light colonel and a three-star general. I think—with absolutely nothing even remotely concrete to back this up—that he's probably running Odessa. He just vanished. He could be looking upward at the grass."

"But you don't think so," Cronley said.

"No. My gut tells me he's running Odessa. Somebody smart is."

"Yeah," Cronley agreed.

"Turning to Skorzeny," Cohen went on. "He realized that the Werewolf operation, fighting to the last man, was nonsense so he turned his considerable talents to setting up escape routes for his friends. Then, on May 16, 1945, he sent a message that he was prepared to surrender, but only to us. He didn't want to wind up in the hands of the French. When I heard this, I went for a look.

"I got there—a road a couple of miles inside Austria, not too far from where he was supposed to fight to the death near Hitler's Eagle's Nest— about ten minutes before he showed up. They took him to a POW collection point. There something very interesting happened. The protocol was that the first field-grade officer who captured a field-grade or up German would make an on-the-spot decision whether the guy was a soldier, in which case he would be sent to a prisoner of war camp, or a Nazi—on the Look For list or not—in which case, he would be turned over to the CIC.

"There was a CIC unit there into whose hands the Army promptly turned Skorzeny. Then the OSS showed up, led by a colonel. He overrode the Army major—and the Look For list, on which Skorzeny was close to the top—and said that Skorzeny was to be treated as a soldier, and that his men would take charge of him, and take him to the special POW enclosure for senior officers at Darmstadt."

"What was that all about?" Cronley asked.

"I've been wondering ever since," Cohen replied. "The best answer I have come up with is that the colonel decided that since Skorzeny hadn't done anything the OSS had done routinely, he was entitled to be treated as a soldier. Fair's fair, so to speak. The OSS colonel who made that decision was Harold Wallace."

"Jesus!" Cronley said, visibly shocked.

"So Skorzeny has been in Darmstadt ever since, rather than here awaiting trial," Cohen said. "And now my lecture turns back to SS-Obergruppenführer und General der Polizei und Waffen-SS Dr. Kaltenbrunner . . ."

"Why the hell would Wallace do that?" Cronley pursued.

"Colonel Wallace, when I raised that question to him, told me it was none of my business," Cohen replied, and then went on: "Toward the end of April 1945, Kaltenbrunner moved his headquarters from Berlin to the Villa Kerry in Altaussee, a small **Dorf** in the Salzkammergut region of Austria. To which **Dorf** I will now turn my lecture, aware that I may be accused of going off at a tangent."

"Colonel, I'm all ears," Cronley said. "And Ziegler better be."

"Altaussee, which had a prewar population of less than two thousand souls, is on the shores of Lake Altaussee. It has the biggest salt deposits of Austria, which have been continuously mined since the middle of the twelfth century. Since 1147, if memory serves."

And I'd bet that it does, Colonel.
And give odds.

"There are miles of tunnels in the mines, so beginning in August 1943, art treasures from Austrian churches, monasteries, and museums were sent to the mines for safekeeping. Then in February 1944 the Sonderauftrag Linz—"

"The what?" Cronley asked.

"It translates to Special Commission Linz, and what it was was the people who were accumulating artworks—sometimes by buying them, but most often by theft—for the planned Führermuseum in Linz. In February 1944, as I was saying before being interrupted, they began to store these artworks in the salt mines. By the end of the war—by the time Dr. Kaltenbrunner moved to Altaussee—there were about six thousand five hundred paintings, as well as many statues, furniture, weapons, coins, and libraries, including most of the Führerbibliothek—Führer's library—in the mines.

"And about this time, a number of high-ranking SS officers—Franz Stangl, commandant of the Sobibór and Treblinka extermination camps; Anton Burger, commandant of Theresienstadt concentration camp; Adolf Eichmann, who was in charge of the Final Solution—people like that—went to Altaussee and placed themselves under the protection of the local **Gauleiter**, August Eigruber, who was a dedicated Nazi.

"When Hitler ordered the scorched-earth-destroy-everything policy, Eigruber somehow got his hands on eight one-thousand-pound bombs and put them in the salt mines. If he had succeeded in setting them off, all the art—Michelangelo's **Madonna of Bruges**, Jan van Eyck's **Ghent Altarpiece**, Vermeer's **The Astronomer** and **The Art of Painting**, all six thousand five hundred works of art—would have been destroyed."

"But they weren't. Our experts—what did they call them, 'the Monuments Men'?—got there in time to save them. Or didn't they?" Cronley asked.

"When the Monuments Men got there, they discovered that the bombs had been disarmed. At the orders of Dr. Ernst Kaltenbrunner."

"Kaltenbrunner?" Cronley asked, visibly surprised.

"There are two common theories about that," Cohen replied. "One is that he isn't as bad a human being as most believe him to be. That, in other words, he couldn't stand idly by and watch Gauleiter Eigruber destroy works of art at the orders of a madman. The second theory is that he didn't give much of a damn about the artwork, but saved it thinking it might do him some good when he was put on trial."

"And which makes most sense to you, Colonel?" Ziegler asked.

"Neither. I have my own theory, to which I will get in due time. In early May 1945, if I have this right, on May eighth, Kaltenbrunner heard that we were getting close to Altaussee, and left Villa Kerry, leaving behind about a hundred and twenty pounds of gold, and headed south. I think—don't know—that he wanted to make his way to Italy, where—I think, don't know—he wanted to make contact with Wilhelm Waneck, whom we know Skorzeny had ordered to establish escape routes.

"He didn't make it. On May twelfth, he and his mistress were arrested by an American patrol. He was turned over to the OSS, who held him until the cells were habitable here. Then he was brought here."

"Two more questions, if it's okay, Colonel," Cronley asked.

Cohen gestured for him to continue.

"The OSS had him, held on to him? When I was in the CIC, the CIC was responsible for big-shot Nazis like Kaltenbrunner."

"I formed the opinion at the time that Colonel Wallace had little faith in the CIC," Cohen said. "An opinion I'm afraid he still holds. Next question?"

"You said you had your own opinions as to why Kaltenbrunner stopped the destruction of all the art."

Cohen paused before answering.

"Answering that will cause you to ask other questions, which will take much longer to answer than either of us has time for right now. I will give you a simple answer now, with the understanding that you won't ask questions until there is time to answer them fully. Agreed?"

"Yes, sir."

"I don't think Kaltenbrunner cared for the art as art, but rather as artifacts necessary to the new religion he and Heinrich Himmler were setting up. I think he's a latter-day apostle gathered around the holy grail."

"'New religion'?" Cronley parroted. "You can't stop there!"

"Give my best regards to Justice Jackson," Cohen said, and stood up. "And I accept your kind invitation to have a drink with you in the bar of the press billet at 1730."

He then marched out of the room.

"What the hell was he saying?" Ziegler said. "Kaltenbrunner is a new apostle? What the hell does that mean?"

"If we're lucky we might find out in the bar of the press billet at 1730." He paused and then added, "What worries me, Augie, is that I don't think he's pulling our leg."

[FOUR]
The Office of the Chief U.S. Prosecutor
The Palace of Justice Compound
Nuremberg, American Zone of Occupation, Germany
1035 21 February 1946

When Cronley and Ziegler walked into Justice Jackson's office, Kenneth Brewster, Jackson's law clerk, politely said, "Good morning, gentlemen."

"Good morning," they replied in chorus.

"There is an officer waiting to see you, Mr. Cronley," Brewster said.

"Who is he?"

"He didn't give his name. A large, very large Negro captain."

Tiny? Here?

Why?

Bearing bad news from Wallace, that's why!

The question then becomes "What bad news?"

"Where is he?"

"In the gentlemen's restroom."

Two doors opened simultaneously. Justice Jackson stood in the door frame of one of them and Captain Chauncey L. Dunwiddie exited the gentlemen's restroom through the other.

"Good morning," Jackson said.

"Good morning, Mr. Justice," Cronley replied.

"Am I interrupting anything here?" Jackson asked.

"Mr. Justice, this is Captain Dunwiddie of DCI," Cronley said. "I don't know what he's doing here."

"Sir, I am reporting for duty, together with two Americans and eight Poles."

"I don't understand," Cronley said.

"Sir, I didn't know where to find you, so I came here," Tiny said.

"Where's everybody else?"

"Parked behind this building, sir, in two ambulances, two jeeps, and a Ford staff car."

"And the Americans are?"

"Miss Miller, sir, and Mr. Hessinger."

Jesus Christ, what the hell is going on?

"And the purpose of your visit, Captain?" Cronley asked.

"Sir, we have been transferred to Detachment A.'"

And what the hell is that all about?

"Tell you what," Justice Jackson said, "why don't you and the captain come into my office? We can have a cup of coffee while the captain tells us what's going on. To judge from Mr. Cronley's normally inscrutable face, he is more than a little curious."

"Thank you, sir," Cronley said.

And what do I do now?

His mouth went on automatic: "Augie, round these people up and take them to the Press Club. Leave the Horch. I'll come out there as soon as I can."

"Yes, sir," Ziegler said.

Mr. Justice Jackson put out his hand to Dunwiddie. "My name is Jackson, Captain. Welcome to the Palace of Justice."

"Thank you, sir."

Jackson waved them into his office, and then into chairs. He then raised his voice. "Ken, would you get us some coffee, please?"

* * *

"You said you've been transferred to Detachment 'A'?" Justice Jackson began his interrogation immediately after Brewster had served the coffee and been waved into a chair.

Dunwiddie looked distinctly uncomfortable.

"Sir, Colonel Wallace, chief, DCI-Europe, apparently felt that Mr. Cronley did not have enough personnel to carry out his mission here."

"I used to be a lawyer, Captain," Jackson said. "Now I'm a prosecutor. Most of the time I can tell when a response to a question, while it may be true, is not the whole truth."

Cronley's mouth went on automatic. "Tell him, Tiny. He's one of the good guys."

"Thank you, Jim," Jackson said.

Ken Brewster flashed Cronley an icy glare.

Dunwiddie looked even more uncomfortable.

"Out with it, Tiny," Cronley ordered.

Dunwiddie visibly organized his thoughts.

"DCI-Europe, at President Truman's order, is about to be tripled, quadrupled, in size," he began. "Most of the new hires, and most of the military personnel now transferred here, are ex-OSS recruited by El Jefe."

"Who is?" Brewster asked.

Well, Jackson told his law clerk to stay.

I guess that means he can ask questions because Jackson wants him clued in on everything.

And that's his call.

I can only hope Brewster doesn't run at the mouth when he's having a drink with his friends.

On the other hand, if he has a running mouth, I don't think he'd be working for Jackson.

"They call Oscar Schultz, who is Admiral Souers's Number Two, El Jefe—the Chief—because he was a chief petty officer," Cronley explained.

"An ex–enlisted man is Number Two in the Directorate of Central Intelligence?" Brewster asked, incredulous.

"Yes, he is. And before that, he was the OSS deputy chief of station for the Southern Cone," Cronley said.

"You were telling us, Captain, why you were transferred here," Jackson said.

"Well, for one thing, sir," Dunwiddie said, "I was deputy chief of DCI-Europe under Cronley. The first three officers El Jefe sent to DCI were two majors and a lieutenant colonel. I think Colonel Wallace wanted the lieutenant colonel to be his deputy. So he transferred me here."

"Why do I still think that's not the whole story?"

"For Christ's sake, Tiny, out with it!" Cronley said, not very pleasantly.

"On the way down here, Hessinger and I talked about it."

"So what did Freddy have to say?" Cronley demanded impatiently.

"Freddy said he thinks Wallace would really not only relieve you, but get you out of the DCI completely. He's afraid to do that for a lot of reasons . . ."

"Such as?" Brewster asked.

"Cronley was appointed chief of DCI-Europe by the President. He's close to El Jefe, and to Cletus Frade . . ."

"Who is?" Brewster asked.

"He was the Southern Cone—Argentina, Chile, and Uruguay—OSS chief of station," Cronley said. "Now the same for DCI."

"Where he handled—handles—the Argentine end of Operation Ost," Dunwiddie said. "So, Freddy theorizes—"

"And who is Freddy?" Brewster asked.

"A younger version of Colonel Cohen," Cronley said. "Now, for Christ's sake, let Tiny finish."

"Freddy thinks that Wallace thinks you're really incompetent, a disaster—which would reflect on him—about to happen. That would get you out of DCI. His problem then is to have clean hands, so that when people come to your aid—including General Gehlen and probably General Greene—he can say, 'Don't blame me. When I suspected he was about to get in trouble in Nuremberg, I sent my deputy down there, my administrative chief, more Poles than he asked for, everything I could think of to keep him out of trouble.'

"Which also caused vacancies in what is now his DCI-Europe headquarters, which he can now fill with his old pals from the OSS," Jackson said thoughtfully. "Very clever."

"What does Colonel Wallace have against you, Mr. Cronley?" Brewster asked. "If you don't mind the question."

"I suspect he dislikes Cronley for the same reasons you do, Ken," Jackson answered for him. "Cronley is much farther up the totem pole of power than someone of his years, in your opinion, should be. Worse, he's usually very good at what he does. I think you should start to consider that both President Truman and Admiral Souers have put him where he is and are quite satisfied with his performance."

Jesus H. Christ!

Brewster looked as if he had been slapped in the face.

"And so, Ken, from the little I've seen of him in action, so am I, with a few minor exceptions, quite satisfied with his performance."

"And I guess you're going to tell me about the exceptions. Right?" Cronley said, and then, having heard what had come out of his automatic mouth, quickly and very awkwardly added, "Mr. Justice, sir?"

"What you should keep in mind, Jim, is that you're not very good at playing politics. You are, in fact, a babe in the woods in that regard. On the other hand, I've spent a great deal of time in Washington and painfully have learned the rules of the game. I've been giving your assignment here some thought. Would you be interested in hearing what I've been thinking?"

"Yes, sir."

"You will not be able to conceal your purpose here from Chief Judge Biddle by saying you're my public relations man. I wouldn't be surprised if he already has heard who you really are and is mulling it over. The first thing I suspect he's thinking is that the President sent you here to keep an eye on him, that I am complicit in that spying, and he's deciding how he's going to deal with it. And Chief Justice Biddle is a master of politics at the highest level.

"So, before he unsheathes his sword and swings it at your knees, we have to do something to prevent that. Would you be interested in hearing what my suggestions are?"

"Yes, sir. Of course."

"The first thing I think you should do is fess up. You're DCI and you're here to protect the senior members of the American contingent at the Tribunal, which would of course mean both Chief Judge Biddle and myself."

"How would I do that? Go see him and tell him that the President has sent me to provide security for him, too? I'd hate to lie . . ."

"And I don't think that will be necessary. Would you like to hear what my suggestions are in that regard?"

"You tell me what to do, Mr. Justice, and I'll do it."

"Actually, it would be me doing something. Would you trust me to act on your behalf?"

"I'd be really grateful if you would, sir."

"Ken, get General Whatsisname, the Nuremberg Military Post commander, on the phone."

"General Kegley, sir," Brewster said, as he walked to the telephone on Jackson's desk. "Major General George Kegley Junior."

He then dialed a number.

"Chief Prosecutor Jackson for General Kegley, please," Brewster said into the phone, paused, and then added, "One moment, please, General, for Mr. Justice Jackson."

Jackson took the phone.

"Good morning, General . . .

"Very well, thank you. Yourself? . . .

"Well, aren't we all getting a little long in the tooth? . . .

"The reason I'm calling, General, is that I have a little problem. This is out of school, you understand. What's happened is that President

Truman has decided that Judge Biddle and I need the DCI to keep us safe—

"The Directorate of Central Intelligence. What used to be the OSS. It's run by Admiral Souers, an old friend. Anyway, when the President speaks, as you can imagine, things happen rapidly. Mr. Cronley, the DCI man in charge, arrived the day before yesterday, and today all of his people arrived . . .

"Neither Judge Biddle nor I got a heads-up. Did you? . . .

"I didn't think so. The problem is they need a place to stay. A secure place, preferably in, or very near to, the Tribunal, and they need it right now. There's about twenty people in all . . .

"Well, what I was thinking, General, was that I would send one of Mr. Cronley's people over to see you and tell you what they need, and then prevail upon you to have a discreet word with the Post housing officer . . .

"That's very good of you, General. Thank you very much—

"When? Right now, if that would be convenient . . .

"I very much appreciate your understanding, General. My regards to Mrs. Kegley."

Jackson hung up the phone.

"Within the next three hours," he said, "every senior officer in Nuremberg will be told, in the strictest confidence, that President Truman has sent the DCI to protect Judge Biddle and myself from the evil minions of the Kremlin. And after General Kegley has a word with the Post housing officer, you and your noble warriors will have a place to rest your weary heads."

"Thank you," Cronley said. "Thank you very much."

"How could I do less, Super Spook, for a man who's trying to keep me alive? I presume you are going to send Captain Dunwiddie to see General Kegley?"

"Yes, sir."

"Ken, would you take Captain Dinwiddie to see the general?"

V

[ONE]
**The Press Club Bar
Farber Palast
Stein, near Nuremberg
American Zone of Occupation,
  Germany
1725 21 February 1946**

Colonel Mortimer Cohen walked up to the table where Cronley was sitting with Dunwiddie, Ostrowski, Hessinger, and Ziegler. Everyone at the table started to get to their feet. Cohen waved them back down, and slipped into a chair.

"Who are they?" he asked, indicating Dunwiddie and Hessinger.

"Colonel Cohen, this is Captain Chauncey Dunwiddie, my deputy. If you call him 'Chauncey,' he will tear your arms off. And Friedrich Hessinger, my chief of staff."

"Jesus, Jim!" Dunwiddie complained. Then he said, "How do you do, sir?"

Cohen extended his hand to both men.

"Why do I think you're a coreligionist, Friedrich?" Cohen asked.

"I'm Jewish, if that's what you mean."

"Born here, or in the land of the free and home of the brave?"

"Here, sir."

"And may I hazard the guess you were CIC before Super Spook here seduced you into the DCI?"

"Yes, sir."

"'Super Spook'?" Cronley asked. "I thought you were Super Spook, Colonel Cohen."

"That was before Mr. Justice Jackson dubbed you that."

"You heard about that, did you?"

"I'm in the CIC, we know everything. Chauncey, I trust the quarters Mr. Justice Jackson asked General Kegley to get you to house your people sent to protect Chief Judge Biddle and himself are adequate?"

"Jesus, you do know everything!" Cronley said.

"Very nice, sir," Tiny said. "A twenty-eight-room fenced-in mansion that had been home to a **Gauleiter** who is now in the Justice compound prison awaiting trial. It had been reserved for an incoming brigadier general."

"Haverty, Richard C.," Cohen said. "As he's to be General Kegley's deputy, I'm sure they'll find suitable accommodations for him."

At that moment, just about simultaneously,

a waiter and Janice Johansen walked up to the table.

"Ah, Miss Johansen," Colonel Cohen said. "Why do I think I'm not going to be able to have the private conversation I had hoped to have with these gentlemen?"

"Maybe you're clairvoyant," she said. "I'm not leaving until somebody tells me what's the skinny on Bonehead Moriarty getting shot in the Compound."

"None of us know what you're talking about," Dunwiddie said.

"Oh, come on, Tiny," Janice said.

"We can't talk about that in here, Janice," Cronley said. "So what I suggest we do is give the waiter our order and have it delivered to the Duchess Suite."

"You're really going to tell her, Captain Death Wish?" Dunwiddie asked.

"You're really going to have to learn, Captain Dumb-Dumb, who you can trust and who you can't. Janice, for example, falls in the former category. Everybody drinking beer?"

[TWO]

"Curiosity overwhelms me," Cohen said, indicating a man in triangled ODs who had a

Thompson submachine gun in his lap. "Why do you have an armed guard in your bedroom?"

"Because there's a SIGABA system in the closet, and General Greene would order my castration if he learned I'd left it unguarded," Cronley replied. "As soon as the waiter shows up with the beer and then leaves, I'll show it to you."

"On that subject," Hessinger said, "Miss Miller called from the Mansion just before you showed up. She suggests we put the SIGABA in her room there."

"Is that what we're calling it, 'the Mansion'?"

"That's what it is," Hessinger said.

"Do it," Cronley ordered.

"Miss Miller is who?" Cohen asked.

"Formerly one of General Greene's finest. Now a DCI cryptographer, SIGABA operator, room debugger, **und so weiter**," Cronley answered.

The waiter appeared pushing a rolling cart on which sat silver wine coolers holding enough Berliner Kindl beer to serve three bottles of each to everyone. He served theirs first, and left.

"Not to worry, Colonel," Cronley said, "Hessinger will charge it to DCI under the 'miscellaneous expenses, hospitality' category. We are plying you with suds to get you and Janice to tell all."

"I know what I want from you," Janice said, "but what do you want from Morty here?"

"Only my friends get to call me 'Morty,' Miss Johansen."

"Then let's be friends, Morty," she said. "What does Jim want you to tell him?"

Cronley held his hand up to keep Cohen from replying.

"When the waiter's finished, Sigmund," he said, "show him out, and then guard the premises from the corridor."

"As you wish, sir," the man with the Thompson said.

When they had left, Cohen said, "He sounds British."

"Sigmund Karwowski served five years in Old Blighty as a Free Polish Army major," Cronley explained. "When we recruited him, he was a watchman—private—in the Provisional Security Organization, guarding groceries in the Giessen Quartermaster Depot. Once the SIGABA is moved, I'm going to put him in charge of Judge Biddle's security team. Good man."

"The Poles really lost the war, didn't they?" Cohen said.

"Turning the conversation to what happened to Bonehead?" Janice said.

"Okay, I'll tell you," Cronley said, and did so.

"Okay," Janice said, when he had finished. "I'll sit on it."

"Thank you."

"And now what are you trying to get out of Morty here?"

"I don't think the colonel would like you to know that."

"I'm about to continue my lecture on the real problem of Nazism," Cohen said. "If you're willing to restrain your journalist's tendency to ask a question every fifteen seconds, you might find it interesting."

"The 'real problem of Nazism'? Lecture away, Morty."

"You missed 'Real Problem 101,' Janice," Ziegler said. "That was a visit with Kaltenbrunner, followed by Colonel Cohen telling us what a three-star bastard he really is. That was followed by the colonel saying, 'You ain't heard nothing yet.'"

"And you haven't," Cohen replied. And then continued: "There is a castle not too far from here near Paderborn I'd like to show you—"

"Wewelsburg?" Hessinger interrupted.

"Yes. What do you know about Wewelsburg Castle?"

"Not nearly as much as I would like to."

"What's the source of your curiosity?"

"Well, I read somewhere that in 1939, Himmler forbade publishing anything about the castle . . ."

"He did."

"And I wondered why, so I started looking into it."

"And?"

"I couldn't find much, except a few vague references to it being . . . I don't know what. Somewhere the high SS brass used to go. I even heard they held marriages and christenings there, according to some Nazi ritual."

"And?"

"I even drove down there. I couldn't get in. There were some CIC people who said it was off-limits, even after I showed them my CIC credentials."

"And what did you think about that?"

"Well, I decided that something was going on there that was highly classified. CIC credentials won't get you into Kloster Grünau or the Compound, either. So I left. I kept looking, but the only thing I came up with is that Himmler ordered that Wewelsburg Castle should become the 'Reichshaus der SS-Gruppenführer,' and I don't even know what that means."

"Well, let me try to fill in some of the blanks in your knowledge—"

"Pay attention, everybody, as one professor delivers a lecture to another," Cronley's automatic mouth said.

"You're free not to listen, of course," Cohen said.

"Sorry, Colonel, that was my automatic mouth."

"The one that seems to get you so frequently in trouble? Perhaps you should consider putting a zipper—better still, a good padlock—on it."

"Sir, I'm really sorry."

Cohen snorted, and then went on: "Wewelsburg Castle is near Paderborn, Westphalia, a little over two hundred miles from here, along some really bad roads. I think, presuming when I finish the lecture and Super Spook wishes to have a look, we'll go there in his illegal airplane."

"Fine with me," Cronley said.

"Much of what is the castle now," Cohen went on, "was built near the site of the Battle of the Teutoburg Forest in 1603 dash '09 for the prince-bishop of Paderborn, Dietrich von Fürstenberg. That battle, in 9 B.C., saw a cluster of German tribes assembled under a man named Arminius annihilate three Roman legions. Most historians agree—"

"That the battle was the greatest defeat the Romans ever suffered and was one of the most decisive battles in history. After it, the Romans never tried to take territory east of the Rhine," Hessinger furnished.

"Correct," Cohen said. "And if you hadn't interrupted me, Friedrich, you would have had a gold star to take home to Mommy."

Cronley laughed aloud, earning himself a withering look from Hessinger.

"Two things are germane here," Cohen went

on. "The German victory near where the castle was built, and, two, that after being hailed as a hero for a while, Arminius was assassinated by jealous fellow tribesmen. Victory and death by assassination.

"During the Thirty Years' War, in 1646, the castle was razed by the Swedes. Death, in other words. In 1650, the Swedes having been chased away, Prince-Bishop Ferdinand von Fürstenberg rebuilt it. Death followed by resurrection. Anyone see where I'm going with this?"

"The castle rose phoenixlike from the ashes?" Hessinger asked. "The first Operation Phoenix?"

"Something like that," Cohen replied. "During the Seven Years' War—1756 to 1763—the basement rooms were used as a military prison. During the eighteenth and nineteenth centuries, it was rarely repaired and became nothing more than another ruin. Such ruins were—are—all over Germany.

"From what I have been able to learn, during Hitler's election campaign in January 1933, Himmler came up with the idea to use a castle to serve as a place—a **Reichsführerschule**—to train senior SS officers.

"On his very first visit to Wewelsburg on November 3, 1933, Himmler decided to buy the castle. When the local government asked what Himmler thought was too much money, he leaned on them, which saw the SS signing a one-hundred-year lease, one reichsmark per annum, for the castle. The SS then moved in, so to speak, with an elaborate ceremony in September 1934.

"Himmler then dubbed the castle the 'Reichshaus der SS-Gruppenführer,' which means something like the national spiritual or symbolic home for SS lieutenant generals and up. Anyway, he began to hold conferences of senior SS brass at Wewelsburg.

"At about this point, the occult enters the Wewelsburg scenario. Irminenschaft—Irminism—starts to raise its ugly head—"

"What the hell is that?" Cronley asked.

"A pre-Christian German religion," Hessinger furnished.

"Correct. Another gold star for you, Friedrich," Cohen said. "Tacitus, the great historian, wrote about it. Irminenschaft comes into the picture via a very interesting character named Karl Maria Wiligut, an Austrian occultist.

"Karl Wolff, chief adjutant of the SS, introduced him to Himmler. Himmler liked what Wiligut had written about the Roman Catholic Church, the Jews, and the Freemasons being responsible for both the defeat of Germany in the First World War and the downfall of the Habsburg Empire.

"Himmler also became fascinated with Wiligut's views on ancient German history, most important that Irminism was the pre-Christian German ancestral religion.

"Himmler took Wiligut into the SS in September 1933, in the rank—colonel—Wiligut had earned by distinguished service in World War One. They quickly became close friends, which resulted in Wiligut's promotion to SS-**Brigadeführer** three years later.

"Wiligut designed the runic symbols used on black SS uniforms and flags, and designed and supervised the manufacture of the gold SS Totenkopfrings, which were passed out to SS officers who had distinguished themselves in some way."

"He's the guy who came up with that skull and crossbones hat insignia?" Ziegler asked.

"I presume you mean the Totenkopf," Cohen replied. "No. That goes back at least to the War of Austrian Succession and the Seven Years' War, when Frederick the Great formed a regiment of Hussar cavalry in the Prussian Army. They wore black uniforms and tall headgear—mirlitons—with a silver skull and crossbones insignia pinned to them."

"Colonel, how the hell do you know all this stuff?" Ziegler asked.

"Some intelligence officers, such as myself, and I suspect Mr. Hessinger and Captain Dunwiddie, find it useful to read military history rather than comic books or novels with strong sexual content. You might want to keep that in mind."

"You have just been cut off at the knees, Augie," Cronley said, laughing. "Throw away all those Superman comic books."

"Let him who is without sin cast the first stone, Cronley," Cohen said. "And, if I may now continue?"

"In the Civil War, the 41st New York Volunteer Infantry, made up of mostly Germans who had emigrated from Prussia, wore a skull and bones insignia," Hessinger said.

"One more gold star, Friedrich, for that historical footnote and for proving my point about the value to intelligence officers of reading military history. I hope you and Ziegler were listening, Super Spook?"

"Augie and I are all ears to just about anything you have to say. Pray continue, Colonel, sir."

"Wiligut had some other noteworthy ideas about history and religion," Cohen said. "He believed, for example, that Germany was settled by people from the lost continent of Atlantis about two hundred and twenty-eight thousand years before Christ, their first settlement being in what is now Goslar.

"He also believed that the events chronicled in the New Testament had occurred in Germany, rather than Palestine. And that Krist—with a K—who had founded the Irminist religion about 12,500 B.C., was the man we now think of as Jesus Christ. He claimed the Wiligut family was directly descended from Irminist wise men whom rival sorcerers had driven into northern Europe, then a wilderness, now Germany, about 1200 B.C."

"This guy sounds like a real candidate for the funny farm," Ziegler said. "And he was pals with Himmler?"

"Wiligut was indeed pals with Himmler. What I haven't been able to find out is whether Himmler knew that Wiligut had been committed at the request of his wife to the Salzburg mental asylum in November of 1924 as a paranoid schizophrenic liable to cause harm to himself and others. He was released from the asylum in 1927, on condition that he leave Austria. He then moved to Munich.

"What I have learned is that 'under the guidance'—which means with the support of— SS-Obergruppenführer Karl Wolff, Himmler's chief adjutant, Wiligut developed the plans to turn Wewelsburg Castle into something like an SS holy place."

"Holy place?" Janice asked.

"Holy place," Cohen confirmed. "This is the point of the lecture, so pay attention. Starting in 1934, the plaster on the exterior walls of Wewelsburg was removed to make the building look more castle-like. They opened a blacksmith operation to make wrought-iron interior decorations. The blacksmiths, and the plaster removers, were concentration camp inmates, mostly Russian POWs, but absolutely no Jews, as Jews would obviously contaminate the place.

"The first official Irministic ceremony at Wewelsburg was a baptism rite for Obergruppenführer Wolff's son, Thorisman—rough translation, Man of Thor, or Thor's son."

"Who is Thor?" Ziegler asked.

"The Nordic warrior god of power, strength, lightning, et cetera," Hessinger said. "That's where we get Thursday—Thor's Day."

"I never knew that," Ziegler said.

"Present at the baptism," Cohen said, "were SS-Obergruppenführer und General der Polizei Reinhard Heydrich and Professor Karl Diebitsch, an artist and, to be fair, soldier—he was an **Oberführer** in the Waffen-SS—who had designed the all-black SS uniform, and was sort of Himmler's artist-in-residence.

"He was also a businessman. He owned the Porzellan Manufaktur Allach, which manufactured not only what one might expect, but also porcelain busts of Adolf Hitler, which good Germans were expected to buy at a stiff price and display on their mantelpieces. The factory was next to the Dachau concentration camp, which provided its labor force."

"Jesus Christ!" Cronley muttered.

"At the risk of repeating myself, Super Spook, you ain't heard nothing yet," Cohen said. "Diebitsch also designed the gold Totenkopfring that Himmler awarded to SS officers and enlisted men who somehow pleased him. I think it was the SS equivalent of our Army Commendation Medal, as they were passed out by the tens of thousands.

"In 1938, at Himmler's order, the Totenkopfrings of SS personnel who had died—the custom was to take the rings from the corpses of the deceased just before burial, so they could be suitably framed and proudly displayed by the family next to the bust of Hitler—were ordered to be sent to Wewelsburg and stored in a ceremonial chest. This was to symbolize the deceased's perpetual membership in the SS-Order. There were approximately twelve thousand such rings. My men have so far been unable to find them."

"Your men?" Hessinger asked.

"My men, Friedrich," Cohen confirmed. "The ones who ran you off. They are now the custodians of Wewelsburg."

"And what, I have to ask, does military government think about that?" Cronley asked. "The CIC detachment in charge of protecting the Tribunal taking over Castle Wewelsburg two hundred odd miles away?"

"They are curious and I suspect displeased. But so far General Greene has been able to keep the situation under control," Cohen replied. "As I said, the rings are gold. Twelve thousand rings represent a lot of gold.

"One scenario is that as soon as the rings got to Wewelsburg, they were melted down and turned, so to speak, into pocket money for Himmler and friends. The upper ranks of the SS were filled with crooks. Reinhard Heydrich, for example, was cashiered from the Navy for conduct unbecoming an officer and a gentleman. And then there's that business of ransoming Jews from concentration camps."

"What?" Ziegler asked.

"Super Spook, since you know about that, you have the floor," Cohen said. "Until I return from the restroom."

"What if I have to go, too?"

"You will have to control your bladder until I return. Rank hath its privileges."

When the bathroom door was closed, Ziegler asked, "Boss, what was he talking about?"

"SS officers, or people working for the SS, would go to rich Jews in London, or New York, wherever, and tell them for a price Uncle Max and family could be taken from Dachau or some other concentration camp and moved to Argentina."

"How did they manage to do that?"

"I got this from El Jefe and Cletus Frade," Cronley said. "What happened was Major Freiherr Hans-Peter von Wachtstein, the acting military attaché at the German embassy in Buenos Aires—"

"Von Wachtstein? The SAA pilot we saw in Berlin when we were getting Mattingly back?" Ziegler asked incredulously.

"One and the same. Hansel tipped Cletus—the OSS—when a German submarine was going to show up at Samborombón Bay south of Buenos Aires carrying some people—SS types—they wanted to smuggle into Argentina, plus chests full of English pounds, Swiss francs, dollars, and gold and jewels.

"It was part of Operation Phoenix, building a sanctuary for high-level Nazis. The plan was that if Germany lost, they would make their way to Argentina, wait until things cooled down, and then rise—phoenixlike—from the ashes of the Third Reich.

"Anyway, when the sub arrived, Clete, and a bunch of gauchos from his estancia, all ex-soldiers, were waiting for it. They grabbed the sub and everybody around. The prisoners were then interrogated. By us and by an Argentine officer, Bernardo Martín, who ran—still runs—BIS, the Argentine OSS and FBI combined.

"Cutting to the chase, the SS guys quickly started to sing like canaries."

"Really? They caved right away?" Ziegler asked.

"Apparently, after watching one of their number being dragged feetfirst across the pampas behind a gaucho on a horse," Cronley explained, "they became cooperative. The BIS has interesting interrogation techniques.

"Anyway, they fessed up all the details of Operation Phoenix, plus all the details of the ransom operation.

"The way that worked was once the ransom had been paid, a couple of mid-level—the equivalent of field-grade officers—SS officers would go to a concentration camp and tell the SS commandant that they had come for prisoners So and So, who were to be interrogated in Berlin.

"They would then take them to Spain, where they would be loaded on neutral ships bound for Argentina."

"So the OSS was able to shut down the scam?" Ziegler asked.

"No. The decision about what to do about it went all the way to the top, to President Roosevelt. Roosevelt decided that if we shut it down, all the Jews in the concentration camps would end up in the ovens. Thousands of them. So it ran until the end of the war."

"Jesus," Ziegler said. "What happened to all the Phoenix money on the sub?"

"Most of it wound up with Tío Juan, but Clete told me he suspected El Jefe took a finder's fee from it before Tío Juan got his hands on it."

" 'Tío Juan'?"

"Juan Domingo Perón. He likes to be called 'Uncle Juan' by Don Cletus Frade, his godson."

"I didn't know that Perón was Frade's god-father," Cohen said as he slipped back into his chair.

"I thought you said you were CIC and knew everything," Janice said.

"I thought you said you wouldn't ask questions."

"I'm a woman and we get to change our minds."

"Point taken. Will you wait until the lecture is over?"

"Sure, Morty."

"The second theory vis-à-vis the missing twelve thousand gold rings," Cohen began, "is that they were taken to a cave near Wewelsburg Castle, and then the mouth of the cave was blown closed. We so far have been unable to verify this.

"As I said, Wiligut was promoted in 1936 to SS-**Brigadeführer**, and with Himmler's blessing undertook a number of projects, some of which made sense, and some which were . . . for lack of a better word, insane.

"Wiligut supervised the building by concentration camp inmates—again, no Jews who would contaminate the premises—of an SS-**Stabsgebäude**, a staff building, and a **Wachgebäude**, a guardhouse, at Wewelsburg. The

North Tower was rebuilt, and a safe for Himmler was placed in the basement of the West Tower. We don't know what was in it. When the castle fell into the hands of the 83rd Armored Reconnaissance Battalion, 3rd Armored Division, on April 3, 1945, the safe was open and empty."

"Insane projects?" Janice asked.

"I will take that question," Cohen said. "Men can change their minds, too, Janice. Many of the modifications Wiligut made to the castle had to do with the number twelve. Himmler apparently wanted to reincarnate the Knights of the Round Table."

"As in King Arthur's Knights of the Round Table?" Cronley asked.

"A German, or Teutonic, version thereof. If you didn't spend all of your time in university reading naughty novels, perhaps you read something about them? How many of them there were, that sort of thing?"

"Actually, Colonel, sir, what stuck in my mind was that Sir Lancelot, one of the twelve knights, got caught fooling around with Guinevere."

"I remember that, too," Ziegler said. "Diddling the King's wife was a no-no for a supposed-to-be-pure-and-noble knight."

Both earned withering looks from Cohen.

"In Nordic mythology," he went on after a significant pause, "there were twelve æsir—sort of gods, including Odin and Thor. When

Himmler re-formed, enlarged, the SS, he set it up with twelve departments—SS-**Hauptämter**. What I have been thinking is that Himmler wanted the castle to serve as the stage for a Nazi version of the Knights of the Round Table. In this scenario, Himmler designated twelve senior SS officers as the knights of his round table.

"What I do know is that the number twelve played a major role in Wiligut's design of the North Tower. Inside it, between 1938 and 1943, Wiligut built two rooms, the **Obergruppenführersaal**—SS Generals' Hall—and the **Gruft**."

"**Gruft?**" Ziegler asked.

"Vault, as in burial vault," Hessinger clarified.

"Their ceilings were cast in concrete and faced with natural stone," Cohen went on. "And he made plans for another hall on the upper floors. They wanted the North Tower to be the **Mittelpunkt der Welt**—the center of the world."

"Morty, sweetheart, this is all for real, right?" Janice asked.

"Yes, it is, Miss Johansen. In the vault, which is held up by twelve pedestals, he had a swastika placed in the center of the ceiling. A gas line leading to the center of the floor was almost certainly going to fuel an eternal flame.

"In the Hall of the Obergruppenführers, there are twelve pillars and niches—the latter probably intended for the eventual interment of Himmler's latter-day knights. There is also a sun wheel with twelve spokes."

"What's a sun wheel?" Cronley asked.

"What looks like a wheel, with the sun in the center," Cohen explained. "In this SS religion they were starting, the sun was the 'strongest and most visible expression of God.'"

"They were actually expecting people to take this new religion seriously?" Janice asked.

"I think, to some degree, that's exactly what happened. That's what is so frightening."

"You want to explain that?"

"I'll be happy to, but please let me finish first."

"Go ahead, Morty, baby."

"If I didn't mention this before, we have learned, credibly, that upper-level SS officers, mostly general officers, would gather secretly at various places in Wewelsburg and there conduct rites of some sort. Religious rites. Or quasi-religious."

"Sounds crazy," Cronley said.

"Unfortunately, they were dead serious," Cohen said. "But speaking of crazy, did you ever hear of the Inner World of Agharti?"

"No."

"It is a world deep under the surface of this world. It's a common myth, on the order of the Lost Continent. You never heard of it?"

Cronley shook his head.

"Edgar Rice Burroughs, who wrote **Tarzan**, wrote about an under-the-earth civilization. He called it 'Pellucidar,' " Hessinger said.

"It was fiction, right? Fantasy?"

"Of course," Hessinger replied.

"What if I told you that beginning in 1941, the SS began construction in Hungary of a vertical tunnel, sort of a mine shaft, that would eventually be equipped with an elevator that would take Himmler and his inner circle ten miles downward to the Inner World of Agharti? Would you consider that fact or fiction?"

"Fiction," Hessinger said.

"Insanity," Cronley said.

"Work on the tunnel went on until November 1944, when the SS ran out of supplies and decided the project would have to wait for the Final Victory."

"You're bullshitting us, right, Morty baby?" Janice asked.

"Janice, baby, to quote Super Spook, I shit you not."

"Incredible," Cronley said.

"Not incredible," Cohen said. "Very credible. I've been there. You would be astonished at the size of the mounds of evacuated earth and stone from a hole two and a half miles deep—that's as far as they got—and, say, thirty feet in diameter creates."

"Boggles the mind," Ziegler said.

"Let me now turn to what happened to Castle Wewelsburg when the Final Victory didn't occur," Cohen went on. "In late March 1945, as the U.S. 3rd Armored Division approached the area, Himmler sent SS Major Heinz Macher, one of his adjutants, to Wewelsburg with fifteen men. His orders were to tell SS General Siegfried Taubert, who was in charge of the castle, to remove, quote, sacred items, end quote, and then blow the place up.

"When Macher got there, he found that Taubert was long gone. He was captured by us as he tried to get to Italy. We've got him in a cell here. He flatly refuses to tell us what he had with him when he left Castle Wewelsburg.

"Macher couldn't blow up the castle, as he didn't have enough explosives. All he had were some tank mines, which he used to take down the southeast tower—the weakest tower—and the guard and SS buildings. Then he tried, unsuccessfully, to burn the castle down.

"Then he took off and tried and failed to make it to Italy. We caught him, and he's now in an SS prisoner enclosure in Darmstadt. That concludes the lecture."

"How much of this can I use?" Janice asked. "It's a hell of a story."

"You can use all of it, but I suggest that you wait until you see the castle for yourself."

"Can I go with you and Super Spook in his illegal airplane?"

"That would be up, of course, to Super Spook. I was going to suggest that you might wish to sit on your story until we answer some more of the questions that need answers."

"Morty, what's your interest in this, pure curiosity?" she asked.

"Nazi evil. My feeling is that this Himmler-inspired Nazi religion made greater inroads into the German people than anyone suspects, and is a greater threat to society than most people recognize."

"I don't think I understand," Cronley said.

"Most Jews want people like Kaltenbrunner, after a fair trial for the murder of the Jews they slaughtered, hung. Simple vengeance."

"What's wrong with that?" Ziegler asked. "I wanted to put a bullet . . . more than one . . . into his ear."

"I think, Mr. Ziegler, that you have a greater understanding of the problem—whether or not you're aware of it—than most people. You said something to the effect that you shot rabid dogs in the head to make sure they didn't bite and infect anyone else before they, I quote, 'got to piss on the pearly gates.'"

"Now I don't understand," Ziegler said.

"Himmler, Kaltenbrunner, and people like

them have already infected the German people with their variation of rabies," Cohen said.

"Now I really don't understand," Ziegler replied.

"The way Himmler and his new religion have influenced the German people is that when we hang Kaltenbrunner, the German people will interpret it as the vengeance of the victors—especially Jewish victors, like me—rather than the punishment of a mass murderer. Instead he will be a martyr to the cause—this foul religion—he helped found.

"Kaltenbrunner and his cult have convinced many Germans—perhaps more than half, maybe sixty, seventy percent of them—that Germans—I should say, Aryan Germans—are a superior race. And that there's nothing morally wrong in protecting that race by eliminating inferior peoples."

"You're saying it was that that sent the Jews to the ovens?" Cronley asked.

"There was a political element in the anti-Semitism. Hitler needed a political enemy to rally the people to his cause. He convinced the people that the Jews were responsible for the unemployment, out-of-control inflation, et cetera, when it was the somewhat justified French vengeance—through the Versailles Treaty—that had caused it."

"And once the German people were satisfied

with that explanation for their plight—there was little public outcry against the **Nürnberger Gesetze**—Nuremberg Laws—of September 1935. Specifically: 'Law for the Protection of German Blood and German Honor.' There were two parts of this law. The Reich Citizenship Law declared that only those of German or 'related blood'—whatever the hell that means—could be citizens of the Reich, and classified everybody else in Germany as 'state subjects,' without citizenship rights.

"The other part of the law was more specifically anti-Semitic. Marriage between Germans and Jews was forbidden. As was 'extramarital intercourse.' So was the employment of females under the age of forty-five in Jewish households."

"That sounds nutty," Ziegler said.

"Nutty and evil," Cohen said. "And since German Jews were without rights as citizens, they could no longer be civil servants, or practice medicine or law, or be schoolteachers, et cetera.

"One would think there would be an enormous public outcry against this, but there was only a negligible protest. I say negligible because the protesters—all bona fide German citizens—were quickly rounded up and placed in 'detention camps,' which were quickly renamed 'concentration camps.'

"Turning to that—immediately after Hitler became chancellor in 1933, the Nazi Party took over all the police in Germany. Reich Interior Minister Wilhelm Frick and Hermann Göring, who was then Prussian acting interior minister, promptly established the first **Konzentrationslager**—"

"Using as a model the 'reconcentration camps' the Spanish general Valeriano Weyler set up in Cuba in 1897," Hessinger interrupted.

"No shit?" Ziegler asked.

"Pray continue, Professor Hessinger," Cohen said.

"For the obvious reason—I almost wound up in one—I've always been interested in concentration camps. And I found it very interesting that a year after the first one was opened, Lieutenant Colonel Teddy Roosevelt and the 1st United States Volunteer Cavalry—the Rough Riders—shut it down."

"And I'll bet you're also going to tell us Lieutenant Colonel Roosevelt went on to become President?" Cohen inquired, more than a little sarcastically.

"Something very much like that happened in Argentina," Cronley said. "Cletus Frade's father commanded the Húsares de Pueyrredón, a cavalry regiment. That's the Argentine version of our 'Old Guard' in Washington. Lots of prestige. They got their start when Pueyrredón, who was Clete's great-great-great—whatever—grandfather, formed gauchos—cowboys—from his estancia into cavalry and chased the English out of Buenos Aires."

"Fascinating," Cohen said. "But if you and Friedrich are through with your little lectures, I would like to continue with mine.

"The first **Konzentrationslager**—Dachau— was set up in 1933 by Himmler to hold Germans—including Aryans—who opposed National Socialism. There was no public out- cry against this. At the time it was called the 'Dachau Protective Custody Camp.'

"Then he started to send what he called 'ra- cially undesirable elements' to Dachau. Not only Jews, but Romani—Gypsies—common crimi- nals, and homosexuals. Among the latter were many actors, writers, musicians, and other intel- lectual types well known, even famous, in Ger- many. And again there was no outcry."

"Maybe because everybody was afraid of Himmler and the SS?" Janice asked.

"That certainly played a part, but I think it's also likely that a substantial portion of German Aryans decided, 'Well, those sort of people are corrupting German purity, such as my own, and deserve what they're getting.'"

"That's a hell of an accusation," Cronley said.

"Unfortunately, it's fair," Cohen replied. "I've come to the conclusion that Himmler saw in the acceptance of what he had done that he could do even more. And even more than he had been doing if he could give the German people, the Aryans, a moral justification for exterminating people. And the way to do that was to give them a new religion. Or at least one that had risen, phoenixlike, from long-forgotten German history."

"And you think that's happened?" Cronley asked softly.

"I think we're further down that road than most people understand. That's why what Jackson is doing is so important. Showing the German people what the extermination of inferior people was really like. Putting the movies of those stacks of dead bodies—only a little more than half of which were Jews—into evidence and showing that Göring and Kaltenbrunner, et al, were responsible."

"Do you think he's going to be able to do that?" Ziegler asked.

"The court is going to find them guilty, there's little doubt about that. What I want to see is for the German people to see—to understand— that the swine hanging from the gallows were criminals, not disciples in a new religion that would have turned Germany into a Germanic Utopia had the evil Americans, French, English, and Russians not interfered."

"And how are you going to do that, Colonel?" Janice asked.

She didn't call him "Morty" or something

else clever, Cronley thought. **He's gotten to her with this.**

Hell, he's gotten to me with this.

"I intend, Janice, to give you everything you need for your story. The more people who know about this, the better."

"Including a tour of this Nazi Vatican?"

"Yes. As soon as that can be arranged."

"That's all?" Cronley asked.

"And, with your assistance, Captain Cronley—or my assistance to you—I intend to witness Odessa being not only brought down, but brought to floodlights before the German people."

Boy, is he serious about that!

Cohen's tone was changed when he went on.

"Not only have I given everyone something to think about, I hope—the lecture is over for the time being—but my stomach tells me it's time to eat."

He stood up as Ziegler distributed more beers.

"I thought you wanted to see the SIGABA device," Cronley said.

"I guess that means my stomach will have to wait," Cohen said. "Duty once again keeps me from what I'd rather do."

VI

[ONE]
The Press Club Restaurant
Farber Palast
Stein, near Nuremberg
American Zone of Occupation,
Germany
1825 21 February 1946

It took two white-jacketed waiters about five minutes to locate two oblong—as opposed to round—tables and then move them to a suitable area, join them, and then lay a tablecloth and other accoutrements on it.

Finally, everyone sat down. The waiters presented menus.

A third and fourth waiter appeared, bearing towel-wrapped bottles in wine coolers and champagne flutes.

"Wrong table," Cronley said in German.

"Courtesy of Colonel Serov, Mein Herr," the waiter replied.

"What?" Cronley asked. Then he saw two Soviet Army officers walking across the room toward them. They were in dress uniform, a light blue single-breasted tunic with shoulder boards showing their rank and branch of service. A gold cloth belt was around their waists, and both wore an impressive display of ornate medals.

One of them, a pleasant-looking blond-haired man in his early thirties, was wearing the shoulder boards of an infantry colonel. The officer with him was wearing infantry major's shoulder boards.

Cronley knew the man wearing the **polkovnik** shoulder boards was neither a colonel nor in the infantry, which made it very likely the man with him was also neither a major nor in the infantry.

"James, I heard you were here, and I was hoping to see you," the man Cronley knew to be Major of State Security Ivan Serov, first deputy to Commissar of State Security Nikolayevich Merkulov, said, extending his hand and smiling warmly. His English was only slightly accented.

"How goes it, Ivan?" Cronley replied, taking the hand. "Why don't you and your friend pull up a chair?"

"I would hate to intrude."

"Not at all, Colonel," Cohen said. "Please join us. I was hoping to meet you."

And what's that all about? "Hoping to meet you"?

Serov made an impatient gesture to the major, who immediately set off to find chairs.

When they were seated, Serov between Cohen, who was at the head of the table, and Cronley to his right, Serov said, "The wine is French, Veuve Clicquot, which is what James and I drank the last time we had dinner."

"Colonel Cohen," Cronley said, "this is Senior Major of State Security Ivan Serov."

"Not any longer," Serov said. "I have returned to my first love, the Queen of Battles, infantry."

You can tell by the look on the bastard's face that he knows we know he's lying, and doesn't give a damn.

"I'm very happy to meet you, Colonel," Serov said. "We're going to be coworkers."

"So I understand," Cohen said.

So you understand? What the hell does that mean?

"Colonel, Major—forgive me, **Colonel of Infantry**—how do I say this?—Serov took care of Colonel Mattingly when he was—"

"In the hands of Thuringian authorities for having over-imbibed," Serov interrupted. "I wanted to thank you for coming up with that scenario, James. It solved many problems for me. Or perhaps I should be thanking Miss Johansen."

"You're welcome, handsome," Janice said.

"You are a credit to the DCI, madam."

"I don't work for the DCI, handsome."

"Of course you don't. I can't imagine why I thought that."

You sly sonofabitch!

Actually, I think I'm thinking that with admiration.

The major began to pour the Veuve Clicquot.

"Gentlemen and lady, this is Major Sergei Alekseevich, my aide-de-camp," Serov said.

"Colonels in my army don't get aides to pour champagne," Cronley said.

"Colonels in my army do when they are given great responsibility."

"Such as?"

"Protecting the Soviet Union's prosecutors, Iona Nikitchenko and Alexander Volchkov, from all harm. As you, James, I understand, are protecting Judge Biddle and Justice Jackson."

"You heard about that, huh?"

"And I also heard what happened to your friend Lieutenant Moriarty. Please accept my condolences on your loss."

The only way he could know about Bone-head is from the mole, or moles, he has in the Compound. And he wants me to know he has moles.

"Well, people should be very careful when cleaning their pistols."

"That's not what I heard happened to the lieutenant."

"What did you hear?"

Major Alekseevich finished pouring the champagne.

Who is this guy?

Really his aide, or someone the NKGB sent to watch him?

The way Polkovnik Dragomirov was watching him the last time he bought me dinner in Vienna?

And now that I think about it, Serov should have been in trouble when the Mattingly–Likharev prisoner swap didn't work.

And he didn't manage to get Major of State Security Venedikt Ulyanov back from us before we found out he was former SS-Brigadeführer Franz von Dietelburg.

So what's he doing here, rather than penance in Lubyanka? Or Siberia?

Is he Commissar of State Security Nikolayevich Merkulov's fair-haired boy? All is forgiven, my boy. Daddy Merkulov knows you gave it the old school try?

Wild thought: Maybe Merkulov hasn't given up on getting the Likharevs back, and sent him here for another try.

Why here?

Because Captain James D. Cronley Jr. is here?

Is the sonofabitch here to kidnap me?

Does he think I'm that important?

I'll be goddamned!

Serov raised his flute.

"Gentlemen and lady," he said, "may I suggest we raise our glasses to international cooperation?"

"Lovely thought, Colonel," Cohen said.

"I know these gentlemen from Berlin," Serov said, tipping his flute toward Dunwiddie and Ostrowski, "but we've never been formally introduced. And I don't have the pleasure of knowing this gentleman." He tipped his glass toward Ziegler.

"Mr. August Ziegler," Cronley said.

Serov offered his hand. Ziegler took it.

"How do you do, Colonel?" he asked.

Cronley pointed to Dunwiddie.

"Captain Chauncey Dunwiddie, my deputy, who for reasons I can't imagine, is often called 'Tiny.'"

"How do you do, Colonel?" Dunwiddie said, as they shook hands.

"And Mr. Maksymilian Ostrowski," Cronley said.

Serov offered his hand. Ostrowski didn't take it.

Ostrowski asked in Russian, "How do you do, Colonel?"

"You speak Russian?" Serov asked, speaking English.

"I'm a Pole," Ostrowski continued, this time

in English. "A great many Poles speak Russian."

"You sound English . . . British."

"Probably because I spent five years in Great Britain as an officer in the Free Polish Army."

"Well, that explains, doesn't it, why James recruited you for the DCI?"

"I suppose it does. And I accepted as it would have been unwise for me to return to Poland now that you Russians have taken it over."

"I don't suppose you would believe me if I said I understood."

"No, I don't think I would."

"Before this gets out of hand, why don't we order dinner?" Janice asked.

"I would be honored to have you all as my guests," Serov said.

"What is it that they say? 'Beware of Russians bearing gifts'?" Cronley said.

"I rather like what they say about 'Never turn down a free meal,'" Cohen said. "I know not what course others might take, Colonel, but as for me, I accept your kind offer."

What the hell is Cohen up to?

"I go along with Morty," Janice said. "Thank you, handsome."

"As for me," Cronley said, "I'll have a Jack Daniel's on the rocks, water on the side, followed by a New York strip, pink in the middle, with a baked potato. Max, what about you?"

"I'll have the same. Except vodka, Russian if you have it, instead of whisky."

"And the same for me," Serov said.

"Why don't we have the same all around?" Cohen asked. "That will produce our dinner quicker, and I will be saved from starvation."

"So what brings you to Nuremberg, Miss Johansen?" Serov said, as they were having a post-dinner cognac. "If I may ask?"

"You may ask, handsome. And since you're buying, you can call me Janice."

"And I would be pleased if you were to call me Ivan."

Janice didn't reply.

After a moment, Serov asked, "Well?"

"Well, what?"

"You said I might ask what brings you to Nuremberg."

"I said you could ask, Ivan, but I didn't say I would tell you."

"Janice wanted to visit Wewelsburg Castle," Cohen said, "and came to see if I could arrange that for her."

Now what? Cronley thought.

"The Cathedral of Saint Heinrich the Divine? That Castle Wewelsburg?"

Cronley laughed.

"Is that what the KGB calls it?"

"That's what I call it."

"That one," Cohen said.

"How many of those obscene rumors one hears about it are true?" Serov asked.

"That would depend on what rumors you've heard," Cohen said.

"I've heard the one about it being the castle where Crown Prince Heinrich gathered his Knights of the SS around the Nazi Round Table. I found that one a bit hard to believe."

"That one's true," Cohen said. "There's even a thirteen-place round table."

"And you're going to write about this, Janice?"

"If it's true—if half of it is true—it's one hell of a story, Ivan baby," she replied.

"And Colonel Cohen holds the keys to the castle?"

"Yes, I do."

"That, you will understand, raises my curiosity. Dare I ask why the CIC is guarding a ruined castle?"

"Primarily to keep tourists from interfering with our search of the place."

"Looking for what?"

"Two things in particular. One, to see what happened to the twelve thousand gold Totenkopfrings that Himmler ordered sent there . . ."

"You just confirmed, thank you, another rumor I have heard," Serov said.

". . . and to see if we can find out what was in the safe that Himmler built in the basement. When we got to the castle, it had been emptied under conditions that suggest it was emptied just before we got there."

"Fascinating. Emptied by Himmler?" Serov asked.

"Not by him personally. And we just don't know if the emptiers were acting on his orders, acting on their own, or even if they were SS. I presume, Ivan, you know what happened to Himmler after Hitler shot himself?"

"I know the official version . . ." Serov began.

"I don't," Cronley admitted.

". . . but I would love to hear yours, presuming, of course, that you would not be revealing any state secrets."

"So would I," Janice said.

"I thought I could relax after my previous lecture," Cohen said. "But what the hell, Ivan, you're picking up the bill."

Cohen's being awfully obliging to Serov, and he obviously knows the sonofabitch is NKGB, so what the hell is he up to?

"Before Hitler committed suicide, he named Grand Admiral Karl Doenitz as his successor—"

"I wondered about that," Cronley interrupted. "Why Doenitz and not Göring?"

"Because Himmler told him Göring was trying to arrange an armistice with Eisenhower, which he was. There is an unconfirmed scenario that Hitler ordered Hermann arrested and shot.

"Doenitz moved the German government to Plön, in Schleswig-Holstein. When Himmler, who was then **Reichsführer**-SS, C-in-C of the Reserve Army, **Reichsminister** of the Interior, and chief of police, showed up there on May 6, 1945, Doenitz, who had hated him for years, fired him from all of his posts.

"Himmler probably was not happy getting canned, but since Doenitz had what was left of the Wehrmacht and the Navy behind him, there was nothing he could do about it.

"On May tenth, he started for Bavaria . . ."

"Was he headed for Wewelsburg?" Cronley asked.

"We don't know. Possibly. We do know that before he left, Himmler and the twelve people in his entourage disguised themselves and equipped themselves with phony ID documents. Himmler's said he was Sergeant Heinrich Hitzinger of a special armored company, attached to the Sicherheitsdienst Field Police, who had been demobilized on May 3, 1945.

"He put on civilian clothing, shaved off his mustache, took off his famous pince-nez eyeglasses, and put a pirate's patch over his left eye."

"That I hadn't heard," Serov said. "Why didn't he get papers saying he was a simple sergeant?"

"Good question," Cohen replied. "I just don't know. Anyway, by October eighteenth, Himmler and entourage moved to Bremervörde, a small **Dorf** on the Oste River.

"On May twenty-second, Himmler and two of his escorts, a Waffen-SS lieutenant colonel and a major, were picked up by an alert British infantry patrol suspicious of their phony documents. They took them to a checkpoint run by British Field Security—the Brit version of the CIC—where they were arrested.

"Did they know who they had?" Cronley asked, and then went on without waiting for a reply. "The reason I ask is that when I ran a CIC checkpoint . . . which seems like fifty years ago . . . we had a list from the OSS of people to look for. Himmler's name, plus a long list of SS officers' names, were on my list, but no enlisted men."

"Apparently, the suspicious identity documents were enough to get them arrested. They didn't know who they had. The three of them were fed and put into a small building at the checkpoint. The next morning, they were sent by truck to the Civil Internment Camp at Barnstedt. On the way, they had to pass through another Field Security checkpoint.

"The officer—a captain, I used to know his name—took a look at the phony credentials and ordered them sent to the Military Internment Camp at Zeven.

"At 1900 that night, Himmler asked to see the camp commandant—Captain Thomas Selvester, who is my source for all this—and when Selvester saw him, fessed up. Selvester then called the G-2 at Headquarters of the British Second Army, who sent an intelligence officer to Zeven with a document bearing Himmler's signature. Himmler signed a blank piece of paper, the signatures were compared, and they now knew who they had.

"He was immediately—he and the other two—taken to 2nd Army Headquarters at Lüneburg, where the G-2, Colonel Michael Murphy—my source for what follows—took over. He immediately ordered a complete change of clothing and supervised two body searches. Murphy knew all about cyanide capsules and was taking no chances.

"He next ordered up a doctor to perform a professional body search. A Royal Army doctor, a captain named Wells, showed up and at quarter after ten started his search. When he got to Himmler's mouth, he saw a small blue object between the teeth and the skin.

"He put his finger into Himmler's mouth to get it out. Himmler bit the doctor's finger, jerked his head away, and bit the cyanide capsule. Ten minutes later, he was dead."

"Ten minutes later?" Dunwiddie asked. "I thought cyanide works immediately."

"That's what they tell people who may have to bite one," Cohen said. "It took Himmler ten minutes to die. They propped the corpse up in a hospital bed, folded his hands on his chest, made a formal identification, performed an autopsy, and then buried him somewhere around three a.m. the next day."

"Where?" Serov asked.

"In a remote farmer's field outside Lüneburg. In an unmarked grave."

"Do you know where, precisely?" Serov asked.

"Colonel Murphy reminded me that the more people who know a secret, the less likely it is that it will remain a secret, and with impeccable British tact told me to butt out."

"Obviously, the Brits didn't want the faithful turning his grave into a shrine," Serov said.

"Too late," Dunwiddie said. "He already has his shrine in Castle Wewelsburg."

"I'm afraid Tiny is right," Cohen said. "Unless we can convince the German people that Wewelsburg is more than just one more place where Nazi nastiness occurred."

"How are you going to do that?" Cronley asked.

"I don't know. Tying it to the smelting of all

those Totenkopfrings back into gold which then went into the pocket of some senior SS officer would help, and so would finding the contents of Himmler's empty safe. My gut tells me it was loaded with a good deal of stuff—probably tens of millions of dollars' worth of stuff—that Himmler stole from the German people."

"Your problem there . . . Am I permitted to comment?" Hessinger asked.

"Why not?" Cohen said.

"When Colonel Frade was in Berlin—"

"What was he doing in Berlin?" Cohen asked.

"Officially, he was there as the captain of an SAA Constellation making a routine flight to Germany. Actually, he came to help with getting Mattingly back."

"I thought he had retired from—" Cohen said, and stopped abruptly.

He suddenly realized he's having dinner with the NKGB, who would be fascinated to hear what he was about to say.

It's comforting to realize that Cohen also makes mistakes.

Correction: almost makes mistakes. He stopped in time.

Which is the difference between him and me.

I almost never am smart enough to stop in time.

"You were saying, Friedrich?" Cohen said.

"I had the chance to ask him about that ransoming operation. He said he had heard and believed that while it went high up in the SS, it didn't go as far as Himmler, that the senior SS officer involved was probably Himmler's adjutant, SS-Brigadeführer Franz von Dietelburg."

"Am I permitted to ask what you're talking about?" Serov asked.

"Rich Jews in the States, England, and some other places were permitted to buy their relatives' way out of the concentration camps and be given safe passage to Argentina, Brazil, and Paraguay. Senior SS officers made a lot of money," Hessinger explained.

"I hadn't heard that story," Serov said. "Not even a rumor. It's amazing how common criminals could rise so high in government."

"Isn't it?" Ostrowski asked. "And how they remain in power by continuing to be criminals."

That was a shot at Russia. At Serov.

I understand why, of course. He's probably thinking of some Free Polish Army buddy who made the mistake of going home to Poland, where he was promptly shot by the Russians.

But I'm going to have to tell him—order him—not to antagonize Serov.

At least until we find out what the sonofabitch is up to.

"What happened to . . . What did you say?

Brigadeführer Franz von Dietelburg?" Cronley asked. "Do we know? Have we got him?"

"No, we don't have him, and no, we don't know what happened to him," Cohen said. "But since he was already skilled in getting people out of Germany, I wouldn't be surprised if he isn't deeply involved—perhaps even running it—with Odessa. He's high on that OSS—now DCI—list of wanted people."

"Maybe he's running it from Spain," Cronley said.

"Possibly," Cohen said. "If he is running Odessa, he's running it from where he thinks he's most safe. Possibly in East Berlin or East Germany."

"You're not suggesting we're harboring this man?" Serov said.

"No, I'm not," Cohen said. "You were saying, Friedrich?"

"I was making the point," Hessinger said, "that if we can't tar Himmler with the brush of common criminal, and make the Germans accept that, he's likely to be thought of as a martyr, and Castle Wewelsburg—"

"Will become his shrine," Serov finished for him. "I'd love to have a look at that place."

"Cronley's going to fly me up there in the morning. Your Storch carries three people, doesn't it, Jim? There would be room for Friend Ivan?"

I didn't say I was going to fly up there to-morrow.

It was going to be sometime in the future.

With Janice.

Who will be highly pissed—at me, not Cohen—if she's bumped by Serov.

So what do I do?

I go along with ol' Morty, who has some kind of agenda vis-à-vis Serov.

"Sure," Cronley said.

"Soldier's Field at 0800?" Cohen asked.

"I'll be there," Serov said. "Thank you, James."

"My pleasure."

"And when do I get to see the Cathedral of Nazism?" Janice demanded.

Cronley's mouth went on automatic: "All things come to he, or she, who waits."

Janice gave him both the finger and an icy glare.

She really is pissed.

Guess who will sleep alone tonight in the Duchess Suite?

"Well, since I'll be flying tomorrow morning, I can't have any more to drink," Cronley said. "I think I'll go have a look at the Mansion."

"What's that?" Serov asked.

"Our newly assigned quarters, formerly the modest home of the local **Gauleiter**. I'm told it has twenty-eight rooms. We got it today, but I've never seen it."

"And I, too, must take my leave of this company," Serov said.

"Where do you live, Ivan?" Cronley asked.

"We have another requisitioned mansion, but like you, James, I have a room here."

So you can keep an eye on me, and pick the right moment to kidnap me?

"Wonderful. We can have breakfast together at, say, seven? And then go to the airfield together. In my Horch. It used to belong to Colonel Mattingly."

"How nice of Robert to turn it over to you," Serov said, as he got to his feet. "I'm a little surprised, frankly. During our chats, I got the impression he didn't like you very much."

Robert? You sonofabitch!

Just in time, Cronley shut off his automatic mouth before asking, **You mean the chats you had with him when you had him chained to a chair?**

Instead he said, "See you here at seven, Ivan."

Serov bowed to everyone at the table and then, with Major Sergei Alekseevich following him, walked out of the dining room.

Cronley waited until they were out of sight, and then said, "Come on, Max. Let's have a look at the Mansion."

[TWO]

It had been Cronley's intention that once they were in the Horch, he would "counsel" Ostrowski about his insulting Serov, but even before they left the hotel Ostrowski put his hand on Cronley's arm and stopped him.

"I'm really sorry for showing my contempt for Colonel Serov and all things Russian. It won't happen again."

"However justified, Max, I'm glad you stopped when you did. Colonel Cohen has an agenda for Serov, and we shouldn't fuck it up."

"Too late, I figured that out. What's he up to?"

"I have no idea, and we won't know until he decides to tell us."

"You think it might have something to do with Cohen suggesting this chap, Brigadeführer von Dietelburg, might be in East Berlin or East Germany?"

"Your guess is as good as mine, Max. Turning to another subject: What do you think of assigning Karwowski as chief of Judge Biddle's security detail?"

"A very good idea. He's a good man. I thought he was really wasted guarding the SIGABA."

"Why didn't you say something?"

"I was going to wait until things settled down."

"Next time, don't."

"Yes, sir."

"I was planning, if you thought giving him the job was a good idea, of introducing him to Biddle tomorrow. But now I'm going to Wewelsburg. Will you handle Biddle?"

"I will if you say so, but I think it's a bad idea."

"Why?"

"My English is good, but I have an accent. Karwowski sounds like the King of England. If I were Biddle, and a man with an accent shows up to introduce his new bodyguard, I'd wonder where the American in charge was, and if he was being snubbed. If Karwowski walks into his office in pinks and greens, flashes his DCI credentials, and announces—looking and sounding as if he graduated from Sandhurst—that he's been named Judge Biddle's chief of security, no problem."

"Good thinking. That's what we'll do."

[THREE]
Offenbach Platz 101
Nuremberg, American Zone of
    Occupation, Germany
2105 21 February 1946

"**Gauleiter**s lived pretty high on the hog, didn't they?" Cronley observed, as he stopped the car before the wide marble stairs leading up to the imposing double doors of the mansion.

"I don't know what 'high on the hog' means," Ostrowski confessed.

"That's Texan for 'like Roman emperors.' "

"Or high priests," Ostrowski said.

As they walked up the stairs, Florence Miller came through the doors. She wasn't wearing her tunic, which revealed the snub-nosed .38 revolver on her hip.

"You must be the lady in charge of tours of the mansion," Cronley greeted her.

"Wait till you see this place," she said. "Unbelievable!"

"Lead on."

* * *

"I saved this for last," she said, pushing open one of the double doors on the second floor. "This is the lair of the laird of the manor, in other words, yours."

Beyond the doors was an elegantly furnished three-room suite, plus an all-marble bathroom. After a second look at the smaller of the rooms, Cronley realized it was a wardrobe.

"Tell you what, Flo," Cronley said, "in addition to your other duties, you are herewith appointed general manager of the Mansion. As such, you get the best room, to share it with the SIGABA."

"Really?"

"I'll take that room under the staircase."

"But it's small and there's no window."

"Making it impossible for anyone to take a shot at me through a window. Anyway, I'm keeping my room at Farber Palast, so the room downstairs is sort of a backup."

"Are you going to tell me why?"

"Because former senior major of State Security Ivan Serov, now sporting the shoulder boards of an infantry colonel, is also staying at the Palast, as is his aide-de-camp, ostensibly an infantry major named Sergei Alekseevich."

"What the hell is that all about?"

"His cover is that he's in charge of the Russian judge's security. Somehow I don't think that's the whole truth."

"Have you seen him?"

"He bought us all dinner, and tomorrow morning, at Colonel Cohen's suggestion, the three of us are going to fly to Paderborn for a look at Castle Wewelsburg."

"Jesus Christ! What's with Castle . . . what you said?"

"Wewelsburg. And while I'm gone, Max can tell you all about it."

"So you're not going to tell me why you're going there? What am I supposed to say if someone—Colonel Wallace—asks where you are?"

"The reason I'm going is because Cohen has got some sort of agenda vis-à-vis Serov. I don't know what, but Cohen isn't taking Serov there to be nice. So far as Colonel Wallace is concerned—**Mr. Cronley didn't share with me, Colonel, sir, where he was going, just that he would be unavailable until 1730. Would you like to speak with Captain Dunwiddie, Colonel, sir?**"

Florence chuckled. "Got it."

"Tomorrow, I want the SIGABA moved here. And tomorrow, once that's done, Sigmund Karwowski becomes chief of security for Judge Biddle, and you're in charge of the SIGABA. See that Karwowski is assigned a room in keeping with his new status, which is Number Two to Max here."

"Got it," Flo said. "Boss, do you think Serov may be here to kidnap somebody else?"

"That unpleasant scenario has flashed through my mind, Flo. I've been wondering if I might be the desired kidnappee. When we got Colonel Mattingly back, Serov had to be humiliated. And I think he blames me. And they still want Colonel Likharev and family back in Mother Russia. He might be thinking kidnapping me is a splendid idea."

"Do you suspect Serov was responsible for Lieutenant Moriarty's . . ."

"Assassination? With Serov, anything is possible. And at dinner he offered his condolences for Moriarty."

"Which means he has a mole in the Compound," Max said.

"And wants us to know he has," Flo said.

"And now, General Manager of the Mansion, I will take my leave," Cronley said.

"I don't like you driving back to the Palast alone," Max said.

"I'm a big boy, Max."

"So I'm going to send somebody with you. I agree with your scenario that Serov may be here because of you."

"Listen to him, boss," Flo said.

"I'm too tired to argue."

"Are you too tired to hear a request?" Flo asked.

"Shoot."

"I'm going to need some ASA type help around here."

"Okay. What? How many?"

"I could use two cryptographers, basically. With debugging skills. Holders of Top Secret clearances you'd feel comfortable to upgrade to Top Secret–Presidential."

"Why do I think you have two old pals from your ASA days in mind?"

"Because I do. I already asked Tiny. He said he'd ask Colonel Wallace, but that he'd have to check with you first. Now you'll be gone tomorrow . . ."

"And you need them right away?"

"I really want to very carefully sweep this place for bugs. And you see how big it is. It will take forever if I do it myself."

"Well, I'm glad you asked me before Tiny called Wallace. We're not going to ask him. Give me the names and I'll get on the SIGABA to General Greene, ask him to put them on temporary duty with Detachment 'A.' He's turning out to be one of the really good guys."

"And Wallace is not?" Max asked.

"I sometimes feel he's turning into Mattingly. Which means he doesn't particularly like me, and that he'll do whatever he has to do to cover his ass. Like deny, or at least delay, adding two female ASA types to us."

Flo reached into her shirt pocket and came out with a slip of paper, which she handed to Cronley.

"You're always selling that Boy Scout line, 'Be Prepared,' boss, so I was. Am."

"I'll call General Greene as soon as I get to the Palast," Cronley said. "Bring on my bodyguard, Max."

[FOUR]
Farber Palast
Stein, near Nuremberg
American Zone of Occupation,
Germany
2155 21 February 1946

Sigmund Karwowski was sitting in a Louis XIV chair in the Duchess Suite when Cronley walked in. A Thompson submachine gun rested against the wall.

"You can go to the Mansion now, Sigmund, and get a good night's rest before assuming your new duties."

"Sir?"

"As soon as you turn over the SIGABA to Flo Miller tomorrow, you, as Number Two to Ostrowski, will be in charge of security for Judge Biddle."

"I don't know what to say, sir."

"Try 'Good night, Jim. Sleep well.'"

Karwowski smiled and shook his head.

"Have you ever heard the expression 'WASP'?" Cronley asked.

"The insect?"

"It stands for 'White, Anglo-Saxon Protestant.' WASPs are sort of the American version of British Landed Gentry. They think of themselves as slightly superior to everyone else. Judge Biddle is known as a Super-WASP. Keep that in mind when you introduce yourself to him tomorrow."

"You're not going to introduce me?"

"I'm going to Castle Wewelsburg with Colonel Cohen tomorrow, and Max thinks his accent would be a problem, but that the judge will be dazzled with your Buckingham Palace accent, so you're on your own."

Karwowski again smiled and shook his head.

"Max thinks I need a bodyguard, so he sent one with me. As you leave, take him with you. There's a car outside."

"And if he doesn't want to go?"

"You are now Max's Number Two. You have that authority to tell him what to do."

"Two questions: Should I leave the Thompson with you, and what's Castle Wewelsburg?"

"Leave the Thompson, you can pick it up in the morning. And Max will explain the Castle

Wewelsburg situation to you when you get to the Mansion."

After a moment, Karwowski said, "Good night, Jim. Sleep well. And thank you."

When the door had closed after him, Cronley went into the wardrobe, hung his tunic on a hanger, and then sat down at the SIGABA.

"Fulda."

"James D. Cronley for General Greene."

"Hold One."

"Greene."

"James D. Cronley for you, sir. The line is secure."

"Put him on."

"Good evening, sir."

"What has Colonel Cohen done to you now, Jim?"

"Actually, sir, we're getting along pretty well."

"Really?"

"Yes, sir. Tomorrow he's going to show Ivan Serov and me Castle Wewelsburg."

"Serov is in Nuremberg?"

"Yes, sir. He is wearing the shoulder boards of an infantry colonel and told us over dinner—which he paid for—that he's now in charge of security for the Soviet judges."

"What the hell is that all about?"

"I don't know, General. I think Colonel Cohen has some sort of agenda."

"He usually does. You're going to Wewelsburg? And taking Serov with you?"

"Yes, sir."

"I gather you've deduced Colonel Cohen is obsessed with Castle Wewelsburg?"

"Yes, sir."

"He's going to be annoyed to learn you called me to tell me about this. Why did you?"

"Sir, I didn't call to do that. I called to ask a favor. You raised the question of how I'm getting along with Colonel Cohen."

"So I did. And you want a favor? Why does that worry me? What kind of a favor?"

"Sir, I need a couple of ASA people. Florence Miller needs some help."

"How is she doing?"

"Pretty well."

"Does she know Serov is in Nuremberg? I'm presuming she knows he's responsible for trying to kidnap her."

"I'm sure she knows both, sir. That's probably why she has a pistol strapped to her hip."

"You're protecting her against the possibility that something like that could happen again?"

"General, she's living in a secure building with at least twenty heavily armed men."

"What kind of a secure building?"

"A fenced-in, twenty-eight-room mansion that used to be the home of the Munich **Gauleiter**."

"A twenty-eight-room mansion? How the hell did you pull that off, Cronley?"

"Mr. Justice Jackson had a word with the Munich Military Post commander on my behalf."

"Which suggests you haven't so far really pissed him off."

"We get along pretty well, sir."

"Why do you need two of my people? What kind of people? And why didn't you go through channels, instead of calling me late at night on the SIGABA net?"

"Sir, I decided that the less I trouble Colonel Wallace with things like this, the better."

"Bullshit. What kind of people is Miller asking for?"

"She gave me two names, sir. Of a tech sergeant and a Spec-6."

"Both WACs?"

"Yes, sir."

"Against my better judgment, you can have them. Give me the names, and I'll have orders cut in the morning. And I won't tell Wallace."

"Tech Sergeant Helene Williamson and Spec-6 Martha Howell."

"Surprising me not at all, two of my best WACs. I will miss them."

"Thank you, sir."

"Anything else, Jim?"

"Sir, what happens to people who use SIGABA for a personal call?"

"It starts with castration with a rusty bayonet followed by a long recovery period in a Fort Leavenworth cell. Who do you want to call?"

"My father, sir."

"Why?"

"Chief Schultz took Lieutenant Moriarty's body from Washington to home. I'm sure he told my father what happened . . ."

"That whoever killed the lieutenant thought it was you he was whacking?"

"Yes, sir. And I want to assure him I'm all right."

"Are you? Are you covering your ass, Jim? Somebody wants you dead."

"I'm all right, sir."

"Famous last words. Your father was a light colonel under Wild Bill Donovan in the First War, right?"

"Yes, sir."

"And Dunwiddie has SIGABA access, right?"

"Yes, sir."

"Have Dunwiddie place the call to Colonel Cronley."

"Yes, sir."

"Fulda Operator?"

"Yes, sir, General?"

"Destroy the recording of my chat with Mr. Cronley, and when you break down the Dunwiddie–Colonel Cronley call, destroy that recording, too."

"Yes, sir. Sir, I'll have to make a report of doing that."

"Yes, son, you will. You are required to. That report will end up in my in-basket. And when I read it, I will read a report of what I just told you to do. Ruminate on that, son."

"Yes, sir."

Before Cronley could say thank you, Greene ordered, "Break it down, Fulda."

[FIVE]

"Fulda."

"Dunwiddie, Chauncey. I need to speak to Lieutenant Colonel James D. Cronley Senior, in Midland, Texas."

"Hold One."

"Vint Hill."

"I need a number in Midland, Texas, for Lieutenant Colonel Cronley."

"Fulda, that'll have to go through the White House switchboard."

"Vint Hill, do it."

"White House."

"White House, this is Fulda. I need Lieutenant Colonel Cronley in Midland, Texas. The line is not, repeat not, secure."

"Wait, please."

"Operator."

"This is the White House switchboard. I need the number for a Lieutenant Colonel Cronley in Midland."

"The White House?"

"This is the White House switchboard."

"Please hold."

"The only Cronley I have is James D. Senior, at the F-Bar-Z Ranch."

"Can you connect me, please?"

"Please hold."

"Hello?"

"This is the White House calling for Lieutenant Colonel James Cronley."

"You're serious?"

"Is this Colonel Cronley?"

"A long time ago it was."

"Fulda, I have Captain Cronley on the line. The line is not, repeat not, secure."

"Dad?"

"Jimmy, good to hear your voice, son. I guess you finally got my message."

"What message?"

"The one I left with Major Kramer . . . where you work."

"Major who?" Cronley asked, and then re-

membered Kramer was one of the ex–OSS officers recruited for the DCI by El Jefe and now
assigned to DCI-Europe.

"He said his name was Kramer, and that you
were not available at the moment, but that he
would try to get word to you to call."

"He didn't. Is everything all right? Is Mom all
right?"

"Physically, she's fine. The question is, how
are you?"

"I'm fine."

"Chief Schultz told us what happened to
Bruce Moriarty. What really happened to him,
as opposed to the 'while cleaning his pistol' version. So we were worried about you and I decided to call."

"I'm all right, Dad. I'm in the Duchess Suite
of a fancy hotel in Nuremberg used to house re-
porters."

"Schultz told me about your new job. How's
it going?"

"Fine. Physically?"

"Excuse me?"

"You said Mom was fine physically. What
does that mean?"

"It means she's a little shaken up, emotion-
ally."

"About what?"

"Well, for one thing Ginger Moriarty lost
control at the funeral."

" 'Lost control'?"

"As she was being led away from the gravesite, she spotted us and screamed, 'If it wasn't for that goddamn hotshot son of yours, my baby would still have his father.' "

"Oh, shit!"

"It was painful for your mother."

"Unfortunately, that's true. I recruited Bonehead for DCI. I thought I was doing him a favor. He was sleeping in what had been my bed when some sonofabitch shot him in the head and six other places with a silenced Colt Woodsman .22, thinking he was whacking me."

"Schultz told us that. So your mother is upset about the scene in the cemetery, and even more upset knowing that somebody is trying to kill you."

"Nobody's going to kill me."

"I think it would be helpful if you personally tried to convince her of that."

"Sure, get her on the phone."

"Before I do—she's taking a nap—there's one more thing. She got a letter from Frau Stauffer yesterday, your cousin Luther's wife. She said that Luther has been arrested on trumped-up charges by some French policeman who hates him because he was drafted into the Wehrmacht. She went on to say she tried to call you to beg you to use your influence to get him set free, but that you have refused to take her calls, to talk to her."

"And she wants Mom to lean on me?"

"That's the sum of it. If you were to tell your mother you'll do what you can . . ."

"Won't happen, Dad."

"Why not?"

"That bitch never tried to call me—and I would have heard if she did—because she knows I know her husband, former SS-Sturmführer Luther Stauffer—"

"You're saying he was in the SS?"

"—did not desert as soon as he could to come home to Strasbourg, but instead was sent to Strasbourg by Odessa—Organisation der Ehemaligen SS-Angehörigen, or the organization of former members of the SS—to facilitate the escape of big-shot Nazis to South America and elsewhere."

"That's a hell of an accusation, Jimmy. Are you sure of your facts? Did this come from some French officer you met who hates Strasbourgers who were drafted into the German Army? I have to ask."

"Cousin Luther was arrested by a friend of mine, Commandant Jean-Paul Fortin, who is probably really a colonel, and who commands the DST—Direction de la Surveillance du Territoire in Alsace-Lorraine."

"And he told you this about Luther Stauffer?"

"No. I already knew. I turned my cousin Luther over to Fortin after my people—**my peo-**

ple, Dad—caught him trying to get two real
Nazi bastards—SS-Brigadeführer Ulrich Heimstadter and his deputy, Standartenführer Oskar
Müller—across the Franco–German border
and then to Spain. These were the sonsofbitches
who massacred all the slave laborers—men and
women, some of whom were buried alive—at
Peenemünde so they couldn't tell the Russians
or us—whoever got to Peenemünde first—what
SS-Sturmbannführer Wernher von Braun and
his rocket scientists had been up to."

"Von Braun was in the SS, too?"

"Yes, he was."

"Why did you turn Stauffer over to this
French officer?"

"Because he asked, and because I knew the
French have interrogation techniques I'm not al-
lowed to use. I really want to get the bastards in
Odessa."

"I don't want your mother to hear this," Cronley's father said softly.

"And I don't want to lie to her. So, what do
I do?"

"I won't tell her we talked. It's a lie, but . . ."

"I'm sorry I'm putting you on the spot, Dad."

"The reverse is true, son. I love you, and I'm
very proud of you."

There was a click on the line, and after a moment Cronley realized his father had hung up.

"Break it down, Fulda," he said.

He sat for several moments at the SIGABA device, inhaling and exhaling audibly.

When he rose and went into the bedroom, Janice Johansen was sitting up in the bed.

"You look, Adonis," she said, "as if you need a little tender care. Why don't you take a shower and come to bed?"

He did.

VII

[ONE]
Soldier's Field
Nuremberg, American Zone of
Occupation, Germany
0805 22 February 1946

When Colonel Serov and Major Alekseevich sat down for breakfast with Cronley and "Casey" Wagner, the Russians were wearing "regular" as opposed to the ornate dress uniforms they had been wearing the night before.

These consisted of a brimmed cap with a black crown and a red band; a high-collared light brown tunic, with the insignia of their rank on tabs at the neck; what Cronley thought of as black "riding breeches"; knee-high black boots; and a brown leather belt. No medals at all. Both had pistols in tan leather holsters, held up by a leather belt across the chest. Major Alekseevich had what looked to Cronley like a leather-cased Leica 35mm camera hanging from his neck.

"Good morning," Serov said. "And who is this handsome young man?"

"Karl-Christoph Wagner," Cronley replied. "We call him 'Casey.' Casey, this is Polkovnik Serov and Major Alekseevich, his aide-de-camp."

The men shook hands as a waiter appeared. After he had taken their order and left, Serov asked, "Why do I suspect, James, that Casey here is your aide-de-camp?"

"Maybe because you have a naturally suspicious nature?" Cronley replied. "Actually, Casey is a DCI agent. I'm telling you that because I know your naturally suspicious nature will make you check him out, and you'd learn that anyway."

"Please don't take offense, Casey, if I say I think you must be the youngest agent in the DCI."

Casey gave him a dirty look, but didn't say anything.

"That's true, Ivan," Cronley said. "But you

shouldn't judge people by their appearance. Casey was responsible for finding out how Odessa was moving people around Europe in **Stars and Stripes** trucks."

"Really?"

"Really, Ivan. And Casey was largely responsible for the entire operation in which we bagged SS-Brigadeführer Heimstadter and SS-Standartenführer Müller."

"And who were they?"

"The guys responsible for massacring the slave laborers at Peenemünde."

"And where are they now? Here?"

"Yes, they are."

"I'd really like to talk to them."

"I'm sure that can be arranged."

"But I'm afraid it would be a waste of my time."

"Why do you say that?"

"You might think me impolite."

"Tell me anyway."

"Your permitted interrogation techniques don't work well on people like that. Especially if Russians, or those of the Hebrew persuasion, are asking the questions . . ."

He's talking about Cohen.

". . . then refusing to answer questions becomes far more than refusing answers beyond the 'name, rank, and serial number' obligation of the Geneva Convention. It becomes, for Nazis like those two, senior SS officers, more like something noble, even a sacred obligation. They would rather be hung, shot, or literally burned at the stake than betray their holy faith by telling of its secrets."

And that's a reference to Castle Wewelsburg and what went on there.

How much does this bastard already know about Wewelsburg?

As the waiter approached with their breakfast order, Serov changed the subject to the superior quality of American waffles over Belgian.

[TWO]

When Cronley stopped the Horch on the tarmac in front of Hangar Two at Soldier's Field Army Airfield, Colonel Mortimer Cohen was waiting for them.

He walked up to it and announced that "When I saw you driving up in that Nazimobile, I was tempted to stick my arm out straight and bellow '**Sieg Heil!**'"

"It's a very nice car, perfect in all details except for a couple of bullet holes in the doors," Cronley replied.

"How are you on this unusually sunny winter day, Polkovnik?" Cohen asked of Serov, who was in the backseat with Major Alekseevich.

Cronley had not been surprised that Serov's aide-de-camp had been with Serov at breakfast, but he was a little surprised when they got to the Horch and Alekseevich got in the backseat with Serov.

Cronley had shut off his automatic mouth in time for him not to say, **There's no reason for you to come out to the airfield, Major. My airplane only holds three people.**

"I'm really looking forward to seeing the castle," Serov said.

"And I see you brought Major Alekseevich along to photograph you as you take off on what—considering what I've heard about Cronley's flying skills—may be your last flight."

"Actually, I thought I would take Alekseevich's camera with me, and photograph all of us for posterity."

"Not only unnecessary, as my people at the castle can do that, but impractical. I don't think there's room for you and the camera in Cronley's little airplane."

In other words, Ivan, Cohen doesn't want you taking pictures in the castle.

And with that lame excuse, he wants you to know he doesn't.

Why not?

Why is he afraid that Ivan wants pictures? Of what?

"Well, if we can get the hangar doors open, can push the Storch outside without giving ourselves a hernia, and I can get it started, why don't we go flying?"

[THREE]
Airstrip Y-97
Paderborn, American Zone of
Occupation, Germany
1035 22 February 1946

Cronley made a second pass over what was obviously a deserted airfield to confirm what he had seen on the first.

"Did you see those great big X's painted at both ends of the runway?" he asked into the intercom. "They mean 'This ain't no functioning airport. Don't land here.'"

"I had the runway so marked to keep the curious away," Cohen replied matter-of-factly.

"So I can land here?"

"Please do. I urgently require the gentlemen's restroom."

Cronley set the Storch down on what was the deserted airfield's only runway, and then taxied to a small, two-story control tower. They had just about reached the tower when two Ford staff cars appeared.

I didn't see them when I passed over the field, which means they were hiding somewhere.

What's that all about?

When they had climbed down from the Storch, Cohen walked quickly to the control tower building, opened the door, and went inside without saying a word to the four men wearing triangled ODs who were now standing by the staff cars.

"Why do I think there's a functioning pissoir in there?" Cronley asked.

None of the four men replied.

"My name is Cronley, and this is Colonel Serov of the Red Army."

Again, none of the men replied.

Cohen came out of the building several minutes later.

"Well, let's get in the cars," he said.

"Who's going to sit on my airplane?" Cronley asked.

"It's perfectly safe here."

"On a deserted airfield? And where am I going to get gas for my airplane?"

"That's the first time that's come up," Cohen said.

"That's because I didn't know we were headed for a deserted airport."

"What kind and how much gas are you going to need?"

"Three jerry cans of regular gas."

"Levinson," Cohen ordered, "you will stay here and protect Mr. Cronley's airplane. And when we get to the castle, you, Davis, will procure three jerry cans of gas and get it out here."

Two of the men said, "Yes, sir," in chorus.

Cohen motioned for them to get in one of the staff cars. He got in the front passenger seat, and Cronley and Serov got in the back. They started off, and the second car followed.

"Colonel, are we going to have time to see the Hermannsdenkmal?" Serov asked.

"The what?" Cronley asked.

"Ivan, I thought we were on a first-name basis," Cohen said.

"And so we are, Mortimer."

" 'Morty,' please," Cohen said. "No, I don't think we'll have time today. Sorry, Ivan, I have to get back to Nuremberg before 2100."

"So it did survive the war?" Serov asked.

"Oh, yes," Cohen said. "Maybe if you talk nice to Cronley . . ."

"I always talk nice to James."

"He'll fly you up here one day and you can have a look at it."

"At what?" Cronley asked.

"It's an enormous statue of Arminius, a.k.a.

Hermann der Cheruskerfürst. The Germans put it up around the turn of the century. It's near Detmold in the Teutoburg Forest."

"The guy who won the Battle of the Teutoburg Forest?"

"One and the same. He became the poster boy for German nationalism. Many Germans are named after him, including Hermann Göring. There's even a statue of him in New York City, called the Hermann Heights Monument."

"And there's a statue of him in New York City? Come on, Colonel!" Cronley said incredulously.

"To use your indelicate phrase, Jim, I shit you not. It was erected in 1897 by the Sons of Hermann, a fraternal organization of German Americans in New York. That fraternal organization evolved into the German-American Bund, which you may recall used to hold meetings, complete with swastikas and enthusiastic singing of 'Deutschland über Alles' in Madison Square Garden. And on the Missouri River there is a town, Hermann, also named for the winner of the Battle of the Teutoburg Forest."

"I'll be damned."

"Probably. But it's never too late to repent. Isn't that true, Ivan?"

"So I have been taught," Serov replied. "Saint Luke tells us 'joy shall be in heaven over one sinner that repents, more than over ninety and nine just persons.'"

What's with this sonofabitch?

First, he goes way out of his way to get those guys Claudette shot full Russian Orthodox funerals, including the right tombstones, and now he's quoting Scripture.

His mouth went on automatic.

"That doesn't say anything about being too late to repent, Ivan."

"No, but it allows me to think there was joy in heaven when this sinner repented, hopefully before it was too late."

Christ, he said that with a straight face!

Is he serious about being a Christian?

That's hard to believe about a senior NKGB officer.

"Diverting this theological discussion to something more appropriate to our visit to Castle Wewelsburg," Cohen said, "may I point out the Germans seem to have a deep affection for their heroic noble forebears, often attributing to them something very close to divinity?"

"Are you suggesting that Himmler thought of himself as divine?" Serov asked. "Or royalty?"

"I don't think royalty, perhaps because he didn't have a son to whom he could pass his crown. But divine? After you take a good look at Castle Wewelsburg, you tell me if you think it's possible he was trying to set himself up as the founder of a new religion."

"You do?" Cronley asked.

"Why don't you wait until you see the castle and then ask yourself that?"

"Political regimes are, relatively speaking, easy to topple," Serov said. "Religions are not, as Stalin and Beria have learned to their chagrin."

And that doesn't sound as if you're unhappy that they've failed.

Is he actually a Christian?

Or is the sonofabitch just trying to make us believe he is, for God only knows what reason?

"How's that going, Ivan?" Cronley asked. "Have Stalin and Beria stopped trying to rid the Soviet Union of the 'opiate of the masses'?"

"They're still working on it."

"And do you think they'll eventually succeed?"

"No," Serov said, with finality.

[FOUR]

"And there it is," Cohen said, pointing out the windshield.

Cronley looked and saw a massive building at the top of a tree-covered hill. At one end, atop a round corner, was a domed tower. At the other end there was a much larger round corner. If there had been a domed top, it was now gone.

He decided, just before Cohen turned on a narrow road and he lost sight of the castle, that the larger round corner had to be the North Tower.

After winding through the trees, they came to the castle. The North Tower was now on the right, connected to the Left Tower by first a two-story structure, and then a three-story structure.

Leading to a tunnel in the center of the two-story structure was sort of a bridge. Two Provisional Security Organization guards armed with Thompson submachine guns stood at the near end of the bridge beside a large wooden sign in German and English: RESTRICTED AREA—ABSOLUTELY NO ADMITTANCE.

Cronley just had time to idly wonder what rank in the Free Polish Forces the guards in shabby dyed black U.S. Army overcoats had once held when he realized the bridge was over what, in bygone times, had been the castle's moat.

They found themselves in a courtyard. There was a three-quarter-ton weapons carrier, two jeeps, and a staff car parked close to the corner of the courtyard, close to a door leading to the interior of the building.

There were at least fifty or sixty five-gallon jerry cans—Cronley thought **a weapons-carrier load**—stacked near the door. **What are they doing with all that gas?**

Cohen led them into a building and then into a makeshift kitchen. There were two middle-aged women tending two U.S. Army field stoves, and there was a Cannon heater, glowing red, in a corner of the room.

"As soon as I have a cup of coffee," Cohen announced, "the tour will begin. Help yourselves."

"Colonel, you said you were CIC and know everything," Cronley said, as he filled a china mug.

"So?"

"So tell me about that Cannon heater. Is that a trade name, or was it intended to heat cannons?"

"You've got me. I've been wondering about that myself, for lo these many years."

"It never occurred to me," Serov said, "how uncomfortable a castle must be in the winter. How do your men put up with it? Do they live here? Or?"

"They live here with stoic devotion to a noble cause."

"The Nazis didn't apply that legendary German technology to make this place comfy in the winter?" Cronley asked.

"They spent a fortune doing just that. But after Sturmbannführer Heinz Macher tried and failed to blow up the castle, he tried, with some success, to burn the insides. And after that, he told the local citizenry they were free to loot the place. Which they did."

"What happened to Macher?"

"I thought I told you. He was captured with Himmler. Originally, they sent him to a prison camp for Less Important SS officers in Darmstadt. I arranged to have him brought to Nuremberg."

"Charged with what?"

"We don't have anything on him that we can charge him with. Being Himmler's adjutant is not in itself a war crime, nor is trying to destroy a castle. I was thinking that maybe, just maybe, being surrounded by people who are going to hang, especially since he believes the victors are taking revenge, might make him cooperative, and he would fess up to what happened to the contents of Himmler's safe and all those golden Totenkopfrings. So far, all he'll give me is name, rank, and serial number."

"Maybe a charming young officer who is not, as Ivan put it, either a Russian or of the Hebrew persuasion, and who speaks German with a Strasbourg accent, could get to him."

"Why do I think you know just such a person, James?" Serov asked, chuckling.

"And why do I think it's worth a shot?" Cohen said. "Finish your coffee, gentlemen, your tour of what's left of the Nazi version of Saint Peter's Cathedral is about to begin."

[FIVE]
The Bar
Farber Palast
Stein, near Nuremberg
American Zone of Occupation,
  Germany
1930 22 February 1946

When he walked into the bar, Cronley saw a faintly familiar face on a tall, thin, middle-aged major of infantry sitting alone at a corner table, but he couldn't remember his name, or where he had seen him before.

"Let's take a table," he said to Serov, Cohen, and Casey Wagner, who had driven them from the airport. "I'm about to quickly have several belts of Jack Daniel's and I don't want to fall off a barstool."

"Something bothering you?"

"And you know what: Castle Wewelsburg."

"Red Army officers such as myself pride themselves on impassiveness in all situations," Serov said. "Having said that, I will tell the waiter to bring a bottle of Jack Daniel's."

"You, too, Ivan?" Cohen said.

"I had the feeling that we were as close to absolute evil—perhaps hell itself—as we are ever going to be in this life."

Well said, Ivan.

But from the guy who tried to kidnap Claudette and Flo?

And kidnapped Mattingly and then kept him chained to a chair?

So I would give him Colonel Likharev and his wife and children so that he could show NKGB officers what happens to NKGB officers and their families if they try to switch sides?

Serov was as good as his word. When the waiter came to the table, he ordered, in fluent German, "Please bring a bottle of Jack Daniel's immediately. On my tab."

Cronley saw that Wagner was all ears.

But smart enough not to ask questions.

The Jack Daniel's was quickly delivered.

Cronley opened the bottle and, ignoring the silver shot dispenser, quickly poured whisky into glasses, half filling them.

"Inasmuch as you have to drive Colonel Cohen to wherever the hell he's going, you don't get no booze, Casey," Cronley said.

"I understand, sir."

Cohen, Serov, and Cronley wordlessly touched glasses and then took healthy swallows from them.

"I guess I should have raised that glass to

your people at the castle," Cronley said. "Christ, imagine having to live there."

"It poses a strain on them . . ."

"I saw that on their faces when we landed. At the time, I thought it was normal CIC agent behavior."

"Excuse me?" Cohen asked.

"When I was—I admit briefly—a CIC agent in Marburg, I noticed that the real agents always tried to keep a stone face, so people would know they were serious."

"That's called 'maintaining a serious demeanor,'" Cohen said. "So far as the strain on my people at Wewelsburg is concerned, I first select the more mature of my agents for that assignment, then I ensure that they spend every third week at Berchtesgaden, with their families, if they have families."

"At Hitler's 'Eagle's Nest'?" Serov asked incredulously.

"No, Ivan. I should have said 'Garmisch.' The Army runs a resort there. And then I get them out of Wewelsburg when they seem to have had all the strain they can handle."

"That place seems more evil to me than even the extermination camps," Cronley said. "And yeah, I've been to Auschwitz-Birkenau, and seen the movies of the others."

"That was mass murder," Cohen said. "The point I've been trying to get across is that a religion that permits, even encourages, mass murder of inferior people in the name of God is actually worse than mass murder itself."

"Don't let this go to your head, Professor, but your lectures and guided tour of Wewelsburg made me a convert to your way of thinking."

"I didn't need to be converted," Serov said. "When I first heard of what was going on at Wewelsburg, I came to that conclusion. However, actually being there . . ."

He left the sentence unfinished.

Cronley picked up the Jack Daniel's bottle and refilled Serov's and his empty glasses. When he turned to Cohen's glass, he saw that it was not only not empty, but that Cohen was holding his hand over it.

"I really have to meet with Colonel Rasberry," Cohen said. "He has a problem with the jail he's asked me to help deal with. And while I'm there, I'll ask him to arrange a chat with Sturmbannführer Macher for you, Jim."

"Thank you," Cronley said.

"Aren't you going to thank me for the tour of Castle Wewelsburg?"

"That would be like me thanking my mother for having taken me to the dentist and having him pull two wisdom teeth. Right now, I wish I had never been in the place."

"Most of what you're feeling, I felt," Cohen said. "Most of it, I suggest, will pass."

"I think if that feeling of mingled contempt, disgust, and fear completely went away, that would make us lesser human beings," Serov said. "People in our line of work have to learn to deal with the scum of the earth, and learn not to have them contaminate us."

Scum of the earth like Polkovnik Sergei Likharev and family, Ivan?

Or, really wild thought, does he mean NKGB scum?

"Good night, gentlemen," Cohen said. "Come on, Casey."

"Meet me for breakfast, Casey," Cronley ordered. "Early—0730."

"Yes, sir," Casey said, and then followed Cohen out of the bar.

"As soon as I finish this," Serov said, holding up his glass, "I'm going to have to leave myself. Are you going to be all right, James? Drinking oneself into oblivion is not wise for people in our business."

"I'll be all right."

"Good," Serov said. He then raised his half-full glass of Jack Daniel's and drained it.

He stood up and said, "A day unfortunately not to be forgotten," and then walked out of the bar.

I am not stupid enough to drink myself into oblivion. I will slowly finish this one and go to my room, have a shower, and then go

to bed, either with good ol' Janice, or by myself. In either case I will probably later have
nightmares about what Castle Wewelsburg is
all about.

Cronley was, literally, staring into his empty
glass when a voice saying "Captain Cronley?"
brought him back to the here and now.

He looked at the speaker and saw it was the
major with the familiar face he had seen when
he came in the bar.

"You are Captain Cronley, right?"

"Yeah, but how do you know that?"

The major produced DCI credentials, identifying him as Anthony M. Henderson. Cronley
now remembered, clearly, where they had met,
in the Schlosshotel Kronberg, and who El Jefe
had said he was, a War II OSS comrade in arms
now in DCI.

"Now I remember you," Cronley admitted.
"Just passing through Nuremberg, are you?"

Henderson smiled. "Harold Wallace sent
me down here to see what you needed. I'm
DCI-Europe's new inspector general. May I sit
down?"

"Why not? Help yourself to the Jack Daniel's.
I'm through for the night."

"Thank you. I will," he said. "Bad day? I
couldn't help but notice you and your friends
didn't look as if you were having a good time."

"Ask away."

"Excuse me?"

"Ask the next question. 'I couldn't help but wonder who . . .'"

"Consider it asked."

"What you saw, Major, was me doing just what Sun-tzu recommended. 'Keep your friends close, and your enemies closer.' The U.S. colonel was Mortimer Cohen, who commands the CIC at the War Trials. The Russian **polkovnik** was Ivan Serov, formerly of the NKGB."

"What was that all about?"

"Major, with all respect, what I suspect is that Colonel Wallace sent you down here to see what I'm up to, particularly what I'm doing wrong."

"Why would he do that?"

"I think the acronym is CYA."

"And you think that he would not be pleased to learn what you were up to with Colonel Cohen and Polkovnik Serov?"

"He is rarely pleased with anything I do."

"He wasn't pleased when you got Bob Mattingly back from Polkovnik Serov?"

"He wasn't pleased with the way I did it."

"Oscar was."

"Oscar? As in Oscar Schultz, executive assistant to Admiral Souers?"

"Right. And El Jefe told me how pleased he, the admiral, and President Truman were with you when you found U-234 at the Magellan Strait and took out SS-Oberführer Horst Lang just before he was going to sell five hundred and sixty kilos of uranium oxide to our Russian friends."

Cronley met Henderson's eyes, but didn't say anything.

"Oscar also told me that your present assignment was not a bone you were tossed when you were relieved as chief, DCI-Europe, but rather at the direct order of the President, who thought—based on the reports of Colonel Mortimer Cohen—that his close friend Justice Jackson was in jeopardy. The President decided that you were just the guy to protect him."

Again Cronley didn't reply.

"Although I am assigned to DCI-Europe, my chain of command up is to my old friend Oscar, not to Wallace. I will, however, report to Wallace that Justice Jackson is completely satisfied with the protection you're giving him, and aside from bedding Janice Johansen almost publicly, you're not doing anything wrong. I will also report to El Jefe that you're up to something with Colonel Cohen and Polkovnik Serov that you don't want to tell me about. I think my report to El Jefe will promptly result in a SIGABA call from El Jefe somewhat angrily ordering you to tell the both of us what the hell you and Cohen are up to with Ivan Serov."

And yet again Cronley didn't reply.

"Your call, Cronley," Henderson said. "You

can either trust me now or wait until El Jefe gets on the SIGABA."

Jesus H. Christ! What do I do?

General Gehlen has told me time and time again how dangerous trusting your gut feeling is.

And my gut feeling is to trust this guy.

My mother used to tell me, "There is an exception to every rule."

So if I break Gehlen's rule, is Henderson promptly going to Wallace?

"Colonel, you won't believe what your loose cannon has been up to."

I could, I guess, get on the SIGABA to El Jefe and tell him.

Oh, fuck it!

"Major, have you heard about Castle Wewelsburg? What Himmler and company were up to there?"

Henderson shook his head, then asked, "Are you going to tell me?"

"Not here. Let's adjourn to the Duchess Suite."

"Fine. Shall we take the Jack Daniel's with us?"

"Why not?"

[SIX]
The Duchess Suite
Farber Palast
Stein, near Nuremberg
American Zone of Occupation,
  Germany
2005 22 February 1946

Cronley walked directly to what had been the wardrobe of the suite and looked inside.

"Why do I think you were not checking to see if your dry cleaning has been delivered?" Henderson asked.

"I was checking to see if the SIGABA has been moved to the Mansion."

"An apt description of your headquarters. I was over there. Just long enough for your people to make me feel unwelcome."

"Sorry."

"Don't be. Your people are taking care of you, which suggests they like you. How did you manage to get that place?"

"I have friends in high places."

"El Jefe?"

"Justice Jackson."

The door to the suite opened and Janice Johansen walked in.

"Why do I think you're not about to take me to dinner, Adonis?"

"I've told you, you're prescient," Cronley replied.

"Who's your friend?"

"Adonis is still making up his mind whether I fit that description, Miss Johansen."

"This is Major Anthony Henderson," Cronley said. "He's the DCI-Europe inspector general."

"Wallace sent you to snoop on Adonis, did he, Tony?"

"I wouldn't put it in quite those words, Janice."

"Well, Adonis, is he or ain't he one of the good guys?"

"About three minutes ago, I decided he is."

"Thank you," Henderson said.

"So what are you and your new friend chatting about in here where no one can hear you? Castle Wewelsburg?"

"We were about to do just that."

"You recall promising to tell me all about it, I hope."

"I do."

"Then I guess I got here just in time."

Where do I start?

At the beginning.

And what do I tell them?

Every last goddamn thing, including that I left there feeling I had just escaped Dracula's Castle.

With Dracula and sixty demons hot on my tail with evil intentions.

"We landed at an airfield near Paderborn Cohen has taken over, and X marked the runways so that nobody will land there . . ."

"My God!" Henderson said. "If it wasn't you and Cohen, I wouldn't believe any of this."

"Janice, I hope you recall that when I told you I'd tell you, I told you you'd have to hold off on writing it."

"I recall. But let me give a brief lesson in Journalism 101. Let's say I knew for a fact—and nobody else did—that Harry Truman fortified himself with half a bottle of Old Crow before delivering the State of the Union speech. Because I have a certain reputation, if I wrote that story it would be on the front pages of a lot of newspapers. That would make the White House hate me and make me a candidate for the Pulitzer Prize.

"If, however, I knew for a fact—and nobody else did—that Bess had caught ol' Harry with a hooker and beat him and the hooker nearly to death with a bottle of Old Crow and wrote the story, it wouldn't get published. Nobody would believe it because they wouldn't want to believe it. So who do you think would want to believe what you just told us?"

"Interesting point, Janice," Henderson said thoughtfully.

"How about the Jews?" Cronley asked. "They know what the Germans did to the Jews here."

"What they did to the Jews here is provable. It was incredible, but then we sent the photographers to the extermination camps and they took pictures of the ovens and the piles of bodies and that made it credible. All you've got to show the Jews—all you've got to show anybody—is pictures of a castle that was burned and looted. Like Tony here, if it wasn't you and Cohen, my professional opinion of what you just told us would be 'Oh, bullshit!'"

"Actually, it's worse than that," Cronley said. "Cohen is so interested—maybe obsessed—with Wewelsburg because he thinks the Nuremberg trials will be pissing in the wind."

"The vengeance of the victors?" Henderson asked softly.

"Particularly the vengeance of the Jewish victors, who as all Germans know, are really running everything."

"What you and Morty need, sweetie, is to get some Nazi big shot—preferably a lot more than one—whom the Germans still adore and get him, them, to fess up convincingly. That's going to be hard because we're going to hang the big shots who could do that for us."

"There's a lot of big-shot Nazis still on the loose," Cronley replied. "Properly questioned, I hope I can get some answers from them. I start tomorrow morning with Sturmbannführer Heinz Macher, who tried to blow up Castle Wewelsburg."

"No offense, Jim," Henderson said, "but do you think you're qualified to do that?"

"No. But since I have an honest face, speak Strasbourger German, and I'm neither Jewish nor Russian, I'm going to give it one hell of a try."

VIII

[ONE]
The Dining Room
Farber Palast
Stein, near Nuremberg
American Zone of Occupation,
   Germany
0725 23 February 1946

Colonel Mortimer Cohen, Captain Chauncey Dunwiddie, and Casey Wagner walked up to the table where Cronley and Major Henderson were about to finish their breakfast.

"Casey I expected. But to what may I attribute the honor of the unexpected presence of you two?" Cronley asked.

"I need your permission to do something," Cohen said seriously, as he sat down.

Cohen needs my permission?
What the hell?

"Good morning, gentlemen," Henderson said.

"Tony, this is Captain Dunwiddie, my executive officer," Cronley said.

"I had the privilege of meeting the captain at the Mansion yesterday," Henderson said.

"You told me. I forgot," Cronley said. "So let me bring him up to date. Tiny, Major Henderson is one of the good guys. He's welcome at the Mansion."

"So Colonel Cohen told me," Dunwiddie said.

"What's going on?" Cronley asked.

"Colonel Rasberry has a problem with his enlisted men," Cohen said.

"He told me," Cronley said. "They're all eighteen years old and don't know how to drive."

"More of a problem than that," Cohen said. "He suspects someone is getting to his enlisted men. No proof, but that gut feeling we're always talking about. Good officers like Rasberry are usually right when they have a gut feeling about their enlisted men."

"Getting to his enlisted men? How? Who?" Henderson asked.

"There's a number of people who want to smuggle things, primarily messages, but God only knows what else, to—and from—the prisoners. Rasberry has a gut feeling that's happening."

"And he wants the CIC to look into it?" Henderson asked.

"What he asked me to do is send a couple of my agents into the 26th Infantry undercover to see what, if anything, is going on."

"Makes sense," Henderson said. "Are you going to do it?"

"I'd be happy to. The problem is—"

"That none of your agents look like eighteen-year-old PFCs?"

"Right."

"Clever intelligence officer that I am, I suspect that this conversation now turns to DCI Special Agent Wagner," Cronley said.

"Yes, it does."

"If Casey's willing, that's fine with me," Cronley said. "Casey?"

"Yes, sir. I'd like to."

"Casey hasn't been in the Army long enough to learn never to volunteer for anything. On the other hand, he's already proved he's damned good at working undercover. That's why he's one of the two youngest special agents in the DCI."

"Who's the other one?" Dunwiddie asked.

"You're looking at him," Cronley said. "So what's Casey going to be looking for in the 26th Infantry Regiment?"

"Find some other PFC who has a lot of money, or who has a romantic involvement with a fräulein," Cohen said.

"Nine out of ten PFCs in the Army of Occupation have a relationship with a fräulein," Cronley said. "This place is the realization of every eighteen-year-old's fantasies. **Shall I pay a Hershey bar to get laid before I go to the movies, or should I go to the movies first and then get laid?**"

"I wonder how many PFCs have a relationship with a handsome eighteen-year-old German male?" Henderson asked.

"A handsome eighteen-year old **queer** German male?" Cronley asked.

Henderson nodded.

"Interesting question," Cohen said.

"Is anyone interested in my scenario?" Henderson asked.

"I think we all are," Cronley said.

"Let's start with the premise the somebody who is trying to corrupt one of Colonel Rasberry's PFCs or corporals is interested in getting him to smuggle things to and from the prisoners.

"Who would want to do that? I suggest someone smart, somebody in Odessa, for example. Or some Nazi, some SS officer not affiliated with Odessa who needs to communicate with a prisoner, or get something to him.

"Anyway, someone smart enough to know that a PFC who suddenly has a lot of money would attract unwanted attention. So how else could one entice a nice young American boy to do something illegal?

"Find one who might be interested in other young males, arrange for them to have an affair, and then take movies of the lovers having at it."

"**And unless you do so-and-so, we'll see that Colonel Rasberry and your parents get the movies of you blowing your boyfriend in the mail, and you'll be court-martialed and sent to prison, and your parents—the whole world—will know why,**" Cronley said.

Henderson nodded.

"Wouldn't that also work for some guy getting a blow job from his fräulein while the cameras rolled?" Casey said.

"A PFC would be far more likely to go to his first sergeant, or even his regimental commander, and confess, **Some Kraut took movies of me getting a blow job from my fräulein and said unless I smuggle**—what? A letter, some kind of medicine in a capsule to Göring—**into Göring or—**"

"He will send the movies to your commanding officer—or parents," Cronley finished for him.

"On the other hand, I think it's far less likely our PFC would go to his first sergeant or his regimental commander and confess that some Kraut had made movies of him locked in the passionate embrace of his boyfriend."

"Casey, do you think you could find a pansy among the troops?" Cronley asked.

"They're not that hard to spot, sir."

"You said 'Kraut,'" Dunwiddie said. "Are we sure Germans are trying to do this?"

"No," Cohen said simply.

"This movie-blackmail scenario smells like something good ol' Ivan would come up with," Cronley said. "That's a comforting thought."

"Comforting?" Dunwiddie asked.

"I thought he might be here to either whack or kidnap me."

"You mean that?" Dunwiddie asked dubiously.

"I think that's a distinct possibility," Cohen said, "and the more religious piety Serov throws at us, the more I tend to believe it. But returning to the immediate situation, we have another problem."

"Which is?" Henderson asked.

"At some effort, Colonel Rasberry got General Seidel to agree that the guards in the prison should not be eighteen-year-olds straight from basic training at Fort Dix. Seidel got the G-1 to change the assignment policy. Instead of sending kids straight from the 7720th Replacement Depot in Marburg, which is where they go when they get off the troop ship, soldiers assigned to the 26th Infantry are reassigned from other units in Germany. The basic requirements for such reassignment are six months in Germany and a Secret security clearance."

"Good idea," Cronley said.

"Except that it means Casey can't just show up at the prison. He has to be transferred from some other unit. Dunwiddie suggests General White might be useful in this."

"Presuming General White will go along," Dunwiddie said. "We take Casey to the Constabulary School. He gets a tour of that, to see what training he would have gone through, and then he sews on the Constabulary patch and is transferred from one of the Constab regiments to the 26th Infantry."

"How long do you think, providing General White goes along with this, doing this will take?"

"If you fly Dunwiddie and Casey to Sonthofen right now, we can have Casey chasing fräuleins or being chased by a handsome young German youth by tomorrow night," Cohen said.

"Is it that important?" Cronley asked.

"More pressing, I think, than your chat with Sturmbannführer Heinz Macher. That can be put off until you come back from arranging to insert Casey into the 26th Infantry.

"Do you still have a duffel bag, Casey? You're going to have to have one to make your arrival at the 26th Infantry look credible."

"It's in the Horch's trunk, sir."

"Am I that predictable? You knew I would be willing to let you stick your neck out like this?"

"I don't know about Casey, Super Spook," Cohen said, "but I can say with absolute certainty that no one else in the intelligence community thinks you're predictable."

[TWO]
Office of the Commanding General
U.S. Constabulary School
Sonthofen, Bavaria
American Zone of Occupation,
  Germany
1055 23 February 1946

"General, Colonel Wilson is here, with some people. Not on the schedule," White's sergeant major, a great bull of a thirty-odd-year-old with a closely cropped crew cut, announced.

"I knew something was going to ruin my day," White replied. "Let him pass, Charley, but keep an eye on him."

Lieutenant Colonel William W. "Hotshot Billy" Wilson, who had been at the airfield when Cronley, Dunwiddie, and Wagner arrived and who had offered to drive them to the headquarters building, marched into the office, trailed by the others.

He came to attention and saluted.

"General, I found these nefarious characters trying to infiltrate my airfield."

"I am always delighted to see Sergeant Wagner, Billy," White said. "It is **Sergeant** Wagner, right, Chauncey?"

"Yes, sir," Dunwiddie said. "He was promoted immediately after a senior officer thought that would be appropriate."

"Wagner, if you tire of these intelligence types, there's always a place for you in the Constabulary."

"Thank you, sir."

"I'm not sure whether I'm delighted to see you, Mr. Cronley. The story I get is that an officer I reluctantly transferred to you shot himself while cleaning his pistol. Accidents happen, but commanding officers can't dodge responsibility for not preventing them. Comment?"

Oh, shit!

His mouth went on automatic: "General, I hold myself responsible for Lieutenant Moriarty's death. Bonehead would not have been in DCI if I hadn't recruited him. But—"

"It wasn't an accident, sir." Dunwiddie finished the sentence, then asked, "May I tell the general, Mr. Cronley?"

"What the hell do you mean, Chauncey?" White flared. "**May** he tell me? He goddamned well better tell me!"

"General, Tiny is—as usual—being a good officer," Cronley said. "The circumstances surrounding Lieutenant Moriarty's death are classified Top Secret–Presidential."

"And I don't have the goddamn Need to Know? Is that what you're telling me, Cronley?"

"No, sir. You have every right to know. And I fuck— Excuse me. I **failed** to bring you into this. I'm very sorry."

"As you goddamn well should be. You also failed to tell me you've been assigned to protect Justice Jackson at Nuremberg."

"Sir, no excuse, sir."

I haven't said that since I was a Fish at A&M.

General White makes A&M upperclassmen tormenting Fish seem like Angels of Mercy.

And how the hell does he know about Nuremberg?

"I read minds, Cronley. You might want to keep that in mind. I knew that you and Chauncey had been sent to Nuremberg because Colonel Wallace told me when he called to tell me he was now chief, DCI-Europe."

My God! He does read minds!

"But he didn't tell you about Moriarty?"

"I can only surmise that he didn't think I had the right to know. So, are you going to tell me? Or are you going to wait until I tell Colonel Wilson to excuse us?"

"No, sir. Lieutenant Moriarty was assassinated. Everything points to me being the intended target. He was sleeping in what had been my bed at the Compound. He was shot—through the window—seven times with a silenced Colt Woodsman .22."

"And who do you think was the assassin?"

"Obviously a mole in the Compound. General Gehlen thinks it's probably one of his people, but it's possible it's one of the Polish guards."

"His people?"

"One or more of them may be under pressure from either Odessa or the NKGB who may have their families."

"And the Poles?"

"Same thing, sir. And, sir, that's why we're here."

"Tell me."

"The commanding officer of the 26th Infantry, who has the guards on the prisoners at Nuremberg—"

"So I've heard. Get to it, Cronley."

"Colonel Rasberry thinks the same thing is happening to his guards. He went to Colonel Cohen, and Cohen came to me."

"To do what?"

"We want to send Wagner to the 26th under-cover, to see what he can find out."

"What's that got to do with me?" White asked. Before Cronley could reply, White raised his voice. "Sergeant Major!"

Then he turned to Cronley.

"Sergeant Major Charles Whaley has a Top Secret clearance, but not a Top Secret–Presidential. Despite that, I think he should hear what you are about to tell me. Objections?"

"No, sir."

"General?" Whaley asked from the door.

"Mr. Cronley is about to ask the Constabulary to do something I suspect will be legally questionable. I think you should hear what that is."

"Yes, sir," Whaley said, and came into the room, and then leaned on the wall beside the door.

"Okay, Mr. Cronley. What probably illegal act, or acts, can the Constabulary do for you?" White asked.

"Sir, replacements to the 26th Infantry—"

"Which is charged, Charley," White interrupted, "with guarding Hermann Göring and his former underlings at Nuremberg. Continue, Cronley."

"Yes, sir. Replacements to the 26th don't come from the repple depple at Marburg—"

"I know," Sergeant Major Whaley interrupted. "Once a month we get a TWX from USFET, levying on us for sometimes as many as six troopers, pay grades E-3 through E-5, with six months in the theater and with Secret security clearances. No MOS requirements. To be transferred to the 26th. There's one on my desk now for four men. Weird."

"Mr. Cronley will now explain that to us," White said.

"The idea is that Colonel Rasberry doesn't want the guards to be fresh out of basic training and just off the troop ship from Camp Kilmer," Cronley explained.

"Let me take a wild guess," General White said. "You want Casey Wagner sent to the 26th as if he's been levied from us."

"Yes, sir."

"Did you volunteer for this, Casey? Or did Mr. Cronley just tell you this is what's going to happen?"

"I'm all right with it, sir. I'm a DCI special agent. This is what we do."

"You're a what?" Sergeant Major Whaley inquired incredulously.

"Why don't you show Charley your credentials, Casey?" White said.

Wagner handed Whaley his credentials.

"And how old are you, son?" Whaley asked, after he had carefully examined them.

"Seventeen. I'll be eighteen next month."

"And even more incredible, Charley," White said, "Casey earned those credentials. Casey is the fellow who figured out how Odessa was moving Nazis around and across borders in **Stars and Stripes** trucks, allowing us to bag those two bastards who massacred the slave laborers at Peenemünde."

"I'll be damned," Whaley said.

Casey Wagner blushed.

"Unless we abandon our sinful ways, Sergeant Major, we all will be damned. Except for Colonel Wilson and Mr. Cronley, who have demonstrated, time and again, they can walk between the raindrops of sin and remain as pure as the driven snow."

"No problem, General," Whaley said. "I was about to cut the orders transferring the levy to the 26th. I'll just put Casey on them."

"It's not quite that simple, Sergeant," Cronley said. "We have to give Casey a cover. He has to know what training he would have had if he had gone through the school. And something about the regiment from which he is supposedly transferring. I mean stuff about which **Gasthaus** he frequented, the nickname of his first sergeant, that sort of thing."

"I understand, sir. But unless we do that right now, I won't be able to put him on the orders I'm about to cut. And so far as familiarizing him with a regiment—"

"Thank you, Colonel Wilson," General White interrupted, "for volunteering to fly Casey to the 10th Constabulary Regiment in Wetzlar immediately after lunch for that background orientation you will arrange for him there with Sergeant Major Donley."

"I hear and obey, my General," Wilson said.

"And speaking of lunch, Charley, call Mrs. White and tell her to set places for lunch for all of us. Drop Captain Dunwiddie's name into the conversation. That will cause her to raise her culinary standards."

[THREE]
The Prison
The Palace of Justice
Nuremberg, American Zone of
Occupation, Germany
1650 23 February 1946

It wasn't until Cronley was actually at the prison checkpoint that a disturbing thought popped into his mind.

Cohen told me that Macher had been sent to the SS detention compound in Darmstadt.

But he knew I was coming here—"your chat with Sturmbannführer Heinz Macher can be put off until you come back from arranging

to insert Casey into the 26th Infantry"—so what the hell is going on?

"If you're going in, Mr. Cronley, I'll have to have your weapon," the captain in charge of the checkpoint said.

"Sorry," Cronley said, as he hoisted his Ike jacket to gain access to his pistol. "Where have you stashed Heinz Macher?"

"Our newest guest is in Cell 12, right upper tier," the captain said. "I know because I had the duty when he arrived."

"When was that?"

"The day before yesterday. They had been holding him in Darmstadt, but I guess the CIC found out he wasn't just one more unimportant SS-**Sturmbannführer**."

Thank you, Captain. You just told me what to say to this guy.

And clever fellow that I am, I just figured out what that clever fellow Cohen has done. Since he and/or his people couldn't get anything out of this guy at Darmstadt, he moved him here—

Did he need anyone's permission to do that?

Or is ol' Morty Cohen another loose cannon?

—where he will see all of the big shots on their way to the gallows and will be thinking of how he can dodge that.

But why didn't Morty interrogate Macher himself once he was here?

Because Macher clammed up in Darmstadt when interrogated by a senior officer of the Jewish persuasion. Answering questions posed by a gottverdammten Juden would be a sin against Saint Heinrich's new religion, and we know that Macher worked for Himmler, and Saint Heinrich himself sent him to see that Castle Wewelsburg was emptied and then blown up.

That means Himmler trusted him. He was too junior to be an apostle, but he damned sure had to be a convert to the new religion. A born-again convert, like someone at a Southern Baptist revival: "Hallelujah, brother. You have been washed in the blood of the lamb!"

In this case, the blood of Jews, Gypsies, Russian POWs, homosexuals, and other Untermenschen.

And when I said I wanted to talk to Macher, Cohen figured, "What the hell, maybe Cronley can do what I couldn't. Improbable, but worth trying."

And so he had Macher moved here.

Does Cohen think I can do what he couldn't?

Is that a vote of confidence in me?

Or is he just grasping at straws?

Almost certainly.

A 26th Infantry sergeant led Cronley up three flights of metal stairs to the upper tier, then past a dozen cells, and then across the bridge to the right tier of cells, and then down it to a door with a sign—"Macher, Heinz"—on it.

"Open it up," the sergeant ordered the PFC who was standing beside the door.

He's about as old as Casey. Casey will fit right in here.

"Fit in"? Bullshit!

Casey should be running around Pennsylvania chasing girls, not risking his neck—his life—trying to outwit some really dangerous people.

And what about you, Super Spook?

Shouldn't you be a Second John, supervising the washing of mud off the tracks of a tank in some motor pool, not trying to outwit some really dangerous and clever people?

"Mr. Cronley?" the sergeant asked.

Cronley saw the door to Cell 12 was open.

"Thanks, Sergeant," Cronley said, and walked into the cell.

A tall, trim, nice-looking man in his late twenties rose from the bed on which he had been sitting.

"Wie geht's, Heinz?" Cronley asked. "How are they treating you?"

Macher didn't reply.

Cronley showed him his DCI credentials.

"I don't know what that is, this Directorate of Central Intelligence," Macher said, after he had carefully examined them.

"Well, it's sort of Abwehr and the Sicherheitsdienst rolled into one. We look into everything from theft to crimes against humanity. You're charged with both."

"What do you want with me?"

"I'm looking for the contents of Himmler's safe you took from Wewelsburg Castle, the twelve thousand—or more—Totenkopfrings you also took from the castle, and most important, for Brigadeführer Franz von Dietelburg."

"As I told the other investigators, Herr Cronley, I stole nothing from Castle Wewelsburg. And I think you know von Dietelburg is dead."

"You and I both know he isn't. And I didn't say you stole the contents of the safe, or the rings. Theft of SS property would violate your SS officer's Code of Honor, wouldn't it? I said you took that stuff from the castle because those were your orders from Reichsführer-SS Himmler."

Macher shrugged, more than a little condescendingly.

"But I know, and you know I know, that you know where all that stuff is. And we want it."

"If I knew what happened to what you're talking about, and I don't, I wouldn't tell you."

"In a way, Heinz, I almost admire your dedication to keeping the faith. But the difference between you and me is that I wouldn't go so far as getting myself hung because I wouldn't cough up some rings and some gold and old paintings. That's not the same thing as betraying the Reichsführer-SS's secrets, is it? You ever hear 'To the victor goes the spoils'?"

Macher didn't reply.

"Well, we won," Cronley said. "We're the victors, and we want those spoils. Think about that, Heinz. What difference does it make? Reichsführer-SS Himmler doesn't need that stuff anymore. He took the coward's way out, didn't he?"

Macher glared at Cronley.

"It is better to die at one's own hand than to be hung by the Jews," he said.

"The Jews weren't going to hang Himmler, Heinz, and the Jews aren't going to hang you. People like me—and I'm half-German, my mother was born and raised in Germany— would have hung him, and unless you come to your senses, will hang you."

Macher didn't reply.

"Think it over, Heinz. I'll be back," Cronley said, and walked out of the cell.

[FOUR]

The sergeant led Cronley back across the bridge to the left tier of cells, and then down the stairs to the second tier and then to Cell 14, on which was a sign: "Heimstadter, Ulrich."

"Open it, soldier," the sergeant ordered.

The guard outside, who looked even younger than Casey Wagner, worked the lock and then the sliding barrier, and Cronley entered the cell.

"And how are you on this snowy February day?" Cronley asked in German.

Heimstadter, Cronley saw, had shaved off the soup-strainer mustache he had on his chubby face when he had been captured.

But the bastard still looks like a postcard Bavarian in lederhosen with Gemütlichkeit **oozing from every pore.**

Heimstadter didn't reply.

"Generals White and Harmon asked me to look in on you," Cronley said.

Major General Ernest Harmon had commanded 2nd Armored Division and, on assuming command of the VI Corps, had turned over Hell on Wheels to I. D. White. Three weeks earlier, on 1 Feburary, White had assumed command of the Constabulary.

When the stone-faced Heimstadter did not respond, Cronley added, "They saw what you and Müller did at Peenemünde and are looking forward to your conviction and hanging."

Heimstadter's face blanched for a moment.

"Victory must be sweet for someone like you," he said.

"I don't think 'sweet' is the word that applies. But a mixture of satisfaction and shame for someone of German blood like me. I will find it uncomfortable to watch my cousin Luther swing with a broken neck under the gallows."

"Your cousin?" Heimstadter blurted.

"My mother's brother's son. You may have met him. Former Sturmführer Luther Stauffer . . ."

That rang a bell! I could see it in his eyes!

"The name does not seem familiar," Heimstadter said.

"The SS sent him home to Strasbourg just as the Thousand-Year Reich was in its final death throes," Cronley said. "They assigned him the duty of helping people they knew we would be looking for to get out of Germany. The French caught him trying to get you and Müller across the border. As soon as the Direction de la Surveillance du Territoire is finished asking Cousin Luther about Odessa, he'll be transferred here for trial and, I'm afraid, the hangman's noose."

"You are a disgrace to your German blood!"

"I'm sure Cousin Luther would agree with you," Cronley replied. "He was deep into Himmler's Nazi Knights of the Round Table nonsense. He even got married at Castle Wewelsburg. But on the other hand, I can sleep at night. The hangman's noose is not in my future."

I don't know where all that came from, but this time, my automatic mouth was right on the money.

I could see it in his eyes.

He met Cousin Luther and he knows what went on at Wewelsburg.

What he's worried about right now is how much Müller is going to tell me.

Which is nothing, because I'm not going to call on Müller.

And when he asks Müller what he told me, and Müller tells him he never saw me, he'll think Müller is a liar, and Müller will start wondering what former SS-Brigadeführer Ulrich Heimstadter told me to try to avoid the noose.

Cronley, you have really learned how to be a devious bastard!

He turned and raised his voice, and then cried in English, "Sergeant, let me out of here!"

[FIVE]
Farber Palast
Stein, near Nuremberg
American Zone of Occupation,
 Germany
1845 23 February 1946

When Cronley walked into the lobby, he saw Lieutenant Tom Winters sitting in an armchair reading the **Stars and Stripes**.

"Please don't tell me you flew Wallace down here," he greeted him.

Winters closed the newspaper and stood up.

"No," he said simply. "I'm reporting for duty. Me and the other Storch. Colonel Wallace told me you would probably eventually come here."

"Let's go in the bar and you can tell me all about it," Cronley said, and then asked, "Why didn't you wait for me in there?"

"Because I knew if I went in there, I would drink more than I should."

"Tell me about it over a double scotch, and then we'll get something to eat."

* * *

They went in the bar and took a table and, when the waiter came, ordered Johnnie Walker, doubles.

When the drinks were served, Cronley took a healthy swallow and Winters a small—very small—sip.

"Did Wallace tell you why he was transferring you to Detachment 'A' and giving me another airplane?"

"He said he wanted to be sure you have all the assets you need," Winters said.

"That was nice of him, presuming he doesn't have an ulterior motive. And, if I have to say this, I'm glad to have you."

"An ulterior motive such as getting the Storch out of the Compound, where if some Air Corps type with stars on his epaulets asks Wallace what we're doing with an illegal airplane, he would have to answer?"

"And if it's—they're—here, and questions were asked, I would have to answer them?"

Winters nodded.

"Not a problem. I have a place to hide the airplanes, and if anybody but General Bull asks what I'm doing with them, I will dazzle them with my DCI credentials."

"They do dazzle people, don't they?"

"How's the baby?"

"When he's on his back getting his diaper changed, he can piss on the ceiling."

Cronley laughed and then asked, "How does Barbara feel about coming down here, moving again?"

Winters looked uncomfortable.

"She doesn't like it?"

"Captain . . ."

"Captain?"

What the hell is this?

"Sir, I might as well bite the bullet."

"So bite it."

"My wife, sir, blames you for Bonehead's murder."

"She's right. So do I."

"And she's afraid the same thing will happen to me. She wants me to go to General White and ask him to transfer me back into the Constabulary."

"Is that what you want to do?"

"No. For two reasons."

"Which are?"

"I think the contribution I can make to DCI is more important than flying an L-4 spotting artillery or flying the brass from Point A to Point B."

"True. And?"

"I'm not going to ask General White to do something like that for me. That's not in my genes."

"I know where you're coming from, Tom. At Bonehead's funeral, Ginger lost it and screamed at my mother, 'If it wasn't for that goddamn hot-shot son of yours, my baby would still have his father.' And unfortunately she had every right."

"I don't suppose it's occurred to you that the Officer of the Day was sleeping on duty in your bed when he was shot?"

"That ran through my head. But Bonehead wouldn't have been sleeping in my bed if I hadn't recruited him for DCI. That's the bottom line."

"No. Bonehead's death is not on your shoulders. Period."

"Thank you. So what are you going to do about Barbara?"

"As soon as we're assigned quarters here, she moves into them. And I will, without much hope of success, continue to reason with her. I just thought you should know the situation."

"Yeah."

"Jesus, look at that. A full-bird Russian. What is this place, anyway?"

"With a little bit of luck, we can get him to pick up our tab." He raised his voice. "Polkovnik Serov! Over here."

Serov, trailed by Major Alekseevich, walked, smiling cordially, up to the table.

Winters quickly stood up. Cronley resisted the Pavlovian urge to stand.

"May we join you?" Serov asked.

"If you're buying, Ivan, we would be honored," Cronley said.

"And this gentleman is?"

"Lieutenant Thomas H. Winters the Third, may I introduce Colonel Ivan Serov and Major Sergei Alekseevich?"

The men shook hands.

Winters said, "A pleasure to meet you, sir."

"The pleasure is entirely mine," Serov said, as he waved for the waiter. "It is always a pleasure to meet a member of a distinguished military family such as yours."

"Excuse me?" Winters said.

"Your father does command the 1st Cavalry Division in Japan, does he not?"

"Yes, sir, he does."

That didn't come out of left field.

That's off Serov's Order of Battle for the DCI.

And he wants me to know he has one, and that it's pretty thorough.

And does that make Tom a candidate for kidnapping?

A U.S. general's son for a defected Russian colonel?

Or a U.S. general's grandson?

And didn't I hear that Barbara is an Army brat?

Isn't she the daughter of a general officer?

A general's daughter and a baby who has two general officer grandfathers for a Russian colonel and his family?

Barbara Winters and baby are safe in the Compound.

But they wouldn't be nearly as safe in ordinary dependents' quarters here.

What the hell am I going to do about that?

"We're all friends here," Serov said. "Isn't that so, James?"

"How about drinking buddies?" Cronley said.

"I would be pleased if you could find your way to call Sergei and myself by our Christian names," Serov said.

The waiter appeared.

"Bring us a bottle of whatever they're drinking, and put it on my tab," Serov ordered.

"Beware of Russians bearing booze," Cronley said.

"Consider the booze to be a small token of my gratitude," Serov said.

"For what?"

"For my tour of that castle."

"Oh."

"What?" Winters asked. "What castle?"

"I gather Thomas is not in the castle loop?"

"Only because he just got here, and I haven't had time to tell him."

"And I wanted to wait until I had your permission before I told Sergei about it."

Oh, bullshit!

"What are you going to tell the NKGB about it?"

"Actually, I'm still thinking about that."

"And if I give you permission to tell Sergei what you probably have already told him, what is he going to tell the NKGB?"

I am pissing in the wind. He told Sergei about the castle as soon as he could after we got back. And by now that report is being read in that building on Lubyanka Square in Moscow.

"Nothing until I tell him to, and then only what I tell him to," Serov said. "You really should learn to trust me, Jim."

"I do."

About as far as half the distance I could throw Tiny Dunwiddie.

"When I saw you, I thought perhaps you would be kind enough to have dinner with Sergei and myself, and we could both bring him into the loop. I think it's important that he hear everything, and I suggest that's also true for Thomas."

"And what would we chat about over dinner?"

"I agree that the tale of the castle would ruin my appetite for anything but spirits, so why don't we drink our dinner?"

"Why not?" Cronley said.

IX

[ONE]
Farber Palast
Stein, near Nuremberg
American Zone of Occupation,
  Germany
1925 23 February 1946

"I never heard anything about this," Tom Winters said. "And now that I have, I'm having a hard time believing it."

And I'm having a hard time believing my gut feeling that this is the first time Sergei has heard about it.

But to judge from the look on ol' Sergei's face, and in his eyes as we revealed the secrets of Wewelsburg Castle, it was.

Which means that ol' Ivan was telling me the truth.

"What about you, Sergei?" Cronley said. "If you heard all this from me, not from Polkovnik Serov, would you believe it?"

"I would have the trouble I'm having to believe it if I heard it from Nikolayevich Merkulov."

"Who's he?" Winters asked, just a little thickly. He had begun sipping scotch five minutes into Serov and Cronley's recitation.

"He's Ivan's NKGB boss, the commissar of State Security," Cronley said.

"I think he's heard something about it," Serov said. "And dismissed it as nonsense . . ."

He didn't challenge that, which is admitting he's still working for Merkulov.

Is that the scotch talking? For every sip Winters took, ol' Ivan took a healthy gulp.

On the other hand, he knows I don't believe the scenario that he's here in Nuremberg to protect the Soviet judges, so why keep up the pretense?

". . . otherwise, the Soviet liaison team, which is authorized to go anywhere in the U.S. Zone, would have taken an interest in the castle. And when Colonel Cohen's people denied them entrance, that would not only increase their curiosity but cause an incident. And a public incident would alert the people we're looking for to our interest. So you will understand, Sergei, why the less Commissar Merkulov hears about what we've been discussing, the better."

Is that to try to convince me that he's not filing a daily After Action Report to Merkulov?

Or does he mean it?

"I understand, sir," Sergei said.

"Who are you looking for?" Winters asked.

Serov looked at Cronley.

"I think there's a connection between the castle and Odessa," he said. "Would you agree, Jim?"

Cronley nodded.

"Gut feeling. But what? Who? Von Dietelburg?"

"Who else?"

"Who's he?" Winters asked.

He's plastered. Because of a combination of what he heard just now, and his problems with his wife. The latter, I think, more than the former, but both.

"Brigadeführer Franz von Dietelburg," Cronley said. "He was Himmler's adjutant. He sent Macher to blow up Wewelsburg Castle. And, Ivan, Cohen, and I strongly suspect, to empty Himmler's safe and do something with those thousands of gold Totenkopfrings."

"And I gather he's among the missing?" Winters said.

"Yeah. Vanished into the blue. I talked to Macher today. He professed to have no idea where the contents of the safe, or the rings, are. And he told me I should know that von Dietelburg is dead. I brought the noose into the conversation, and he may eventually have a change of mind. But we can't wait for that to happen, can we?"

"So what are you thinking, Jim?" Serov asked.

"I'm going to have another chat with Commandant Fortin and my cousin Luther. I also had a chat with Heimstadter today. I saw something in his eyes when I mentioned the former Sturmführer Luther Stauffer."

"Good idea," Serov said. "Actually, any idea right now is a good idea."

"If you're going to be flying, you better lay off the booze," Winters said, more than a little self-righteously.

"Polkovnik Serov," Cronley said, "Lieutenant Winters is reminding me that U.S. Army aviators are prohibited from flying U.S. Army airplanes if they have imbibed intoxicants within the previous twelve hours."

"Sounds like a reasonable regulation."

"But since I am not a U.S. Army aviator, and will be flying an illegal airplane, that regulation obviously does not apply to me. I will follow the rule for Texas aviators, which is that if you can climb into the cockpit without assistance, and can find the master buss switch in less than five minutes, you're sober enough to fly."

"So you're going to continue drinking?" Sergei asked.

That's genuine concern, not just disbelief, in his voice.

Truth being stranger than fiction, can Sergei be one of the good guys?

Or are both of them playing me for the fool they know I am?

"Sergei, my friend, that was what is known as Texas humor. What I am going to do is have a glass of Cabernet with the enormous steak I am about to eat in the dining room. And then I'm going to bed, from which I will rise with the roosters and fly to Strasbourg. Presuming, of course, that God is willing and the creek don't rise."

[TWO]

There was a note Scotch-taped to the mirror in the toilet of the Duchess Suite:

They caught two colonels—one a chaplain—black-marketing big-time in Heidelberg. Got to cover it. Be back tomorrow. Wash behind your ears. J.

"Fortune smiles on the pure of heart," he said aloud.

I really didn't want to explain where I've been and with whom, and I really am in no shape for bedroom gymnastics.

He stripped out of his clothes, intending to shower.

"Shit!" he said. "First things first."

He went naked into the bedroom, sat on the bed, and picked up the telephone.

"Nuremberg 4897," a slightly accented voice answered.

"Get Captain Dunwiddie on here, please."

"There's no one here by that name."

"This is Cronley."

"One moment, sir."

"Captain Dunwiddie."

"Tiny, Winters is on his way there. Pretty well bombed. Make sure he gets into a bed all right."

"You corrupted Winters?"

"He corrupted himself. With good reason. Barbara is really unhappy that Wallace transferred him to us. She wants him to go to General White and ask to be returned to the Constab."

"I can't imagine him doing that."

"He's not going to. That's his problem. And I told him about Castle Wewelsburg."

"Why did Wallace transfer him?"

"I think (a) to get him out of the new DCI-Europe headquarters, and (b) to cover his ass by sending the other Storch down here. If El Jefe were to ask, he would say, 'I wanted Cronley to have all the assets he needed.'"

"I hate to admit this, but I think you're right."

"See what you can do about getting them some really secure quarters. Really secure in Barbara's eyes."

"And what will you be doing when I'm on my knees before the Nuremberg Military Post housing officer?"

"Don't go to him, go to the post commander."

"While you're doing what?"

"Having a chat with my cousin Luther in Strasbourg."

"I knew you would have a credible excuse for dumping your commanding officer's responsibilities on my weary shoulders."

"Carry on, Captain Dunwiddie," Cronley said, and hung up.

[THREE]
The South German Industrial
Development Organization
Compound
Pullach, Bavaria
American Zone of Occupation,
Germany
0915 24 February 1946

Cronley had indeed risen with the roosters intending to get to Strasbourg as early as possible and was at Soldier's Field before seven. At seven-twenty, he was at the threshold of Runway Two Four, cleared for a VFR flight to Strasbourg.

He had an epiphany.

Goddamn you, Tiny, for so subtly reminding me of a "commanding officer's responsibilities."

Then he had picked up the microphone.

"Soldier's Departure Control, Army Six One Six."

"Six One Six. Go."

"Change of flight plan. Scrap VFR Soldier's-Entzheim. File VFR Soldier's-Schleissheim."

"Six One Six, sir, you're required to go to Flight Planning to change your flight plan."

"Soldier's, if you do this for me, you will be rewarded in heaven. It's important."

After a thirty-second pause, Soldier's Departure Control came back on the air.

"Army Six One Six is cleared for VFR Soldier's-Schleissheim and for immediate departure Runway Two Four."

"Six One Six rolling. **Muchas gracias**, which means **Vielen Dank**!"

Barbara Winters answered the door with Thomas H. Winters IV in her arms.

"What's happened to Tom, Jim?"

"Aside from being hungover, Mrs. Winters, Lieutenant Winters is fine."

"Then what are you doing here?"

"They call it 'the counseling of the wives

under one's command,' Mrs. Winters. May I come in?"

"Frankly, Jim, you're not welcome here."

"Nevertheless, Mrs. Winters, your husband's commanding officer is at your door. May I come in?"

She stepped aside and gestured with her head for him to enter.

"The reason Lieutenant Winters had too much to drink last night, Mrs. Winters, is because you asked him to do something he finds it difficult to do."

"I have no idea what you're talking about."

"Forgive me, Mrs. Winters, but I think you do. And what you asked him to do does not, speaking frankly, reflect well on you."

"If you mean my asking him to go back to the Constabulary—"

"I mean your asking him to go to General White to ask for that. Surely you know he doesn't want to do that."

"You tell me why he doesn't, Captain Cronley."

"Surely, as the daughter of a general officer . . . your father is a general officer, correct, Mrs. Winters?"

"My father is . . . He's deputy commander of Fort Knox. What's that got to do with anything?"

"I presume he's a friend of General White?"

"He commanded the 175th Armored Field Artillery of Hell on Wheels. Until he was wounded in Normandy."

"Then I presume he's also a friend, at least an acquaintance, of General Harmon?"

"Yes, he is. A friend, more than an acquaintance."

"That makes you an Army brat, doesn't it?"

"I don't like that term, frankly."

"Like it or not, Mrs. Winters, that's what you are. And as such, if you haven't considered what would happen if Lieutenant Winters went to General White asking for a transfer back to relatively safer duties in the Constabulary, I suggest you should."

"What I'm trying to do, Captain Cronley, is keep my husband alive."

"At what price?"

"Excuse me?"

"Have you considered what would happen to your husband's career if he goes to General White?"

"What I have been considering, Captain Cronley, is what's very likely to happen to him, I mean losing his life, if he stays in the DCI. Doing God only knows what incredibly dangerous things."

"If Lieutenant Winters goes to General White, the general will do one of several things. In my judgment, he'll tell Lieutenant Winters that when a good officer is given an order, he salutes and says, 'Yes, sir,' and carries out that order to the best of his ability. Not tries to get out of it because his wife wants him to. And he was ordered to the DCI."

"Because you asked for him. And for Bonehead. And we know what happened to Bonehead, don't we, **Captain** Cronley?"

"Yes, we do. I think it's entirely likely that General White would call me and tell me Lieutenant Winters was in his office, asking to be relieved of his assignment, and asking me what I know about it.

"And I would tell him what I know, that he's there because he wants to do what his wife wants him to do. And I think General White would ask me what I think he should do. Then I would be forced to say that I don't want anyone in DCI who doesn't want to be there. And that if General White doesn't take him back, I will see that he's transferred elsewhere."

"So?"

"How long do you think it will take for General Winters and General . . . **whatever his name is** . . . your father . . . to learn what's happened to their son and son-in-law? For the story of your husband trying to use family connections to get out of an assignment his wife didn't like to make its way, via the Officers' Ladies Intelligence Network, around the Army establishment? The Regular Army establishment?"

"You sonofabitch!"

"As an Army brat, you should know that an officer's lady should not call her husband's commanding officer a sonofabitch. And now, having concluded counseling you, I will say, good morning, Mrs. Winters."

"What the hell do you want me to do?"

"You're an Army brat. Figure it out yourself."

Cronley turned and walked out of the house.

Well, I gave it my best shot.

Which probably fucked things up more than they were already fucked up.

[FOUR]
Hôtel Maison Rouge
Rue des Francs Bourgeois 101
Strasbourg, France
1305 24 February 1946

Commandant Jean-Paul Fortin was sitting where Sergeant Henri Deladier told Cronley he would find him, having lunch with Captain Pierre DuPres in the Maison Rouge.

When Fortin saw him, he righted one of the upside-down glasses on the table and poured wine into it.

"Sit down, James, and have a glass of wine while you tell us what you did to lose your job."

"You heard about that, huh?"

"I'm a senior officer in the Direction de la Surveillance du Territoire, I hear a lot of things. Are expressions of sympathy in order?"

"No, my Colonel. And I'm surprised that a senior officer in the Direction de la Surveillance du Territoire believes everything he hears."

"As I have told you many times, I am but a lowly commandant, not a colonel."

"I'm surprised that you have risen as high as you have. You lack an essential requirement for someone in our business. You're a lousy liar."

Fortin stood up and went to Cronley and embraced him.

"When I heard, James," he said, "I was distressed that I'd never see you again."

Deladier also rose and embraced Cronley.

The Frogs are always kissing each other, so why am I touched by this?

"Are you hungry?" Fortin asked, and without waiting for an answer, called for a waiter.

As Cronley cut his first bite from the grilled pork tenderloin that had been quickly laid before him, Fortin asked, "So what happened, **mon ami**?"

"I am now in charge of security for Judge Biddle and Justice Jackson at the War Crimes Trials in Nuremberg."

"That's not your basic area of expertise, is it?"

"President Truman and Justice Jackson are old friends. The President decided he needed more protection than the CIC sitting on him was providing. He selected me."

"That must have been flattering for a very junior captain."

"I went right out and bought a bigger hat."

"So it wasn't a demotion?"

"DCI-Europe is being tripled, quadrupled in size. It can no longer pretend to be commanded by a very junior captain."

"So Colonel Wallace took over?"

"And I think was very happy when the President ordered me, and my people, to Nuremberg."

"Henri de Vabres introduced me to Colonel Cohen . . ."

What? He knows Morty Cohen?

"Who?"

"The French chief judge. He is concerned with the safety of the prisoners. He wanted me to have a look at what Colonel Cohen had set up."

"That must have been flattering for a lowly major."

"Henri and I served together during the war. He speaks very highly of Cohen, and I was impressed with him. Not charmed. Cohen is a difficult man. But I could find no flaw in what he'd set up to protect the prisoners, and their judges."

"Colonel Cohen was not pleased when I told him what I had been sent to Nuremberg to do."

"Then I suggest you be careful, James. Colonel Cohen—I say this with admiration—is not the sort of man a very junior captain should annoy."

"Truth being stranger than fiction, Jean-Paul, Morty Cohen and I have become chums."

"That I find hard to believe. First that he would allow a man known to be—what is it General Seidel calls you? 'A dangerous loose cannon'?—to get close to him, and second that you would believe that his offered friendship did not have an agenda."

"Oh, he had an agenda, all right. Have you ever heard of Castle Wewelsburg, Jean-Paul?"

"I have heard some frankly absurd rumors."

"That Himmler was trying to establish a Nazi religion there?"

Fortin nodded.

"All true, Jean-Paul."

"Nonsense."

"All true, Jean-Paul. And Colonel Cohen wanted to—has—recruited me to join his noble crusade to cut its head off."

"If you're—what do you say?—'trying to pull my leg,' I am not amused."

"I am not trying to be clever, Jean-Paul. I've seen the evidence."

"And what is Colonel Cohen's interest in this Nazi nonsense?"

"I like to think it's because he's a good intelligence officer, but his being a Jew also has a lot to do with it."

Fortin made a **Come on** gesture with both hands.

"For one thing, when they hang Göring and company, he wants the German people to know they're being hung as criminals, mass murderers, not because the Jews won the war and are extracting vengeance.

"That's the Jewish angle. As an intelligence officer, Cohen thinks Brigadeführer Franz von Dietelburg, whom we know was deeply involved—an apostle, so to speak, in Himmler's new religion—is the guy running Odessa."

"Very interesting."

"What comes next is my scenario. Cohen doesn't even know that I was coming here."

"You don't want him to know? Why not?"

"I didn't say that. What I was trying to get across is that my scenario didn't come from Cohen."

"I would be more interested if it had, but let's hear it anyway."

"I think Cousin Luther is a disciple in the new religion."

Fortin said nothing.

"Think about it, Jean-Paul. We now know

that he didn't desert from the SS as the war was ending. He was sent here by Odessa, possibly even by von Dietelburg himself."

"My opinion is that your cousin Luther is an opportunist. He joined the Légion des Volontaires Français contre le Bolchévisme to avoid being sent to Germany as a laborer, not because he had anything against the Communists. And then he did the best he could to please his German masters."

"He was, in other words, what we Americans would call a born-again German?"

"Yes. In one of our conversations—we were talking about his treason—he said that his father was responsible for his problems. He said that after World War One, when Strasbourg became French, his father could have elected to keep his German citizenship, but instead opted to be French.

"He said that if his father had not 'betrayed' his German blood, he would be a prisoner of war, not a traitor."

"My mother thinks of herself as German, ex-German," Cronley said. "As an American, I never even thought much about my German blood until I saw what the Germans did. Now, when I think about it, I'm a little ashamed about it. That people 'of my blood' could do what the Nazis did."

"I'm still ashamed that so many Frenchmen

were crying 'Better Hitler than Blum' just before the war started, but I don't think Luther Stauffer thought of himself as a German. If he had, instead of deserting, he would have gone to Berlin with the French SS Division Charlemagne and died fighting for the Thousand-Year Reich."

"You ever wonder where that came from, 'the Thousand-Year Reich'?"

"From Josef Goebbels, the propaganda minister. It has a nice ring to it."

"It also fits what Himmler was trying to do. Did. Start a new religion that would last a thousand years. A religion that sanctions the elimination of the **Untermenschen** so that the Aryans own everything."

"And you and Cohen believe this? All of it, including the religious devotion to it?"

"Yeah, we do."

"You may be on to something," Fortin said. "Just before the war was over, and anyone who could find his derriere with both hands had to acknowledge the Germans had lost, we captured—"

"Who's we?"

"General Leclerc's 2e Division Blindée. I was the G-2."

"I thought division G-2s were colonels. What did you do to get demoted?"

Fortin glared at Cronley and then shook his head in resignation.

"Just outside Strasbourg, we captured a dozen Frenchmen wearing the uniform of the Charlemagne Division. When we interrogated them, we got nothing. They stuck nobly to name, rank, and serial number. And they didn't seem frightened.

"I told my general we had them, and he said he wanted a look. So we marched them from the POW enclosure here. To this very room, which was then General Leclerc's headquarters.

"As we marched them through town, French citizens of Strasbourg started throwing things—the contents of chamber pots, garbage, that sort of thing. Under the circumstances, one would assume they would cringe. To the contrary, one of them called attention and then gave the order, **Vorwärts, marsch!** And, backs straight, heads held high, they marched the rest of the way here.

"I confess that I was more than a little annoyed with my countrymen for attacking helpless prisoners, and felt more than a little admiration for what I saw as the maintenance of discipline in trying circumstances.

"When I marched them into General Leclerc's office, he looked at each one of them and then asked, 'Why are you Frenchmen wearing German uniforms?'

"Their senior officer, an SS-**Hauptsturmführer**, the one who had called them to attention, replied, 'And why are you, a French general, wearing an American uniform?'

"The general was uniformed as I am, in American ODs with French shoulder boards and wearing his kepi."

"What did Leclerc say?"

" 'If you're through with them, Colonel, shoot them.' "

"And did you? Without a trial?"

Fortin pointed toward the ceiling.

"In the parking lot outside. They died bravely. No pleas for mercy, or anything like that. At the time, I thought I saw a sort of a parallel with the SS execution of Colonel Claus von Stauffenberg in the courtyard of the War Ministry after the bomb plot failed. As I understand it, he died bravely, shouting, 'Long live Germany.'

"Now I see I was right. Von Stauffenberg died believing in his faith, that of the Roman Catholic Church. And the men, the traitors to France, as von Stauffenberg was a traitor to Hitler—like everyone else in the Wehrmacht, he had sworn an oath to follow Hitler to death . . ."

He paused, gathered his thoughts, and then went on: "I now think it's entirely possible that the men I had executed here believed they would be martyrs to this new Nazi religion. That's frightening."

"The more you get into it, the more frightening it gets," Cronley said.

"What makes you think you can talk your cousin Luther out of it?"

"What you said just now. The bastard is primarily an opportunist. He is far more interested in Luther Stauffer than in being a disciple in the new religion. He doesn't want to hang."

"We don't have enough on him to send him to Nuremberg."

"He doesn't know what we have. And I'm going to offer to send him to Paraguay."

"Paraguay?"

"There's a colonel there who thinks there's nothing wrong with National Socialism except Nazis, who he believes fucked it up."

"What the hell are you talking about?"

"You ever wonder what happened to the Nazis we shipped to Argentina?"

"I was too polite to ask."

"Well, we had a bunch of them, and their families. And we couldn't keep them all locked up, and we couldn't shoot them . . ."

"Why not?"

". . . and we couldn't turn them over to Juan Domingo Perón, who would have kissed them on each cheek and then welcomed them to Argentina. But then ol' Bernardo—General de Brigade Bernardo Martín, who runs the BIS, the Bureau of Internal Security, which is something like the Direction de la Surveillance du Territoire, and is a pal of my pal Cletus Frade

and a really nice guy—came up with Paraguay."

"You are losing me."

"We send our Nazis to Paraguay. The guy
who really runs Paraguay is a colonel named
Alfredo Stroessner. His parents were German
immigrants. He loves Germany and National
Socialism, but doesn't like Nazis, who, if you
were listening, he thinks fucked up Germany.
He **really** doesn't like Nazis. When he comes
across anyone we sent him from Operation Ost
who is still holding his breath waiting for Nazism
to rise from the ashes—Operation Phoenix—he
has them shot. By firing squad. In a public ceremony. Tied to a stake, blindfolded. What's that
phrase of yours? **Pour encourager les autres?**"

"As incredible as that sounds, I have a strange
temptation to believe you."

"Cross my heart and hope to die, Jean-Paul,
Boy Scout's honor, it's the truth."

"Would you really want to send him to South
America, or are you just going to dangle that
carrot in front of his nose?"

"I really want to send him."

"Because of the family connection?"

"Yes. I'm hoping that Stroessner will shoot
him. Then I can tell my mother that I did all in
my power for Cousin Luther."

"It's not nice to lie to one's mother."

"I'd rather lie to her than have to tell her a friend of mine shot him in the knees and elbows with a .22 and then threw him in the Rhine."

"Which would have already happened were we not friends. I got nothing out of the **fils de pute** even after employing my best interrogative techniques. He resisted me with what I'm now thinking was a religious fervor."

"Why don't we go see him, and see if I can talk him into accepting the good life in Paraguay instead of waiting to see what Himmler's Heaven will provide?"

"I don't see what either of us has to lose. Capitaine DuPres, would you please call the Sainte Marguerite and have Stauffer taken to an interrogation room? Naked and in shackles. He can have a blanket."

"Oui, mon colonel."

"What did Henri call you, Jean-Paul? **'Mon colonel'?**"

"To use my favorite American phrase, 'Go fuck yourself, **mon ami**.'"

"Saint Marguerite? Who's she?"

"That's where we have your cousin Luther, James. In the loving arms of Saint Marguerite."

[FIVE]
Sainte Marguerite Prison
Strasbourg, France
1410 24 February 1946

From the outside, Sainte Marguerite Prison looked more like a hospital or a school than a prison, but once they went inside, there were barred corridors and windows and an unpleasant smell.

A guard led them down a corridor through three barred barriers to a small room furnished with a simple table and three wooden straight-backed chairs. There was a lined pad and a pencil on the table.

"Bring him in," Fortin ordered curtly.

"Oui, mon commandant."

Luther Stauffer was led into the room a minute later by two guards.

He was naked under a gray blanket. There were shackles around his ankles and wrists. Cronley could see no bruises or other signs of physical abuse.

"Put him in the chair," Fortin ordered.

Stauffer was shuffled to the chair at the table and sat down in it.

"Wie geht's, Herr Sturmführer?" Cronley asked.

"And how are you, Cousin James?"

"Well, there are no shackles around my wrists and ankles and I'm wearing a lot more than a dirty blanket to keep me warm, so I'm obviously doing better than you."

"Are you going to tell my aunt Wilhelmina you came to gloat over me?"

"Well, Herr Sturmführer, since we have you in here, I think I'm entitled to gloat. Odessa has lost the services of a valuable member. Whether or not I tell my mother that I've paid you a visit depends on how you react to the offer I'm about to make."

Stauffer didn't reply.

"I'm sure Brigadeführer Franz von Dietelburg has told you about our Operation Ost—"

"Who?"

"I'm sure you remember him. He was Himmler's adjutant, the officer who ordered you to Strasbourg."

"I don't know what you're talking about."

"One more display of that SS arrogance, Luther, and I will leave you to Colonel Fortin, who wants to shoot you in the elbow and knees with a .22 and then see how well you can swim."

Stauffer didn't reply.

"I don't think of you as anything other than one more despicable SS officer, Stauffer. And the offer I came here to make has nothing to do with the unpleasant fact that my mother is your father's sister. Do you understand that?"

Stauffer, after a moment, nodded.

"As I was saying, Herr Sturmführer, I'm sure Brigadeführer von Dietelburg has told you about Operation Ost. We do what von Dietelburg is doing and what you failed to do—send Nazi swine to South America so that they can escape the noose. Or a swim in the Rhine.

"Do you know where Paraguay is, Herr Sturmführer?"

"Of course."

"There is a colonel named Stroessner in Paraguay. There's a president, but he serves because Colonel Stroessner permits him to. Stroessner, who was born in Paraguay to German immigrant parents, is a devout believer in National Socialism. Not Nazism. He believes Hitler, Göring, Himmler, and company betrayed National Socialism and are the cause of the failure of the Thousand-Year Reich.

"We send the Nazis—and their families—we took to South America to Paraguay, to Colonel Stroessner. He sets them up on farms, or in business. In a new life, in other words. We are comfortable in doing this because we know that these Nazis will be stood against a wall and shot in a public ceremony if Colonel Stroessner finds out—or even deeply suspects—that they are holding their breath waiting for Nazism to rise phoenixlike from the ashes.

"Are you following me, Herr Sturmführer?"

"I don't know why you're telling me this."

"Because—I'm a little surprised, Herr Sturmführer, that you haven't figured this out—because I'm offering you—and of course your devoted wife—the opportunity to go to Paraguay. In exchange for telling me where I can find Brigadeführer von Dietelburg."

"I don't know where he is. And if I did, why should I trust you?"

"Because the only other option you have is taking a swim in the Rhine, which would, of course, leave Ingebord a widow."

"Your mother would hear that you were complicit if something like that happened to me."

"To which I would reply that I had no influence with the French, in how they deal with traitors."

Stauffer glared at Cronley but said nothing.

"And I would tell her that I had no influence with Colonel Stroessner should you and Ingebord be shot in Paraguay for not behaving.

"Think it over, Herr Sturmführer. Von Dietelburg's not even going to try to rescue you from Sainte Marguerite. It would be too risky for him, for Odessa. Talk it over with Ingebord. I understand Colonel Fortin has denied her permission to visit. So I will ask him to allow her a visit. One visit. You have twenty-four hours from right now—it's now two-thirty-five—to make up your mind."

He met Stauffer's eyes and said, "In case we don't meet again, **auf Wiedersehen**, Herr Sturmführer."

"Get him out of here, out of my sight," Fortin ordered.

When the guards had led Stauffer, shuffling, out of the room, Fortin said, "Don't let this go to your head, James, but you did that rather well."

"When you bring his wife here, let her sit here for at least an hour and worry about what's going on before you let her see him."

"I had planned to do just that, James."

[SIX]
Soldier's Field Army Airfield
Nuremberg, American Zone of
Occupation, Germany
1705 24 February 1946

Lieutenant Tom Winters came out of the hangar and helped Cronley and the 26th Infantry guards push the Storch inside.

"I drove your Horch out here. Was that the right thing to do?" Winters asked.

"Since Casey is otherwise occupied, fine. But do I detect an agenda?"

"I have to ask for a favor."

"Shoot."

"Can Barbara stay at the Mansion until we get quarters?"

When Cronley did not immediately reply, Winters went on.

"There's a hotel for transient junior officers. A madhouse."

"When is she coming down?"

"She called just after lunch. She said she'd thought things over, that her place was to be with me, supporting me in whatever I want to do, and that she doesn't want me to go to General White."

"Well, as my mother often told me, women have a God-given right to change their minds."

"Thank God! Remember what Lee said before he went to surrender at Appomattox Court House? 'I would rather die a thousand deaths'? I felt that way about going to Sonthofen."

"When is she coming?"

"She's going to drive down tomorrow morning. It's only about a hundred miles. All autobahn."

"All autobahn covered with ice and snow," Cronley said. "Let me tell you, Lieutenant Winters, what your commanding officer, ever mindful of the welfare of his subordinates, is going to do. We are going to rise with the roosters and fly you to the Compound and you can drive your family down the snow-covered autobahn. And I'm going to tell the ladies resident in the Mansion to prepare suitable quarters for your wife and Thomas H. Winters the Fourth."

[ONE]
Near Soldier's Field Army Airfield
Nuremberg, American Zone of
Occupation, Germany
1710 24 February 1946

"Where the hell are we going?" Cronley asked when, on leaving the airfield, Winters took a left turn. "The hotel's thataway."

"Casey Wagner found a shortcut and told me."

Two minutes later, Cronley said, "Christ, it's narrow, winding, and cobblestone."

"And will save us fifteen minutes getting to the hotel."

"If we don't skid off the icy cobblestones in the dark and run into a tree."

"Oh ye of little faith!"

Five minutes later, Cronley said, "It looks like someone else has discovered your private autobahn. How are you going to get around that truck?"

"With superior driving skill," Winters replied.

Two minutes later, Winters said, "Now the son-ofabitch is stopping. What the hell!"

"Tom, I don't like this!" Cronley said.

He turned in the seat and saw a car, a small Audi convertible, headlights off, was coming up behind them.

The truck stopped, forcing Winters to slam on the brakes. The Horch skidded into the rear of the truck.

The Audi pulled up behind the Horch and stopped. A man got quickly out of the passenger seat and raised a shoulder weapon.

"Watch it, Tom!" Cronley cried, as he pulled the latch on his door and then rolled out of the car.

There was a burst of submachine gun fire and then another as Cronley, now lying on his side, fumbled through his trench coat and Ike jacket to get at his pistol.

He finally found it, rolled onto his stomach, flipped off the safety, and holding the .45 in both hands, found the man standing next to the Audi and fired three times.

The man disappeared in the darkness.

Cronley could not tell if he had hit him or not. He took aim at the windshield of the small sports car and emptied his magazine at it. Then he fumbled again through the layers of clothing until he found the spare magazine in his holster.

He heard the sound of the truck driving off as he fed the magazine into his pistol.

Now there was silence.

"Tom?" he called.

"Under the car. You all right? Did you get him?"

"I don't know. Stay where you are!"

Cronley crawled to the rear of the Horch.

Now he could see by the right front wheel of the Audi, a man's booted feet. After a moment's thought, he fired at them. There came a muffled scream. Cronley raised his head and looked at the Audi's windshield. There were four bullet holes in it, but he couldn't see the driver.

"Jim?" Winters called.

"I think I got both of the bastards. Stay where you are."

He crawled to the man down by the wheel. The man was moaning in pain. Cronley could now see the weapon, and recognized it as a Maschinenpistole 40. He jumped forward until he could grasp the barrel, and pulled it to him.

Then, holding the .45 in both hands, he slowly got to his feet and, stepping around the man on the ground, looked into the Audi.

A man—a very young man—wearing a hooded jacket was lying across the seat with his head in a pool of blood and brain tissue that was leaking from a bullet hole in his forehead.

Jesus Christ, he's even younger than Casey.

"I got both of them, Tom."

Winters appeared at his side a moment later.

"That one's alive," Cronley said. "That one isn't."

Winters dropped to his knees and examined the man on the ground.

"You got him twice, once in the shoulder, once in—I dunno, in the side, waist level. He's bleeding pretty badly."

"Three times. I also shot him in the foot," Cronley said. "Can you stop the bleeding? I want the bastard alive."

"I can try," Winters replied. "What do we do now?"

"Well, since I don't think waiting on Casey's autobahn for a friendly Constabulary patrol to come along and render assistance will do us much good, we're going to have to go to the hotel."

"What do we do with this guy?"

"We take him with us. We take both of them with us."

"The dead kid, too?"

"Maybe we can find out who he is. Was. You grab this one's shoulders, I'll grab his legs."

They carried the man, who was moaning, to the car and laid him on the backseat.

"Not only is my upholstery going to be really fucked up, but my nearly new sixty-nine ninety-five trench coat already is," Cronley said.

"Looking on the bright side, you're alive."

"And look at the fucking windshield! Half a dozen fucking holes!"

"As I said, looking on the bright side . . ."

"Yeah. Let's go get the kid."

"My God, this is a woman!" Winters said.

Cronley looked and saw that when Winters had begun to pull the body out of the Audi by the feet, the hood had come off the head. Not only could Cronley now see an obviously feminine face, but blond hair braided and pinned to the skull.

The next thing he knew, Winters was helping him to his feet, and trying to put his arms around him.

"I threw up," Cronley said.

"I can smell it."

"I just shot a blond teenage girl with braids in the middle of the forehead."

"You were defending yourself, Jim."

"Against a blond teenaged girl with braids?"

"Come on, let's go. I already have the body in the Horch."

"How long was I down there, crying like a baby and throwing up everything I ever ate?"

"Not very long, and just for the record, I tossed my cookies, too, after I got her in the car." He paused. "We have to go, Jim."

[TWO]
The Bar
Farber Palast
Stein, near Nuremberg
American Zone of Occupation,
   Germany
1810 24 February 1946

A military police captain walked in the bar, looked around, and then marched to Tiny Dunwiddie, who was sitting with Cronley and Major Tony Henderson at a table.

"Are you Captain Cronley?" he asked Dunwiddie.

"I am," Cronley said.

"You're not wearing bars," the MP captain said.

"I suggest we wait until the provost marshal arrives before this goes any further," Henderson said.

"With respect, sir, this is a military police matter."

"No," Henderson said, "it's not."

He handed his DCI credentials to the captain, who examined them and then replied, "Major, I don't know what this is."

"The provost marshal will explain what they are when he gets here," Henderson said.

"I don't think I should wait for that."

"I'm a major and you're a captain. Consider that an order."

After a moment the captain said, "Yes, sir."

"Is he still alive?" Cronley asked.

"The wounded man?"

"Yes, the wounded man."

"He was alive when they put him in the ambulance. They're taking him to the 385th Station Hospital."

"And the officer who was with him? Captain Winters? Where is he?"

Before the MP captain could reply, Winters came into the room. He walked to the table and sat down. Cronley slid a glass half full of whisky to him.

"I waited until they sent another ambulance for . . . the body," Winters said.

"Tiny, get on the horn," Cronley ordered. "I want people sitting on the wounded man and the body."

"Yes, sir," Dunwiddie said, and went in search of a telephone.

Winters picked up his glass and drained it. Cronley slid a bottle of Johnnie Walker across the table to him.

"Go easy, Tom. You're going to have to fly yourself to the Compound in the morning."

Winters looked at him, but said nothing.

"Barbara should hear about this from you," Cronley said. "If she changes her mind about coming here tomorrow, which seems a distinct possibility, we'll work something out."

"I don't have to go up there."

"Consider it an order, Lieutenant, and say, 'Yes, sir.'"

Winters shook his head and said, "Yes, sir. Thank you, sir."

Colonel Mortimer Cohen trailed by a full colonel in pinks and greens and two stone-faced CIC agents walked into the room and to the table. The MP captain and Winters stood up. Cronley and Henderson did not.

"When I saw the ambulance, I was afraid it might be one of you," he said.

"It almost was. My Horch looks like a sieve. A blood-covered sieve."

"What the hell happened?" the MP colonel asked.

"Before this gets started, Colonel," Henderson said, and handed him his credentials.

"As the senior DCI officer present, sir, I inform you that this incident involves national security, that the DCI is taking over this investigation, and that all details are classified Top Secret–Presidential. Do you understand that, sir? And you, Captain?"

"Colonel Cohen brought me up to speed on the DCI," the MP colonel said. "Which then raises the question, why am I here?"

"To bring you up to speed on what happened, to tell you its classification, and to ask you to provide what assistance may be required."

"I understand," the colonel said.

"Okay, Jim," Henderson said, "tell everybody what you told me."

Augie Ziegler hurried into the room.

"Jesus Christ, what the hell happened? Are you all right, boss?"

"I'm doing as well as can be expected for someone who just shot a blond teenaged female in the forehead," Cronley said. "And shot a guy

I'd already put two bullets in once more. This time in the foot."

"I told you, Jim, those were acts of self-defense," Winters said. "And I meant it."

"The guy, sure. The teenaged blonde? Hell, no. All she was doing was driving the Audi."

"Mr. Cronley," Henderson said, "I will not ask 'what Audi?' and instead ask you to start at the beginning."

"Winters met me at the airport. We started for the hotel taking a back route that Casey came up with. We were a couple of miles down the road when we came up on a truck. A German truck. Tom couldn't get around it.

"Then the truck slowed and stopped. We skidded into it.

"I looked over my shoulder and saw an Audi sports car, headlights off, pulling up right behind us. So I bailed out of the Horch as a man got out of the Audi and started shooting at us with a Schmeisser.

"I finally got my .45 out and shot at him. I thought he went down, but I wasn't sure. I then emptied the .45 at the driver's windshield, and then reloaded. Then I crawled up near the Audi, saw a boot on the ground, and put a round in it. The guy screamed, so I knew I hit him. I heard the truck drive off, and then I got up and had a look."

"Where were you, Winters, during all this?" Cohen asked.

"Under the Horch. When Cronley rolled out the right side, I rolled out the left."

"You didn't have the opportunity to use your weapon? Super Spook did all the shooting?"

"I didn't have a weapon, sir."

"I'm sure you've already considered that wasn't very smart of you," Cohen said.

"That occurred to me, sir, as I crawled under the Horch."

"And then what, Cronley?" Henderson asked.

"We loaded the man, and the body of the driver, which we now knew was a girl, into the Horch, pushed the Audi off the road, which fucked up the fender of the Horch, and came here. I left Tom with the wounded guy and came in here and called Colonel Cohen."

"Not Captain Dunwiddie?"

Max Ostrowski and two Poles came into the bar.

"Hail, hail, the gang's all here. So who's minding the store?" Cronley said, as he reached for the bottle of Johnnie Walker.

"If I were you, I'd think about going easy on that, Jim," Henderson said.

"But you didn't just shoot a teenaged girl in the forehead, did you?" Cronley replied, as he filled his glass.

"A teenaged girl?" Ostrowski asked.

"Yeah, Max, a teenaged girl. I got her right here." He put his index finger on his forehead. "It made a large exit wound in the rear of her cranium."

"What the hell happened?"

"My current scenario, Mr. Ostrowski," Cohen said, "is that parties unknown—most likely Odessa, but we cannot exclude other possible parties—attempted to assassinate Super Spook. They did so by intercepting him and Lieutenant Winters as they took a shortcut back road from Soldier's Field airfield."

"Did you take that shortcut road to the airfield, Winters?"

"Yes, sir."

"Did you notice anyone following you?"

"No, sir."

"That suggests to me that the malefactors knew that Cronley had gone off somewhere in his airplane, and that he inevitably would return. When Winters got in Cronley's Horch . . . which was here, right?"

"Yes, sir," Winters said.

"Whoever Odessa—or whoever—has here in Farber Castle assumed he was headed for Soldier's Field, and would take the shortcut road back here once he picked up Cronley. And he—or maybe she—got on the telephone and told them to put their in-place assassination scenario into play."

"Yeah," Henderson said softly.

"May I ask questions?" the MP colonel asked.

"What I want you to do for us, Bruce—"

"In other words, Morty, I don't get to ask questions?"

"I may not answer your questions, but go ahead."

"Why does whoever did this want to kill Mr. Cronley?"

"A lot of people, with good reason, would like to see Super Spook sent to Fiddler's Green. Now what I want you to do, Bruce, is see if you can find out who owns the Audi, and see if you can find out who the man in the 385th Station Hospital is. And who the young woman is."

"I'll get right on it," the MP colonel said.

"Mr. Ziegler is ex-CID," Cronley said. "Can I send him with you?"

"Why not?" the MP colonel said.

"What I have to do is get on the SIGABA and get the word to Colonel Wallace and General Greene," Henderson said. "And I suggest that the rest of you move your discussion somewhere where you know no one's listening. Did you think about having your room here swept, Cronley?"

"It gets swept once a day."

"Good thinking."

[THREE]
The Duchess Suite
Farber Palast
Stein, near Nuremberg
American Zone of Occupation,
Germany
1835 24 February 1946

The door opened and Janice Johansen walked in.

"They threw you out of the bar, right?" she greeted the men in the room, who were sitting in chairs gathered in a rough circle around the enormous bed.

No one replied.

She went to the dressing room and returned with a chair and joined the circle.

"So what are you talking about that you don't want anyone, especially me, to hear?"

"Something we don't want to see on the front page of **Stars and Stripes**," Cohen said.

"Okay, what?"

"Somebody tried to whack me," Cronley said.

"Well, they apparently missed. Who somebody?"

That's all of her reaction?

Not "Oh, my God! Are you all right, Adonis?"

Or words to that effect?

"You came in at the tail end of a long discussion in which it was decided we don't **know**," Cohen said. "The suspects are Odessa and the NKGB."

"Why would the Russians want to whack Cronley?"

"I embarrassed ol' Ivan when we got Mattingly back. Am I forgiven, or did he come to Nuremberg to kidnap, or whack, me?"

"I confess I've been a little curious about his piety," she said. "Why is Odessa pissed at you? I mean, specifically at you."

"Probably because they know I'm after von Dietelburg. Maybe I'm getting close, and that's why they want to take me out."

"The word that he's been asking the wrong kind of questions could have come out of the prison. They know you talked to Kaltenbrunner and Macher," Ostrowski said.

"Actually, Max," Cohen said, "I've always been more worried about things being smuggled out of the prison than getting smuggled in. Orders, for example. In this case, to Odessa. **This new man, Cronley, is asking the wrong kind of questions. Take him out.**"

"I'm not saying you're wrong, Colonel," Ostrowski replied. "You're right. What I saw was how easy it is for the prisoners to get messages out. Orders to Odessa or somebody else. Not necessarily written. Verbal. And even coded verbal. 'PFC Smith, please get word to my wife that I have no further problems with my ingrown toenail.'"

"Obviously, you've been giving some thought to the prisoners and their guards?" Cohen said. It was a question.

"I've been nosing around ever since I heard Casey was going to be undercover. I really like the youngest DCI agent."

"And?"

"Well, the guards are just kids. Not nearly as smart as Casey. And that Casey, unless he's far more clever than we have any right to expect him to be, is in some danger. And it would be a lot easier to whack him than it would be to whack Cronley, especially since Cronley will now have one of my people around twenty-four hours a day covering his back."

"What?" Cronley asked.

Ostrowski smiled at Cronley.

"I was playing chess with Justice Jackson when Tiny called to give me a heads-up on what had happened to you. When I told Justice Jackson what had happened, he asked, 'What about Jim's bodyguard?' I told him you didn't think you needed one. To which he replied, 'Get him one right now, and keep one on him from now on.' To which I replied, 'Yes, sir, Mr. Justice, sir.'"

Cohen chuckled.

"Janice, Jim was just about to tell us what happened in Strasbourg," Cohen said.

"How'd you know I was in Strasbourg?"

"I'm CIC. We know everything about everything."

"Well, since you asked, I told Cousin Luther that he has until two-thirty tomorrow to give me von Dietelburg or I will let Colonel Fortin have him. He knows that Fortin has expressed an interest in shooting him in the knees and elbows with a .22 and then seeing how well he can swim."

"You think he'll cave under a threat like that?" Dunwiddie asked. "It doesn't seem very credible to me. The caving or the .22s in the knees."

"There is a legend, one that I'm sure Cousin Luther has heard. It alleges that shortly after the French returned to Strasbourg, a priest was sent swimming that way. The legend further alleges that the priest—for the good of the Catholic Church—didn't do enough to try to convince the Milice and the SS that Fortin's family really didn't know where Fortin was. I also offered him a new life in bucolic Paraguay. That, I think, may work."

"And if he doesn't cave? You're going to let

Fortin throw him in the Rhine?" Dunwiddie pursued.

"I'll cross that bridge when I come to it, to coin a phrase."

"Wallace told you to offer him Paraguay?" Cohen asked.

"Actually, the subject never came up between us."

"So you're not going to send him to Paraguay?" Cohen asked.

"If he gives me von Dietelburg, I am. I have high hopes that Colonel Stroessner, once he gets to know Cousin Luther, will put him in front of a firing squad. He does that to unrepentant Nazis."

"And you don't believe Cousin Luther is repentant?" Dunwiddie asked.

"Tiny, I know a little something about Colonel Fortin's interrogation techniques. Anyone who doesn't tell Fortin what he wants to know is a fool, or thinks he is responsible to a higher power. Cousin Luther has many character flaws, but he's not a fool."

"You think he's part of this Nazi religion crap?" Dunwiddie asked.

"He may be. What I do know is he thinks he's still alive because Fortin doesn't want to annoy the chief, DCI-Europe—the **former** chief, DCI-Europe—by sending his cousin for a swim. I have now told him Fortin will get him if he doesn't come up with von Dietelburg by half past two tomorrow. I suspect Cousin Luther could give Wallace lessons in How to Protect One's Own Ass, and will see the light."

"Two questions, Super Spook," Cohen said. "How are you going to get him to Paraguay? And how are you going to Cover Your Ass— presuming you're successful—when Colonel Wallace finds out what you've done without his permission?"

"I'm going on the SIGABA tonight and tell Ashton and Frade in Buenos Aires that I will require passage on the next available flight for a French Nazi and his wife who want to go to Paraguay. That will probably see Cletus or von Wachtstein in the pilot's seat on the next SAA flight to Berlin.

"Fortin will transfer Cousin Luther and wife to the French Zone of Berlin. If by then we have von Dietelburg in the bag, the Stauffers will get on the plane."

"And if Colonel Wallace finds out what you're up to before you have von Dietelburg and/or before they get on the plane?"

"I will cross that bridge—those bridges—if I get to them."

"I can't imagine why General Seidel and Colonel Wallace think of you as a dangerous loose cannon," Cohen said, and went on. "You didn't answer my question. What do you think Wallace is going to do when he finds out what you've done?"

"If it works, he'll take credit for the success of DCI-Europe in taking out Odessa's head man."

"And if it doesn't?"

"He can truthfully tell Oscar Schultz that I didn't tell him anything about what I was doing. And that if he had known, he would have stopped me, as my trying to take down Odessa was not only not my business, but would distract me from my primary duty of protecting Justice Jackson."

"Have you thought about that? That your primary duty **is** protecting Justice Jackson?" Cohen asked.

"That was all I thought of until you took me on a tour of Wewelsburg Castle. That changed things. And Max doesn't need my help to protect Justice Jackson."

"I really would like to see that place. As promised," Janice said.

"So would I," Tiny said.

"Colonel, Winters could drop them off tomorrow morning on his way to the Compound," Cronley said.

"Okay. I'll call and tell my people to give them the tour."

"But how would they get back?" Cronley said. "I suspect that my morning will be occupied chatting with Wallace, and I have to stick around here to hear from Fortin, or maybe even have to fly to Strasbourg."

"How to get back is one of those bridges to be crossed when we get to it," Janice said.

"I think I better tell El Jefe what happened before he hears it from Wallace," Cronley said. "So I think I better get on the SIGABA right now."

When Cronley went into the corridor outside the Duchess Suite, there was a Polish special agent of the DCI sitting there with a Thompson submachine gun in his lap.

"There's a car outside?" Max asked him.

"Two, sir. Yours and one for Mr. Cronley."

"Fine."

The man with the submachine gun stood up and followed them as they went down the curving stairway to the lobby and then outside. As they went down the stairway outside the hotel, two Ford staff cars pulled up to them.

Ostrowski walked to the first car and opened both doors.

"You may sit, sir, wherever it pleases you."

Cronley looked in the front seat, saw that a Thompson was lying across it, gave Ostrowski the finger, and then got in the backseat.

"There's more room back here," he said to the man who had followed him from the Duchess Suite.

[FOUR]
The Mansion
Offenbach Platz 101
Nuremberg, American Zone of
   Occupation, Germany
2020 24 February 1946

"Fulda, Cronley, James, for Schultz, Oscar, in Washington."

"Vint Hill."

"Cronley, James, for Oscar Schultz."

"DCI."

"Cronley, James, for Oscar Schultz."

"Schultz."

"James Cronley for you, sir. The line is secure."

"Put him through."

"Mr. Cronley, Mr. Schultz is on a secure line."

"What's up, Jimmy?"

"Somebody tried to kill me a couple of hours ago."

"Who?"

"Probably Odessa."

"You okay?"

"More or less."

"Who does Wallace think was responsible?"

"I don't know. I haven't talked to him."

"You want to explain why you called me and not him? You ever hear of command channels?"

"Tony Henderson called him a few minutes ago."

"Tony works for me. Not Wallace. If he called anybody, he should have called me." He paused. "Oh, shit! Okay. Starting at the beginning, tell me what happened."

"I had been in Strasbourg—"

"What the hell were you doing in Strasbourg? You're supposed to be sitting on Justice Jackson."

"And when I came back, Tom Winters met me at the airport. On the way to the Farber Palast—"

"To the what?"

"On a back road, we were bushwhacked. Very professionally."

"Not **very** professionally. You're still alive. What happened to the bushwhackers?"

"I killed one, and wounded—I don't know how bad—the other one."

"When Justice Jackson hears about this, he'll shit a brick."

"He already knows."

"And?"

"He told Max Ostrowski to put a bodyguard on me."

"You should have thought about doing that ten seconds after you heard they whacked Moriarty. They were after you, not that poor sonofabitch. That brings us to who are they?"

"As I said, probably Odessa."

"I was thinking the Russians. You made an ass of Serov, getting Mattingly back. Made an ass of him in front of his bosses. He might think taking you out would restore his reputation. I don't believe his story that he's in Nuremberg to sit on the Russian judges."

"I think it's Odessa."

"Why?"

"Because I'm getting close to von Dietelburg. Or think I am. That's what I was doing in Strasbourg."

"The guy you think is running Odessa? Wallace sent you to Strasbourg to look for him?"

"No. He didn't know anything about me looking for von Dietelburg. Or going to Strasbourg."

"Jesus Christ, Jimmy. You're as bad as Cletus Frade! A fucking three-star loose cannon. And you didn't get to grab von Dietelburg in Strasbourg? Or even get any idea where to look for him, right?"

"I find out tomorrow, before half past two, whether or not I'm going to be told where to look for him."

"Reliable source?"

"If he tells me anything at all, I think it'll be reliable."

"Turn him over to that Frog, the one who runs DST. What's his name?"

"Commandant Fortin."

"I hear he's really a colonel. And also that he could take a rock from the Kremlin wall and have it singing 'La Marseillaise' in fifteen minutes. I know you know him, so the question, Loose Cannon, is how well? Is he in that legion of people you've royally pissed off, or will he do us a favor?"

"He'll do us a favor. Actually—"

"Mr. Schultz, it's Vint."

"What the hell do they want?" Schultz snapped.

"Fulda has a Colonel Wallace on the line, sir. He insists on speaking to you immediately. He says it's urgent."

"Does he know who I'm talking to?"

"No, sir."

"Make sure he doesn't find out. Hold One, Vint Hill."

"Yes, sir."

"Jimmy, give your source to Fortin. Tell him I said to do whatever it takes to make your source give us von Dietelburg. I really want to close down Odessa and the way to do that is nail this sonofabitch. Say, 'Yes, sir.'"

"Yes, sir."

"I'll get back to you, Jimmy. Vint Hill, put Colonel Wallace through."

"Fulda, Vint Hill. I have Mr. Schultz on a secure line for Colonel Wallace."

Cronley's line went dead.

[FIVE]

When he came out of the bedroom closet in which Florence Miller had installed the SIGABA system, he found her sitting on her bed.

She got quickly to her feet.

"Sit," Cronley ordered. She remained standing.

"I heard what happened," she said. "Are you all right?"

"I'm all right. How did you hear? And what?"

"I put that major . . . Henderson? . . . on the SIGABA and happened to overhear what he told Colonel Wallace."

"Major Anthony 'Tony' Henderson is one of the good guys, Flo. He reports to Oscar Schultz, not Wallace. What did he tell Wallace?"

"That when Lieutenant Winters was driving you from the airport to the Farber Palast, somebody opened up on you with a Schmeisser."

"And?"

"Colonel Wallace said he's not going to drive here at night in a snowstorm, but that he'll be here as soon as he can in the morning. And he told the major to make sure you and Winters were available."

"Winters won't be. He's flying to the Compound first thing in the morning to tell his wife what happened. I wanted her to hear it from him, not Wallace."

"You think she'll still come down here?"

"I dunno, Flo. But keep whatever you set up for her here in place."

"Yes, sir."

"From now until we get this situation straightened out, I don't want you and any of the girls to go anywhere, and I mean anywhere, alone. And take your pistols with you."

"I already told them. Can I ask who you think did this?"

"Probably Odessa, but maybe the same people who went after you and Claudette."

"Can I tell her what happened?"

"Why do I think you've already told her?"

Florence looked very uncomfortable.

"I thought I had made it clear that Claudette's in the loop."

"I wasn't sure."

"The next time you're not sure, ask."

"Yes, sir."

[SIX]
The Bar
Farber Palast
Stein, near Nuremberg
American Zone of Occupation,
  Germany
2120 24 February 1946

Cronley more or less expected to find Janice in the bar when he walked in with his bodyguard. She wasn't. Polkovnik Ivan Serov and Major Sergei Alekseevich were.

Cronley pointed to an empty table, an order for his bodyguard to sit there, and then walked to Serov's table.

Serov stood up, smiled, and put out his hand.

"I heard what happened," he said.

"I'll bet you did," Cronley said, taking the hand.

"I'm glad you're all right, James," Serov said.

"I'm fine."

I'm not fine. If I were fine, my brain would be functioning on all four cylinders and I would be able to guess whether the sonofabitch is really glad to hear I'm all right,

or whether he's sorry the assassins—his assassins—failed.

"Sit down, have a little Johnnie Walker, and if you feel up to it, separate the facts from the rumors that are circulating through the Palast."

Cronley sat down.

"I am glad you're all right, Mr. Cronley," Alekseevich said, and offered him his hand.

And if my brain were functioning, I'd be able to guess if ol' Sergei means that, or is nearly as accomplished a liar as ol' Ivan.

"Thank you," Cronley said, as he took the hand.

Alekseevich stood up and walked to the bar.

"That's a good idea, James," Serov said, nodding toward the bodyguard. "One you should have thought of immediately when you lost your friend."

"Actually, Ivan, the bodyguard is Justice Jackson's idea. Our roles seem to be reversed."

Serov chuckled.

"That trench coat doesn't do much to conceal his weapon, does it?" Serov asked. "What is it, a Thompson?"

"The U.S. M1A1 Caliber .45 ACP submachine gun, commonly called 'the Thompson' or 'the tommy gun,' is a splendid weapon, Ivan. Our gangsters really love it. But it weighs about ninety pounds, kicks like a mule, and it is a bit difficult to hide under a trench coat."

Serov laughed.

Alekseevich returned to the table holding three whisky-filled glasses with two hands.

He set them on the table. Serov picked up his.

"To assassins who miss," he said.

"I'll drink to that," Cronley said, and touched his glass to Serov's.

"Who do you think was responsible?"

As if you don't know.

"Well, the first thing that came to mind was the NKGB."

"James, if it was the NKGB, they would have consulted me first."

I'll be a sonofabitch! That sounded sincere.

Serov crossed himself and then raised his right.

"Before God, my friend, I swear on my mother's grave, I know nothing about this!"

My brain is really upgefukt. I believe him.

"And then I thought it was probably Odessa. I think I'm getting close to von Dietelburg, and they know it."

"Thank you," Serov said.

"For what?"

"For believing me. I could see in your eyes that you do."

Jesus!

"Say nighty-night to your pals, Adonis. It's get-tucked-in time," Janice Johansen said.

No one had seen her enter the bar.

"I was about to ask James to have dinner with us, Miss Johansen," Serov said. "We'd love to have you join us."

Janice gave him the finger.

"Why? So you could put cyanide in his soup? On your feet, Jimmy boy!"

Cronley stood up. Janice took his arm and propelled him toward the door.

The bodyguard followed them out of the bar.

XI

[ONE]
The Mansion
Offenbach Platz 101
Nuremberg, American Zone of
 Occupation, Germany
1005 25 February 1946

Brigadier General Homer P. Greene was sitting with Colonel Mortimer Cohen, Max Ostrowski, and Cronley in the sitting room of the Mansion, when Colonel Harold Wallace and another officer walked in.

"Good morning, General," Wallace said.

Greene answered Wallace's unspoken question. "I drove down last night. Morty thought talking about this over the phone was a bad idea."

"Everybody knows everybody, right?" Wallace said.

"I don't know this officer," Cohen said.

"Sorry, this is Lieutenant Colonel Bill Conroy, my operations officer," Wallace said. "Another OSS retread. We served together in London, then in France."

The two shook hands.

"Congratulations, Cronley," Conroy said. "You're still alive. I just saw the Horch."

"My bullet-ridden Horch, you mean? The one with all the blood on the upholstery?"

"I had it towed here," Cohen said. "It was causing too much interest at the Palast."

"What Palast?" Wallace asked.

"The Farber Palast. Where Cronley rests his weary head at night," Greene said. "The chief of protection for Justice Jackson couldn't be expected to sleep in a tawdry room in this tawdry dump."

"Sir, with respect, you seem to find some of this amusing. May I ask what?" Wallace asked.

"Some things I've heard here are amusing. Cronley sleeping in the Duchess Suite in the Palast makes me smile. And Janice Johansen turning down Colonel Ivan Serov's invitation to buy dinner for Cronley and her by giving him the finger and asking, 'Why, so you can put cyanide in his soup?' I wish I'd been there to see that. And some things I've heard are the direct opposite of amusing. Frightening. Sickening."

"Ivan Serov offered to buy Cronley dinner?" Wallace asked incredulously.

"Oh, you haven't heard that Morty, Cronley, and Serov have become pals? You're really in the dark, Harold."

"I'd like to come into the light, sir. Can we start the debriefing? I'd like to get the facts to Mr. Schultz as soon as possible."

"Done deed," Greene said. "I just got off the SIGABA with him. Cronley thought he'd place more credence in my report than in his."

Wallace gave Cronley a dirty look.

"Obviously, Cronley didn't think I would be interested."

"Sir, Major Henderson suggested that since we didn't have any intel but the basic facts, it would be better to wait until you got here," Cronley replied.

"Where is Henderson? And where is Winters?"

"Henderson is taking a tour of Wewelsburg Castle, and Winters is at the Compound telling his wife what happened."

"That obviously means Conroy and I are the only ones in the dark."

"You won't know how dark, Harry," General Greene said, "until Morty brings you up to date on Wewelsburg Castle, a.k.a. the Heinrich Himmler Cathedral."

"I've heard those rumors, General, and found them hard to believe. Is there something I don't know?"

"Yes, indeed," Greene said. "Not some **thing**, Harold. **Lots** of things."

"So what happened, Cronley?" Wallace said. "Tell me what I don't know."

"Yes, sir. When I came back from Strasbourg—"

"What the hell were you doing in Strasbourg? You were sent here to protect Justice Jackson, nothing else."

"I guess one of the things you didn't know is that Schultz told him to take down Odessa," Greene said.

"How do you know that?"

"Oscar told me," Greene said. "I wonder why he didn't tell you?"

"I have no idea."

"Cronley, hold off telling Colonel Wallace why you were in Strasbourg and tell him what happened when you came back," Greene ordered.

"Yes, sir. Winters met me in the Horch at the airport. We were taking a shortcut to the Palast on a back road. We came up behind a slow-moving truck Winters couldn't get around. An Audi, headlights out, came up behind us. The truck stopped. Winters bumped it hard. The Audi pulled behind us, a guy got out and started shooting at us with a Schmeisser."

"And?"

"I got out of the Horch and took him down."

"Is he still alive?"

"Yes. He's in stable condition at the 385th Station Hospital," Cohen answered for him. "He is former SS-Obersturmbannführer Günther Kuhn. The girl is—was—his daughter Elfriede."

"What girl?" Conroy asked. "And how did you identify him, them, so quickly?"

"The girl was driving the Audi," Cohen said. "She died during the ambush."

"How?" Conroy pursued.

"I shot her," Cronley said. "In the forehead." He pointed with his index finger.

"How were you able to identify them? Positively? So quickly?" Wallace asked impatiently.

"I am always delighted to explain CIC techniques to a fellow intelligence officer," Cohen said sarcastically. "What we did, Colonel, was check the prewar records of the Bavarian Motor Vehicle Bureau for a 1939 yellow-and-black Audi soft-top.

"There were complete records for one hundred fifty-three such vehicles. One hundred forty-nine of them had either been requisitioned by the Todt Organization or reported as destroyed. There were four whose records said they had been stolen. One of the four was registered to SS-Obersturmbannführer Kuhn.

"He was on your list of senior SS officers to be looked for, probably, I thought, because he had been on the personal staff of Reichsführer-SS Himmler. Such senior officers often reported their personal cars stolen just before the Todt Organization requisitioned them. Since they were senior SS officers, the Motor Vehicle Bureau took them at their word. The vehicles then disappeared under a haystack on a farm somewhere, from which they would rise phoenixlike after the Final Victory.

"We knew that SS-Obersturmbannführer Kuhn had a farm not far outside Nuremberg, because we had gone there looking for him. So I sent one of my men, dressed as a Nuremberg policeman, to the farm. He told Frau Kuhn that her daughter had met her fate in an auto accident and she would have to identify the remains. My guy then took Frau Kuhn to the German hospital to which I had moved the body.

"When the sheet was pulled from the girl's corpse, Frau Kuhn screamed at my guy, 'You stupid sonofabitch of an American lackey! This was no auto accident. My daughter was shot! Shot by your goddamned Jewish masters.'

"Or words to that effect. At that point, Frau Kuhn was taken into custody."

"You arrested her?" Wallace asked. "On what charge?"

"The German authorities arrested her. She is charged as an accessory before the fact with murder. The Germans also arrested former SS-Obersturmbannführer Kuhn for murder."

"But neither Cronley nor Winters were hurt," Wallace challenged.

"Their daughter was killed. Under German law, anyone involved in a crime is responsible for anything that happens during the commission of that crime. Their daughter was unlawfully deprived of her life, which is the definition of murder, during Kuhn's attempt to unlawfully deprive Mr. Cronley and Lieutenant Winters of their lives. Since there is no longer a death penalty in Germany, the punishment for murder is life imprisonment at hard labor. If the Kuhns do not understand this law, their court-appointed attorneys will explain it to them at the earliest opportunity.

"The funeral will be delayed until her parents can attend her interment. Until, in other words, we can shackle her father, who will be dressed in prison clothes, to a wheelchair, which Frau

Kuhn, also shackled, and wearing a prison dress, will be permitted to push to the gravesite.

"I will have people at the cemetery to see who shows up for the burial of a fallen heroine of the Himmler cult, and to check their **Kennkarten** to see if that's who they really are. We may get lucky.

"Following the interment, the Kuhns will be returned to their solitary confinement cells, where they will have time to think about their future. After they have had what I consider to be sufficient time to do that thinking, either Cronley or I will visit them and offer a reduction in the charges against them to manslaughter, which carries a penalty of five to twenty years if they give us former Brigadeführer Franz von Dietelburg."

"You or **Cronley**?"

"I haven't made up my mind whether they will react better to a nasty Hebrew colonel or to a nice young man who speaks fluent German with a Strasbourg accent and who looks like a poster boy for an SS recruitment poster."

"Thanks a lot!" Cronley protested.

"You said, 'Himmler cult.' What's that?" Wallace asked.

"It's the religion Himmler set up, with Castle Wewelsburg as its Vatican," Cohen said.

"You're telling me you're placing credence in that nonsense?"

"Oh, yes. And so do persons of much higher pay grade than you and I."

"What persons of higher pay grade? Chief Schultz? The admiral?"

"When I was telling Schultz what Super Spook the poster boy—"

"Jesus Christ!" Cronley said.

"—had come up with in Strasbourg, he brought the subject up. He said the admiral had told him Justice Jackson had told the President that he was worried that all that hanging Göring and company was going to do was give the German people martyrs to Nazism. The President said that Jackson had heard from me about what had gone on at Castle Wewelsburg and he wanted the admiral to get to the bottom of it.

"So the admiral told Schultz to get on it. So Schultz asked me what we were doing, and I told him what Cronley and I were doing. And he said, 'Keep Cronley at it. Give him whatever he asks for.'"

"What else did he say?"

"All right. What Schultz actually said was, 'Cronley is a lot smarter than most people think. So give him what he wants and keep out of his way until he does something really dumb.'"

Wallace obviously regretted asking the question, but he didn't reply directly, instead asking, "What did go on at this castle?"

"Prepared to be disturbed, Harold," General

Greene said. "Tell him, Morty. Just the high points. We don't have time for the full lecture."

"Yes, sir," Cohen said. "Harold, this is where we are in looking into Castle Wewelsburg and what went on there, what we think is still going on. It now seems beyond doubt that Heinrich Himmler was trying to start—hell, **started**—a new religion using the castle as its cathedral . . ."

"And you believe this?" Wallace asked perhaps five minutes later when Cohen had finished.

"Yeah, I do," Cohen said. "More important, Harold, so do the admiral and Schultz."

"And you think Odessa is connected with it?"

"I think Odessa is an integral part of this. If we can shut down Odessa, we just might be able to shut down this cult. And the way to do that is to get our hands on SS-Brigadeführer Franz von Dietelburg. He's the connection between Odessa and the cult. That's what Cronley was doing in Strasbourg."

"Tell me about that."

"The floor is yours, Super Spook," Cohen said.

"We now know my cousin Luther was sent to Strasbourg by von Dietelburg to set up an Odessa escape route through France. And we know he was in touch with Odessa—which means with von Dietelburg—recently because when we caught him he was trying to get SS-Brigadeführer Ulrich Heimstadter and SS-Standartenführer Oskar Müller across the border into France. That was an Odessa operation. We also know that Cousin Luther is into this new religion business. At least to a certain degree."

"What do you mean by that? 'To a certain degree'?" Wallace asked.

"He has so far resisted answering questions posed to him by Commandant Fortin. Fortin thinks Luther could only keep his mouth shut, quote, **if he was answering to a higher court**, close quote, which we think is the Himmler religion."

"So what are you going to do?"

"I told him that unless he gives me von Dietelburg by half past two today, I'm going to give him to Fortin."

"Fortin already has him."

"But has not applied his full arsenal of interrogation techniques, because Cousin Luther and I are kin."

"What's the full range consist of?"

"I don't want to know, but at the end of the list, Fortin shoots the one being interrogated in the knees and elbows with a .22 and then tosses him in the Rhine to see how well he can swim."

"And you're willing to turn your cousin over to Fortin, knowing he's going to do this?"

"I'll cross that bridge when I get to it," Cronley said.

"What I think we should do is bring him here and see if we can make him talk."

"That's Cronley's call," Greene said.

"Excuse me?"

"Harold, weren't you listening when Cohen said Schultz told him to keep out of Cronley's way until he does something really dumb?" Greene asked. "That sounded like an order to me."

"Cronley's a loose cannon," Wallace said.

"Agreed. But a loose cannon out of whose way we have been ordered to get."

"And you agree with Schultz?"

"I'm a simple soldier, Colonel. When I get an order, I salute and say, 'Yes, sir.'"

"Are you going to tell me what you're going to do next, Cronley?" Wallace snapped sarcastically "Or have you decided I don't have the Need to Know?"

"Temper, temper, Harold," Greene said.

"Sir," Cronley said, "I'm going to Strasbourg to see what Cousin Luther has decided to do."

"Take your bodyguard with you, Cronley," Greene said.

"What bodyguard?" Wallace asked.

"Justice Jackson suggested Cronley needed a

bodyguard, Harold," Cohen said. "Somewhat reluctantly, Super Spook took this as an order."

"Colonel, I need a minute in private with you and Ostrowski before I go," Cronley said.

"Whatever your little heart desires, Super Spook," Cohen replied, and followed Cronley and Ostrowski out of the sitting room and into the foyer.

[TWO]
Entzheim Airport
Strasbourg, France
1255 25 February 1946

"Who's he?" Commandant Jean-Paul Fortin asked, as Cronley's bodyguard handed him his Thompson before climbing down from the Horch.

"DCI Special Agent Cezar Zieliński is my bodyguard."

"You need a bodyguard?"

"All very important Americans have body-guards. I'm surprised you don't know that."

Zieliński reclaimed the Thompson.

"Cezar, this is Colonel—"

"Commandant," Fortin corrected him.

"—Jean-Paul Fortin. You may have run into him in England, where he was in G-2 at Free

French Army headquarters when you were doing the same thing at Free Polish Army headquarters."

"**Mon colonel,**" Zieliński said, coming to attention.

"I like people who didn't surrender," Fortin said. "I also like people to think I'm a commandant. And I also doubt you're my American friend's bodyguard. Who are you really?"

"My chief assigned me to see that no harm comes to Mr. Cronley."

"Why would he do that?"

"Because Justice Jackson suggested I needed one," Cronley said.

"And, prefacing this by saying I'm already growing weary of your American humor, why would Justice Jackson think you need a bodyguard?"

"Probably because when I returned to Nuremberg from here yesterday, Odessa tried to kill me and Tom Winters as Tom was driving me from the airport to the Farber Palast."

"Somehow I think you are now telling the truth."

"Boy Scout's honor, Jean-Paul," Cronley said. "First, they used a truck to stop us, and then an Audi pulled in behind us. Former SS-Obersturmbannführer Günther Kuhn got out of the Audi and let loose with his Schmeisser."

"But missed you. What about Tom?"

"He's all right. He managed to get out of the line of fire by crawling under my Horch."

"And?"

Zieliński answered for him. "Mr. Cronley took Kuhn down, and killed the Audi driver."

"Who, if we needed any further proof that members of Odessa are really not nice people, was his daughter," Cronley added.

"His **daughter**?" Fortin asked incredulously.

"His very good-looking daughter. She was nineteen at the time of her demise."

"**Mon Dieu!** What kind of swine would involve his young daughter in something like that?"

"The Odessa type of swine," Cronley said. "But just before we came here, I heard something from Colonel Cohen that I am hoping will mitigate my guilty feelings about shooting a teenaged blonde in the forehead. Morty got the German cops to charge her poppa with murder."

"He's alive?"

Cronley nodded. "It seems German law holds anyone involved in a crime guilty of whatever happens during that crime. Since Poppa was committing a crime when his daughter was sent to Nazi Valhalla, Poppa is guilty of murdering her, not me."

"I find myself agreeing with German law for once," Fortin said. "James, you are not responsible for that young woman's death."

"That's what I keep telling myself, but I am having a hard time believing me."

"Why did Colonel Cohen get the Germans to charge Poppa Nazi with murder?"

"The penalty is life at hard labor. Both for Poppa and Momma. She's charged with being an accessory before the fact. Cohen will offer them reduced charges if they tell us where we can find von Dietelburg."

"Is Poppa a practicing member of Himmler's cult?"

"I think so. Because of his daughter. They were doing Saint Heinrich's good works."

"Then he probably won't give von Dietelburg up. And to further ruin your day, I've come to conclude that Cousin Luther really thinks of himself as a Mormon."

"A Mormon?"

"Don't they call themselves 'Latter-Day Saints'?"

"And I have a questionable sense of humor?"

"I spoke with your kinsman, told him you were coming. He said, 'It'll be a waste of his time.'"

"Let's go see him anyway. Maybe learning we have Kuhn will change his mind. And if it doesn't, I have yet another idea on how to deal with the sonofabitch."

"After we have our couscous."

"Have our what?"

"Our couscous. Sergent-chef Ibn Tufail has been laboring on it all day in the Hotel Gurtler-hoft kitchen. You and Zieliński arrived just in time to profit from his labors."

"I gather it's something to eat?"

"A Moroccan delicacy. Steamed flour particles, onto which a stew—chicken, lamb, vegetables—is ladled, and then sprinkled with almonds, cinnamon, and sugar. In Morocco, they think lamb's eyeballs should go into the stew, but I told Sergent-chef Ibn Tufail to leave them out. I find them disconcerting."

"And while we're eating, I will tell you what lamb's eyeballs I'm going to put on Cousin Luther's plate if he doesn't give me von Dietelburg," Cronley said.

[THREE]
Sainte Marguerite Prison
Strasbourg, France
1415 25 February 1946

Former SS-Sturmführer Luther Stauffer was led shuffling into the warden's office. His wrists and ankles were shackled and he was unshaven.

Commandant Jean-Paul Fortin was sitting behind the warden's desk. Cronley, Zieliński,

and the warden were bent over a table, affix-
ing their signatures to documents that the warden snatched from them as quickly as they were
signed.

"Put him in that chair," Fortin ordered.

Two guards put Stauffer in a wooden straight-
backed chair facing the warden's desk.

Cronley and Zieliński took two identical
chairs from a row of chairs against the wall and
moved them to either side of Fortin behind the
desk.

"Can I talk you out of your chair, Commandant?" Zieliński asked. "It's going to be difficult
transcribing this unless I can get my legs under
the desk."

Fortin rose from his swivel chair and waited
for Zieliński to get out of his. Finally, both sat
down. Zieliński picked up a pencil and held it
over a pad of lined paper.

"Anytime you're ready, Mr. Cronley," he said.

"Final interview of former SS-Sturmführer
Luther Stauffer in connection with the case of
former SS-Brigadeführer Franz von Dietelburg.
Interview held at 1420 hours, 25 February, 1946,
at the Sainte Marguerite Prison, Strasbourg,
France. Present are Commandant Jean-Paul
Fortin, director of the Direction de la Surveil-
lance du Territoire for the Département du Bas-
Rhin, DCI Special Agent Cezar Zieliński, and

DCI Supervisory Special Agent James D. Cronley Junior.

"Tell me, Stauffer, are you a married man?"

"You know I am, Cousin James."

"Were you married when you joined the Légion des Volontaires Français contre le Bolchévisme?"

"No."

"Then you were married later. After you joined the SS?"

"Yes."

"Which would mean after you renounced your French citizenship and became German?"

"**Resumed** my German citizenship, Cousin James. I was born, as your mother was, a German. My father, your uncle Hans-Karl, foolishly chose to be a Frenchman after the First World War when the Versailles Treaty stole Elsass-Lothringen from Germany."

"I don't know where you went to school, but I was taught that Elsass-Lothringen—Alsace-Lorraine—was stolen from France in 1871 after the Franco–Prussian War and then returned to France after Germany lost World War One. And then Hitler stole it back just before World War Two. And, when Germany lost World War Two, France took it back again. Isn't that the case?"

Stauffer didn't reply.

"But that's going off at a tangent, isn't it? I was

asking about your career in the Schutzstaffel, the SS. No. Come to think of it, we were talking about you getting married. When did that happen?"

"In 1942."

"After you returned from your service in Russia?"

"While I was in Germany, in Berlin, on temporary duty."

"And what was that special duty?"

"Stauffer, Luther. **Sturmführer**, 4848329."

"Not a problem. We already know what that duty was. You don't have to violate your SS officer's honor by telling me. But that's where you first came under the command of SS-Brigadeführer Franz von Dietelburg, right?"

"Stauffer, Luther. **Sturmführer**, 4848329."

"Let's return to something that doesn't pose a question you feel uncomfortable answering. Were you married in a Roman Catholic church? Since my mother was raised as a Roman Catholic, I'm presuming you and Ingebord were."

"We were married in a civil ceremony."

"In Berlin?"

"No. Not in Berlin."

"In Castle Wewelsburg?"

"Stauffer, Luther. **Sturmführer**, 4848329."

"I must confess I'm impressed. I didn't think you were important enough to be honored by getting hitched in Castle Wewelsburg. Or was letting you get married there sort of a pat on the head? 'We have plans for you, Stauffer. And to prove it we're going to let you get married by a senior SS officer in the SS Vatican, a.k.a. Wewelsburg Castle.'"

Stauffer didn't say anything.

"Do you remember the name of the SS officer who presided over your nuptials? Was it maybe SS-Obersturmbannführer Günther Kuhn?"

Stauffer didn't reply.

"I just met him. Lousy shot."

"Wie, bitte?"

"He had a Schmeisser. All I had was my pistol. But guess, since I'm sitting here and he's in a hospital bed in the Munich prison, who won?"

"I have no idea what you're talking about."

"I think you do. I think you got word somehow to Odessa that I was asking questions about the Organisation der Ehemaligen SS-Angehörigen that were getting dangerous. That I had connected you with von Dietelburg, for example. And they were already annoyed with me because I was responsible for you getting caught trying to get Heimstadter and Müller across the Franco–German border. So they told Kuhn to take me out.

"He wasn't at all good at that. He's lying in a hospital bed with three bullet holes in him.

His daughter is dead. And he and his wife are charged with murder because she was shot while involved in the assassination attempt and that makes them liable."

"Who shot the daughter?"

"Did you know Fräulein Elfriede, Luther? Good-looking nineteen-year-old blonde?"

"Who shot her?"

"So you did know her?"

"Stauffer, Luther. **Sturmführer**, 4848329."

"Interview interrupted at 1435 hours by Supervisory Agent Cronley. Did you get it all, Zieliński?"

"Yes, sir."

"I shot Elfriede, Luther," Cronley said. "In the forehead." He pointed with his index finger.

"You sonofabitch!"

"When I get back to Nuremberg, I'm going to tell the Kuhns that you confessed all, including where I can find von Dietelburg, and as a result have been turned over to the people that deal with unimportant Nazis, instead of being hung as a war criminal. I'm going to offer them the same deal, as I feel bad about taking their only child from them. Give me von Dietelburg or spend the rest of your life in jail.

"And, last chance, Cousin Luther, I'm offering you the same deal. 'Give me von Dietelburg or go to the gallows.'"

"Stauffer, Luther. **Sturmführer**, 4848329."

"Wrap him up, Cezar. Give him five minutes to say goodbye to his wife, and then put him in the truck. With a bag over his head."

[FOUR]
The Prison
The International Tribunal
  Compound
Nuremberg, American Zone of
  Occupation, Germany
2305 25 February 1946

When Second Lieutenant Paul J. Dowsey, a member of the class of 1945 at West Point, had four days before being transferred to the 26th Infantry, 1st Division, from the 18th Infantry of the division, where he had been a platoon leader in Baker Compound, 1st Battalion, Colonel James T. Rasberry, who commanded the 26th Infantry Regiment, had given him a surprisingly cordial and informal welcome.

"Pull up a chair, Dowsey, and have a cup of coffee while I give you the skinny on what we do here."

He had begun by telling Dowsey that "Jack Mulaney"—by which he meant Colonel Jackson Mulaney III, commanding officer of the

18th—had selected him for transfer because, of the five second lieutenants taken out of the Infantry Basic Officer Course at Benning before graduation because of a severe officer shortage and flown to Germany and assigned to the 18th, he was "the only one who seemed to be able to find his gluteus maximus with either hand and without supervision."

"While I'm sure the Officer Basic Course is nice to have, I've always felt that it was sort of a waste of time for people like you and me, who had already been taught at Hudson High which end of a Garand the bullet comes out of.

"There are a large number of really despicable people in our prison, the most notorious of whom are Hermann Göring and Ernst Kaltenbrunner, whom we have been charged with keeping fed, locked up, and alive until the trials are over and we can hang them.

"You will be one of a dozen company-grade officers who serve as assistant wardens. You will be the junior of them, the others having been in the Army about a year longer than you have. You will have the privilege of commanding a fine group of enlisted men, seventy percent of whom are yet to celebrate their nineteenth birthday and fifty percent of whom have yet to learn how to drive.

"But thirty percent of your troops are fine noncommissioned officers. I'm sure you remember being told on the Plain that sergeants are the backbone of the Army, and that a wise second lieutenant is he who keeps his mouth shut and his ears open when around a good sergeant.

"Welcome interview over. Sergeant Major Kinsey, one of the latter, will now turn you over to First Lieutenant Paul Anderson, the senior assistant warden, who will not only clue you in further but almost certainly quickly remind you that Norwich graduates are commissioned into the Regular Army with the same date of rank as those who graduate from West Point. You are dismissed, Lieutenant Dowsey."

Dowsey jumped to his feet, popped to attention, and raised his hand to his temple.

"Permission to withdraw, sir?"

"Welcome interviews like this traditionally end with the commanding officer saying, 'My door is always open.' This interview differs from the traditional in that I mean it about my door always being open."

Lieutenant Paul J. Dowsey watched as the ex–U.S. Army ambulance with its red crosses painted over and bearing French Army markings pulled up to the door of the prison.

"Here it comes," he announced unnecessarily to the soldiers with him, a technical sergeant, a sergeant, a corporal, and two PFCs.

"I can see it, Lieutenant," Technical Sergeant Woodrow Thomas said, which reminded Dowsey what Colonel Rasberry had said about how second lieutenants should behave in the company of Regular Army sergeants.

And Sergeant Thomas was a splendid example of that breed. A Combat Infantry Badge was pinned to his Ike jacket breast. Below it were colored ribbons representing the Silver Star, the Bronze Star, and the Purple Heart. The latter two had insignia representing the second award of both medals.

He had seen the sergeant in Colonel Rasberry's outer office awaiting with three other teenaged soldiers to be welcomed to the 26th. His youthful face did not fit with the sergeant's chevrons, and Dowsey decided he had to be older than he looked.

The next time he had seen him was when Sergeant Rasberry had introduced him.

"Lieutenant, this is Sergeant Wagner. The colonel assigned him as our interpreter. He speaks fluent Kraut."

"You're German, Sergeant?"

"Pennsylvania Dutch, sir."

"Put those Thompsons at Port Arms, for Christ's sake!" Tech Sergeant Thomas snapped. The two PFCs obeyed the order.

A jeep and then a Ford staff car rolled up beside the ambulance.

Lieutenant Anderson got out of the jeep and an enormous, very black captain got out of the staff car.

"Good evening, sir," Anderson said. "How may I be of assistance to the captain?"

Dowsey thought, **That sounded sarcastic, almost impertinent**.

"Try signing for the prisoner, Andy," the captain said. "You're in charge, I'm just observing."

A French **capitaine** and a French sergeant got out of the ambulance. The **capitaine** walked up to the black captain, saluted, and handed him a clipboard.

"After we're sure the prisoner is alive, Lieutenant Anderson will sign the receipt," the black captain said. "I am presuming, Anderson, that you arranged for a doctor?"

"I did."

"Your response should have been 'I did, **sir**.' Think 'role reversal.' Say, 'Yes, sir.'"

"Yes, sir."

"Close your mouth, Lieutenant," Captain Dunwiddie said to Dowsey, "or you'll catch flies and look like Lieutenant Anderson."

"Yes, sir," Dowsey said.

The **capitaine** gestured for his sergeant to open the rear doors of the former ambulance.

When they had been opened, Dowsey saw the ambulance held three men, two French soldiers, and a third man in shackles with a black bag over his head.

"Get him out of there," the black captain ordered. "Leave the bag over his head."

The prisoner was, with some difficulty, extracted from the ambulance.

"Anybody speak German?"

"I do, sir," Sergeant Wagner said.

"Ask him if he's all right."

"I demand to know where I am," Luther Stauffer said in English.

"Herr Sturmführer, you're not allowed to ask questions," Dunwiddie said.

"I demand to know where I am," Stauffer repeated.

"Duly noted," Dunwiddie said. "Anderson, you told me you had arranged for a doctor."

"I don't know where the hell he is," Anderson said.

"Well, while we're waiting, and if you're satisfied that the prisoner is alive, why don't you sign the receipt for him?"

"Yes, sir."

"A question, Lieutenant Anderson," Dunwiddie said. "After you've signed for him, do you want everybody to stand around here waiting for the doctor, or are you going to take the **Sturmführer** to the examination room and get him out of his clothing?"

Another jeep rolled up and a pudgy captain with the Medical Corps caduceus on his lapels got out.

"Who's in charge?" he demanded.

Dunwiddie and Anderson pointed to each other.

"I'm just a spectator, Doctor," Dunwiddie said. "The **Sturmführer** with the bag over his head is the man you're to examine. Lieutenant Anderson will show you where."

"I know where the examination room is," the doctor said.

"And while you're doing that, I would like a word with the interpreter. What did you say your name was, Sergeant?"

"Wagner, sir."

"I take it, Captain, sir, you're not going to observe the body search?" Anderson asked.

"I don't like looking at Nazis when they're fully dressed. Seeing one naked with his rear end exposed for the doctor's examination would be just too much for my delicate stomach."

When the guards had Stauffer shuffling toward the prison entrance, Dunwiddie went to the French officers.

"The officers' mess is two streets down and one over. They expect you, and they'll feed you and get you a place to sleep. And when you get back to Strasbourg, please give my respects to Commandant Fortin and say, **Merci mille fois**."

* * *

"So how'd you get to be the interpreter?" Dunwiddie asked when the French ambulance had driven off.

"Colonel Rasberry said it would give me a chance to move around."

"He knew what you're doing here?"

"I guess Colonel Cohen did. Or maybe Mr. Cronley."

"How's it going?"

"I just got here."

"Did you hear what happened to Cronley and Winters?"

"Mr. Cronley had to shoot some fräulein in the eye."

"In the forehead. And he didn't have to. It just happened. He shot at the windshield and she was on the other side. It bothers him. Which leaves me worried about both of you."

"I'm all right."

"Casey, these people kill people. Including nice young Pennsylvania Dutchmen. That makes me worry. Ostrowski is also worried."

"I'll be all right."

"Since Cronley would pass it down to me, I'd have to write the letter to your mother saying you were no longer with us. Don't make me have to do that, Casey."

"I will try very hard to stay alive," Casey replied. "What's with you and Lieutenant Anderson? I expected you to stand him tall, the crap he gave you just now."

"I know you know about Norwich, so I will tell you."

"How do you know I know about Norwich?"

"Because General White told me he had explained its virtues to you. And that, when General Harmon is allowed to retire and become president of Norwich, he will arrange a scholarship for you. When that happens, you will be honorably discharged from the Army for the purpose of enrolling at Norwich. And General White has charged me with encouraging you to do so. That means I have to keep you alive or face the wrath of General White, something I don't like to consider."

"That doesn't answer what's with you and Lieutenant Anderson."

"Freshman students at Norwich are called 'rooks,' as West Point freshmen are called 'plebes.' Rooks are introduced into such subjects as close order drill by upperclassmen, with the hazing part of that instruction left to sophomores.

"Lieutenant Anderson was a year ahead of me at Norwich. He pushed me over the edge, primarily, I believe, because he doesn't like people with my complexion, and so one day I beat the crap out of him. He, of course, turned me in.

Other upperclassmen came to my aid, and the result was that I wasn't expelled, and he was told to leave me alone. Which he did.

"After I resigned, I have been reliably informed, he expressed pleasure that, quote, the nigger is finally out of here and will be an enlisted man the rest of his life, end quote. Or words to that effect.

"And then we both wind up in Nuremberg. Me with railroad tracks, and him with a brand-new first john's single bar. That was very hard for him to take. What I suspect the sonofabitch was up to just now was to have me deck him again. Rooks can beat up second classmen in some circumstances. Captains cannot assault junior officers under any circumstance. Get the picture?"

"Yes, sir. I get it."

"What I just told you goes no further. Understood?"

"Yes, sir."

"Not even to Cronley."

"Yes, sir. And to change the subject, what happens next?"

"We give Stauffer and the Kuhns a couple of days to think things over. Then we offer them a deal, give us von Dietelburg or spend the rest of your life in jail. If that doesn't work, we'll just have to keep trying."

Casey nodded his understanding.

"You better go in there and watch the doctor stick his finger up Cousin Luther's anal orifice."

"Yes, sir."

Dunwiddie punched Casey affectionately on the arm.

Twenty minutes later, Sturmführer Stauffer was led, naked and shackled, into a cell in the upper tier of the prison.

The shackles were removed, and the guards handed him prison-issue shirt and trousers and a small carton containing soap, a toothbrush, Colgate toothpaste, two towels, and a roll of toilet paper.

He asked for a razor and Casey Wagner told him, in German, that he would be permitted, under supervision, the use of a safety razor every other day.

Then Wagner and the guards left him alone in the cell.

XII

[ONE]
The Dining Room
Farber Palast
Stein, near Nuremberg
American Zone of Occupation,
  Germany
0815 26 February 1946

Lieutenant Tom Winters and his wife and their baby walked into the dining room, followed by a bodyguard holding a Thompson submachine gun at his side.

Winters looked around until he found what he was looking for, then nudged his wife, indicating the table at which Cronley, Ostrowski, and Dunwiddie were sitting with Janice Johansen. They walked to it.

The men at the table rose.

"Mrs. Winters," Cronley said. "What a pleasant surprise."

"Tom drove us down yesterday," Barbara Winters said.

"If Captain Dunwiddie knew about that, he apparently didn't think I would be interested."

"May we join you?" Barbara asked.

"Certainly. Have you had breakfast?"

"I want to thank you for saving Tom's life, Jim."

"You heard about that, huh?"

"Tom told me all about it."

"Well, we men of A&M feel a deep moral obligation to take care of West Pointers."

"I'm Janice Johansen," Janice said. "Since Super Spook is not good at making introductions."

"Sorry," Cronley said. "Miss Johansen, this is Mrs. Winters. And this, Barbara, is Max Ostrowski."

"Charmed," Ostrowski said.

"He only sounds like an Englishman, he's actually a Pole."

"Tom brought me up to speed on who's who on the way down here," Barbara Winters said.

A waiter appeared and took their order.

"Feed him, too," Cronley ordered, pointing at the table at which the Winterses' bodyguard had taken a seat beside Cronley's bodyguard.

"Did we interrupt a private conversation?" Barbara asked.

"Actually, I just charged Max with an important task," Cronley said. "Finding someone in the indigent population who can fix the bullet holes in my Horch and get the blood and brain tissue off the upholstery."

"Clever fellow female that I am, Mrs. Winters, I detect some tension between Super Spook and you," Janice said. "What the hell's going on?"

"Captain Cronley, Miss Johansen, told me I was a selfish bitch and a lousy Army wife," Barbara said.

"I can see where that might cause a little tension," Janice said.

"He did what?" Dunwiddie asked incredulously.

"And when I thought it over, I realized he was right. So I want to thank you for that, too, Jim."

"Thank him for what?" Dunwiddie asked.

"Why don't we change the subject to something pleasant?" Cronley said.

"Like what? The blood and brains on your upholstery?" Janice asked.

"I have some good news," Dunwiddie said.

"Out with it," Janice said. "Quick!"

"Yesterday afternoon, when I was talking with Colonel Rasberry about Casey, I dropped into the conversation that Tom and Barbara needed quarters . . ."

"You're staying in Nuremberg?" Cronley asked.

"That's where my husband is stationed," Barbara answered. "Where else would I want to be?"

Dunwiddie continued: ". . . and he said he

would explain the special circumstances to the post commander."

"What special circumstances?" Janice asked.

Dunwiddie nodded to the two bodyguards.

"Oh," Janice said. "Those special circumstances."

The waiter appeared with a fresh pot of coffee.

"If you'd like, Mrs. Winters, I'll hold that while you're drinking your coffee," Janice said.

"It's a him, not a that, Miss Johansen," Barbara said. "He even has a name."

She handed Thomas H. Winters IV to Janice.

"Good-looking kid," Janice said. "Beautiful. You're sure Tom is the father?"

"Jesus Christ, Janice!" Tom exclaimed.

"I'm sure, Miss Johansen," Barbara said.

"In that case, I think you qualify to be a member of Super Spook's Merry Band of Outlaws. And I think you should start calling me Janice, and I will call you Barbara."

"Thank you, Janice," Barbara said.

"Yeah, welcome, welcome, Barbara, we're glad to have you," Cronley said.

"Thank you, Jim," she said, her voice on the cusp of breaking.

"And now, if you will excuse me," Cronley said, "my bodyguard and I have to get on the SIGABA."

[TWO]
The Mansion
Offenbach Platz 101
Nuremberg, American Zone of
  Occupation, Germany
0855 26 February 1946

"Buenos Aires, Fulda. Captain Cronley for Colonel Frade. Require secure line."

"Buenos Aires understands Captain Cronley for Colonel Frade on a secure line," a heavily Spanish-accented voice replied.

"Affirmative, Buenos Aires."

"Hold One, Fulda."

Holding One took about two minutes.

"Fulda, Colonel Frade is on. The line is secure."

"This better be important. I dislike rising with the roosters to answer the phone."

"It is."

"I understand people have been shooting at you."

"How'd you hear about that?"

"El Jefe thought I should know they missed."

"And they were trying hard. The sonofabitch

had a Schmeisser. My Horch is full of bullet holes."

"What's on your mind, Little Brother?"

"I need to talk to Colonel Niedermeyer. Can you get him on here?"

"No."

"Oh, shit! Why not?"

"He's not here. He's in Munich."

"What's he doing in Munich?"

"I probably shouldn't be telling you this, but General Gehlen found out Gábor Péter's AVO has Niedermeyer's wife in Budapest—"

"Clete, what the hell are you talking about?"

"I thought everybody's now calling you Super Spook. And you don't know what the AVO is?"

"I don't have a fucking clue."

"Okay, from the beginning: Otto Niedermeyer's wife is Hungarian. She was in Budapest when the Russians took over."

"Why wasn't she with Niedermeyer in Argentina?"

"She was looking for her brother. The AVO, which stands for Allamvedelmi Osztaly, which is the Russian-controlled secret police, and which is run by a guy named Gábor Péter, already had him. And knew that Scheiberné Zsigmond, the Hungarian brother, had been Oberstleutnant Sigmund Schneiber when he worked for Abwehr Ost. So they used him to bag Károly Niedermeyer, who we called Carol when she was in

Argentina with Otto. They want to use her to bag Otto and maybe others in Gehlen's organization."

"She left Argentina to look for her brother in Hungary? With the Russians there? That sounds pretty stupid."

"Perhaps. If you weren't such a prick, Jimmy, you might think it was an act of familial love. Like your mother is showing for your cousin Luther. Not too bright but understandable, even commendable. How is your cousin Luther, by the way?"

"Right now he's in a cell here. I'm trying to get him to give me von Dietelburg."

"Who is?"

"The guy I think is running Odessa."

"Before I forget to say this, don't tell Wallace about Niedermeyer's wife. He thinks he's over there to talk to Gehlen."

"Okay. So why is he in the Compound?"

"Gehlen's staging an operation to get Frau Niedermeyer and her brother out. He wants to be in on it. I don't think Wallace would approve."

"What about El Jefe? Does he know?"

"I didn't tell him, but I'm sure he does."

"There are those who might think that makes you a loose cannon."

"I bear that description proudly, Little Brother, when I think I'm doing the right thing. Niedermeyer told me about what goes on at 60 Andrassy Place in Budapest."

"What's that?"

"AVO headquarters. When they execute people in the basement, they stand them on a little stool, put a noose around their necks, and then kick the stool away, so that they can watch them strangle to death. According to Niedermeyer, even the Russians don't do that. The NKGB standard execution procedure, according to Sergei Likharev, is to take people into the basement of that building on Lubyanka Square in Moscow, stand them over a drain in the floor, and then shoot them in the neck. You can understand why Niedermeyer wants to get his wife out, and why Gehlen is trying hard to help him. I don't think Wallace would."

"Either do I."

"So tell me how you're doing trying to take Odessa down. Any luck?"

"Not much. I told you I have Cousin Luther in a cell in the Tribunal Compound. I hope he thinks we're going to hang him unless he gives me von Dietelburg, and we're going to offer the guy I took down when he came after me with the Schmeisser the option of giving me von Dietelburg or spending the rest of his life in a German jail."

"How'd you get Cousin Luther into the Tribunal jail?"

"Colonel Cohen, who runs the CIC at the Tribunal, arranged it."

"He's the guy who dubbed you 'Super Spook'? El Jefe likes him. What's his interest? Just being a nice guy?"

"No, Clete. The Germans, the Nazis, were—Himmler was—trying to start a new religion."

"A new religion?"

"And Cohen thinks that when we hang Göring and the others, the Germans will think they're martyrs, not criminals, hung by the Jews just because we won the war."

"A new religion? Sounds like bullshit to me."

"It's not. They even have a Saint Heinrich Himmler Cathedral. Castle Wewelsburg. Cohen showed it to me. Cousin Luther was even married there in a New Nazi Religion ceremony."

"Tell me all about it."

"As much as I would love to, I don't have time. I'm off to the Compound."

"Goddammit, Jimmy, tell me about it."

"You've got four of Gehlen's guys there. Okay, three with Niedermeyer here. I'll bet at least one of them—probably all three—knows all about Castle Wewelsburg. I know Gehlen does, and that he agrees with Cohen."

"I never heard anything about this Nazi religion from them. Why not?"

"Probably because they didn't think you'd believe it. Unless I'd seen Castle Wewelsburg myself, I wouldn't believe it. Ask them to tell you all about it."

"I'm asking you."

"Nice to hear your voice, Clete. Tell von Wachtstein I said 'Howdy.' Break it down, Fulda."

[THREE]
The South German Industrial
Development Organization
Compound
Pullach, Bavaria
American Zone of Occupation,
Germany
1255 26 February 1946

There was a BITTE NICHT BELÄSTIGEN!! sign on the closed door of the Senior Officers' Mess in Kaserne Two.

Cronley said, "Shit!" under his breath and then opened the door.

General Reinhard Gehlen, former colonels Ludwig Mannberg and Otto Niedermeyer, former major Konrad Bischoff, Colonel Harold Wallace, and Major Anthony Henderson were sitting at a table about to begin their lunch.

"What's that expression?" Mannberg asked. " 'Speak of the devil'?"

"You're just in time for lunch," Gehlen said.

"I thought you knew enough German to know that **bitte nicht belästigen** means 'Please don't disturb,' " Wallace said.

"Major," Cronley said, ignoring Wallace, "if I'd known you were coming here, you could have flown up with me."

"I had the staff car," Henderson said. "I don't think that would fit in your airplane."

"Henderson and I were briefing General Gehlen on the assassination attempt. Trying to make sense out of it," Wallace said.

"Sit down and have some lunch," Gehlen said. "Or have you eaten?"

"Thank you," Cronley said, and sat down next to Niedermeyer.

A waiter almost immediately set his lunch before him.

"Cletus told me you were here," Cronley said to Niedermeyer. "Good to see you, Colonel."

"And you, James."

They shook hands.

"Why do you think they tried to kill you?" Wallace asked. "And who do you think they are?"

"I think Odessa thinks I'm getting too close to Brigadeführer Franz von Dietelburg," Cronley replied. "That's why I'm here. I thought that Otto might be able to tell me something about him, or one of the other Argentine Germans could. When I called Colonel Frade, he told me Otto was here. So here I am."

"If it's the same man—Himmler's adjutant—I knew him years ago in Vienna," Niedermeyer said. "He's Austrian. Viennese. Many SS officers were. But I haven't seen him since . . . since he went to Berlin to be Himmler's adjutant. That was in 1939 or 1940. What I primarily remember about him is that he had an eye for the ladies. He set up a Vienna Opera ballet dancer, a spectacular beauty, in a villa on the Cobenzlgasse."

"You remember her name? What's the Cobenzlgasse?"

"No, I remember her, but not her name. I remember the villa, on Cobenzlgasse, but not the number. It's a street in Grinzing, a Vienna suburb, lined with villas and leading up to the Cobenzl, the top of the hill, from which, legend has it, Ernst Rüdiger von Starhemberg directed the Battle of Vienna in 1683. That victory kept the Muslims from taking Vienna, and is generally regarded as the start of the end for the Ottoman Empire in Europe."

"And the beginning of the Viennese coffeehouse, Otto," Gehlen said. "Don't forget that."

"How could I, Herr General? James, when the Turks retreated, they left behind bags of brown beans . . . tons of them. Somebody said he had heard that the Turks first roasted and then ground up the beans and finally boiled them in water, which produced an aphrodisiac drink. And much as the Spanish brought the tomato from the New World to Europe—it was originally called 'the Passion Fruit'—as an aphrodisiac, coffee became an instant success. There's a coffeehouse—or the ruins of one—on every block in Vienna."

Everyone except Colonel Wallace chuckled and smiled.

"Can we get back to the significance of Odessa trying to kill two DCI officers?" he asked.

"I think we've heard enough from both James and Major Henderson to answer that, Colonel," Gehlen said. "Odessa wants him eliminated because he's getting too close to them, to Brigadeführer Franz von Dietelburg."

"How close are you, Cronley?" Wallace asked.

"Not close enough. General, would you ask all of your people where I can at least start looking for von Dietelburg?"

"I've already asked. We're as much in the dark as you are. I was—Admiral Canaris, me, Mannberg, all of Abwehr Ost, was—under SS suspicion after the bomb attempt on Hitler's life. And I suspect Odessa wasn't set up until after that operation failed. The SS was able to keep everything about Odessa to themselves."

"Well, I tried. So I will get back to Nuremberg."

"And protect Justice Jackson, which is why I sent you there," Wallace said.

Just in time, Cronley shut off his automatic mouth before he said, **Oscar Schultz sent me to Nuremberg, not you**. Instead he said, "And I have to get out of here right now. Colonel Niedermeyer, can I have a minute in private? I need you to tell Frade something when you get back to Argentina."

"Why don't you send him a message on the SIGABA?" Wallace asked.

Cronley ignored him, stood up, nodded at everybody, and walked out of the dining room. Niedermeyer followed him. They walked to an empty corner of the main dining room.

"Otto, Cletus told me about your wife. If there's anything I can do . . . ?"

"Prayer might help, Jim. But thank you. I find myself again turning to General Gehlen, and reminding myself how competent he is in solving problems like mine."

"Still, there might be something I can do for you."

"I can't think of a thing, but again, thank you. And now that I think about it, there is something I can do for you. I'm going to Vienna. When I'm there, I'll ask around and see if I can come up with the name of von Dietelburg's ballerina. And at the very least, I'll take a ride up to the Cobenzl and get you the address of that villa."

"Where are you going to stay in Vienna?"

"Cletus got me DCI credentials, and told me they'll get me into the Hotel Bristol. You know it?"

"When are you going?"

"Tomorrow, or the day after."

"I'll see you at the Bristol, Otto. You can show me where von Dietelburg stashed his girl-friend."

[FOUR]
The Mansion
Offenbach Platz 101
Nuremberg, American Zone of
Occupation, Germany
2230 26 February 1946

A soldier was walking slowly down Lorenzer Strasse, approaching the medieval twin-towered Saint Lorenz Church, when a Ford staff car turned onto the street and drove up to him. It stopped. The soldier went quickly to the car and jumped into the backseat. The staff car drove quickly away.

"**Wie geht's**, Casey?" Cronley inquired from the front seat. "If I didn't know what a God-fearing Christian you are, I would suspect you were looking for a little Hershey bar romance."

"Not funny," Max Ostrowski, who was driving, said.

"No offense, Casey," Cronley said. "Just a little joke."

"None taken, sir," Sergeant Wagner said.

"Just in case the bad guys are watching, Casey . . ."

"They are," Ostrowski said.

". . . lie down on the seat. We're almost there, and we don't want them to see you," Cronley finished.

"Yes, sir."

The car stopped before the gate at Offenbach Platz 101. Ostrowski blew the horn three times. The solid twelve-foot-high gate rolled out of the way, and then, when the car had passed, rolled back in place.

"Okay, we're home," Cronley said. "Let's go inside."

"Sir, should I bring the Thompsons?" Casey asked.

"That's probably a good idea," Ostrowski said drily. "One never knows when one will have need of a Thompson."

Dunwiddie and Augie Ziegler were waiting for them in the library of the Mansion, which quickly had been changed into a bar. Both shook Wagner's hand, and Dunwiddie affectionately patted his shoulder.

"Now that you've got him here, how are you going to get him back to the Tribunal Compound?" Ziegler asked.

"Dunwiddie and you are going to take the younger Pennsylvania Dutchman to the **Bahnhof**—take him a couple of blocks from the **Bahnhof**—and discreetly drop him off. He will then walk to the **Bahnhof** and take the Army bus to the Compound," Cronley ordered. **"Verstehen Sie?"**

"Jawohl, Herr Captain."

"We don't have much time," Ostrowski said. "So let's get to it."

"Casey, we need to know what's going on in the prison, how it's done and by who," Ziegler said. "Start anywhere you want to."

"Lieutenant Anderson knows," Casey began, "and has made the sergeants understand that the guards are teenagers who don't have a clue how important what they're doing is.

"One of them, for example, was caught smuggling in a camera so that he could get a picture of him with Hermann Göring. I was with Lieutenant Anderson when Sergeant Jenkins dragged him in. He asked him—Lieutenant Anderson did—why he wanted a picture of him and Göring. He said he did it because Göring was famous and he wanted the picture to send to his mother. Lieutenant Anderson asked him if he knew why Göring is famous, and he didn't have a clue."

"What's going to happen to him?" Ziegler said. "Court-martial? Company punishment?"

"Company punishment. Busted to PFC and thirty days' restriction to the barracks. Plus 'Jenkins punishment,'" Casey said, chuckling.

"And what is that?" Cronley asked

"He has to shine the boots of everybody in his squad as long as he's on restriction."

"That's clever," Cronley said. "And this guy Anderson, who has to know about that, also knows enough to look the other way. Where'd he come from?"

Wagner looked at Dunwiddie.

"Norwich," Dunwiddie said.

"Now I'm sorry I asked," Cronley said. "You knew him there?"

"Yes."

"Casey, how did they catch this guy smuggling a camera in?" Ziegler asked.

"To keep people from smuggling things, all the pockets on our uniforms are sewed up, except one shirt pocket. That's for a handkerchief."

"That's clever. Who thought that up?" Ostrowski asked.

"It was Sergeant Jenkins's idea. He took it to

Lieutenant Anderson, who took it to Colonel Rasberry, who got the quartermaster to issue the guards two more sets of ODs. With sewn-up pockets."

"I hate to say this," Cronley said, "but for a Norwich graduate, Lieutenant Anderson seems very competent. He probably can even read and write."

Dunwiddie gave Cronley the finger.

"Go on, Casey," Ostrowski said.

"So when we go on duty, or come off, the sergeants pat us down. The only way to smuggle anything in or out would be to put it in your jockey shorts. Then you would move whatever's in there between your legs. The sergeants usually don't pat you down around your private parts."

"So they could smuggle practically anything small enough to hide under their balls in and out. Very interesting," Cronley said. "You went to Norwich with Anderson, Captain Dunwiddie. Tell him to tell his sergeants to start checking their men under their balls."

"I'll do that, Captain, sir," Dunwiddie said.

"What else have you learned about your fellow guards, Casey?" Ostrowski asked. "Including the sergeants."

"About half the sergeants are married. Off-duty, I guess they go to their quarters. The unmarried non-coms mostly do their drinking at the 26th NCO Club. And the corporals and PFCs go to the 26th EM Club."

"What about fräuleins?"

"Just about all of the unmarried sergeants have one," Casey replied. "And maybe half of the others."

"They have rooms someplace?"

"Yeah."

"And how do they pay for the rooms?"

"With their PX rations and packages from home."

"Containing coffee and cigarettes, et cetera?"

"What I hear is that the APO guys—or the CID, whoever is checking packages for black market stuff—don't check small packages very much. They're looking for twenty pounds of coffee, twenty cartons of cigarettes, not a couple of pounds of coffee or a couple of cartons of Lucky Strikes."

"Did you see Janice Johansen's story in **Stars and Stripes**?" Dunwiddie asked. "They caught a full bird chaplain in Heidelberg getting regular shipments of Bibles and other religious materials that turned out to be coffee and silk stockings."

"I saw it," Casey said. "That was pretty despicable for a man of God."

"Well, look at the bright side," Cronley said. "After his general court-martial, he can save souls in Leavenworth."

"Some fräuleins will spread their legs for a couple of Hershey bars," Ostrowski said. "Others command a higher price for their services. Do you know if any of the sergeants or the others have higher-priced girlfriends?"

"I've only been there a couple of days, Mr. Ostrowski. I've been looking for things like that, but so far . . ."

"Casey, you are a bona fide spook now. Marching in the footsteps of our leader, Super Spook. You can call me Max."

"Yes, sir."

"Super Spook Junior, you're doing a great job," Cronley said. "Keep it up, and for Christ's sake, watch your back. We're dealing—you're dealing—with some nasty sonsofbitches."

"Yes, sir."

"And on that cheerful note, let's get you to the **Bahnhof**. Unless somebody has something else?"

No one did.

[FIVE]
The Prison
The International Tribunal
  Compound
Nuremberg, American Zone of
  Occupation, Germany
0750 27 February 1946

Luther Stauffer was sitting on his bed when Cronley walked into his cell.

"**Wie geht's**, Cousin Luther? Looking forward to another day of staring at the walls?"

"**Leck mich am Arsch!**"

"'Kiss my ass' is language unbefitting a **Sturmführer**. Shame on you. What would Brigadeführer von Dietelburg think?"

Stauffer didn't reply.

"How's the food? Did the powdered egg omelet you had for breakfast make you homesick for Strasbourger cuisine?"

"**Geh zur Hölle!**"

"Unless I reform my sinful ways, going to hell is a distinct possibility for me. You going there isn't a possibility, it's a sure thing. As is your spending the next fifteen to twenty years staring at the walls of your cell."

Stauffer just looked at him.

"Luther, Hitler is dead. The oath you took to him no longer has any meaning. Himmler is also dead. He took the coward's way out. He chose to bite on a cyanide capsule."

"Better to die at one's own hand, Cousin James, than to let the Jews and their lackeys hang you. Lackeys like you."

"I don't think he was worried about being hung. Everybody dies. I almost died a couple of days ago. It was close. Elfriede and her father almost killed me. But they didn't. Elfriede's dead. Her father and mother are still alive, and while they stare at the walls of their prison cells for the next twenty years or so, they'll have plenty of time to wonder if sacrificing their only daughter on the altar of Himmler's phony religion was worth it.

"Your idol, Luther, Reichsführer SS Himmler, didn't bite that capsule because he was afraid of being hung. What he was afraid of was being locked in a cage for the next twenty years while people laughed at him. He was far more afraid of public humiliation than dying."

"The German people will never humiliate Reichsführer-SS Himmler. He is the keeper of the faith."

"That's what the German people thought before we showed them what the Reichsführer-SS did at Buchenwald and Dachau and Treblinka and Sachsenhausen, **und so weiter**. And of course show **dem guten katholischen Volk** of Bavaria, and **dem guten evangelischen Volk** of Hesse what Saint Heinrich was up to at Castle Wewelsburg. Both **das evangelisch Volk** and **das katholische Volk** regard that sort of nonsense as heresy. And if you practice, or even tolerate, heresy, both believe that gets them a one-way ticket to hell."

"The German people will recognize it for what it is, Jewish propaganda."

"But it's not Jewish propaganda, Luther, and you know that. And so did all **das gute Volk** of the towns near the concentration camps who we forced to pick up the corpses, the thousands of decaying corpses, the SS didn't have time to bury or burn before they fled to save their necks. Those Germans, those good Nazis, had to face the fact that the day before the Americans and English and Russians had arrived, the SS-Totenkopfverbände had been running the camps. Even we efficient Americans hadn't had the time to round up thousands of people, move them to the camps, and then murder them. Then who else?

"Come on, Luther, use your head. You did your duty to the end. But the end is here. The Thousand-Year Reich lasted . . . what? Eleven, twelve years. You're going to spend more time than that staring at the walls of your cell unless you give me von Dietelburg."

"Stauffer, Luther. **Sturmführer**, 4848329."

"Oh, come on, Luther!"

"Stauffer, Luther. **Sturmführer**, 4848329."

"Well, I tried."

I really did.

And I failed.

And my reaction to my failure isn't mostly disappointment, or anger, although God knows there's that.

What I'm really feeling most now is sympathy for my cousin Luther, the miserable stupid sonofabitch.

And for me. How the hell am I going to tell my mother that I looked into her nephew's welfare in his cell?

Where I put him, and where he's going to be for the next decade or so.

Cronley walked to the door of the cell and gestured to the eighteen-year-old soldier looking through the window to let him out.

[SIX]
Suite 407
The Hotel Bristol
Kaerntner Ring 1
Vienna, Austria
1930 27 February 1946

When there was a knock at the door, Cronley got off a couch and went to open it.

"Hello, Charley," he said, and then, "Good evening, sir. Thank you for coming. Please come in."

Colonel Carl Wasserman, who commanded the Vienna CIC, and Lieutenant Charles Spurgeon walked into the suite, shaking Cronley's hand as they passed him.

Otto Niedermeyer and Cezar Zieliński rose from the couch. Zieliński was wearing pinks and greens, as was Cronley. Niedermeyer was wearing a superbly tailored double-breasted suit made for him by a tailor on Buenos Aires' Avenida Florida.

"Colonel Carl Wasserman, Lieutenant Charley Spurgeon, these are DCI agents Otto Niedermeyer and Cezar Zieliński."

The men shook hands.

"As you may have guessed from Otto's absolutely gorgeous suit, all DCI agents are not created equal. Otto, formerly **Oberst** of Abwehr Ost, and formerly General Gehlen's man in Argentina, is now working there for Cletus Frade. Cezar, formerly captain of the Free Polish Army, now has the unpleasant duty of being my bodyguard."

"I heard you need one," Wasserman said. "And, to judge from those violin cases, which I don't think hold violins, you are taking appropriate precautions."

"Those are actually violoncello cases," Zieliński said. "Thompsons don't really fit in violin cases. So I bought these on the free market, and now have two really beautiful violoncellos that I have absolutely no idea how to play."

"On the other hand, we didn't terrify the people in the lobby by walking in with Thompsons slung from our shoulders."

Wasserman chuckled and then asked, "What brings you to Vienna?"

"Brigadeführer Franz von Dietelburg," Cronley replied. "And it's probably a wild-goose chase, but I'm desperate. What happened was that Cletus Frade told me Otto was at the Compound doing some business with General Gehlen, so I went to see him, to see if he could help. He told me that he hadn't seen von Dietelburg since before the war, when he left here to become Himmler's adjutant."

"I actually knew von Dietelburg rather well," Niedermeyer said. "Well enough to remember his lady friend, a strikingly beautiful ballerina, and that he had set her up in a villa on the Cobenzl. Unfortunately, I can't remember her name, or the address on Cobenzl. But I thought if I was in Vienna, my memory might be triggered, and knowing how much Jim wants von Dietelburg, I thought it would be worth coming here."

He's lying—we're both lying—to one of the good guys.

Who is also a damned good intelligence officer, and damned good intelligence officers can generally tell when people are lying.

But we certainly can't tell him he's in Vienna trying to help Gehlen get his wife and her brother out of the AVO jail in Budapest. Gehlen has to get Wallace's permission to stage any kind of an operation, and Gehlen knows that Wallace would judge—with justification—that since Otto's wife and her brother contribute zilch to DCI, the risk of DCI getting caught breaking them out of an AVO jail in Budapest was not justified.

So we have no choice but to lie to one of the good guys.

"And have you had any luck with your memory?" Wasserman asked.

"Not so far. But just now I was thinking of walking over to the Hotel Sacher to see if that triggers anything. I used to spend many hours drinking there with von Dietelburg and his lady friends. Friends, plural. There were many."

"Any names you could come up with might be helpful," Cronley said.

"Unfortunately, Jim, in those days they were called **Schatzi** or **Liebchen**. And won't be in the telephone book."

"Well, at least we can have a Sachertorte," Wasserman said.

"You've apparently been here long enough to know about Sachertorte," Niedermeyer said.

"I had my own version of 'What to do in Vienna.' Written by my mother. 'Eat Sachertorte. Do not drink Slivovitz.' She was raised here. My mother's an Austro-Hungarian."

"So is my wife," Niedermeyer said.

"She's with you in Argentina?"

"My wife has grown very fond of Lomo and Cabernet Sauvignon from Clete's vineyards."

"Let me propose this," Wasserman said. "We walk over to the Sacher—you can leave the fiddle cases here. When you called, I decided to bring some of my guys with me. We'll have a snort of Slivovitz and have a piece of Sachertorte and see if that triggers your memory. Then we'll get something to eat. And tomorrow, say eleven-fifteen, Charley and I will pick you up and take you to lunch. There's a nice restaurant atop the Cobenzl. And as we drive slowly up the Cobenzlgasse, you can spot the villa where von Dietelburg stashed whatsername, his **Schatzi**."

"You're more than kind, Colonel," Niedermeyer said.

XIII

[ONE]
The Hotel Bristol
Kaerntner Ring 1
Vienna, Austria
1120 28 February 1946

As Cronley, Zieliński, and Niedermeyer walked out of the revolving door of the hotel to get in Wasserman's staff car, Cronley saw a well-dressed Viennese matron, a woman pushing sixty, coming toward the hotel. She was wearing an ornate feathered hat, a Persian lamb coat, and was leading a dachshund on a leash.

But Cronley knew she was not really a Viennese matron, but rather an NKGB colonel

known to the Gehlen Organization as Rahil—
Rachel—who had been given the code name
Seven-K.

Seven-K, for $200,000, had smuggled Nata-
lia Likharev and her sons, Sergei and Pavel, out
of their Leningrad apartment to East Germany,
where Cronley and Kurt Schröder had flown
across the border and picked them up in Storchs.

Gehlen had told Cronley Seven-K would, in
her dual role as an agent of Mossad, the Jewish intelligence organization, use the money to
smuggle Zionists out of the Soviet Union and to
Palestine.

Cronley had last seen her when he had been
in Vienna to meet Ivan Serov, who wanted to
swap Colonel Robert Mattingly for Colonel Sergei Likharev and his family.

When they came back from their dinner meeting at the Drei Husaren restaurant, Seven-K had
been sitting, dachshund in lap, having a coffee
in the Bristol lobby.

Although their eyes had met—for no more
than two seconds—Cronley knew she had recognized him. But that had not been the time to
cry, **Well, look who's here!**

And Cronley instantly decided neither was
this.

**If she wants to see me, she'll be taking cof-
fee in the lobby again.**

And maybe I'll have the chance to ask her

**if another $200,000 will get Otto's wife and
her brother out of the AVO prison in Budapest. If DCI won't spring for that, Cletus and
I will.**

Otto Niedermeyer got in the front passenger
seat beside Charley Spurgeon, and Cronley got
in the back with Colonel Wasserman, and Spurgeon started off down Ringstrasse past the ruins
of the Vienna Opera.

"Somebody got to the Ford family," Wasserman said.

"Excuse me?"

"The Fords are going to pay for the rebuilding
of the Opera."

"Really?"

"And they started a fund to rebuild St. Stephen's Cathedral. I guess this city really gets to
people. It's gotten to me."

"It got to my wife," Niedermeyer said, turning in the front seat. "I met Carol here, proposed
to her here, and we got married in St. Stephen's.
We were supposed to go to Venice for the wedding trip, but we never got further than the Im-
perial Hotel, where she had made reservations."

"Pity you couldn't have brought her here with
you," Wasserman said.

"Yeah, it is."

Niedermeyer was still sitting so he could look
into the backseat. Cronley averted his eyes. He
didn't want to look at him.

* * *

"Well, here we are in Grinzing," Spurgeon said. "And there's Cobenzlgasse."

Cronley saw they were in a sort of square. To the left, the streetcar tracks leading from Vienna ended. There was a circular section of track that permitted the streetcars to turn around for return to Vienna.

The square was lined with stores, many of which had hanging signs reading HEURIGER.

"What's a **Heuriger**?" he asked.

"A place where you can get a monumental headache drinking wine made from grapes that last week were hanging from the vine," Niedermeyer said. "It's a sacred Viennese custom."

Spurgeon started driving up the cobblestones of Cobenzlgasse. Almost immediately he saw that the left side of the road was lined with very large houses behind fences. To the right there were snow-covered vineyards.

"Not too slow, Charley," Colonel Wasserman cautioned, "we don't want to appear too curious."

Spurgeon accelerated.

Cronley had just noticed a **Heuriger** on the left side of the road, apparently closed for the winter, when Niedermeyer said, "Olga Reithoffer, her name was Olga Reithoffer. And there it is! Number 71."

"Bingo!" Zieliński said.

"No wonder you had trouble remembering it," Cronley said.

He looked at number 71 Cobenzlgasse and saw that it was a large masonry building behind a fence. He saw that the fence had sheet metal attached to it, which blocked a good view of the lower floor of the building. The closed French doors opening on the building-wide balcony were heavily draped, except for one, which was half open.

"Damn! A privacy fence," Wasserman said. "Which makes me wonder how long it's been up."

They continued up Cobenzlgasse to the top and pulled into the parking lot of a restaurant whose wrought iron grape-bedecked sign identi-fied it as the Restaurant Cobenzl.

"They used to serve a nice **Wiener Schnitzel mit Ei** in here," Niedermeyer said.

"They still do," Wasserman said. "But I hope you brought a lot of money."

"I thought Charley invited us," Cronley said.

"Charley doesn't have any money," Wasser-man said. "He has his own ballerina, and they don't come cheap."

"Colonel," Spurgeon protested, "I don't have my own ballerina. I happened to meet a young lady who was a ballerina and is helping to support herself by helping me improve my German and by showing me around Vienna."

"That's why I said you don't have money," Wasserman said. "That sort of service can't be cheap."

"Charley," Cronley asked, "why do I get the idea this is the first you knew Colonel Wasserman knows about your ballerina slash tour guide?"

Spurgeon didn't answer.

"A word of advice, Charley," Cronley went on. "If things go the way I'm sure you're hoping they will with your 'tour guide,' make sure nobody's making movies of your mattress gymnastics."

"Screw you, Cronley."

"Maybe Cronley is speaking from experience," Wasserman said.

"Under the Fifth Amendment to the Constitution of the United States . . ."

Niedermeyer, Wasserman, and Zieliński laughed.

They were shown to a table by the windows that provided a spectacular view of Vienna.

When the waiter appeared, Wasserman said, "I think **Wiener Schnitzel mit Ei** for everybody, right?"

"Thank God it's winter and I can't be tempted

into a **Heuriger**," Niedermeyer said. "But I think a nip of Slivovitz is in order to celebrate the return of my memory."

"What did you say was the name of von Dietelburg's 'tour guide'?" Wasserman asked.

Cronley saw that he had taken a notebook and pencil from his pocket.

"Olga Reithoffer."

"Spell it, so I can write it down."

Niedermeyer did so.

"Charley," Wasserman ordered, "go fetch that telephone."

He pointed to a socket in the center of the table, and then to a telephone sitting on a sideboard. He saw Cronley's curiosity.

"Plug-in telephones. Very convenient. We would have them in the States if Bell Telephone, for reasons I can't imagine, didn't insist that their telephones be securely wired to the wall."

Spurgeon delivered the telephone. Wasserman plugged it in and dialed a number.

"Write this down," he said, without any preliminaries. A moment later, "Olga Reithoffer. I'll spell . . .

". . . She used to live at 71 Cobenzlgasse in Grinzing. Find out everything you can about her and that address. I'll ask Wangermann to do the same. Which brings us to him. Get on the radio to him and tell him I'd like to buy him

lunch. Right now. I'm at the Restaurant Cobenzl. And prioritize a list of our guys according to the importance of what they're doing. I'm
going to need a bunch of people to handle what
I've got going. Other things are going to have to
wait. Got all that?"

There was a reply, which Wasserman didn't
acknowledge. He simply hung up.

"Wangermann?" Niedermeyer asked.

"Walter Wangermann, the Vienna cops' chief
of intelligence. Good man. The Russians and
the Organisation der Ehemaligen SS-Angehörigen like him about as much as they like Cronley.
About a month ago, one or the other put a bomb
in his Mercedes."

Thirty minutes later, a muscular man in
his late thirties stepped into the room, looked
around carefully, and then made a **Come ahead**
gesture. A stocky, florid-faced man in his fifties,
in a suit that looked two sizes too small for him,
came into the room, followed by another well-
dressed, muscular man in his thirties, this one
holding a Schmeisser along his trouser seam.

The older man walked to the table and sat
down. One of his bodyguards sat at a nearby
table. The one with the Schmeisser pulled a
chair near the door, turned it around, and then
sat down on it.

"Walter, these are my friends Otto Niedermeyer, Cezar Zieliński, and James Cronley," Wasserman said. "And this is my friend Walter Wangermann."

Wangermann offered his hand first to Niedermeyer and then to Cronley, both of whom politely said, **"Wie geht es Ihnen?"**

"I can't decide if you're a Berliner or a Viennese," Wangermann said to Niedermeyer. "The boy is obviously a Strasbourger. He has a worse accent than my sister-in-law. And this one's obviously an Englishman."

"The boy"?
Fuck you!
Why is this guy so rude?

"Actually, I'm a Pole," Zieliński said.

"And I'm a Texan, Herr Wangermann," Cronley said. "My mother is from Strasbourg."

"Well, at least she taught you to speak German. Most Amis can't."

There he goes again!
Is he just naturally a rude sonofabitch?
Or does he have an agenda?

"A bit of each, actually, Herr Wangermann," Niedermeyer said.

"Been traveling, have you? That suit didn't come from either Berlin or here."

And once more!
Is he trying to show us how clever he is?
Or to make the point that he can say any-

thing he wants to us because he knows we want something from him?

"No, it didn't," Niedermeyer said coldly.

And now Otto is getting pissed off!

"And what brings you to Vienna, Captain Strasbourger?"

"I'm looking for former SS-Brigadeführer Franz von Dietelburg."

"A lot of people are looking for that **Hurensohn**. Maybe if your people sent somebody a little older and more experienced looking for him—"

"**Hurensohn**, Jim," Niedermeyer said, "is Viennese patois for 'sonofabitch.'"

"Actually, 'son of a whore' is grammatically correct German." Cronley's mouth ran away with him. "But for all we know, that **jämmerlich Missgeburt**'s mother could be as pure as the driven snow."

"Despicable monster?" Wangermann said. "I agree, but hearing that from you, Captain Strasbourger, is a little surprising."

"Because I'm young? We Americans are quick learners, **Herr Wiener Schnitzel**."

"I like him!" Wangermann exclaimed. "I'm very surprised, but I like him."

"Jim is a very surprising fellow," Wasserman said. "Jim, why don't you show Chief Inspector Wangermann your credentials?"

Wangermann examined them carefully.

"Very impressive," he said. "But what do they mean?"

"They mean when Jim comes to Vienna to see me and asks for something, I am under orders from General Greene to give him everything he asks for. And everything includes calling in all favors you owe to me."

"Carl, you know how much I would love to see von Dietelburg hanging from a noose," Wangermann said. "But I don't have a clue where the bastard is."

"Jim may have found him, Walter," Wasserman said.

"Here? Now that's really surprising. Is that what this is about?"

"That's what this is about."

"We don't have much," Cronley said, "but we're clutching at all straws. This straw is that Otto remembered that when he knew von Dietelburg here he had a girlfriend—"

"You were in the SS with von Dietelburg?" Wangermann interrupted.

"I was a Wehrmacht officer assigned to Abwehr Ost."

"Under Reinhard Gehlen?"

Niedermeyer nodded.

"I knew him. Good man. I was pleased when he didn't show up at Flossenbürg with Admiral Canaris."

"What were you doing at Flossenbürg?"

"The SS decided I wasn't doing enough to round up the Jews they were looking for. Fortunately, they didn't know I was working with Gehlen, so I didn't wind up hanging from the gallows beside Canaris. I was surprised when I got a list from Wasserman of the people you've got in Nuremberg, that Gehlen and his deputy—Mannberg? Yeah, Ludwig Mannberg, another nice guy—weren't on it."

"There's a reason for that," Niedermeyer said. "General Gehlen and Ludwig Mannberg are alive and well, running the Süd-Deutsche Industrielle Entwicklungsorganisation."

"So Abwehr Ost by another name is alive and well? And you still work for it?"

"I used to. General Gehlen sent me to Argentina to work with the OSS. When DCI came along, I was asked to join, and I did."

"Wasserman, you sonofabitch, you never told me anything about this."

"You didn't have what we Americans call 'the Need to Know.'"

"And now I do?"

"Now you do."

"If you expect me to say **Danke schön**, don't hold your breath," Wangermann said, and then turned to Cronley. "Okay, so Niedermeyer knew von Dietelburg had a girlfriend. Pick it up from there."

"Otto couldn't remember her name, but he remembered the villa where von Dietelburg stashed his ballerina. Not the address, just somewhere on Cobenzlgasse."

"So you came here on the strength of that?"

"We're clutching at straws."

"Her name was Olga Reithoffer, and von Dietelburg had her set up at 71 Cobenzlgasse," Niedermeyer said.

"I would call that a straw," Wangermann said.

He raised his hand above his head and snapped his fingers.

The bodyguard at the table jumped to his feet and hurried to Wangermann.

Pointing at the telephone, Wangermann ordered, "Plug this in somewhere else. Then get on it and tell them, one, I want everything we have on 71 Cobenzlgasse and a woman who may still live there named Olga Reithoffer. Two, get Bruno Holzknecht up here ten minutes ago."

The bodyguard nodded acceptance of his orders and reached for the telephone plug.

"Holzknecht is my surveillance man," Wangermann said. "Good man. We were in Flossenbürg together. Lucky for him the SS didn't find out he's a Jew. So am I going to have to do this myself, or are you going to help?"

"Tell me what you want me to do," Wasserman said.

"What pops into my mind is that we pair one of your men—with his radio—with one of mine."

"Done."

"Did you notice if one of those closed-for-the-winter **Heurigen** is anywhere near 71 Cobenzl-gasse?"

"There's one right across the street," Cronley said.

"Very nice," Wangermann said. "And now, while we're waiting for Holzknecht, I think I'll have the lunch Wasserman offered to pay for."

Bruno Holzknecht, a very ordinary-looking man in his late forties, came into the restaurant thirty minutes later.

"Should we find someplace private, Herr Chief Inspector? Or are your companions privy to what's going on?"

"**Wie geht's**, Bruno?" Wasserman said.

"This one I know is particularly untrust-worthy," Holzknecht said, nodding toward Was-serman.

"You can speak freely, Bruno. You ever hear of the DCI?"

"The replacement for the OSS?"

"Say hello to Otto Niedermeyer, Cezar Zieliński, and James Cronley of the DCI."

The men shook hands.

"This one I remember from the bad old days," Holzknecht said. "He was a major about to be an **Oberstleutnant**."

"Your memory is better than mine. I don't remember you."

"You ran around with an SS sonofabitch named von Dietelburg. You had a good-looking Hungarian girl. He had a ballerina."

"I married the Hungarian girl," Niedermeyer said.

"And went on to be an **Oberst** in Abwehr Ost," Wasserman said. "Which, in case you haven't heard, is alive and well as the . . . what's it called, Otto?"

"The Süd-Deutsche Industrielle Entwicklungsorganisation."

"I always wondered how Gehlen managed to keep out of the cells at Nuremberg," Holzknecht said. "So he's working for the Americans? That explains it."

"The reason he's not locked up waiting to be hung," Niedermeyer said, "is that he's not a war criminal. Quite the opposite. He was involved in the bomb plot that failed to take out Hitler. And other failed schemes to get rid of Der Führer. The SS didn't learn that until the war was almost over. If the SS had found him then, he would have been on the Flossenbürg gallows with Admiral Canaris."

"I knew the Russians really wanted him, but I didn't know about the SS," Holzknecht said. "I'm glad to hear it. I always professionally admired, and personally liked, Reinhard Gehlen. The next time you see him, please give him my regards."

"I will."

"Now what's your interest in 71 Cobenzlgasse?" Holzknecht asked.

"We're trying to find von Dietelburg," Wasserman said.

"And you think he might be there?"

"It's unlikely but possible," Cronley said.

"What would that sonofabitch be doing in Grinzing?"

"The Reithoffer woman lives there."

"What's that got to do with anything?"

"She was von Dietelburg's **Schatzi**."

"You're kidding? Olga Reithoffer was von Dietelburg's ballerina?"

"She was," Niedermeyer said.

"How the hell did I miss that?" Holzknecht said.

"You've been looking at her?" Wangermann asked.

"For the past three weeks I've had my people in that closed-for-the-winter **Heuriger** taking pictures of 71 Cobenzlgasse and Fraülein Reithoffer."

"Why?"

"Because of her relationship with Colonel Gus Genetti."

"Who the hell is he?" Cronley asked.

"He's the U.S. Forces Austria troop information officer."

"I don't understand," Cronley said. "She's his **Schatzi**?"

"Maybe more than that. Give me a minute. Von Dietelburg and Odessa having a connection never entered my mind before just now."

"While you're thinking, throw Castle Wewelsburg and Himmler's new religion into the mix," Cronley said. "Von Dietelburg is a high priest in that."

"I already knew that," Holzknecht said. "But I am impressed that you do, Captain Strasbourger. Let me finish my thinking."

That took him just over a minute.

"Okay. Starting with basics. During the war, there was the Axis. Germany, Italy, and Japan. Forget the Nipponese. Here it was Germany—which then included Austria—and Italy. The Italians surrendered during the war. The Allies said Italy was liberated. After Germany surrendered, Austria again became more or less a free country, in which the Allies—Russia, England, France, and the U.S.—stationed troops. But we—Austria—were also declared liberated. I never understood that, but that's the way it is."

"Where are you going with this, Bruno?" Wasserman asked.

"There is also Trieste," Holzknecht went on. "For centuries it was part of the Austro-Hungarian Empire. Then Mussolini grabbed it. At the end of the war, Tito and the Yugoslavs moved in. The Germans refused to surrender to anybody but the Allies because the Yugoslavs habitually shot POWs. So the Allies sent in New Zealanders, to whom the Germans surrendered as promised. The New Zealanders promptly turned over Trieste to Tito and company, who promptly began to shoot anyone they suspected might not be a Communist. This offended the Americans. The British said they didn't want the problem all to themselves, the Americans had to be involved. Result: Trieste is now occupied by the Brits and the Americans. The Americans sent in a reinforced infantry regiment and named it Trieste United States Troops, acronym TRUST."

"Fascinating, but so what?" Wangermann asked.

"I have been asking myself what do Germany, Austria, Italy, and Trieste have in common? Answer: They all have American troops who read the **Stars and Stripes**."

"Which is delivered to them daily on **Stripes'** trucks," Cronley said. "Which are not usually suspected of carrying anything but newspapers."

"Off the top of your head, my new young American friend, or do you know something?"

"We caught Odessa trying to get two SS guys across the Franco–German border in **Stars and Stripes** trucks."

"Several questions, if you don't mind," Holzknecht said. "Was this luck, or did you know Odessa was going to try the smuggle?"

"One of my men figured it out."

"I'm impressed."

"Would you be even more impressed if I told you Sergeant Wagner is seventeen years old?"

"Am I supposed to believe that?"

"That's up to you."

"And who did you and this seventeen-year-old catch Odessa trying to get into France?"

"The bastards who murdered all the slave laborers at Peenemünde, SS-Brigadeführer Ulrich Heimstadter and SS-Standartenführer Oskar Müller."

"Senior and nasty SS. That smells like Odessa."

"There's no question in my mind," Cronley said.

"Can we get back to the business at hand?" Wangermann asked.

"There is a place in the inner city," Holzknecht resumed, "two doors down from the Drei Husaren restaurant, if any of you Amis know where that is."

"They do a very nice **paprikás csirke**," Cronley said.

"You constantly amaze me, young fellow. I'm already starting to believe the incredible yarn about your seventeen-year-old."

"What about this place?" Wangermann asked impatiently.

"The more prominent of Vienna's black marketeers and money-changers go there to gamble away their ill-gotten gains and then console themselves in the arms of high-priced ladies of the evening. Two of the bartenders and one of the croupiers—if that's the proper nomenclature for a vingt-et-un dealer—are kind enough to keep me apprised of things in which I might be interested."

"Or go to jail?" Wasserman chuckled.

"Precisely. One of the things they brought to my attention was that an American Army officer, a colonel, was an habitué at the vingt-et-un tables, that he gambled with U.S. currency rather than script, and that, until he settled on one of the girls and moved in with her . . ."

"At 71 Cobenzlgasse?" Cronley asked.

"Ah, you clever fellow! Until he moved in with Fraülein Reithoffer, he was very generous to whichever young lady consoled him for his losses at the table. With U.S. currency. And that he generously tipped, with a fifty-dollar bill, the chap who looked after his Buick Roadmaster convertible automobile while he was at the tables.

"Naturally, this piqued my curiosity. So I got the numbers on his license plate and the provost marshal ran it and told me the car was owned by a Colonel Gus T. Genetti, of Headquarters U.S. Forces in Austria, which are here in Vienna. I learned further that Colonel Genetti is the troop information officer for USFA."

"What the hell is that?" Cronley asked.

"You don't know? I'm amazed!" Holzknecht said.

"What it sounds like, Jim," Wasserman said, "there's a once-a-week hour-long session for all enlisted men, during which they are told what the troop information officer thinks they should hear about world events. And what the command wants them to do, such as avoid shady ladies, and not get into the black market."

"I also learned, Carl, that his duties involve serving as sort of the commanding officer of the **Stars and Stripes** news bureau in Vienna, which involves making sure the USFA generals appear, frequently and favorably, on the front page, and that the newspaper is delivered on time. He is also charged with supervision of the Blue Danube network radio station, which serves Americans all over Austria, and in Naples and Leghorn, Italy, and Trieste. You apparently thought I wouldn't be interested."

"Bruno, this guy is what we call a 'chair warmer.' When the brass finds themselves with a full colonel who can't find his ass with either hand, they assign them as housing officers, public relations officers, and troop information officers."

"Carl, this colonel is up to something dirty."

"Like what, for example?"

"For a long time, ever since I started looking at him, I knew he was dirty. Since I had no idea what, I put my people in that closed-for-the-winter **Heuriger** across the street from 71 and started them out by having them take pictures of everybody who goes in or out."

"And?"

"We now have more pictures for our files of heavy-duty money guys and black marketeers. Plus two or three of Fraülein Reithoffer's brother Alois, who is a used-car dealer in Braunau am Inn, Upper Austria. I checked him out. He has the usual sterling reputation of used-car dealers, but otherwise he's clean. He buys cars there and sells them here in Vienna."

"So you've got nothing," Wangermann said.

"Until just now, I didn't have. But now . . ."

"What?" Zieliński asked. "Now what?"

Holzknecht didn't reply directly, instead continuing: "We know that Odessa has money. But they have to have been spending it like it's on fire, so most of what they started out with—I'm talking about currency, English pounds, Swiss francs, and U.S. dollars—is probably gone. We also know they have gold. But gold is not the same thing as money. You can't sit down at a vingt-et-un table and lay a gold bar on the table.

"So you have to convert gold to currency. And you don't want to buy reichsmarks, as they're just about useless. So is the Austrian schilling. You want either Swiss francs or U.S. dollars. The Swiss don't want to buy any gold that might come from Nazis. Not that they've got anything against either Nazis or gold, but because—according to Wasserman—they don't want to piss off Uncle Sam."

"There's about two hundred FBI and Secret Service agents in Switzerland looking for Nazi gold and hanky-panky by Swiss bankers," Wasserman said.

"So where could Odessa be swapping their gold for currency?" Holzknecht asked rhetorically. "Three places pop into my mind. Leghorn, Naples, and Trieste. All seaports where the U.S. Army has bases and the port is full of ships of all sizes doing business with places like Saudi Arabia and Persia. The Saudis and the Persians have trunks full of U.S. hundred-dollar bills they got from the Americans in exchange for their oil.

And what have the Persians and Arabs been putting away for a rainy day for centuries? Gold."

"I still don't know where you're going with this," Wasserman said.

"Let me guess," Cronley said. "Odessa is sending gold to one or all of three places on **Stars and Stripes** trucks, and then bringing stacks of dollars back on the return trip."

"And can you guess, my new young Ami friend, who drives to all three places in his Buick automobile on a regular basis? To keep an eye on the radio station, to make sure the **Stars and Stripes** is being delivered daily? And of course to make sure your soldiers are properly indoctrinated?"

"I didn't know Colonel Wasserman has a Buick," Cronley said.

"I think I'll have a chat with Colonel Genetti," Wasserman said. "When he realizes he's looking at ten to twenty years in Leavenworth, I suspect he'll sing like a canary."

"No," Cronley said. "That's the last thing we want to do."

"Why?" Zieliński asked.

"Because I don't give a damn about this slimy colonel. I'm looking for von Dietelburg, and through him, Odessa. And I don't think von Dietelburg or anyone in Odessa is going to take the risk of dealing directly with an American colonel."

"Point taken," Wasserman said.

"I don't think he's personally taking gold to Italy and bringing dollars back. He's just checking to make sure things are going smoothly. And I don't think he knows Odessa is involved. If he even knows what Odessa is. He thinks he's dealing with the clever characters around the blackjack table to make a quick buck. The questions in my mind center around Fraülein Reithoffer. Has she just latched onto an Ami colonel with a Buick and lots of money? Or did she just happen to introduce him to somebody who could make him a lot of money? Or did sleazy characters introduce him to her, so she could keep an eye on him?"

"So how do you suggest we proceed?"

"We've got to move up the food chain," Cronley replied. "First, find out if he's dealing with one of the sleazy characters. If he is, then who is the sleazy character dealing with? Find out who Fraülein Reithoffer sees when he's not around. Eventually, we'll find a connection to von Dietelburg. Or somebody who has a connection with von Dietelburg."

"This will take a lot of manpower," Holzknecht said. "But I think it's worth it. I really would like to get that bastard."

"Whatever you need, Bruno," Wasserman said.

"I'd really like to get someone in the Viktoria Palast," Holzknecht said. "As a player."

"That's the vingt-et-un place?" Cronley asked. Holzknecht nodded.

"Say hello to Cezar Zieliński," Cronley said, and then when he saw he had the attention of the others, went on, "who after he escaped from the displaced persons camp in Würzburg made a lot of money in the Munich black market, and loves both a friendly game of vingt-et-un and the ladies who gather around the table."

"That just might work," Holzknecht said.

"Cezar?" Cronley asked.

"I'd need money. Lots of money. Preferably U.S. dollars."

"Five thousand?" Niedermeyer asked. "Ten?"

"Ten would be better than five."

"I have it back at the Bristol," Niedermeyer said.

Which you brought with you in case you need it to get your wife out of Budapest, Cronley thought. **So what are you going to do if you do need it?**

"Otto, as soon as I can get on the phone," Cronley said, "I'll have some cash sent down from Kloster Grünau. There's probably time to get someone on the Blue Danube."

"Thank you," Niedermeyer said simply.

"You've got that kind of money?" Wasserman asked.

Cronley nodded.

"The DCI finally coughed up what I provided

to pay Seven-K. I'm hiding it under the chapel at Kloster Grünau."

"So we start this operation as soon as possible," Holzknecht said. "Which means who's going to be in charge?"

"You are," Wangermann said, and then corrected himself. "**We** are. With the support of our American friends."

"Agreed, with thanks," Wasserman said.

"The—what did our young friend call him? 'that **jämmerlich Missgeburt**'?—is an Austrian. So it's only fair that we Austrians catch him, and then let the Americans hang him. So here's what I think we should do—"

"What we should do first," Holzknecht interrupted him, "is have a chat with the chap who owns the Heuriger Oscar."

"That's the one across the street from 71?" Wasserman asked.

Holzknecht didn't reply directly, instead saying, "During which I will tell him to tell all his friends that he has decided to renovate Heuriger Oscar and that the renovation will start tomorrow morning. Early tomorrow morning, a small army of renovators will appear . . ."

"Some of whom will be your guys," Cronley said.

". . . who will have with them one of Wasserman's people, each with one of those marvelous U.S. Army radios."

"Done," Wasserman said.

"The radio in Heuriger Oscar will serve Operation Headquarters. There will be radios here in the Restaurant Cobenzl and in a van parked innocuously near the Grinzing streetcar turnaround. Radio Heuriger Oscar will report anyone leaving 71 Cobenzlgasse either on foot or by car or motorcycle, and whether they are going up Cobenzlgasse or toward the trolley turnaround. In either event, persons of interest will be trailed.

"To do that effectively, we will need motorcycles, bicycles, and unmarked cars. I can provide motorcycles and bicycles, but . . ."

"Tell me how many cars you need, and where you want them," Wasserman said.

"Six?"

"Done."

"I think two here, and the rest at the trolley turnaround. Will they have radios?"

"Yes," Wasserman said.

"Good," Holzknecht said. "That should cover everything, unless Oberst Niedermeyer has . . ."

"You seem to have covered everything," Niedermeyer said.

Cronley's mouth went on automatic.

"Except giving a serious pep talk to all concerned," he said.

"About what?" Wasserman asked.

"The moment anybody coming out of 71 Cobenzlgasse even suspects they're being surveilled, the whole operation is blown."

"You have a point, my young friend," Holzknecht said.

Cronley's mouth continued on automatic.

"Lieutenant Spurgeon and I were taught all about surveillance at Camp Holabird, the CIC school. By an officer who forgot to practice what he preached about the surveillor taking care to make sure he's not being surveilled and wound up under a freight train in the Munich Hauptbahnhof."

"Major Derwin," Spurgeon said softly.

"Odessa?" Wasserman asked.

"Either Odessa or the NKGB," Cronley said.

He thought, **But most probably agents of the former Abwehr Ost, now known as the Süd-Deutsche Industrielle Entwicklungsorganisation.**

Maybe—even probably—the same guys who are trying to get Frau Niedermeyer and her brother out of Budapest.

"If we're finished here, I've got to get on the phone," Cronley said.

[TWO]
The Hotel Bristol
Kaerntner Ring 1
Vienna, Austria
1605 28 February 1946

"Charley and I have some things to do," Wasserman said as the staff car pulled up to the hotel. "So why don't we just drop you guys off, and then meet later in the bar? Say at half past seven?"

"Done," Cronley said.

"Are you mocking me, Cronley?"

"Didn't your mother ever tell you, Colonel, sir, that imitation is the most sincere form of flattery?"

Seven-K was sitting with the dachshund puppy in her lap at a table in the lobby. Their eyes met briefly.

On the elevator, Zieliński wondered aloud, "I wonder what she's up to?"

"She may be keeping an eye on us," Niedermeyer said. "But it is equally possible that she's keeping an eye on someone else. And just as possible that the NKGB is keeping an eye on her while she's keeping an eye on us or someone else. Or that she is keeping an eye on an NKGB agent who is keeping an eye on us or someone else."

"Do you ever get the feeling that we live on the other side of **Alice in Wonderland**'s mirror?" Cronley asked.

"Here in Vienna I do," Niedermeyer replied. "Things are much simpler in Argentina."

"You are both warned," Cronley said, as the elevator door opened, "when we get to the room, not to get between me and the bathroom door. My back teeth are floating."

Cronley came out of the bathroom and was just about to lower himself into an armchair near the telephone when the door chimes sounded. When he saw that Zieliński and Niedermeyer were in the kitchenette of the suite, he went to the door and opened it.

Seven-K was standing there, holding the puppy in her arms.

"Let me in quickly," she said, as she pushed past him.

Cronley looked down the corridor to see if anyone was in it, and when he saw no one, closed the door.

"Otto," Seven-K called.

Niedermeyer appeared in the kitchenette door.

"Rahil?"

"As quickly as you can, have General Gehlen call off the operation," she said. "It's too late."

"What do you mean, 'too late'?"

"They knew it was coming. You have a mole, Otto."

"How do you know it's too late?" Niedermeyer asked.

Seven-K handed him a small envelope.

"I'm really sorry, Otto," she said.

She walked to the door.

"Young man," she ordered, "check the corridor."

Cronley did so.

"Clear," he reported.

Seven-K pushed past him and went quickly down it to the stairwell.

Cronley saw that Niedermeyer had taken photographs from the envelope Seven-K had given him.

"Ach, Gott im Himmel," Niedermeyer said, and threw the photographs to the ground.

Zieliński picked them up, looked quickly at them, and then handed them to Cronley.

"Ach, Gott im Himmel," Niedermeyer said again, softly. **"Mein Károly. Mein Schätzchen, mein Liebling!"**

Cronley looked at the photographs. One of them showed a man hanging from some simple indoor gallows. He was obviously dead, but from strangulation, not a broken neck. The second showed a woman hanging from the same gallows, obviously strangled by her noose. The third showed the man and the woman hanging side by side from the gallows.

Cronley looked at Niedermeyer. His head was bent and he was obviously trying and failing to suppress sobbing.

Without thinking about it, Cronley went to him and wrapped his arms around him. After a moment, Zieliński crossed himself and then went to Cronley and Niedermeyer and wrapped his massive arms around both of them.

XIV

[ONE]
Kloster Grünau
Schollbrunn, Bavaria
American Zone of Occupation,
  Germany
0905 1 March 1946

Cronley handed Niedermeyer two neatly wrapped packages of currency. The binders on each read $5,000 over and over in red lettering.

"El Jefe would have repaid me for what I loaned you in Vienna," Niedermeyer said.

"When you see him, tell him DCI owes me ten thousand, but let's not complicate things now. Follow my sacred principle."

"What sacred principle is that?"

"When somebody offers you money, take it."

"Jim, there's a car here. You don't have to fly me to the Compound."

"If Colonel Wallace doesn't already know we're here, he will soon. I don't want him to think I'm sneaking around. Besides, General Gehlen may have some thoughts about Vienna."

"Whatever you say."

"I'll ask—you don't have to tell me—what you're going to talk about with Gehlen."

"Well, you already know some of it. Seven-K showed us the proof that it's too late to execute that operation. But there were two parts to it, the second being taking out Gábor Péter. He may still want to carry that out. I want to dissuade him from doing so. Now is not the time. That may be difficult as my brother-in-law, former Oberstleutnant Sigmund Schneiber, was not only one of his best agents, but close to him personally. He wanted him back badly, and now that he's dead, I'm afraid the general will want to take out Gábor Péter both professionally—it will send a message to both the Allamvedelmi Osztaly and the NKGB—and personally. In your terms, Jim, Gábor Péter is a three-star son-ofabitch."

"You don't have to answer this, either. How much is El Jefe involved in this?"

"Oscar operates on gut feelings. He thinks—and you know we have no proof either way—that the NKGB killed your friend Moriarty. Oscar wanted to take out—he used the phrase 'tit for tat'—Ivan Serov. I dissuaded him. So he asked me what NKGB surrogate most deserved elimination. I told him Gábor Péter. This was before he had taken either my brother-in-law or my wife. Oscar asked why Gábor Péter, and I told him it would send a message to both the NKGB and to their Hungarian surrogates that we have people everywhere.

"I called him when my brother was arrested, and again when they took my wife. His reply was, 'Well, with a little luck, maybe Gehlen's guys can get them back at the same time they take out Gábor Péter.'"

"What does Wallace know about this?"

"Oscar apparently decided he doesn't have the Need to Know. He told me not to tell him unless I have to. It's a delicate situation."

"Delicate?"

"Wallace believes he's running the Gehlen Organization as chief, DCI-Europe. Oscar—and more important, the admiral—look at the Gehlen Organization as a DCI asset that can—

and should—be used around the world. The Soviets are causing trouble in Japan, Korea, and all over South America. When he learns this, Wallace is likely to think he's been demoted."

"So you're going to tell him?"

"As soon as the right moment arrives in Munich."

"Am I going to be in the way? I could just drop you at the Compound."

"Since I'm going to tell Wallace what's going on, you probably should be there when I tell him Oscar told me to make it clear to him that you're chasing Odessa and von Dietelburg at his orders, and Wallace isn't to interfere."

[TWO]
The South German Industrial
Development Organization
Compound
Pullach, Bavaria
American Zone of Occupation,
Germany
1015 1 March 1946

As he shut down the Storch, Cronley saw that Colonel Harold Wallace was waiting, hands on his hips, for them.

Otto Niedermeyer climbed down from the

Storch first. He and Wallace shook hands. Cronley climbed down.

"Where the hell have you been?" Wallace demanded.

"Good morning, Colonel, sir. And how are you this morning?"

"I asked where you've been, Cronley."

"In Vienna. Looking for von Dietelburg."

"And where's your bodyguard?"

"In Vienna. Looking for von Dietelburg. You seem a bit upset. May I ask why?"

"At quarter to eight, Justice Jackson called and asked if I knew where you were. And of course I had to tell him you were supposed to be in Nuremberg providing his security and I had no goddamn idea where you were."

"Did he say what he wanted?"

"He said he had just been informed that Sturmführer Luther Stauffer—your cousin Luther—had committed suicide by biting on a cyanide capsule in the mess hall and he thought you should know."

Jesus Christ!

Luther killed himself?

The last time I saw him, he was an arrogant SS officer.

How the hell am I going to explain this to Mom?

"Interesting," Cronley said.

"What I found interesting is that he was

in the Tribunal prison. You want to explain that?"

No, I don't.

"I had him transferred there. For interrogation."

The look on Wallace's face showed that he didn't like—or believe—Cronley's answer.

"I suppose it's really futile to ask what you and Oberst Niedermeyer were really doing in Vienna."

"It's no longer Oberst Niedermeyer, Colonel," Niedermeyer said.

"Excuse me?"

"I should have told you this earlier, I'm sorry."

"Told me what?"

"I'm no longer a former German soldier employed by the Süd-Deutsche Industrielle Entwicklungsorganisation."

"I don't understand . . ."

"I'm an Argentine national employed by the Argentine-American Tourist Board."

He handed Wallace an Argentine passport and a business card.

When he had examined them, Wallace admitted, "Now I'm really confused."

"It was Schultz's idea," Niedermeyer said. "And he talked his friend General Martín of the Argentine Bureau of Internal Security—BIS—to go along with it. Now when I'm wandering around Argentina—for that matter, the world—what I'm doing is promoting American tourism in Argentina, and vice versa."

"Makes sense," Wallace admitted.

"Schultz had another idea—this is what I should have told you—that I should take over certain DCI objectives. High on that list is the destruction of Odessa and putting the Odessa leadership in the Tribunal prison. And at the top of the list of Odessa leaders is former SS-Brigadeführer Franz von Dietelburg. Schultz has given me the authority to draw on any DCI assets to carry this out. He also told me that he had charged Cronley with taking out Odessa and suggested that I should get together with him."

"No one told me anything about any of this," Wallace said.

"Until I asked for your help with something, there was no need to tell you," Niedermeyer said. "I'm only telling you now because you're questioning Cronley about his being in Vienna with me. But since that question has come up, Cronley was there because I wanted him to help me find von Dietelburg."

"He's supposed to be in Nuremberg protecting Justice Jackson."

"He's supposed to do whatever Mr. Schultz—or Mr. Schultz's agent—tells him to do."

"And you're 'Mr. Schultz's agent'?"

"I was the first Abwehr Ost officer sent to Ar-

gentina. Schultz was then Colonel Frade's deputy. I became Schultz's deputy . . . not formally,
but in practice. Colonel Frade's OSS Buenos
Aires station was run the way Frade and Schultz
wanted it to run. Apparently when Schultz went
to Washington as Number Two to Admiral
Souers, he thought I would be more useful to
DCI as his deputy there as Argentina was by
then pretty much under control. The problem
was that a former German officer serving as
Schultz's Number Two would raise eyebrows all
over the Washington intelligence community.
So it was decided that his Number Two would
be based in Argentina, with the Argentine-
American Tourist Board as his cover."

"In other words, you are Schultz's deputy?"

"Yes, I am."

"I'm a little annoyed that I wasn't told about
this," Wallace said.

"El Jefe told me to tell you when the moment
was right. This is the moment. You know what
they say, the more people who know a secret, the
quicker it gets out."

"Does General Gehlen know about this?"

"I'm about to tell him what he doesn't know."

"And then you're going back to Argentina?"

"Via Tokyo and Seoul, South Korea. The nose
of the Russian bear is under our tent there, too."

"I don't understand your role in that."

"There are two kinds of intelligence officers,

the brash and the cautious. Schultz is the former, and I'm the latter. The greatest service I provided him in Argentina—and what the admiral hopes I will provide in my new role—is to keep him from acting impetuously."

"I don't think I understand."

"It's come to the admiral's attention that General Gehlen wishes to—has plans to—assassinate a Hungarian named Gábor Péter, who runs the Allamvedelmi Osztaly for the NKGB."

"Gehlen has plans to do what?"

"When the admiral asked me what I thought, I told him Gábor Péter deserves to die, but now is not the time."

"How did the admiral know about this?"

"General Gehlen told him."

"Gehlen went over my head to the admiral? That sonofabitch!"

"The admiral, and El Jefe . . . speak with General Gehlen frequently. Gehlen is doing things for DCI that have nothing to do with DCI-Europe."

"And the admiral and Schultz didn't think I should be told?"

"I'd offer the guess—both of them admire you—they thought you would know this was standard practice."

Wallace was silent for thirty seconds—which seemed longer—and then he said, "Well, I've kept you long enough."

Then he turned and walked back to his jeep.

"That didn't go well, but it could have gone worse," Niedermeyer said. "And I know if somebody told me what I just told him, I'd be just as unhappy."

"He's also pissed at me," Cronley said. "And I didn't go over his head to talk to El Jefe or the admiral, and nobody asked me if I wanted to go after Odessa and von Dietelburg."

"Well, let's go chat with General Gehlen," Niedermeyer said, "and see how he reacts when I order him to call off the elimination of Gábor Péter. I was his Number Three—or Four—in Abwehr Ost. And as Ludwig Mannberg will tell you, he didn't at all like unsolicited suggestions from his Number Two, much less orders."

[THREE]
Headquarters, 26th Infantry
**   Regiment**
The International Tribunal
**   Compound**
Nuremberg, American Zone of
**   Occupation, Germany**
1635 1 March 1946

Tiny Dunwiddie was waiting for Cronley at Soldier's Field.

"I've got my bodyguard, where's yours?" he greeted Cronley.

"In Vienna, looking for von Dietelburg."

"So we better stop by the Mansion and get you one before we go to the Tribunal Compound."

"One isn't enough?"

"Justice Jackson thinks you should have one. We're liable to run into him when we go to the Compound, and I don't think you want pissing him off added to your problems."

"Why are we going to the Compound?"

"Because Colonel Cohen and Colonel Rasberry are waiting there to discuss the demise of your cousin Luther."

Cronley was surprised when Rasberry's sergeant major led them past Rasberry's office and to the day room. When he got inside, he saw why the meeting was not being held in Rasberry's office; it just wouldn't fit.

Sitting on chrome-and-plastic chairs around a pool table that was covered with a black plastic sheet and on which sat a coffeemaker and plates of doughnuts were maybe twenty people, the soldiers among them ranging in rank from sergeant (Casey Wagner) to four colonels, including Cohen and Rasberry. There were half a dozen bodyguards. And one man Cronley didn't expect to see, Justice Robert Jackson.

"Super Spook," Cohen greeted him. "How good of you to find time in your busy schedule for us."

Cronley ignored him, instead saying, "Mr. Justice."

"Before this starts," Jackson said, "I'd like a private word with Mr. Cronley and Colonels Cohen, Rasberry, and Thomas. May we use your office, Colonel Rasberry?"

"Of course."

"And will you please join us, Mr. Ziegler?" Jackson asked. "And you, too, Ken?"

Cronley hadn't noticed Kenneth Brewster, Jackson's law clerk.

"As this is a quasi-legal proceeding, may I usurp your desk, Colonel Rasberry, to serve as my bench?"

"Of course, sir," Rasberry said.

Jackson sat at Rasberry's desk, and the others found chairs.

"Everyone knows everyone, correct?" Jackson asked.

"I haven't met this gentleman before, Mr. Justice," Colonel Thomas said, indicating Cronley.

"Mr. James Cronley of the Directorate of Central Intelligence," Jackson said. "Colonel Tom Thomas, the Nuremberg Military Post provost marshal."

The two wordlessly shook hands.

"Let me set the stage politically before we ask Mr. Ziegler to tell us what he has learned so far," Jackson began. "About an hour after I learned—at about eight this morning—of the death of former Sturmführer Luther Stauffer, I had a telephone call from Admiral Souers.

"Admiral Souers, Colonel Thomas, is the director of the Directorate of Central Intelligence— the DCI—and is a close personal friend of President Truman and myself. The admiral said it had come to the attention of the President that a prisoner in the Tribunal prison had committed suicide by cyanide capsule.

"I think it germane to put delicacy and discretion aside and tell you, verbatim, what Admiral Souers then said: 'Bob, Harry's really pissed off. He told me to get you on the horn and tell you he wants to know, quote, What incompetent sonofabitch let this happen? I want to hang those Nazi sonsofbitches, and I can't do that if they're committing suicide, unquote.'"

Cronley saw on Colonel Thomas's face that he was shocked and made very uncomfortable by what Jackson had just said.

"Colonels Cohen and Rasberry tell me they did not inform anyone of Stauffer's suicide, pending an investigation, so I am wondering, Colonel Thomas, if you told anyone."

"Sir, the protocol is that whenever something

like this, anything significant, happens at the Tribunal prison, I am to immediately notify the USFET provost marshal. I did so. I can only presume that he relayed this information, probably by telephone, to the provost marshal general of the Army."

"Who then rushed over to the White House," Jackson said. "Let me say that I don't think that either Colonel Cohen or Colonel Rasberry are incompetent, and I have no intention of hanging either of them out to dry unless there is clear evidence that I'm wrong. But I do intend to get to the bottom of this. So, Mr. Ziegler, you have the floor. What have you learned so far?"

Cronley's mouth went on automatic.

"Sir, can I suggest we start with Sergeant Wagner?"

"Jesus Christ, Super Spook!" Colonel Cohen protested.

"Who the hell is he?" Colonel Thomas asked.

"Why?" Justice Jackson asked.

"Sir, because he was there when whatever happened happened."

"Ziegler, have you talked to Sergeant Wagner?" Jackson asked.

"Yes, sir. He was the first guy I talked to."

"And?"

"I think Jim is right, sir. It would probably be valuable for everyone to hear his take on what went down."

"Ken," Jackson ordered, "please go to the day room and ask the sergeant to join us."

Sergeant Casey Wagner walked into the office, took a quick look around, and then marched to precisely eighteen inches from Justice Jackson's desk, where he came to attention, saluted, and then barked, "Sergeant Wagner reporting as ordered, sir!"

"You don't have to salute me, son," Jackson said, smiling. "Take that chair and tell us what happened in the prisoners' mess this morning."

"Yes, sir."

"I have to ask," Colonel Thomas asked, "just who is this sergeant?"

"He works for me, Colonel," Cronley said.

"Son, where were you when the cyanide incident happened?" Jackson asked.

"In the prisoners' mess, sir."

"Doing what?"

"Mostly listening, sir. And looking for anything that looked funny—out of the ordinary."

"And who told you to go to the prisoners' mess to listen and look for things out of the ordinary?"

"Captain Cronley didn't order me to do that specifically—"

"What does he do for you, Captain Cronley?" Colonel Thomas asked.

"Let him talk, Tom," Colonel Rasberry said.

"Whatever I tell him," Cronley said. "Go on, Casey."

"Yes, sir. Mr. Justice Jackson, sir, when Captain Cronley suspected that messages and other stuff were being smuggled in and out of the prison, he sent me in there to see what I could find out. That's what I was doing in the prisoners' mess."

"And what happened there? What did you see happen there?" Jackson asked.

"All of a sudden, Stauffer grabbed his throat and fell backwards off the bench at his table."

"How did you know it was Sturmführer Luther Stauffer?"

"Mr. Cronley told me who he was, and asked me to watch who he talked to. He said he was connected with Odessa."

"Am I hearing," Colonel Thomas interrupted, asking incredulously, "that Captain Cronley believes that Odessa nonsense and has passed that nonsense on to this boy?"

"Colonel, I don't mean to be rude," Justice Jackson said icily, "but that was the last time you will say a word that is not in reply to a question that either I or Mr. Cronley have posed to you. Do you understand?"

Thomas's face flushed.

"Yes, sir," he said.

"Go on, son," Jackson said.

"Yes, sir. So I took a look at him, and he was . . . bubbles were coming out of his mouth, and I remembered what I had heard about what cyanide pills do to you. So I went to the kitchen door and called for the sergeant of the guard and told the PFC on the door to call for the medics—"

"The sergeant of the guard wasn't in the prisoners' mess?" Cronley asked.

"No, sir."

"Why not? Are you saying you were the only American in there?"

"There was a PFC at the door, and when I opened it to yell for help, there was another one outside."

"Where was the sergeant?"

Wagner shrugged.

"And then what happened?" Cronley pursued.

"Well, when the sergeant—Sergeant Brownlee—came, he—"

"How long did it take him to come into the mess?" Colonel Cohen asked.

"I guess two, three minutes, sir. Maybe a little longer."

"He should have been in the mess," Colonel Rasberry said.

"You were telling us, son," Jackson said, "what the sergeant did when he came into the mess."

"Yes, sir. He took a look at Stauffer and told me to call the medics. I told him I already had. And just about then, the medics showed up.

They took one look at Stauffer and loaded him on a stretcher and hauled him off."

"And what, if anything, did you and the sergeant do then?" Jackson asked.

"The sergeant told me not to let anybody leave and to wait for Lieutenant Anderson . . ."

"Who is?" Jackson asked.

"One of my officers, sir," Rasberry said. "He has a platoon of prison guards. He was officer of the day at the time of this incident."

"And how long did it take for Lieutenant Anderson to arrive at the prisoners' mess?" Jackson asked.

"About fifteen minutes, sir."

"And what did you do while you were waiting for him?"

"I called for the corporal of the guard, and when he showed up, I told him to lock up the kitchen crew someplace, and then return the prisoners to their cells."

"They were all there having breakfast when this happened?" Jackson asked. "Göring, Kaltenbrunner, Speer . . . all of them?"

"Yes, sir."

"And what was their reaction when Stauffer fell to the floor, frothing at the mouth?"

"I don't know how to answer that, sir. It was like they were watching a dog that had been run over by a car."

"No one tried to help him?"

"No, sir."

"Anyone say anything, Casey?" Cronley asked.

"Kaltenbrunner was sitting at a table with Göring. There's two tables—like picnic tables—in each row. Stauffer was sitting at the table furthest from the wall. Göring and Kaltenbrunner were at the table nearest the wall.

"They looked over their shoulders when Stauffer fell off his bench. Kaltenbrunner said to Göring, 'Well, at least someone has access to those capsules.' Göring sort of laughed. Chuckled."

"I think we should determine the cause of death," Jackson said. "Ken, would you please get the doctor in here?"

"Yes, sir," Brewster said. And then added, "Come with me, Sergeant. I'll take you back to the day room."

"Unless Justice Jackson objects, I think Casey should stay," Cronley said.

"Please change chairs, Sergeant," Jackson said, "so the doctor can sit there."

"Yes, sir."

Brewster ushered the pudgy medical officer whom Cronley remembered had strip-searched Luther when he arrived at the Tribunal prison, into the chair Casey had given up.

"You won't be sworn, Doctor," Jackson said. "This is an informal inquiry. But we do want the truth, the whole truth, and nothing but. All right?"

"Yes, sir."

"When did you first learn what had happened in the prisoners' mess?"

"I was having my breakfast in the 26th mess when a soldier came to me and said I was needed right away in the Dispensary."

"That would be Sergeant Brownlee, the sergeant of the guard?"

"No, sir. It was some PFC. I didn't get his name."

"And then?"

"So I went to the Dispensary. Stauffer was on the table—"

"You knew who he was?"

"Yes, sir. I strip-searched him when he came to the prison."

"So you're fairly certain he didn't have a cyanide capsule concealed in a body cavity when he entered the prison?"

"I examined him thoroughly, sir."

"Go on, please."

"He was dead when I got there, and from the froth at his mouth, I suspected cyanide poisoning."

"What did you do then?"

"I had the body moved to the 385th Station

Hospital, which has the necessary facilities to conduct an autopsy."

"You did this on your own?"

"He was there," the doctor said, indicating Ziegler. "He thought that was the thing to do."

"Did he say why?"

"The phrase he used, sir, was that 'the shit's really going to hit the fan about this—they'll want an autopsy first thing.'"

"From the time you found Stauffer on the Dispensary table, was the body ever out of your sight, your control, until you performed the autopsy? I'm presuming you performed the autopsy."

"Mr. Ziegler and I rode in the ambulance with the body from the Tribunal Compound to the hospital, and when we got there, two men were waiting for us. Mr. Ziegler told them they were not to let the body out of their sight, and to let no one but me and people with me near it."

"Who were these men?"

"DCI agents, Mr. Justice," Ziegler said.

"And then you performed the autopsy? And what did you determine?"

"Death by cyanide poisoning."

"Anything else?"

"The contents of the stomach showed that he had had scrambled eggs, sausage, and cherry cobbler for breakfast. I also found the remains of a gelatin-like capsule, which showed teeth marks and held traces of a concentrated solution of potassium cyanide."

"You're suggesting he waited until he had finished his breakfast before he took his own life?"

"I think when he took a bite of one of the cherries in his cobbler, he got the cyanide capsule," Ziegler said.

"Now that's interesting," Cronley said. "Lay that out for us, Augie."

"My scenario is that the capsule—probably capsules—were smuggled into the kitchen mess, loaded into the cherry cobbler, and then when Stauffer went down the chow line, he got that piece of cherry cobbler."

"You don't think it was suicide, Mr. Ziegler?" Jackson asked.

"No, sir. Stauffer didn't know what was in his cherry cobbler."

"Sergeant?"

"I go with Augie, Mr. Justice, sir."

"Colonel Cohen?"

"Mr. Justice, in my experience, people contemplating suicide rarely serve themselves a hearty last meal."

"Let's go down that path," Jackson said. "Stauffer died as a result of biting into a capsule of potassium cyanide that had been put into his cherry cobbler. How do we know that capsule was intended for him? And not for Göring or someone else?"

"We don't," Cohen said. "But I suggest that if Göring wanted a pill, he would have gotten it by now."

"Casey," Cronley asked, "who do you think smuggled the cyanide in?"

Casey did not immediately reply.

"How well are the kitchen personnel searched before they get into the mess?" Jackson asked.

"Sir, they make them take a shower," Casey replied. "It's not a body search, but it's almost."

"But a cyanide capsule could be hidden?" Jackson pursued. "In the mouth? Or the anal cavity?"

"In the mouth, perhaps . . ." the doctor said.

"They look in their mouths," Casey said, and then quoted, " 'Stick out your tongue and then spread your cheeks.' "

"Who is 'they'?" Jackson asked.

"Sir, sometimes the sergeant of the guard, but most times one of the guards."

"The temperatures in the anus," the doctor said, "would probably melt the gelatin capsule."

"Unless it's a special gelatin, designed to resist the temperatures in the anal cavity," Cohen said.

"Answer my question, Casey," Cronley ordered. "Who do you think smuggled the capsule into the kitchen?"

Again, Casey did not reply.

"Casey, why do I think you think Sergeant Brownlee is the villain?"

"He's a good guy, Captain. Not too smart, but a good guy. I can't see him giving a cyanide capsule to anybody."

"What if he didn't know what he was smuggling into the mess was a cyanide capsule?" Cronley pursued.

"I didn't think about that," Casey admitted.

"I think we should have a talk with Sergeant Brownlee," Justice Jackson said.

Ken Brewster led Sergeant Robert J. Brownlee Jr. into the office and put him in the chair the doctor had just vacated.

Cronley thought, **He's a nice-looking twenty-odd-year-old with crew-cut light brown hair who knows he's in trouble**.

"I guess you know you're in the deep shit, Sergeant," Cronley said.

Brownlee did not reply.

"You know Sergeant Wagner, right?"

"Yes, sir."

"I should have said, 'You think you know Sergeant Wagner,'" Cronley said. "Because you really don't. Wagner, show Sergeant Brownlee your credentials."

Brownlee examined the folder, looked confused, and then confessed, "Sir, I don't know what this is, this DCI."

"Few people do," Cronley said. "It is an organization answerable only to the President. Among the responsibilities President Truman has given the DCI is the protection of Judge Biddle, Justice Jackson, and the prisoners in the Tribunal prison. With me so far?"

"Yes, sir. I think so."

"It is the desire of President Truman that, after a fair trial to prove what monsters Göring and the other people in the prison are, that they be hanged for their crimes. You understand, I hope, that a President's desires are legal orders?"

"Yes, sir."

"When it came to our attention that messages and other items were being smuggled into and out of the prison, I sent DCI Special Agent Wagner into the prison, with the cover of translator, to determine who was doing the smuggling.

"He had already determined before the death of former Sturmführer Luther Stauffer this morning that you were the smuggler."

The poor bastard looks like he's going to faint. Or throw up.

I think I've got him.

"The decision was made by Colonel Cohen and myself that, rather than arrest and court-martial you immediately, that Sergeant Wagner would keep you under observation and see where that led.

"That decision was bad luck for you, Sergeant. If we had arrested you yesterday, all you would have been charged with would have been failure to obey standing orders, dereliction of duty, something like that. Special court-martial charges, maybe a year in the Frankfurt stockade. Now, following the murder of Stauffer, you'll be charged, in a general court-martial, with being an accessory before the fact to first degree, that is to say, premeditated murder."

Sergeant Brownlee threw up on the floor, narrowly missing Justice Jackson's desk.

Cronley waited until Brownlee had wiped his face with a well-used handkerchief before continuing, "There's no use, Brownlee, in denying what you did. We know."

"I didn't know it was cyanide," Brownlee said. "I swear to God."

"What did you think it was?"

"Laxative. Like German Ex-Lax."

"Laxative?" Cohen said. "You thought you were smuggling laxative into the prison?"

"Come on, Brownlee!" Cronley said.

"Sir, I swear to God that's what I thought it was. Trude's uncle has constipation, and our medics won't give him anything."

"Trude?"

"My fiancée, sir. We've applied for permission to get married."

"And Trude's uncle is?"

"His name is Macher."

"I know him," Cohen said. "I had him transferred here from Darmstadt when we learned of his connection to Castle Wewelsburg."

"Bring me up to speed on that, please, Colonel," Justice Jackson asked.

"I think Cronley has told you what was going on at Castle Wewelsburg?"

"The Vatican, so to speak, of the new religion Himmler was trying to establish? Oh, yes, Jim told me all about it. Just as soon as I can, I'm going to have a look at that place. What is this man Macher's connection with that?"

"Himmler and/or von Dietelburg sent him to blow the place up when 3rd Armored Division was getting close. His orders were to tell SS General Siegfried Taubert, who was in charge of the castle, to remove, quote, all sacred items, end quote, and then blow the place up.

"When Macher got to the castle, he found that Taubert had left, presumably with the sacred items. But when we captured Taubert trying to get into Italy, no sacred items. He stashed them somewhere—we're still looking."

"Macher didn't have enough explosives, couldn't blow up the castle," Cohen said. "He used what he had—anti-tank mines—to blow up—take down—the southeast tower and the guard and SS buildings. Then he tried, unsuccessfully, to burn the castle down. Then he took off for Italy. We caught him, not knowing who he was, and the CIC put him in the unimportant-SS-prisoner enclosure in Darmstadt. When I heard he was there, I had him moved here.

"Castle Wewelsburg, the people who ran that, Cronley and I believe, are the people running Odessa. And yes, Colonel Thomas, Odessa is real, active, and dangerous."

"So your **fiancée's** uncle, it would seem, Sergeant Brownlee," Cronley said, "is not some gentle soul suffering from constipation, but rather somebody who participated—almost certainly at the orders of former SS-Brigadeführer Franz von Dietelburg—in the murder of Sturmführer Luther Stauffer, almost certainly because Stauffer was in Odessa and they were afraid he'd start talking to us.

"Does this give you any idea of how your incredible stupidity has fucked things up?"

Brownlee didn't reply.

"Who did you pass the cyanide capsules to?"

"Wilhelm."

"Wilhelm who?"

"I don't know his last name. He runs the chow line."

"Wilhelm Reiss," Casey furnished.

"Right," Brownlee confirmed.

"The idea being that he would pass the Ex-Lax to Macher as he went through the chow line?"

"Yes, sir."

"Casey, was this guy Reiss in the chow line among the people you ordered locked up?"

"Yes, sir."

"Brownlee, give Mr. Ziegler your fiancée's name and address."

"Trude didn't know the laxative pills were cyanide—she's a good woman."

"Your loyalty to your beloved is touching, Sergeant," Cronley said.

"Are you through with Sergeant Brownlee, Mr. Cronley?" Colonel Rasberry asked.

"Just as soon as he gives Ziegler his girlfriend's name and address, I will be."

"Mr. Justice Jackson, sir?" Rasberry asked.

"I have nothing to ask him at this time," Jackson said.

"Then with your permission, sir, I will place Sergeant Brownlee under arrest, pending proceedings under Article 31 of the **Manual for Courts-Martial 1928**."

"That seems to be the appropriate action, Colonel."

"Sergeant Major, take Sergeant Brownlee into custody and place him somewhere where he cannot make contact with anybody and ensure that someone is watching him twenty-four/seven to make sure he doesn't hurt himself."

"Yes, sir. Let's go, Brownlee."

Sergeant Brownlee, tears running down his cheeks, stood up.

"Would anyone care to offer odds," Cronley asked, "on whether Wilhelm Reiss has somehow slipped away from where Casey ordered he be locked up, or that when we get to Sergeant Brownlee's love nest, his fiancée will have departed for parts unknown?"

There were no takers.

"And I don't suppose anyone knows where I can acquire a coffin at a reasonable price?"

"Why do you want to buy a coffin?" Colonel Thomas asked.

"The late Sturmführer Luther Stauffer was my cousin, Colonel. My mother would want me to see that he receives a proper burial."

XV

[ONE]
The Bar
Farber Palast
Stein, near Nuremberg
American Zone of Occupation,
   Germany
1955 1 March 1946

Miss Janice Johansen of the Associated Press was sitting at a table when Cronley walked in with Tiny Dunwiddie and their bodyguards.

"I wonder how long Guinevere has been patiently—maybe impatiently—waiting for her Galahad to come home," Dunwiddie asked softly.

"Fuck you," Cronley said, and then as they approached the table, "Well, if it isn't Miss Johansen of the Associated Press. What a pleasant surprise!"

"Sit down, Super Spook, and tell me all about Murder in the Tribunal Prison."

"You know he can't talk about that," Tiny said.

"After I have a double Johnnie Walker Black on your tab and you swear on your mother's grave that you won't file it until I tell you you can," Cronley said.

"Deal," she said, and waved to attract the attention of a waiter. "I'll even buy one for Tiny."

As the drinks were being served, Ivan Serov and his aide-de-camp, Major Sergei Alekseevich, approached the table. Alekseevich was carrying a large bundle of flowers and Serov two bottles, one champagne and the other vodka.

"And now I wonder how long they've been waiting," Tiny said softly.

Alekseevich handed the flowers to Cronley, and Serov set the bottles on the table.

"With the compliments of General Iona Nikitchenko," Serov said.

"I'm flattered that the Number Two Soviet

judge sends me flowers, but you're going to have to tell him that Janice has already won my heart," Cronley said.

Alekseevich's face tightened at the implication. Serov laughed heartily.

"The general knows we're chums . . ."

Chums?

Is that what we are?

My trouble with Comrade Ivan is that while my brain knows what an unmitigated—and dangerous—sonofabitch he is, I still like him.

Like him? I'm actually fond of the sonofabitch!

". . . and hopes that I can take advantage of our relationship and have you tell me about what happened to your cousin, former Sturmführer Luther Stauffer."

"In other words, Justice Jackson wouldn't tell him?"

"I think the general would like confirmation of what Justice Jackson has told him."

"Well, chum, I guess General Nikitchenko knows the way to have me abandon my virtue is to send me flowers and champagne. So what do you want to know?"

"My God, Jimmy," Dunwiddie blurted, "it was agreed that this couldn't get out of the tent."

"And I have just decided Ivan gets into the tent," Cronley replied.

"Tiny," Serov said, "the Soviet Union considers it immensely important that the Nazis in the Tribunal prison not be allowed to become martyrs to National Socialism by taking their own lives before we can prove them in court to be common criminals, and hang them—publicly—as such."

"So does the President of the United States," Cronley said.

"So what happened, Jim?" Serov asked.

"A well-meaning young sergeant, because his fiancée asked him to, smuggled what he believed to be laxatives into the prison intended to provide relief, which our medics cruelly refused to supply, to our sergeant's girlfriend's uncle for his constipation."

"And the constipated uncle is?" Serov asked.

"SS Major Heinz Macher."

"The one Morty Cohen brought here from the Darmstadt compound?"

"One and the same."

"Because Morty thought there was an Odessa connection?"

"Correct."

"So Odessa—von Dietelburg or Burgdorf—wanted Macher eliminated?"

"'Or Burgdorf'? Who the hell is Burgdorf?" Cronley asked.

"General der Infanterie Wilhelm Burgdorf. Another former personal adjutant to Hitler,"

Serov replied. "Specializing in eliminating threats—real or perceived—to Der Führer."

"Wasn't he one of the generals who went to Stuttgart? . . ." Tiny asked.

"At Hitler's orders to convince General Rommel that biting on a cyanide capsule was his best option under the circumstances? That was Burgdorf," Serov said.

"I thought Burgdorf committed suicide in the Führerbunker. That you found his body there," Dunwiddie said.

"That was his intention. That we find his body outside the Führerbunker. And stop looking for him."

"I never heard any of this before," Cronley confessed.

"Why is it so important to you that you find this guy?" Dunwiddie asked.

"Because of his relationship with Operation Phoenix, with Odessa, Himmler, and what went on at Castle Wewelsburg."

"What was his connection with Himmler?" Cronley asked.

"I've heard he was the only man Himmler feared," Serov said. "Toward the end, when Hitler became really paranoid—especially after the bomb von Stauffenberg planted at his Wolf's Lair failed to take him out—Hitler began, with some reason, to distrust not only Wehrmacht and Navy officers—Rommel, most notably, and Canaris—but others high in the Nazi hierarchy. Göring, Himmler, and others.

"But not Burgdorf, whom Hitler—correctly—believed to be absolutely devoted to National Socialism and to himself, personally," Serov said. "One credible scenario is that Hitler began to take a closer look—sent Burgdorf to take a closer look—at what was going on at Castle Wewelsburg under Himmler's adjutant von Dietelburg.

"This scenario suggests that Burgdorf turned von Dietelburg, who was—is—an opportunist of the first order. A variation of this scenario suggests that when Burgdorf put his nose in Wewelsburg, von Dietelburg went to him and proclaimed that his loyalty was to the Führer, not Himmler. And that he suspected, but could not prove, that Himmler planned to use Odessa to escape Germany if the situation seemed to be going wrong."

"And you didn't think I would be interested in any of this? That this Burgdorf guy didn't die in the Führerbunker, or either scenario?" Cronley challenged. "I thought we were chums."

Serov made a gesture—both hands extended, palms up—of helplessness.

"If we had told you—DCI or USFET intelligence—that Burgdorf was still alive and on the run and almost certainly involved with Odessa, he would learn of this from an Odessa mole either in the Farben Building or Gehlen's compound."

Cronley didn't reply.

"And we know there are moles, don't we?" Serov asked. "One of them killed your friend." He paused. "Thinking it was you."

"Point taken," Cronley agreed.

"So, now that I have told you, can we get back to the details of what happened? General Nikitchenko really wants to know."

"I was about to say, 'providing it doesn't go any further than your general,'" Cronley said, "but if I did that it would once again reveal my naiveté, wouldn't it?"

Serov made another both-hands-palms-up gesture of **You've got me!**

"And you, Janice, if I let you sit here and listen to what I tell Ivan, will I see it on the front page of tomorrow's **Stars and Stripes**?"

"If you're asking, Super Spook, will I sit on it until you say I can write it, no, I won't. I will sit on it for ninety-six hours or until the story breaks, which I'm sure it will. Deal?"

"Deal. Thanks. Okay, Ivan, what do you want to know?"

"The details."

"Casey Wagner's scenario—and I think he's on the money—is that Sergeant Brownlee smuggled what he thought—what his **Schatzi** told him—was laxative—"

"Her name?" Serov asked.

"Trude Wahlheim," Cronley said. "Or that's what she told Brownlee."

Sergei Alekseevich scribbled this into a notebook.

"Ivan, my chum, how about letting me give you Wagner's scenario and then you ask your questions?"

"Sorry."

"Brownlee smuggled what he thought was German Ex-Lax into the prison by hiding it under his balls in his underwear. He then passed it to the guy—a German named Wilhelm Reiss—in charge of the chow line. Reiss would then pass the Ex-Lax to Macher as he passed through the chow line.

"What we have cleverly figured out is (a) the Ex-Lax was really one or more capsules of potassium cyanide, (b) that instead of passing the cyanide capsules to Major Macher, Reiss put one of them into a slice of cobbler and put that slice on Cousin Luther's tray as he passed through the chow line. **Auf Wiedersehen**, Cousin Luther."

"I suppose it's too much to hope you have this Reiss chap?" Serov asked.

"He and the sergeant's **Schatzi** are not to be found," Cronley said.

"So what are your plans?" Serov asked.

"The general wants to know that, too, huh?" Cronley replied, and then went on without wait-

ing for a reply. "I'm going to give the sonofabitch a Christian burial. I know how important
Christian burials are to you."

Serov ignored the reference to the Russian Orthodox burials he had asked Cronley
to provide—and Cronley had provided—for
the NKGB agents whom DCI agent Claudette
Colbert had killed when they attempted to kidnap her and Tech Sergeant—now DCI agent—
Florence Miller.

"I thought the disposal protocol for the remains of Tribunal prisoners was cremation, with
the ashes then to be secretly scattered into the
Neckar River," Serov said.

"That's my understanding," Cronley replied.
"But Cousin Luther wasn't a Tribunal prisoner
awaiting trial and the gallows. He just thought
he was. I brought him here thinking that he
might decide giving me von Dietelburg was a
better option than the gallows."

"I would hazard the guess that Odessa was
concerned that Stauffer would give him up,"
Serov said.

"That scenario has run through my mind,
Ivan."

"And now?"

"Somewhat reluctantly, Colonel Fortin has
agreed to help me give former Sturmführer Luther Stauffer a Christian burial."

"What's the point of that?" Tiny asked.

"I could lie and say I want to see if anybody interesting shows up for the funeral, but the truth is that I want to be able to tell my mother that after her nephew Luther—her last living relative—was murdered, I saw to it that he was buried next to his parents."

"Your mother knows he was in the SS?" Serov asked.

"No. And I hope I don't have to tell her," Cronley said. "What happened was that when I first came to Germany and was a very junior CIC agent manning a roadblock in Marburg an der Lahn, I got a letter from my mother asking me, if possible, to put some flowers on the graves of my grandparents.

"She said they were buried in the family plot in the Sainte-Hélène Cemetery, in a little **Dorf** called Schiltigheim just outside Strasbourg. Until I got that letter, I had never considered that I had grandparents over here—or any grandparents at all. My father's parents died long before I was born.

"Anyway, as soon as I could, I got a three-day pass and drove to Strasbourg. That's a long ride in an open jeep in the winter. It took me some time to find the cemetery, and even longer to find flowers to place on my grandparents' graves, but eventually there I was. It was—the Stauffer plot was—surprisingly well maintained. There's a monastery nearby, and I guessed they maintained the cemetery.

"There were two fairly new graves, with tombstones. Josef and Maria Stauffer. Clever fellow that I am, from the dates I deduced this was the grave of my mother's brother—and therefore my uncle—and his wife. I knew that when my mother married my father, her family disowned her, and I knew this bothered her. So, standing at my grandparents' and my uncles' and aunts' graves, I shifted into Boy Scout mode . . ."

"Which means?" Serov asked.

"I decided to see if there were any other relatives. If I could find somebody, I would go to him or her and say, 'I'm Wilhelmina Stauffer's son, and your cousin, nephew, whatever, and I think it's high time you and my mother made up.'

"So I went to the Strasbourg Police Station—"

"Why didn't you go to the DST?" Tiny asked.

"Because I had never heard of the Direction de la Surveillance du Territoire. So I asked the cop, a sergeant, in German, which was probably a mistake, making him wonder about an American speaking German with a Strasbourg accent, if he could help me find any members of the Stauffer family living in Strasbourg.

"I could see that got his attention. He asked me why I wanted to locate such people. I told him my mother was from Strasbourg, and her maiden name had been Stauffer.

"He said he would make inquiries. So I stood there with my thumb up—you know where—for maybe twenty minutes until he came back. He had a French Army captain with him—starchy sonofabitch—and he demanded—not asked—for my identity card. So I flashed my CIC credentials and then he asked what was the interest of the CIC in the Stauffer family. So I went through the whole story again for him.

"He said, 'Give me a minute and I'll see what I can find for you.' Twenty minutes later—maybe half an hour—he came back and said sorry, he couldn't find any record of any living Stauffers, but if I gave him my address and phone number, he would look further and be delighted to let me know if he found anything.

"So I got back in my jeep and drove back to Marburg through a snowstorm. I never heard from him. I decided there were no more Stauffers and forgot about it.

"Then a couple of months or so later, I was at . . . a military installation not far from Munich—"

"The Pullach Compound or Kloster Grünau?" Serov asked.

"I have no idea what you're talking about, Colonel Serov."

"Then I guess you're not going to tell me how

one day you're a second lieutenant manning an unimportant checkpoint in Hesse and three months or so later, you're a captain—and chief, DCI-Europe—in Bavaria?" Serov asked.

"I have no idea what you're talking about, Chum Ivan, but even if I did, I couldn't talk about it because something like that would be classified Top Secret–Presidential."

Serov laughed.

"As I was saying, when I was in this place outside Munich, I got a letter from my mother saying she had gotten a heart-wrenching letter from her nephew—my cousin Luther—who said he'd finally made it home to Strasbourg from the war but didn't have a job, or any prospects, and practically nothing to eat, and if there was anything she could do to help . . . et cetera. She said she had made up some packages of food and had mailed them to me, and if there was any way I could get them to him, it was obviously the Christian thing for me to do.

"Four huge packages arrived a couple of days later—canned hams, chicken, coffee, sugar, you name it. They had been opened by the Army Postal Service and had 'Evidence' stamped all over them in large red letters.

"They were delivered not by the APO, but by a CIC agent who worked for Colonel Mattingly. He handed a memo—an interagency memorandum—to me with copies to General

Seidel, the USFET provost marshal, the Munich provost marshal, and some other brass . . . including El Jefe. It said that the next time I felt it necessary to import such items from the States in connection with my duties as . . . with my duties, I do so through him."

"He meant your duties as chief, DCI-Europe?" Serov asked.

Tiny answered for him: "The obvious purpose of the memorandum was to suggest to everybody on the **Copies To** list that Cronley was a black marketeer."

"You mean that he meant to suggest that the chief, DCI-Europe, was—"

"Fuck you, Chum Ivan," Cronley said.

Serov chose to ignore him.

"And who is El Jefe?" he asked.

"My boss, Chum Ivan, but that's all you get," Cronley said, and then went on. "My first reaction was to throw the packages away, but then I decided to deliver them. Or at least one of them.

"But then Fat Freddy and Tiny intuited something smelled."

"Fat Freddy is?"

"You met him, Chum Ivan. Here. He's my chief of staff. Sort of a younger version of Colonel Cohen."

"I'd forgotten."

"Freddy thought that we should learn more about Cousin Luther, and that showing up in a staff car with Twenty-third CIC painted on the bumpers was not the way to do that. So I put on a gold bar and quartermaster insignia, and we drove down there in one of our ex-ambulances that had 711th MKRC painted on the bumpers."

"Which meant?"

"Originally—my idea when I thought we had to paint something other than Twenty-third CIC on the bumpers—it stood for Mess Kit Repair Company, but Fat Freddy made me change that to 711th Mobile Kitchen Renovation Company."

Serov chuckled and said, "Clever. What could be more innocent than a kitchen renovation company?"

"So we went to Strasbourg and met with Cousin Luther and his wife, Ingebord," Cronley continued. "And gave them two of my mother's packages. They were suitably grateful. And then Freddy started talking about there being more PX black market goodies available, if Luther knew anyone who would pay for them and make sure no one learned about it.

"Cousin Luther said he'd see what he could come up with, and then we left.

"On our way out of town, we were congratulating ourselves on how clever we were. Cousin Luther, we cleverly deduced, was up to his ears in the black market, and we would work our way up that chain of command and at least be able to nab a serious black marketeer or two, and possibly somebody, or something, more important.

"And then we were stopped by French **police militaire**, who escorted us to the headquarters of the Direction de la Surveillance du Territoire—which even if we had heard of it, we knew next to nothing about it—and where Commandant Jean-Paul Fortin was waiting for us.

"Cutting to the chase, Commandant Fortin said he knew there was no unit called the 711th Mobile Kitchen Renovation Company because he had asked his good friend Brigadier General Homer Greene—"

"The USFET counterintelligence chief?" Serov asked.

Cronley nodded.

"So what the hell were we doing in Strasbourg talking to Luther Stauffer?

"**When you can't think of anything else, tell the truth.** So I did. Fortin then showed me a photograph of my cousin Luther getting married. He was in uniform. That of a **Sturmführer.** We later learned the wedding took place in Castle Wewelsburg.

"Fortin said that General Greene had told him something else. That the story going around the intelligence community that DCI-Europe was sort of a joke, and not a serious intel operation, the proof being that its commander was a very junior twenty-two-year-old captain, was obfuscation.

"So, Fortin said, he was going to tell me of DST's interest in my cousin Luther. Luther's story was that he had deserted the SS in the last days of the war and made his way home. Fortin believed Luther had been sent there by Odessa, specifically by SS-Brigadeführer Franz von Dietelburg, whom he suspected was running Odessa, to facilitate the escape of senior SS officers and other Nazis from Germany into France, and then, via Spain, to South America.

"He said my snooping around Luther was going to interfere with his surveillance of him, so butt out unless you learn something that might help me catch von Dietelburg. So I dropped contact with Cousin Luther until Casey Wagner figured out how Odessa was using **Stars and Stripes** trucks to smuggle Nazis into France through a little **Dorf** on the border called Wissembourg.

"So I got in contact with Fortin and told him what Casey had come up with. He said that was very interesting, because Cousin Luther was spending a lot of time in Wissembourg. Cutting to the chase, we caught Odessa trying to smuggle two really bad Nazis across the border, and Fortin caught Cousin Luther waiting for them on the other side.

"So he's been trying to get **Where's von Dietelburg?** intel from Luther ever since. With-

out much success. According to Fortin, he resisted with a 'religious-like fervor,' which of
course made us think of what went on at Castle
Wewelsburg.

"When I suggested to Fortin that the threat
of the hangman's noose might seem more real to
Cousin Luther if he was in the Tribunal prison
and could take his meals with Göring and company, whom he knows we're going to hang, he
agreed to let me bring him here.

"Where Odessa took him out with a cyanide
capsule."

"So where do you—we—go from here?"
Serov asked.

"I don't know about you, Chum Ivan, but I'm
going to Strasbourg tomorrow to bury my beloved
cousin Luther beside his parents in the Sainte-
Hélène Cemetery. And right about now, I think,
a Strasbourg policeman is going to visit Ingebord
in her cell and tell her she's a widow. One of Jean-
Paul's policemen, if I have to say that.

"He will tell her she will have to get Fortin's
permission to attend the interment. The idea
being to see how quickly—and via whom—the
word gets out that he's dead and that there will
be a funeral at Sainte-Hélène's. Whether or not
she goes, Fortin will cover the cemetery with his
people to see who turns up."

"Do you want me to go with you?" Janice
asked.

Cronley considered that a moment.

"As a friend or the AP needing a ride?"

"Both."

"Okay," Cronley said.

"Thank you, Jim, for your candor," Serov said.

"As I said before, Chum Ivan, the way to get me to run at the mouth is to ply me with champagne and flowers."

[TWO]
Sainte-Hélène Cemetery
Schiltigheim, near Strasbourg,
France
1605 2 March 1946

There was a small chapel Cronley hadn't noticed during his first visit to the cemetery. The monks of the monastery were using it to perform the mass of Christian burial for Luther Stauffer.

Cronley, Janice, DCI Special Agent Max Ostrowski—who was filling in as Cronley's bodyguard as Cezar Zieliński was in Vienna—Commandant Fortin, and Captain Pierre DuPres were standing in the shadow of a large mausoleum a hundred yards away. They had watched as the Widow Stauffer arrived in a prison van. First a wheelchair had been unloaded from the van, and then Frau Stauffer, who was dressed in a prison-gray dress. Two burly matrons had seated her in the wheelchair, then handcuffed her to it.

She had then been wheeled into the chapel past a small crowd of people—some with umbrellas against a light snowfall—gathered outside. Next, the ex-ambulance that had carried Luther Stauffer's remains from Nuremberg rolled up. A half dozen monks took the casket from the ambulance and carried it into the chapel. They were followed by a procession of monks, and finally by perhaps the dozen remaining people who were standing outside.

"Full house," Cronley observed.

"How long is this going to take?" Janice asked. "My tuchus is freezing."

"Long enough, I hope," Captain DuPres said, "for our photographers to get good pictures of the mourners."

The mass took about forty minutes before a procession of monks preceded the casket out of the chapel. The procession headed for the burial site as the civilian mourners made their way out of the building. Finally the widow was rolled out. She was not handcuffed, but there was a matron on either side of her.

She looked around the cemetery and spotted Cronley.

Oh, shit!

She jumped out of the wheelchair, pointed at

Cronley, and screamed, **"Meurtrier,** sonofabitch **meurtrier, j'espère que vous brûlerez en enfer!"**

One of the matrons grabbed her hand and shoved a hypodermic through the gray prison dress. A moment later she sagged, and the matrons settled her in the wheelchair.

"What was she yelling?" Janice asked.

"It was unpleasant, **mademoiselle**, not important," Fortin said.

"Murderer, sonofabitch murderer," Cronley softly made the translation. "I hope you burn in hell."

"Oh, Jimmy!" Janice said.

"Let's get the hell out of here and go home," Cronley said.

[THREE]
The Duchess Suite
Farber Palast
Stein, near Nuremberg
American Zone of Occupation,
** Germany**
0805 3 March 1946

Lieutenant Tom Winters knocked at the door of the Duchess Suite, the expression on his face making it clear that he wished he could be doing something—anything—else.

He had to knock three times before there was a response.

"What?" Cronley called, not at all pleasantly.

"Lieutenant Winters, sir. May I come in?"

Cronley called, "Wait a minute," and then turned to Miss Janice Johansen, with whom he was sharing the enormous bed.

"You can either make a dash for the bathroom or hide under the covers."

"Why?" she asked. "Tom already suspects—hell, knows damned well—that I'm in here."

She rolled onto her back and pulled the sheet up under her chin.

"Come!" Cronley called.

Winters entered the room, carefully keeping his eyes away from the bed.

"You can say hello to Janice, she thinks you already know our shameful secret."

"Hi, Tom," Janice said. "How's every little thing?"

"This better be important," Cronley said. "I had a very bad day yesterday, from which I have by no means recovered."

Winters crossed the room and handed Cronley an envelope.

"What's this?" Cronley asked, then took a closer look at the envelope. It was postmarked Vienna, with the name and address of the sender, neither of which Cronley recognized. It was addressed to **Herr J. D. Cronley, Offen-**

bach Platz 101, München**, which was the address of the Mansion.

"It came first thing this morning," Winters said.

"You didn't open it?"

"It's addressed to you."

"But you decided I should have it right away?"

"I had one of those 'go with your gut' feelings you're always talking about."

Cronley opened the envelope. It contained a single sheet of paper.

"Typewritten," he said. "Unsigned. In English." And then he read it: "'Inasmuch as I believe I have found what you're looking for, I strongly suggest you join me as soon as possible, letting as few people as possible know you're doing so.' No signature."

"Zieliński?"

"Who else?" Cronley asked. "But why didn't he get on the phone? Why a letter sent through the Austrian postal system?"

"Gut reaction?" Winters asked.

Cronley made a **Come on** gesture with his right hand.

"He probably thinks he's being surveilled, that he doesn't have access to a secure phone, and that there are moles both in the Austrians you've been dealing with and even in Colonel Wasserman's CIC operation."

Cronley grunted.

After perhaps fifteen seconds, which seemed longer, he said, "That gut feeling you mentioned, Tom?"

"What about it?"

"My gut tells me that we should get in our airplanes and go listen to some Johann Strauss music."

"We? Now?"

"We. Now. Get on the horn to the airfield."

"Why do I get the feeling I'm not going?" Janice asked.

"Because you're not."

He threw off the sheet covering him and marched naked to a chest of drawers in search of underwear.

[FOUR]
Suite 330
The Hotel Bristol
Kaerntner Ring 1, Vienna, Austria
1405 3 March 1946

"Thank you for coming so quickly, sir," Cronley said to Colonel Carl Wasserman, the chief, CIC-Vienna.

Wasserman, trailed by Charley Spurgeon, quickly entered the room and closed the door behind them.

Tom Winters and Oskar Wieczorek, an enormous blond-headed Pole who was filling in for Cezar Zieliński as Cronley's bodyguard, rose from the couch on which they had been sitting.

"If I'd known you were coming, I'd have sent a car to Schwechat," Wasserman said.

"Take a look at this, sir," Cronley said, as he handed him Zieliński's letter, "and then I'll tell you why I didn't want you, or anyone, to know we were coming. And as far as 'we' are concerned, Colonel, this is Tom Winters and Oskar Wieczorek."

Both men said, "Sir."

Wasserman waved them back onto the couch.

"Tom, Oskar, I already told you the colonel is one of the good guys. And this is Charley Spurgeon. We were at the Holabird School for Boys together."

Wasserman shook his head at the irreverent reference to the U.S. Army Counterintelligence Center and School at Camp Holabird, Maryland.

"If you're who I think you are, son," Wasserman said to Winters, "I used to work for your dad. And come to think of it, I think I also know your father-in-law. Right, Thomas Winters?"

"Guilty, sir," Winters said.

"How did a nice boy like you wind up with the Loose Cannon?" Wasserman asked, then quickly added, "Don't answer that. I don't think

I want to know. But when you write, give my regards to your mother and dad."

"I'll do that, sir," Winters said.

Wasserman turned his attention to the letter. When he finished, he held it out toward Spurgeon. "Okay with you, Loose Cannon?"

"Yes, sir. And if it pleases the colonel, the captain prefers 'Super Spook' to 'Loose Cannon.'"

"Duly noted," Wasserman said. "From Zieliński? When did you get this?"

"Who else?" Cronley replied. "It was delivered early this morning."

"Do you think by 'what you're looking for' he means von Dietelburg?"

"I certainly hope so."

"If Zieliński has found von Dietelburg," Spurgeon said, "he must have been in the Viktoria Palast—and wearing a name tag—the first time Zieliński walked in—and that's only been a couple of days."

"The question should be directed to Zieliński," Cronley said. "And where the hell is he?"

There was a knock at the door.

"What the hell is that?" Cronley asked impatiently, and then ordered, "Tom, answer that."

Winters had just opened the door a crack when it was pushed open so quickly and hard that it struck him in the face. He staggered backward.

Cronley reached for his pistol, as Wieczorek

retrieved a Schmeisser machine pistol from under the couch.

Then he said, as he signaled Wieczorek to lower the Schmeisser, "Shit! Jesus H. Christ! What the hell?"

"Sorry, young man," a middle-aged grandmotherly woman wearing an ornate hat and holding a dachshund puppy against her ample breast, said to Winters. "I didn't think I had time to stand in the hall and explain myself."

"What the hell is going on, Rahil?" Cronley asked.

"I have reluctantly concluded that Nikolayevich Merkulov is on to me," she said. "Cronley, you have to get me out of Vienna to somewhere safe."

"I don't believe I've had the pleasure," Wasserman said.

"Can I tell him?" Cronley asked.

"Since I just told you Merkulov is on to me, why not?" the grandmotherly woman said. She put out her hand to Wasserman, as if she expected him to kiss, rather that shake, it.

"I know who you are, Colonel," she said. "My name is Rahil—that's Rachel in English—Rothschild. General Gehlen—and of course Cronley—call me 'Seven-K.'"

Wasserman rose to the occasion. He bowed over her hand and kissed it.

"**Enchanté, madame,**" he said.

"I have been—I suppose, for the moment, still am—a **polkovnik** of the NKGB. I am also an agent of Mossad. I confess the latter because I know you're also a Jew."

"One whose allegiance, Polkovnik, is to the United States," Wasserman said.

"I'm not too fond of Mossad myself right now. The Vienna station chief—an American, by the way—told me yesterday that not only can't he risk his operation here by helping me avoid the NKGB, but refused to let me appeal to Reuven Zamir."

"Who's he?" Cronley asked.

"I'm surprised you don't know, James, that he's the chief of Mossad."

"In other words, this sonofabitch, this **American** sonofabitch, threw you under the bus when you asked for help?"

"I'm not familiar with that phrase, but I think I take the meaning. Yes, he threw me under the bus."

"How'd you learn the NKGB is on to you?"

"I am not—was not—the only Mossad agent in the NKGB."

"Okay. The question now becomes how do we get you out of here?"

"The NKGB has people on the staff of the hotel. They report when anyone is occupying the CIC's home away from home," Wasserman said. "If the NKGB is looking for . . . this lady, there's a good chance—almost a certainty—they know she's in here."

"Then we have to get her out of here," Cronley said. "As soon as possible."

"Out of here to where?"

"To Schwechat. From which Tom will fly her and Wieczorek to the Compound and turn her over—without telling Wallace, Tom—to General Gehlen for safekeeping."

"I think we need a word in private, Captain Cronley," Wasserman said.

Captain Cronley?

Oh, shit! Is he going to cause me trouble?

Is he trying to cover his ass?

"Colonel Wasserman, I think everybody has the Need to Know what you want to say to me."

Wasserman's face whitened before he replied.

"Have you considered that the NKGB wants you, as well as this lady, dead? Or, now that I think about it, really would like to have both of you in a basement cell on Lubyanka Square in Moscow?

"And that they are probably perfectly willing to suffer the ire of the Americans—and maybe the English—on the Quadripartite Commission for doing one or the other in the lobby of the Bristol?"

"Or risk that ire by bursting into the suite here and blowing us away right here. Without witnesses," Cronley argued. "That's an even worse scenario."

There was a long silence. Then Cronley sighed and spoke.

"This is what I'm going to do, presuming Tom and Oskar are willing to go along. If the NKGB or Odessa is finally successful in blowing me away, they're going to cause a stink, hopefully a great big stink, when they do.

"They're going to have to blow me—and Tom and Rachel and Oskar—away in the lobby of the Bristol Hotel. Or on the sidewalk outside as we get in a taxicab. Or on the way to Schwechat. They're not just going to fade into the darkness.

"The NKGB guy—or the Odessa guy—who shot Bonehead Moriarty in the head with a silenced .22 thinking it was me disappeared into the darkness. Round One to the NKGB or Odessa. There were three Odessa people who tried to whack Tom and me on the airport road. I took out one of them, and wounded one. The other got away. In my book, that gives Round Two to the Good Guys.

"This is Round Three. If I'm going to go down—and that seems likely—I'm going to go down fighting. Remember the Alamo."

"I can't believe you actually said that," Tom Winters said.

"What's the Alamo?" Oskar asked.

"Pay attention, Oskar," Cronley said. "Texas History 101, 1836. The bad guy then was a Mexican general named Antonio de Padua María Severino López de Santa Anna y Pérez de Lebrón. He led an army into what is now the Great State of Texas—"

"That was really his name?" Tom asked, chuckling.

"I'm shocked they didn't teach you this at Hudson High," Cronley replied. "Yes, it was. Pray let me continue. This bad guy, commonly known as Santa Anna, led an army—a very large army—across the San Antonio River with the intention of quelling the restless natives—most of them Southerners, but with a sprinkling of Yankees—who had the odd notion they didn't want to be Mexicans.

"He encountered one hundred sixty of them who had turned an old mission building called the Alamo into sort of a fort. He called upon them to surrender, pointing out that he outnumbered them about twenty-five to one, and that he had cannons and they did not.

"They gave him the finger.

"So from February twenty-third until March sixth, Santa Anna's cannons bombarded the one hundred sixty guys in the Alamo. Then early in the morning his troops assaulted the Alamo. The first attack was repulsed. And so was the second. The third succeeded. Every one of the one hundred sixty defenders died. Most Texans—including this one—believe Santa Anna shot the few survivors, in other words, the wounded unable to lift a rifle.

"There were between six hundred and sixteen hundred—give or take—Mexicans KIA."

"KIA?" Oskar asked.

"Killed in action," Wasserman explained.

"The fighting to the death—or the murder—of one hundred sixty of their friends and neighbors at the Alamo mightily pissed off the other Americans in the area, and using **Remember the Alamo** as their battle cry, they raised an army under General Sam Houston.

"On April twenty-first, ol' Sam and the boys defeated Santa Anna's army at the Battle of San Jacinto. We Texans say, **We whupped their ass real good**. We also captured Santa Anna himself. After he surrendered, we forced him to march his army back across the river into Mexico.

"**Remember the Alamo** was also popular during the Mexican–American War of 1848, during which we again whupped their ass real good, and which ended with their surrender at Guadalupe.

"So, yeah, Tom, I said, 'Remember the Alamo.' Would you rather get whacked in here, or take the chance the NKGB won't try to whack us as we walk through the lobby?"

"Frankly, I would rather be back at Hudson

High having dreams of winning glory on some distant battlefield. When are we going?"

"This is as good a time as any," Cronley said. "I don't like the idea of them coming through that door."

"Give me fifteen minutes, please, Cronley," Wasserman said.

"Sir, with respect, I suggest the best thing for you and Charley to do is stay out of the line of fire."

"I want to go with you, Jim," Spurgeon said.

"Not wise, Charley," Cronley said.

"I think I can get enough people here in fifteen minutes to even the odds," Colonel Wasserman said, as he picked up the telephone.

XVI

[ONE]
Suite 330
The Hotel Bristol
Kaerntner Ring 1, Vienna, Austria
1655 3 March 1946

When there was a knock at the door, Cronley rose from the armchair in which he was sitting, moved to the bedroom door, and leveled a Schmeisser machine pistol at the door.

"Charley," he ordered softly, "back against the wall. Then open the door quickly and wide."

Spurgeon nodded.

"Make sure the safety is off," Cronley added.

Spurgeon flung the door open quickly and wide, revealing two men, Walter Wangermann, the chief of intelligence of the Vienna Police, and Bruno Holzknecht, his chief of surveillance.

When he saw Cronley's leveled Schmeisser, Wangermann dove for the floor of the corridor. Holzknecht raised his hands in surrender.

"Well, look who's here," Cronley said. "Bruno, why don't you help Walter get up and bring him in?"

"Gottverdammt Amerikaner!" Wangermann muttered, not quietly, as he got, unaided, to his feet and entered the room.

"I was just about to call you," Cronley said. "To see if you know where our friend Cezar Zieliński is."

"Where's Oberst Wasserman?" Wangermann demanded.

"I already asked him," Cronley said. "He doesn't know."

"I asked where he is."

"You just missed him," Cronley said. "He didn't say where he was going, but he said he'd be back in time for dinner."

"And what are you doing in Vienna?"

"I came to see how much of my money Cezar Zieliński has lost at the vingt-et-un tables at the Viktoria Palast."

"A lot," Holzknecht said, chuckling.

This earned him a dirty look from Wangermann.

"My sources tell me that at about half past two this afternoon, eight of Wasserman's men came here in three staff cars. Further, that they rode the elevator to this floor, suggesting they were headed for this suite. They reappeared in the lobby three minutes later, now brandishing submachine guns and forming a protective shield around an old woman—the same woman, from her description, who sips tea by the **gottverdammt** hour with a **gottverdammt** dachshund in her lap in the lobby—and marched her through the lobby. They put her in the middle staff car and all three took off, sirens screaming, down the Ring.

"Wasserman's cars were later located as they were leaving the Schwechat airfield. The old woman was not in the cars, nor in the airfield terminal, which is interesting because no aircraft of any airline had left the airport in the previous three hours. You want to explain any, preferably all, of this, Captain Strasbourger?"

"Do you want me to bullshit you?"

"You arrogant little sonofabitch!"

"I'll take that as a 'no,'" Cronley said. "Hypothetically speaking, Herr Wangermann—"

"'Hypothetically'?" Wangermann asked sarcastically.

"Let's say, just for the sake of conversation, that a lady in her middle years—a Jewish lady, that's important—came to you and said she had just escaped across the border from Gábor Péter's Allamvedelmi Osztaly in Budapest, and requested asylum—"

"I'm surprised, Captain Strasbourger, that you even know what the AVO is, much less that sonofabitch Gábor."

"I'm DCI, we know everything."

"Scheisse," Wangermann said, but he was unable to control his smile.

"So you are about to grant her wish when the Russian member of the Quadripartite Commission goes before the whole commission and says, 'It has come to our attention that your Vienna Police, specifically Herr Walter Wangermann, is holding a notorious Hungarian criminal, by the name—let's say—of Rachel Rothschild, and we demand that she be immediately turned over to us so that she can face Hungarian justice. Pulling the wings off flies and letting your dachshund piss on state-controlled fire hydrants is conduct that simply cannot be tolerated.'"

"Why does the AVO really want her?"

"I have no idea that I can share with you."

"In other words, she's been working for you? For the DCI?"

"There's a rumor going around that she's friendly with Reinhard Gehlen. But getting back to my hypothetical. What would you do under these hypothetical circumstances? Turn her over in handcuffs to the Communists?"

Wangermann didn't reply.

"Or, maybe, since we both know that Gábor Péter executes people he doesn't like by slow strangulation, would you maybe let her escape, thus giving the Reds the finger?"

"What finger?"

Cronley demonstrated.

"Let me give you another hypothetical," Cronley went on. "Let's say our hypothetical nice Jewish lady with a dachshund didn't go to you. Let's say she met a fellow dog lover, say an American tourist—"

"You're not an American tourist."

"Let's say this American tourist has a passport identifying him as a tourist, which satisfied the Austrian authorities when he landed at Schwechat. In his private airplane—"

"That black Storch with identification marks that can't be read from twenty feet," Wangermann said. "I should have guessed that was yours."

"And let's say this nice Jewish lady told this American tourist that she had a problem.

This got to the American tourist because he had been a Boy Scout, and there is nothing that makes a Boy Scout happier than when he is able to help a nice old lady. To get across the street, for example, or to get her puppy out of Austria and into another country even if the puppy didn't have the proper papers to satisfy the authorities.

"Now, hypothetically, of course, if the American tourist had arranged for the nice old lady and her pooch to get discreetly out of Austria and into another country, she would not have had to appeal to Walter Wangermann for asylum and Walter would have been able to look the Soviet member of the Quadripartite Commission in the eye and declare, 'I don't know nothing about no Jewish lady and her dachshund.'"

"And what would you have done, Captain Strasbourger, if the NKGB had wanted the nice old Jewish lady so bad they tried to take you down in the lobby of the hotel? Or on the sidewalk?"

"Shot back," Cronley said. "But I thought it was worth the risk. They like the odds in their favor. I didn't think they'd have more than four bad guys. We had eight of Wasserman's people, plus Tom, Charley, Oskar, and me."

Wangermann considered that a moment, and then asked, "So she's out of Austria?"

Cronley nodded.

"To where?"

"If I told you that, you wouldn't be able to say, 'I have no idea where this woman you're talking about is.'"

Wangermann nodded.

"Bruno," he ordered, "tell him what you know about Zieliński."

Holzknecht chuckled as he gathered his thoughts.

"As I said before, Captain Cronley, he's having a good time losing a lot of your money and being consoled by our ladies of the evening. This, if he shows up at the Viktoria Palast as he usually does between eight and eight-thirty, will be his fifth night there. On the second night, he won a bundle, but on the other nights he lost. Heavily. He has spent every night—actually every **morning** after three or four a.m.—with a different whore."

"At this place? At the Viktoria Palast?"

"No. It's not a brothel. He goes with them. And that's what's made it difficult—impossible—to surveil him."

"I don't understand."

"The girls use private apartments—not theirs, apartments of ordinary people down on their luck who really need the money—or the carton of cigarettes, pound of coffee—the girls give them for the use of a room. My people can follow him until he enters a usually bomb-damaged and yet-to-be-repaired building. But they don't know where he's going in the building. Or if he is going through the building to another location. Get the picture?"

"Yeah."

"So, my people lose him at, say, three or four o'clock in the morning and don't pick him up again until he shows up at the Vik at eight or eight-thirty that night."

"Which means you don't know where he is."

"What I can do, Captain, is have one of my men intercept him as he's about to enter the Vik and whisper in his ear that you're here in the Bristol."

"Or I could go to this place."

"You know better than that, Captain Strasbourger," Wangermann said.

"I don't look like a successful black marketeer? Is that what you're saying?"

"No offense, but you and Lieutenant Spurgeon look like those Boy Scouts you're always talking about."

"That leaves us only Bruno's guy whispering in his ear when he shows up at the Viktoria tonight."

"That's what it looks like to me," Wangermann said. "If you're worried about the NKGB bursting in here, I can send you some company."

Cronley considered that a moment.

"Thanks, many thanks, but no thanks. Maybe one guy, or two, drinking tea in the lobby. I don't think Joe Stalin's evil minions will try to whack us if they see you're watching over us."

Wangermann, who had been sitting in an armchair, rose with a grunt.

"**Auf Wiedersehen**, Captain Strasbourger," he said.

"**Auf Wiedersehen**, Herr Wiener Schnitzel. **Vielen Dank.**"

[TWO]
Suite 330
The Hotel Bristol
Kaerntner Ring 1, Vienna, Austria
1715 3 March 1946

"I have just had a very dangerous thought," Cronley said to Spurgeon. "We could probably, with Wangermann's guys by now sipping tea in the lobby, manage to get across the lobby into the bar, for a cold Pilsen and pretzels without getting blown away."

"Should we take the submachine guns with us?"

"If we take them with us, it will not only look as if we are looking for a fight, but cause consternation among the other guests in the lobby."

"I vote for causing consternation," Spurgeon said.

"Decisions, decisions," Cronley said. "Let me ponder . . ."

There was a knuckle rapping at the door.

"Shit," Cronley said as he picked up the Schmeisser. Spurgeon grabbed his Thompson and quickly ran to the door, putting his back against the wall beside it.

"Say when," he said.

Cronley positioned himself in the bathroom door and leveled the Schmeisser at the door.

"If I forget to mention this, Charley, it's been nice knowing you. When!"

"Likewise," Spurgeon said, and pulled the door open.

Cezar Zieliński walked through it.

"I'm tempted to shoot you on general principles," Cronley greeted him. "Where the hell have you been?"

"Waiting in a broom closet down the hall for you to finish with Wangermann and Holzknecht. I don't suppose you have a beer?"

"There's plenty of beer, all room temperature. The ice machine down the hall is on the fritz."

"I learned to drink warm beer in Ol' Blighty," Zieliński said. "I also learned that you can cool beer by putting it outside one's room on the windowsill."

"You're in a chipper mood."

"I had a very good night last night," Zieliński

said. "How much of my winnings with your money do I get to keep?"

"How much have you left after paying the hooker?"

"Lots. Do I detect a tone of moral disapproval? And how did you hear about the hooker?"

"Hookers, plural. From Holzknecht."

There came another knuckle rap at the door.

"Jesus Christ, now what?" Cronley said.

"The NKGB apparently saw you come out of the broom closet," Spurgeon said, as he walked to the door and put his back to the wall beside it.

"If I had one of those, I could probably be of some assistance," Zieliński said.

Cronley took his pistol from its holster and tossed it to Zieliński, who immediately saw that the hammer was cocked and locked.

"A round in the chamber? Jesus Christ! You are dangerous!" he said, then took up a position behind one of the armchairs.

"Now, Charley," Cronley ordered.

Tom Winters came through the open door.

He raised his arms above his head and said, "I surrender."

"You're supposed to be in the Compound sitting on Rachel," Cronley said.

"General Gehlen is sitting on Rachel. She's safe. But I didn't think Gehlen could protect me from Colonel Wallace."

"Wallace knows about Rachel?"

"He had a guy at the Compound airstrip. He showed up in Gehlen's quarters about three minutes after I got there with Rachel. The shit immediately thereafter began to strike the blades of the fan."

"Go on."

"Wallace wanted to take Rachel. Gehlen wouldn't give her up. Wallace is sputtering. For a moment, I thought . . . I don't know. Anyway, they got on the SIGABA to Mr. Schultz, and Wallace unloaded on him. Schultz said (a) Gehlen was to protect Rachel, and (b) he thought he had best come to Germany to see what the hell was going on."

"Schultz is coming to Germany?"

"Arriving sometime tomorrow."

"Jesus!"

"And he asked where you were. Wallace said he didn't know, which was embarrassing. Wallace then called Nuremberg and they said they didn't know where you were. He then asked me if I knew where you were, and I said, 'Probably in Vienna,' and when I truthfully said I did not know where in Vienna you were, said answer did not satisfy him.

"After saying 'We'll see how General Seidel feels about this debacle,' or words to that effect, he stormed out of Gehlen's quarters. I then went out the back door of Gehlen's quarters, got on the general's bicycle, and pedaled to the air-strip, where they had just finished refueling the Storch. And here I am. What's going on?"

"Cezar," Cronley said, "I'm afraid to ask this question. Do you know where von Dietel-burg is?"

"Not at the moment, but I'm fairly sure he'll be at the Viktoria Palast at, say, nine o'clock."

"You've seen him?"

Zieliński nodded.

"And you didn't tell Wasserman or Wanger-mann?"

"No. And I thought I'd better explain why in person. That's why I sent that letter . . . by ordi-nary mail."

Cronley made a **Let's have it** gesture with his hands.

"Okay. Von Dietelburg has been hiding in plain sight right under our—and more impor-tant, Wangermann's and Holzknecht's—noses. He's Olga Reithoffer's brother, Alois, the used-car dealer."

"Jesus! You're sure?"

Zieliński nodded.

"The first night, I lost a little over five thou-sand of your dollars and met Colonel Gus Ge-netti, his friend Alois Reithoffer, and Inge—I never learned her last name. Inge cost you three hundred of your dollars, but she was worth every penny. Not only was she a skilled practitioner of her chosen profession, but when we were finished bringing the **Kama Sutra** to life, she confided in me a naughty story about Olga Reithoffer, Colonel Genetti, and Alois. Inge was Colonel Genetti's devoted **Schatzi** as long as he was in town, but the minute he left, Alois moved into 71 Cobenzlgasse."

" 'He's her brother, what's wrong with that?' I challenged.

"Inge told me, 'His name isn't really Reithoffer. It's von something. He's a Nazi on the run.' So naturally I asked her how she knows that—"

"Why is she telling you all this?" Winters asked.

"When I was in London, there were posters on just about every wall. **Loose Lips Sink Ships.** I took that to heart, slightly modified— **And booze loosens lips**. Inge likes champagne. French champagne. It's fifty dollars a bottle. I took two bottles with us to our love nest.

"So Inge says she knows because she's heard Willi call him Franz. So I ask, 'Willi who?' And she says she doesn't know, just that Franz calls him 'Herr General.' "

"Just maybe," Cronley said thoughtfully, "General der Infanterie Wilhelm Burgdorf?"

"Inge says that sometimes Willi brings cars from the country to Vienna. Anyway, I thought I should bring this to your attention."

"I would much rather have had a telephone call,

saying that with the cooperation of the Austrian authorities, former SS-Brigadeführer Franz von Dietelburg has at long last been apprehended. Why the hell didn't you go to Wangermann?"

"That's what I wanted to talk to you about face-to-face."

"Start talking."

"Did you know that fifty percent of the SS officer corps were Austrian?"

"I heard sixty, but so what?"

"You knew that Wangermann and Holzknecht almost got themselves hung by the SS?"

Cronley nodded. "There is a point, right?"

"Good Austrians—like Wangermann and Holzknecht—are embarrassed about Austria's role with Nazism starting with the Anschluss. They would really like to put von Dietelburg on a Nuremberg-style trial to show the world that Austria—"

"I get the point. So what?"

"The Vienna prison is not the Tribunal prison. Von Dietelburg has answers to a lot of questions—about Odessa, Wewelsburg Castle, what happened to the contents of Himmler's safe, **und so weiter**. Even if we grab von Dietelburg, there will still be faithful Odessa people out there. And if they could whack your cousin Luther in the Tribunal prison, they could damn sure whack von Dietelburg in Wangermann's jail to close his mouth permanently."

Cronley didn't immediately reply.

"It's your call, Jim. Do you want to have Wangermann put him on trial here? Or do you want to take the sonofabitch somewhere where we can get answers?"

"What are you proposing, Cezar?"

"That we snatch him as he arrives at the Viktoria Palast, take him to the airport, load him into a Storch, and fly him to the Compound. After Gehlen interrogates him, we announce his capture, lock him up in the Tribunal prison, and then try him."

"I don't want to rain on your parade, Cezar," Tom Winters said, "but have you considered the collateral damage your kidnap scenario will probably cause?"

"Collateral damage to who?"

"To Jim, me, Charley, and you. If we got away with this, Wangermann would want our heads."

"Your call, Jim," Spurgeon said.

"There's no time to get on the SIGABA and ask El Jefe what he thinks is there?" Cronley asked.

"'General Greene, this is ASA Fulda. Captain Cronley just said something to Mr. Schultz that I thought I should bring to your attention immediately,'" Spurgeon said.

"Whereupon Greene would call Wasserman and tell him to sit on us to prevent an international incident," Cronley said.

"Your call, Captain," Zieliński said.

"Tell me the lay of the land around the Viktoria," Cronley said.

"There's an alley next to it. Valet parking. You drive in, get out of your car, and walk back to the entrance on Weihburggasse and go in the Viktoria. The valet then parks your car."

"Where?" Winters asked.

"Various places. They don't have a garage."

"The valets drive further down the alley? What's down there?"

"I don't know. All I know is they drive further down the alley."

"How do you get your car back?"

"They deliver it to the front of the Vik."

"Do they bring it out of the alley, or does it show up on the street?"

"You sound as if you intend to go along with Cezar's kidnapping scenario," Winters said.

"I don't think if we're this close to von Dietelburg we can let him go," Cronley said, and then asked, "How bad do we need him? How many people have been looking for him? For how long?"

"Point taken," Winters said. "**Points** taken. Reluctantly."

"I'm open to suggestion, Tom," Cronley said.

Winters shrugged and threw up his hands in a gesture of helplessness and resignation.

"I think we should take a walk down Weihburggasse and see if we see what's at the end of the alley."

"We're not going to look very innocent if I'm carrying a Thompson," Spurgeon said.

"Then you better leave it here with Cezar."

"You don't want me to go?"

"Yours is a familiar face, Cezar. Don't worry. Both Charley and I passed the Techniques of Surveillance course in Spy School."

[THREE]
Near the Viktoria Palast
Weihburggasse, Vienna, Austria
2105 3 March 1946

A dark blue—almost black—1938 Mercedes-Benz 320B Cabriolet turned off Weihburggasse into the alley beside the Viktoria Palast.

"Nice," Cezar Zieliński observed. "I wonder how long that was hidden in a haystack on some ex-**Standartenführer**'s farm?" And then he immediately added, as he saw a second Mercedes, this one slightly smaller than the first, come into the alley, "Shit, there's another one!"

"I'll take the second," Cronley said, "you make sure von Dietelburg is in the first."

The first convertible drove halfway down the alley and stopped. The second pulled in behind it.

Two men quickly appeared, one going to each car and opening its driver's-side door.

"Hände hoch!" Cronley and Zieliński ordered just about simultaneously as they stepped away from the wall where they had concealed themselves. They held pistols in their hands, moving them from the faces of the men who had opened the doors, and those of the one man who had gotten out of his car, and the one still behind the wheel of the first.

"Guten Abend, Herr von Dietelburg," Cronley said in German. "I've been looking forward to meeting you for some time." He raised his voice. "I've got von Dietelburg!"

"And I think I have General Burgdorf," Zieliński called back.

Tom Winters and Charley Spurgeon, both carrying Thompsons, ran down the alley toward them.

"Pat him down, Tom," Cronley ordered, "while I deal with the valets."

There came the sound and the muzzle blasts of a Thompson firing short bursts.

"What the hell?" Cronley called.

"Spurgeon just took out two guys who appeared out of nowhere carrying Schmeissers," Zieliński called.

"If von Dietelburg tries to get away, Tom," Cronley ordered, "kill him."

He turned to the valet.

"On the ground. On your belly. If you move before we're out of here, you're dead."

He went to the first car in time to see Charley Spurgeon first examine the corpses of the men he had killed and then throw up on the closest one.

Cronley looked at the corpulent man behind the wheel of the first car.

"Out, General," he ordered, and then to the second valet, "On your belly on the ground!"

"You're making a mistake," the corpulent man said.

Zieliński grabbed his arm and jerked him out of the car and began to pat him down. He came up with a revolver, and showed it to Cronley.

"A Smith & Wesson .38," Cronley said. "Favorite weapon of Nazi big shots. Göring had one. So much for the famed Luger Parabellum." Then he raised his voice. "Charley, when you finish tossing your cookies, your services are required. We need the adhesive tape!"

"I'll drive this one with Spurgeon," Zieliński said. "And you the other one with Tom. Okay?"

"Do we adhesive-tape Chubby here or after we get him in the backseat?"

"He's not going to fit in the backseat. He'll have to go in the trunk."

Spurgeon appeared.

"Sorry," he said, and then made sort of an explanation. "The one I threw up on had his eyes open and looked surprised."

"Tape him good, Charley, and then put him in the trunk."

Not more than three minutes later, both Mercedeses drove to the end of the alley, turned right, and wound their way through several alleys until they emerged on Kaerntner Ring, where they turned left and headed for the Schwechat airport.

[FOUR]
The South German Industrial
   Development Organization
   Compound
Pullach, Bavaria
American Zone of Occupation,
   Germany
0405 4 March 1946

There was no air-to-ground radio link between the two Storchs and the Compound airstrip, which meant Cronley and Winters could not ask for the runway lights to be turned on. It was necessary to make several low-level passes before the lights flickered on.

Cronley was therefore not at all surprised, as he taxied up to what served as combined control tower and base operations, to find Colonel Harold Wallace and several members of his staff waiting for him. He also saw General Gehlen and former Obersten Ludwig Mannberg and Otto Niedermeyer. They were not standing with Wallace.

Cronley climbed down from the Storch, and Charley Spurgeon climbed down after him.

"Now what, Loose Cannon?" Wallace greeted him.

"Lieutenant Spurgeon, this is Colonel Wallace, chief of DCI-Europe," Cronley said.

"Who the hell is he?"

"He was formerly Colonel Wasserman's assistant."

"Formerly?"

"Colonel, if you would please summon a squad—a platoon would be better—of the security force, I will introduce our other passengers."

"Who are?"

"I'd really rather not say until we get a platoon out here."

"Goddamn you! Who?"

"If you insist, sir. I have former SS-Brigadeführer Franz von Dietelburg in my aircraft and former General der Infanterie Wilhelm Burgdorf neatly trussed up in Lieutenant Winters's aircraft."

"Are you drunk, Cronley?"

"No," Cronley said. "And while you're summoning the troops, you'd better get Dr. Williamson out here."

"Somebody injured, Cronley?" Dr. Williamson asked from the rear of the pack gathered around Wallace. Cronley hadn't seen him.

"There's some injured ego, Doctor, but what I need you to do for me is to body-search my guests. We were in sort of a rush leaving Vienna, and there wasn't time to do it there. And I don't want either of the bastards to bite on a cyanide capsule."

A jeep and a three-quarter-ton weapons carrier loaded with large black soldiers rolled up.

First Sergeant Abraham L. Tedworth got out of the jeep.

"Honest Abe, I'm really glad to see you!" Cronley said. "There are two characters in the Storchs who need to be taken to my former quarters, where Doc Williamson will body-search them."

"Yes, sir."

"If they give you any trouble, do not, repeat not, kill them. Break an arm, maybe, but we need these bastards alive."

"Yes, sir."

He made the **Join on me** gesture—balled fist held over his head in a pumping motion—and a dozen soldiers jumped out of the weapons carrier.

They went to the aircraft and removed the passengers, both wrapped in what looked like miles of adhesive tape. As they did so, General

Gehlen and former Obersten Niedermeyer and Mannberg walked up.

"What the hell?" Wallace asked.

Gehlen looked down at former General Burgdorf.

"Back from the dead, are you, Wilhelm?" he said.

"You treasonous swine!" Burgdorf said.

"I suppose that depends on your point of view," Gehlen said.

The soldiers put them in the bed of the weapons carrier, which then very slowly started off, with the soldiers trotting along beside and behind it.

[FIVE]
Office of the Military Government
Liaison Officer
The South German Industrial
Development Organization
Compound
Pullach, Bavaria
American Zone of Occupation,
Germany
0450 4 March 1946

"What we have, Cronley," Dr. Williamson said, "is two well-fed naked Germans who did not have anything like cyanide capsules concealed in their body's orifices. What do I do with them now?"

"Honest Abe," Cronley said, "after he has instructed his stalwart troopers, three of each, not to take their eyes off them for two seconds, will get them GI fatigues—no boots or shoes—to hide their nakedness. And come to think of it, Abe, it might be a good idea to put a couple of troopers outside the window of my former bedroom."

"Way ahead of you, Captain," Tedworth replied. "I've got two jeeps with pedestal .50 calibers sitting out there."

"Lieutenant Winters," Wallace said coldly, "since Captain Cronley doesn't seem to understand what a direct order is, this direct order is to you. Neither he, or you, or this officer"—he pointed to Spurgeon—"or Zieliński is to leave this building for any purpose until further orders. You understand?"

"Yes, sir."

"Sergeant Tedworth," Wallace went on, "you will see that they comply with my order."

"Yes, sir."

Wallace walked out of the building, with his staff trailing.

Cronley looked at Tedworth.

"Why are you smiling, Honest Abe?"

"That Kraut is the one everybody's been looking for?"

Cronley nodded. "And the other one is his boss."

"So why is Wallace so pissed at you?"

"I don't think he likes me."

"That's what they call an understatement. I happened to overhear what he said to General Seidel on the telephone."

"Which was?"

"'That loose cannon sonofabitch has caused an international incident. If Schultz wasn't on his way here, I'd have him locked up in the Fulda Stockade awaiting general court-martial.'"

"Speaking of telephones," Cronley said, and reached for the one on the desk.

"Get me Miss Janice Johansen at the Farber Palast Press Center in Nuremberg," he ordered.

[SIX]
0720 4 March 1946

"So you're telling me you left two dead men in that alley?" Major General Bruce T. Seidel, the USFET G-2, asked. "And then left without telling Colonel Wasserman or the Viennese police what had gone down?"

Wallace had ordered everyone but Winters, Spurgeon, Zieliński, and Cronley out of the room—which meant outside the building into lightly falling snow—when he had entered with Seidel.

"Yes, sir," Cronley admitted.

"My God! What the hell were you thinking?"

"Sir, I wanted to get von Dietelburg and Burgdorf out of Vienna."

"You shot the— What did you say, gambling casino guards?"

"I did, sir," Spurgeon said.

"That could be interpreted as murder. Kidnapping people is a felony, and any act in . . ."

He was drowned out by the roar of aircraft engines. A heavy roar, much louder than that of an L-4 or Storch.

"What the hell is that?" Seidel asked.

"Sounds like a C-45 to me," Cronley said.

"Can a C-45 land on that little airstrip?"

"I don't think I'd try it when it's snowing. But Colonel Wilson—"

"You think that's General White's C-45?"

"I think it's possible that General White—or at least his airplane—was waiting for Mr. Schultz at Rhine-Main, in order to bring him here."

"The only thing that could make this situation worse is for Hotshot Billy to kill Mr. Schultz in a crash landing," Seidel said.

About four minutes later, there was a knock at the door.

"Well, I guess he got it on the ground in one piece," Cronley said.

"Sir, there's a lady out here . . ." a trooper said.

He was pushed out of the way by Miss Janice Johansen of the Associated Press.

"You really have grabbed von Dietelburg, sweetheart?"

"Miss Johansen, I'm sorry, but you're not welcome here," Seidel said. "I'm going to have to ask you to leave."

The enormous trooper Janice had pushed aside now entered the room and put his massive hands on her arms, as if to pick her up.

"How about this, General," Janice asked. "Quote, Major General Bruce T. Seidel, the USFET G-2, had this reporter forcibly removed from the building where this reporter was verifying that former SS-Brigadeführer Franz von Dietelburg, sought for war crimes since the end of the war, had been finally captured by James Cronley of the DCI. End quote. You want that on the front page of the world's newspapers tomorrow morning?"

Seidel didn't reply, instead turning to Cronley.

"Did you tell Miss Johansen that you had captured . . . this wanted war criminal, Captain Cronley?"

"No, sir. Not by name. But I did tell her that she might find visiting here interesting."

"That's a distinction without much of a difference," Seidel said.

"One of Tiny's Troopers told me, quote, Super Spook has nabbed some Kraut named von Dietelburg that everybody's been looking for. End quote," Janice said.

"By Super Spook, presumably, he meant Captain Cronley?"

"That's what—for obvious reasons—Tiny's Troopers call him," Janice said.

"I have a deal with Janice, General," Cronley said. "She won't file her story until I tell her she can."

"Somehow, Captain, I don't find that at all reassuring."

"We've got the sonofabitch—and his boss. Why should that be a secret?" Cronley challenged.

Seidel literally had his mouth open to reply, but stopped when Major General I. D. White, followed by his aide-de-camp, Mr. Oscar Schultz, and a third man in a business suit, entered the room.

"General Seidel," Schultz said, "this is Colonel Cletus Frade, USMCR, who is deputy director for South America of the DCI. Clete, you know Colonel Wallace. And Super Spook."

"You got both of these characters, Jimmy?" Frade asked.

"Leaving dead bodies and outraged Austrian police in his wake," Wallace said.

"I wasn't talking to you, Colonel," Frade said coldly.

"Where's General Gehlen?" Schultz asked.

"I presume in his quarters," Wallace said.

"Ask him, Oberst Mannberg, and Mr. Niedermeyer to join us, please," Schultz said.

Wallace walked out of the room.

"What the hell are you doing here, Clete?" Cronley asked.

"I was in Washington admitting to my grandfather that I'm taking Howell Petroleum to the brink of financial ruin as its new president when El Jefe found me and told me he needed a ride over here. And why. So we got in the Howell Petroleum Constellation and here we are."

"I understood Mr. Schultz to say you were DCI deputy director for South America," Seidel said.

"That we don't talk about," Schultz said. "Take notice, Janice."

"My lips are sealed," she said.

Five minutes later, Gehlen, Niedermeyer, and Mannberg came into the room.

"Okay. We're all here," Schultz said. "Let's start with hearing Super Spook's version of what happened. I've already heard Wallace's and Wasserman's somewhat hysterical versions.

"Okay, Super Spook, start with Rachel, a.k.a. Seven-K."

"She came to me saying she had been outed—"

"Who are we talking about?" Seidel asked.

"She is—or was—an asset of mine. An NKGB colonel and also a Mossad agent," Gehlen said.

"Not an asset of yours, General," Schultz said. "An asset of DCI. As the Süd-Deutsche Industrielle Entwicklungsorganisation is a DCI asset."

"I stand corrected."

"Go on, Cronley."

"She came to me and said the NKGB was on to her, and she had to get out of Vienna. She said the Vienna Mossad guy had thrown her . . . had refused to help her."

"You knew she was an asset, correct?"

"Yes, I did."

"So you got her out of Vienna?"

"Yes."

"And where is she now?"

"In my quarters," General Gehlen said.

"And what do you think we should do with her now?"

"Argentina," Cronley said.

"She's still Mossad, a Nazi hunter. What about . . ."

"Our Nazis?" Cronley said. "She said she'd leave ours alone, that there were more than she could handle in Argentina already there under the Phoenix Program."

"General Gehlen?" Schultz asked.

"She's a woman of her word."

"General Seidel, do you have any problem with this?"

"I never heard of this person until just now."

"General White?"

"I'll go along with General Gehlen. Obviously, we can't continue to hide, to protect her here."

"Turning to von Dietelburg and Burgdorf. Cronley, why didn't you at least tell Colonel Wasserman what you planned to do?"

"I thought he'd order me to tell Wangermann that we thought we had him, and that Wangermann would grab him himself."

"Why would that be bad?"

Cronley told him.

"Anybody think that was a bad call?"

For a moment it looked as if Colonel Wallace had something to say, but in the end he was silent.

"Okay," Schultz said. "This is what's going to happen. It is not open for discussion. I say that because I had a long talk on the phone with Chief Justice Jackson when we landed at Rhine-Main. He already had heard from Colonels Wallace and Wasserman how Super Spook had fucked up by the numbers. But he also thought Cronley probably had good reasons for what he had done, and he made pretty good guesses as to what they were.

"Seven-K goes to Argentina. So do Cronley, Spurgeon, Zieliński, and the Winterses. They will go right now, immediately, to Rhine-Main in General White's C-45, with a quick stop in Nuremberg to pick up Mrs. Winters and the baby. Captain Dunwiddie will take over protection of Justice Jackson. While Clete makes a quick round-trip to Buenos Aires, I will go— and I'd like you to come with me, General Seidel—to Vienna and put out the Wangermann volcano eruption by pouring money on it. General Gehlen, you have as long as Seidel and I are in Vienna—no more than seventy-two hours—to interrogate von Dietelburg and Burgdorf. Then Colonel Wallace will take them to the Tribunal prison in Nuremberg. Once they're in there, you can work out further interrogation with Morty Cohen. Any questions?"

There were none.

[SEVEN]

LONG-SOUGHT NAZIS ARRESTED

By Janice Johansen
Associated Press Foreign Correspondent

Munich, Oct 8—

Major General Bruce T. Seidel, USFET's chief
intelligence officer, announced today that former Major General Wilhelm Burgdorf and former SS-Brigadeführer Franz von Dietelburg are
now in cells of the Allied War Crimes Tribunal
in Nuremberg.

Seidel said their arrests "somewhere in Austria" were the result of a combined operation
involving the U.S. Army Counterintelligence
Corps, the super-secret U.S. Directorate of
Central Intelligence, and Austrian authorities.

"I cannot fully express how grateful we are for
the cooperation of the Austrian authorities,"
Seidel said. "We could not have made the arrests without their help."

Burgdorf, one of the two generals sent by Hitler to Stuttgart late in the war to offer General Erwin Rommel the choice between a cyanide capsule and hanging for his role in the failed plot to kill Hitler, was reported to have died in the Hitler bunker and been buried in the Chancellery Garden.

"We knew this was a ruse," said Colonel Harold Wallace, the chief of DCI-Europe, and the only member whose name is made public, "but we allowed him to think he had fooled us so we could catch him. His arrest, and that of his deputy von Dietelburg, removes the leadership of the so-called Odessa Organization, which has tried, without much success, to help other Nazis escape to South America and other locations."

Von Dietelburg, according to General Seidel, was heavily involved in a Nazi religious cult headquartered in Wewelsburg Castle.

"And now that we have him in a cell, we can investigate this fully," Seidel concluded.

When pressed by this reporter for the name of at least one DCI agent, he replied, "Well, there's one they call Super Spook," but would go no further.